Shadow Sabotage

Nicole Gardner

Chapter One

Claire

Am I seriously going to do this? I glanced around, double-checking to make sure the forest was still and silent, then slipped out of the last stitch of clothing covering my body. A thrill ran up my spine. I was alone and naked in the Wyoming wilderness.

I ran as fast as I could, ignoring the sting of sharp pebbles on the soles of my feet, then dove into the cold river. I gasped as the icy water covered my body. My chest constricted, my skin stung, my feet ached.

None of it mattered.

It had been too long since I'd felt freedom like this. And somehow, the fact that I'd lose my job if I got caught made the thrill even better.

I splashed and swam until I couldn't take the cold any longer, then made my way back to the bank, shaking when the cold breeze hit my bare skin. The sun still lingered in the sky. I turned my face toward it, grateful for the bit of warmth it offered. After toweling off, I pulled on the jeans and green flannel shirt I'd left on the creekside. I squeezed as much water as I could from my blonde curls, shoved my frozen feet into my boots, and began the hike back to my campsite.

Shadows lengthened as the sun began to slip behind the trees. I stirred the coals from the fire I'd had earlier, adding just enough wood to keep them going. Then I pulled out the food I'd prepped at home and tucked the foil packs into the coals. It didn't take long for them to start sizzling. I wasn't much of a cook, but the way I saw it, two things made food taste incredible: hunger and being cooked over a wood fire. Camping took care of both.

I sank blissfully into my camping chair. This was heaven. An entire day off of work, free to do whatever the hell I wanted. I couldn't remember the last time I'd had a whole day to myself.

The bridge to the campground rattled as a vehicle approached. I glanced at my watch and smiled. Rhett and Cheyenne were right on time. The familiar truck slowly drove around the bend, searching for my campsite. I stood and waved, getting their attention, then waited while they parked.

Cheyenne, my lifelong best friend, hopped out of the driver's seat. Her dark hair hung in two long braids over her red flannel shirt. She held the door open for Ash, her shepherd-mix dog, who jumped out of the truck with a canine equivalent of a grin on her face, as eager as we humans were for the camping trip. Rhett, my brother, swung down from the passengers' side, brushing his long hair back from his face.

In the looks department, he and I were about as different as two siblings could get. My hair was still the light blonde I had been born with; his was even darker than Cheyenne's. I was barely over five feet tall; he was nearly six. My eyes were green; his were a rich brown. The only thing we had in common was the skin that turned to bronze every summer. But despite how different we looked, he was the sibling I'd always been closest to—and the one who was most like me where it counted. He was another wild soul in our family, and I was happy as hell that he'd moved back home this year.

He said hi to me, gave Cheyenne a quick kiss, then headed back to the truck to grab their gear.

"You already started dinner," Cheyenne said, her face lighting up as she spotted the fire.

"I figured it was only fair, since you had to work today and I didn't."

Ash ran up to me, vibrating with excitement. I squatted down and let her lick my face, scratching her behind the ears as Cheyenne clipped a leash onto her collar.

"Great site," Rhett said when he joined us, as he tossed their tent bag onto the ground and handed a camping chair to Cheyenne. "I can't believe you found a campground this empty this time of year. We only saw a couple other campers out here."

"Well, the main campground is full," I explained. "But not many people go for the primitive sites. Most people want bathrooms and RV hookups."

"*Primitive*," Cheyenne repeated, laughing. "If they only knew."

"Right?" I grinned.

Cheyenne and I were longtime members of the Sage County Search and Rescue team. We were used to camping in a hell of a lot more primitive conditions than this, with only the supplies we could carry on our backs. Bringing camping chairs, pre-cut firewood, and a cooler of food made this "primitive" campground feel like glamping to us.

Cheyenne sank down into her chair, the way I had minutes before. "Ahhh." She sighed in satisfaction. "We needed this."

"We did," I agreed, taking my seat beside her. "Two full days of relaxation and enjoyment."

"No tourists to take care of," she said, smiling.

"No wannabe cowboys to babysit," Rhett added, plopping down into his chair with a grin.

"And no breaking up bar fights, responding to domestics, or doing a lick of paperwork." I flipped open the top of my cooler and pulled out three bottles of my favorite stout. "Food will be ready in about thirty minutes. In the meantime, want a drink?"

Rhett reached over and grabbed one from me. "Hell yeah."

Cheyenne eyed me. "I thought the sign out front said no alcohol."

I grinned, gesturing at the empty campsites around us. "Who's going to tell?"

She laughed and reached for a beer. After she cracked it open and took a sip, she poked Rhett. "Shouldn't you be setting up our tent?"

"I'll flip you for it." He gave her a wicked grin.

"Deal." She pulled a quarter out of her pocket. "Heads or tails?"

"Heads."

She tossed the coin into the air, then smacked it down on the back of her wrist. When she pulled her hand off, she smirked. "Sorry. Tails. You're up."

"How do you always win?" He gave her a mock scowl as he put his beer down and headed over to set up their tent beside mine.

She winked at me. "He'll never learn."

As darkness fell, we feasted on steaming baked potatoes and foil packs of ground beef, onions, celery, and carrots. I felt happy in a way I hadn't in ages. When we had been kids, the three of us had done this kind of thing all the time. But then Rhett left Wyoming, he and Cheyenne broke up, and our trio remained fractured for over ten years. When he returned and they got back together, I thought we'd pick up right where we left off. But we had a lot more responsibilities these days. Seemed like we only saw each other in passing or at SAR training.

I'd missed this. A lot.

Part of me worried I'd never have it again once Cheyenne and Rhett got married—an event that was coming up way too soon. I'd already felt the gap between me and Cheyenne grow while she focused on planning their wedding. Instead of the three of us, they were becoming a pair with a life together that wouldn't include me.

I was happy for them. But I also felt the absence of the closeness we used to share, and I wondered what would happen when they moved into a new life stage completely. If they'd leave me behind altogether when they start popping out kids and acting like, well, grownups.

Which, at nearly thirty, we were. But I sure didn't feel like one yet. And I wasn't ready for things to change again.

I grabbed the special foil pack I'd made for Ash—one without salt or onions—and checked to make sure it had cooled off before unwrapping it and placing it on the ground in front of her. A long string of drool dripped from her mouth, but the polite dog sat and waited for permission.

"Go ahead," I said, encouraging her. "It's yours."

She gave me a look of pure gratitude, then gobbled it up, her tail thumping the leaves behind her.

"You'll be her favorite now," Cheyenne laughed.

"I'm counting on it." I grinned, plopping back into my seat and taking another long swig of stout.

This was the life. The smell of woodsmoke, the crisp evening air, the stars popping into the sky one by one—this was Wyoming at its best. Figured there wasn't another place on earth as pretty as this. I was here with my favorite people and the world's best dog. It was perfect.

Ash started whining, looking at Cheyenne with big eyes.

"Potty time." Cheyenne stood, shrugging. "And you know she's too polite to go anywhere near the campsite. I wish I could just let her off-leash."

"Do it. I won't tell anyone," I said, laughing.

She smirked, but her eyes were full of affection. "You know, you really are the worst deputy."

I winked. "Don't I know it."

It was a sentiment we repeated often. It didn't bother me coming from Cheyenne because I knew she didn't mean it—even if everyone else did.

Truth was, being a deputy in the sleepy little town of Wildwood didn't require all that much. But I had very little patience for rules that didn't take individual circumstances into account, which meant that the sheriff and I didn't always see eye to eye. I thought of him like a second dad, but that didn't mean we always agreed.

This kind of thing was a perfect example. Ash was a highly intelligent, well-trained dog who would never run off or make trouble. Cheyenne was a great owner who would never allow her to. Seemed silly to force rules onto them just because some people weren't smart enough to know how dogs should behave in public.

But unlike me, Cheyenne was a rule follower who wouldn't think of letting Ash roam freely inside the park. So poor Ash was stuck on a leash that wasn't worthy of her.

She started sniffing around, tugging Cheyenne toward the edge of the tree line.

"Sorry," Cheyenne called. "Looks like we'll be a minute. She smells something she wants to explore."

"I'll come with you," I said, jogging over toward them. Ash's nose was to the ground, her tail down as she sniffed and pulled on the leash. "She's got quite a nose on her."

"I know. I'm thinking of training her for SAR work and starting a canine unit here. She's got the nose and the drive. She'd be good at it."

She said it casually, but it hit me like a gut punch.

Cheyenne and I had always worked SAR together—it had been that way for over ten years, even with Rhett now on the team too. But that would be over if she started a canine unit.

I didn't have a dog that would qualify. Frankly, I didn't have time to learn to be a handler even if I did. Our team already cross-trained. Cheyenne and I specialized in horses, but we could also run ATV searches, rope rescues, air evacuations, swift water rescues, and more. But canine units were different. A canine and a handler were a team of their own, and they trained constantly on those skills. Between my normal SAR responsibilities, working full-time, and helping the family on the ranch, I barely had time to think. There was no way I could add something like that to the list.

I'd already lost my place as her best friend. But to no longer be her SAR partner? It would be the end of an era.

I swallowed hard. "Well. You're right about one thing. We could use a canine unit here."

"I know," Cheyenne said, apparently missing the way my voice had come out all strained. "We've needed one so many times lately, and having one in our county would significantly decrease our response times to those calls. Besides, it's really fascinating work. I've been chatting with Deborah, the head of the canine unit over in Park County. She evaluated Ash and agreed we're good candidates. She offered to let us come train with her."

"That's great." My words were hollow, but she didn't seem to notice.

She frowned and pulled a flashlight out of her pocket, shining it on the path ahead. "Speaking of Ash, she's really onto something right now."

"She is," I said, realizing how far away from the site we were. We were heading down a steep incline, completely out of sight from Rhett and the rest of the campground. The woods had grown dark. Cold air stung my exposed skin. I added my flashlight to the mix and stuck my other hand into my pocket, following as Ash picked up speed.

At the bottom of the hill, the dog started digging frantically.

"What on earth has she found?" Cheyenne stepped forward.

I swung my flashlight in their direction. My heart nearly stopped when I saw what she was doing.

"Pull her back," I commanded.

Cheyenne's head jerked at my sharp tone, but she did what I'd said.

I stepped forward and swung my light over the area, my heart sinking as I did.

"What is it?" Cheyenne crouched, holding Ash back.

Nearly hidden by the brush and pine needles was a pile of bones. That wasn't an uncommon sight in the wilderness. The Bighorns were full of predator animals, and I'd seen my fair share of both fresh kills and old bones that had been stripped of meat and left scattered on the forest floor.

But this felt different. Maybe it was gut instinct, or maybe I'd just seen enough animal remains to realize something was off. Whatever it was, my alarm bells were going haywire.

I grabbed a stick and poked at the pine needles covering the area.

Out rolled a human skull.

Chapter Two

Claire

While Cheyenne stood guard over the area, I raced back up the hill. The incline had me out of breath by the time I reached the campsite. As soon as Rhett saw me, he jumped up from his chair, fear in his eyes.

"Where's Cheyenne? What happened?"

"She's fine," I said, holding up a hand as I fought to catch my breath. "But Ash found something out there. I need to call the sheriff."

"The sheriff?" Rhett blanched. He wasn't a big fan of law enforcement, having been on the wrong side of it too many times as a teen.

I ignored him, walking toward the road to get a better signal. When my cell phone had three bars, I hit the number for the station. Andrea, our administrative assistant, answered.

"You're supposed to be on vacation," she said, humor in her voice.

"Yeah, well, looks like the universe has other plans for me."

Her voice changed instantly. "What's wrong?"

"Got a problem up here. Cheyenne's dog, Ash, just uncovered human remains near our campsite."

The line was silent for a beat. "Did you say *human* remains?"

"'Fraid so. Gonna need the sheriff and whoever's on duty. I'd go ahead and call Wendy, too."

"On it," she said, her voice brisk. "What else do they need to know?"

I closed my eyes, picturing the scene. "It's just bones left. That's not my field, but I'd say we aren't dealing with anything real recent. Body was at the bottom of a steep incline. Could have been a camper or a hiker who fell." I mentally scanned the files of our unsuccessful SAR missions but couldn't come up with one that matched the location.

"Got it. Where are you?"

I gave her the GPS coordinates for our site, then ended the call. When I turned around, Rhett was standing with his arms crossed. Despite the gravity of the situation, I cracked a smile. He looked like some sort of superhero with his long hair blowing in the breeze, his biceps bulging, and a stance that said he was ready for anything.

Sometimes I looked at him and still saw the kid he'd been. Moments like this reminded me that ten years had passed since he'd first left Wildwood. He'd grown into a man. A good, responsible, fierce man who loved my best friend with every ounce of his being.

I wondered what he saw when he looked at me. Did he see the years that had passed, the skills I'd learned, and who I was becoming? Or did he still see me as the teenager he'd left behind ten years ago?

Sometimes I felt like I hadn't grown up at all.

"What do you need me to do?" he asked.

"Stay here," I said, walking past him to my truck. "I'm going to take a closer look. I'll send Chey back up here to you. When the cavalry arrives, she'll be able to lead them to the site."

"Got it. Hey." He grabbed my arm, made me look him in the eye. "You okay?"

"Not my first dead body, Rhett."

The worry on his face didn't budge. "I know. Cheyenne's told me about some of the recovery missions you've both done. Still can't imagine it's easy."

"I'm fine. I promise."

I was. But I didn't know how to explain that this felt a thousand times easier than any of those recoveries. This was bones, something that looked more like the plastic models in a science lab than an actual person. I knew technically it was a human, but with the defining features gone, it was easy not to think of it that way.

The coroner would figure out a way to identify the person, and then it would feel real. Then there would be a face and a name and a story that might haunt me. But for now?

This was nothing like being face-to-face with the decomposing body of someone you'd failed to save.

I grabbed my SAR backpack, service weapon, and badge from my truck. Then I hiked back down to the site and sent Cheyenne up to Rhett.

As she disappeared into the woods, I felt a wave of nerves. This was my first police investigation that involved a deceased individual. I'd only been a deputy for a little over a year, and I'd never dealt with anything like this. Odds were, it would be a simple case of accidental death. But I still didn't want to screw up.

At least not any more than I probably already had when I'd poked the mess of pine needles and inadvertently moved that skull.

I used my flashlight and my cell phone to take the best photographs I could and marked off the area with the orange flagging tape we used to flag clues on a search. I second-guessed that decision—this probably wasn't the scene of an actual crime, and the guys would likely make fun of me for treating it like one. But I didn't want to take any chances.

After that, I sat and waited.

Two hours passed before I finally heard a scuffle of rocks and muted voices as Cheyenne led the response team down the hill. Sheriff McGrath approached first, eyeing my tape with a dubious expression. Sergeant Trey Collins—my least favorite coworker—was with him. I stifled a groan as he snickered over my makeshift crime scene.

Sheriff McGrath came over and put a hand on my shoulder. "What do we have going on here? Andrea said you found some remains?"

"That's right," I said, trying to ignore Trey's smirk. "We were walking the dog and she uncovered them. I figured they were animal bones, but upon taking a closer look, we found a human skull."

"So just bones?"

"Just bones," I confirmed.

"Hmmm." McGrath eyed the steep bank and whistled. "One wrong move and that would be a hell of a fall. People have died from less. We'll have to see if Wendy can tell us how old the bones are, cross-reference that with any missing campers thought to have been in this area."

"That's what I was thinking," I said, nodding. "But I've been working SAR for ten years, and every mission we've had in this area has been successful."

He shrugged. "This could be someone who fell fifteen, twenty years ago—even longer. We'll just have to wait and find out. It could also be someone who was never found because they were thought to be somewhere else. Regardless, good work here. Hopefully we're about to bring closure to a family somewhere."

"Yeah, hopefully," I agreed. But even though he was voicing the same thing I'd thought earlier, I found myself unconvinced.

The remains weren't *that* far from a campsite. It was a lesser-used, primitive campsite in a park that didn't get a ton of traffic, sure. But still. A few dozen people camped here every year. Plenty of them brought dogs, like we had. I knew from SAR work that human remains could easily go overlooked, even with diligent search efforts. But it was hard to imagine that the bones would go undiscovered for *that* long in a place frequented by campers.

Sheriff McGrath checked his watch. "Wendy should be here any minute," he said, shoving his hands into his pockets.

"I'm already here." Her voice came from the hill as she gingerly stepped her way down. One hand carried her bag, while the other gripped a tree as she navigated the steep terrain.

Wendy James, our coroner, was a real gem for Sage County. She'd worked as a forensic investigator for over twenty years in Omaha before moving to Wyoming in search of peace. She was vastly overqualified for the job. But the real reason I loved her was because, like me, she was short and blonde. Her hair was spiky, she had a diamond stud nose ring, and most days you could spy her rose tattoo peeking out from the collar of her shirt. She looked like the kind of woman you wouldn't expect to be taken seriously. Yet, unlike me, she was well-respected—even by Mayor Evans and Judge Barrington, the rest of the boys' club that, along with Sheriff McGrath, made up our local government.

Probably didn't help that they remembered me competing in "Little Miss Wildwood," stomping around town in glitter-covered cowboy boots during my pageant phase. Even now, I still heard myself referred to by that name under their breaths. Sheriff McGrath was the only one who seemed to take me seriously as a deputy.

Wendy looked approvingly at the tape. "You were the first one here, Hawkins?"

"That's right."

"Nice work blocking this off," she said. "Glad you recognized the need to do so."

"Thanks." I beamed.

Trey nearly choked.

She pulled gloves and booties from her bag and slipped them on before ducking underneath the tape. Her deputy coroner, Wes, set up a floodlight to illuminate the area, then followed behind her with a large camera, taking photographs of the area that would put my cell phone snaps to shame.

"Now you're just doing our job for us," McGrath joked, rocking back in his boots.

We all knew he was more than happy for Wendy to take point on this. Sheriff McGrath had been in law enforcement a long time, but Wendy still had more crime scene experience than the rest of us put together.

She grinned at him and winked. But her face sobered as she turned back to the skeletal remains. The mood shifted, tension growing as she began to methodically examine the area. Several times we saw her point to something and exchange glances with Wes. Little by little, she uncovered the rest of the bones, taking care to document exactly where they'd been before moving them. The rest of us stayed quiet, the gravity of the situation hitting as we watched her work.

She finally rose and came over to us with a small baggy in hand.

"Well?" McGrath asked.

"The remains are definitely human," she confirmed. There was a weariness in her eyes that I'd never seen. She pushed her short hair away from her forehead and shifted her weight to her other leg.

McGrath frowned. "Male? Female? Age?"

"Based on the pelvis and other details at the scene, I believe the victim was female. Probably a young adult. But I'm not ready to say definitively."

"Cause of death?"

She rolled her eyes. "You know I can't give you that yet. Not until the autopsy is complete. But...I have a suspicion. I'll let you know."

"I have a suspicion too," he said, grinning. "I have a suspicion that some poor soul tumbled off that ridge up there."

She gave him a long look. "I don't think that's what happened."

The hairs on my neck prickled at the intensity on her face. "You think this was murder, don't you?"

But she didn't answer my question.

"There's something you should know." She held the baggy up.

"What's that?" Sheriff McGrath frowned.

"A charm bracelet," I said, staring at it. I recognized it instantly.

"That's right." Wendy's eyes met mine.

The bag held a silver charm bracelet with only three charms—a football, a jeweled crown, and the letter K.

"Oh my God," I whispered, moving my hand to my mouth. "We just found Katelyn Brown."

All the blood drained from Sheriff McGrath's face.

"That's not an official identification," Wendy cautioned. "We'll use dental records and DNA to confirm. But it's certainly a possibility. A strong one. The size of the bones, the age of them..."

"Katelyn Brown was wearing that the night she disappeared," I added, still unable to keep my eyes off the bracelet—a bracelet that had just made those bones entirely too human.

"Nearly identical," Wendy agreed. "The only difference is that Katelyn's had four charms, not three. But a fourth might have broken off during a struggle."

The sheriff's hand trembled. "I have to make some calls," he said gruffly. "No one touches anything else. We're going to have to bring in Wyoming DCI. They'll want to process the scene themselves. I..." He shook his head, trailed off, then turned and headed up the hill without finishing his sentence.

Trey and I exchanged glances. He kept his expression professional, but I could see the excitement in his eyes. This was the biggest thing to happen in Sage County in years, and he was right in the middle of it.

Katelyn Brown. Seven months ago, she'd stormed out of a college party, driven to her apartment, packed a bag, and left town. She'd never been seen again, causing a flurry of speculation, rumors, and fears. According to the news reports, there had been no real leads. After a few months, everyone had moved on and forgotten about her.

I knew in my gut it was her.

But what the hell was she doing in a park outside of Wildwood?

Chapter Three

Claire

Sheriff McGrath's lips were pressed into a tight line when he returned. "DCI is sending an agent. He's a few hours out though, won't be here until morning. Wendy, I'm sorry, but they're asking you to leave the remains in place for tonight. That means you'll have to come back tomorrow, meet them here."

"It's not a problem," she reassured him.

"We'll have to keep the scene secure overnight," he said, his voice oddly gruff. He was staring at the bones with a faraway look, like he couldn't believe that this was happening in his county.

"I can do that," I volunteered. "I was already planning on camping tonight, anyway."

"You sure?" Sheriff McGrath asked, turning toward me with a look of concern. "It's your day off. I know you were looking forward to it and I hate to ruin that for you."

"It's really not a problem," I said. It wasn't like I would be getting any real sleep anyway—not with the adrenaline that was running through my veins.

"That will work out well," Trey said smoothly. "I'm on duty tomorrow. I can be here in the morning to take over watch until DCI arrives."

And kiss the agent's ass. I fought back an eye roll. Everyone knew that Trey's dream was to work for DCI as a special agent. He'd already applied once and had gotten passed over for lack of investigative experience. He was probably chomping at the bit to work a high-profile homicide case with whoever DCI was sending us.

I'd have given anything for them to send a woman. Watching Trey attempt to flatter and impress her would keep me laughing for years.

Sheriff McGrath hesitated, then put his hand on my shoulder. "You're really sure you'll be okay handling this alone?" His eyebrows furrowed as he searched my eyes.

"Why wouldn't I be?" I shrugged. "I do this all the time."

He shook his head. "Sitting with remains isn't the same as bedding down on the trail. You don't have to volunteer for this. I can ask one of the guys to do it."

Ah. So there it was. I could read between the lines. Since I was the only female deputy, Sheriff McGrath often tried to shield me from the rougher parts of the job, never noticing that his doing so just made things harder for me in the long run. I'd never earn any respect if I didn't have a chance to prove myself.

Not that I should have to. I'd proven myself time and time again on the SAR team. But none of that seemed to count when it came to the badge.

I bit down my frustration and plastered on an easy grin. "No need to mess up their beauty sleep. I've got this."

He relented with a nod. "Alright. Call in if you need anything."

I gave him a reassuring nod.

"Deputy Hawkins will keep the scene secured," he said, raising his voice so the others could hear. "The rest of you should get some sleep. Plan on meeting back here at eight sharp. And I know I don't have to say this, but not a word to *anyone* about what—*who*—we may have discovered. This goes nowhere. Got it?"

We all nodded our understanding. News like this would spread like wildfire if we weren't careful.

The others packed up their supplies and headed up the hill, leaving me at the bottom, listening to their low voices slowly fade away. Then there was just that unique silence of the wilderness—a quiet filled with the small noises we normally tuned out when other humans were around. Twigs cracking in the distance, the chirp of crickets, the small rustling noises that meant critters nearby.

It was my favorite kind of quiet. The kind where you could finally hear yourself think.

But it felt unnerving tonight.

Movement in the trees startled me. Then Cheyenne appeared from where she'd apparently stayed close by, waiting for the team to leave. She took a wide path around the area I'd marked off, quiet as she looked at the uncovered remains.

"Want me to stay with you?" she asked, nudging me.

"Nah. No reason to make Rhett sleep alone. He's probably worried sick up there, waiting for you to come back."

"We can both come down here," she said quietly.

I waved her off. "Best to keep Ash up there, away from the scene. I'll be fine. I promise. It's no different than any other day at work."

She wrapped me in a hug. "Just give a shout if you change your mind. You don't have to do this alone."

"It's fine," I said, acting like it was nothing. And I was convincing enough that we both believed me.

But when Cheyenne finally trudged back up the hillside to where Rhett and Ash were waiting for her beside a warm fire, reality set in.

I was alone in the cold, underneath a dark sky, keeping vigil for the scattered bones of a girl who had disappeared without a trace.

And when I finally allowed myself to doze off, I dreamed of all the faces of the ones I'd searched for—and failed to bring back alive.

I startled awake at the sound of twigs snapping. It was dawn, not yet time for everyone to gather, but low voices and movement on the trail told me that people were headed this way. I rubbed the sleep out of my eyes and blinked, trying to orient myself. It had been a mostly sleepless night and my body was crying out in exhaustion.

I relaxed when I caught a glimpse of Cheyenne's red flannel shirt moving through the trees. She and Rhett must have gotten up early and decided to check on me. If I was lucky, maybe they had brought hot coffee—and food. Bacon, sausage... My stomach rumbled just thinking about it.

But when Cheyenne emerged from the trees, she was accompanied by a stranger.

Unlike my gigantic brother, this man was toned and athletic in a way that looked built for speed. He moved with a precision that reminded me of the sleek movements of a mountain lion. He had a chiseled face and piercing blue eyes that stared me down as he approached.

Everything about him looked expensive, from the leather jacket he wore over a black T-shirt and dark jeans to the high-end hiking boots on his feet. His rich brown hair was neatly groomed on the sides, with a classic wave on top.

He looked like Hollywood.

Not Wildwood.

Cheyenne hung back, shooting me an unreadable look as he walked up to me and crossed his arms.

He scanned me up and down. "Who are you?"

"Deputy Claire Hawkins," I said, scrambling to my feet as I noted the DCI badge on the black leather belt that hung low on his hips.

"Where's your uniform?"

I snorted, unable to help myself. "Where's yours?"

A flash of humor seemed to flicker in his eyes, but it was gone as quickly as it had come, making me wonder if I had imagined the whole thing. He stared at me with an unimpressed look that urged me to explain myself.

"I was off duty last night. My friends and I were camping when we found the remains. Since I was already here with outdoor gear, I volunteered to stay and keep watch."

His eyebrows rose. "You were asleep." The accusation was clear.

My cheeks flushed with anger as much as embarrassment. "Yes, I was." I squared my shoulders, hoping to leave it at that.

But he kept pushing. "Do you often fall asleep on duty, Deputy Hawkins?"

"As a matter of fact, yes, I do," I said, crossing my arms and mirroring his stance.

The answer threw him off. "What?"

I kept my face straight. "I'm the Sheriff's Office liaison for the Sage County Search and Rescue team. During tourist season, half my job is sleeping in the woods. I do it all the time."

His face relaxed, and that humor flickered in his eyes again. "Fair enough. But if you volunteered to keep watch, you should have followed through."

The reprimand irritated me even more than his accusation. He didn't even know me, and he was acting like I'd failed at my job.

I was getting damn sick of it.

"My ears are the sharpest in Sage County," I said between gritted teeth. "I know how to sleep light, how to listen for the telltale sounds of an intruder approaching. Years of sleeping in bear country will do that to you. Based on the condition of those brand-new hiking boots you're wearing, I'm guessing you wouldn't know much about that."

I didn't bother keeping the disdain off my face as I sized up the six-hundred-dollar shoes that looked like they'd never seen terrain more than a thousand yards from a parking lot.

"Hmm." His lips twitched before he turned his head and looked at the area I'd marked off with flagging tape.

I shot Cheyenne a look behind his back that forced her to fake a cough to cover up the laugh that slipped out.

He glanced at her, then turned back to me with an expression that said we hadn't pulled a thing over on him. Cheyenne mouthed *good luck* before making her escape.

He watched her climb the hill and waited until she was out of earshot before his attention came back to me. His arms remain crossed, his tone clipped. "Tell me what happened."

I explained about how we had been camping, how Cheyenne's dog had found the bones, and about the bracelet Wendy had found. He listened carefully, his eyes scanning the scene. They landed on the skull, still visible even from here.

I shuddered seeing it again, though I was grateful it was less distinctive in this light. It had been impossible to miss late in the night, when moonlight had glinted off the white bone, drawing my gaze to it no matter how hard I tried to look away.

I wasn't sure what had been worse. Sitting awake, unable to stop my eyes from focusing like a laser on that skull ... or the nightmares that ensured I slept so lightly I wouldn't miss a sound.

The DCI agent tilted his head toward me, his brow furrowing as another shudder ran through me.

I bit the inside of my cheek, annoyed I had let him see me flinch.

He waited a moment before speaking again. His tone was slightly softer when he did. "You saw the remains up close. Was there any soft tissue remaining?"

"Not that I saw," I said, blinking quickly, as if it could erase the images that flashed through my mind at his words.

"Show me the charm bracelet."

"I can't. Sorry. Wendy, our coroner, had already bagged it before the sheriff called DCI."

"That's fine," he said absently, his eyes as focused on that white piece of bone as mine had been the night before. "You said it looked similar to the one Katelyn Brown was wearing when she went missing."

"It's *identical* to the one she was wearing," I corrected. "Except that it only had three charms instead of four."

"Which three?" He looked at me again.

"A football, a crown, and her initial. K."

"You're sure?"

"Positive."

"Hmm." He turned back to the scene. "The fourth charm. Do you know what it was?"

"Yes." I could remember the picture of her that had blown up all over the news when she went missing, the one where she had posed with her hand under her chin, showing off perfectly manicured nails and that silly charm bracelet. Her blue eyes had stared daringly at the camera with a coy look that cut straight through, like she was looking right at me.

Now, I felt the agent's eyes on me. Studying me.

"What was the fourth charm?" he asked.

I sighed. It made me sad in a way, because it was the one thing in that photo I could relate to.

"It was a horse," I said, remembering the pretty charm that looked so much like one I used to wear. "A silver horse."

"That's right."

I realized he'd known all along.

For a long moment, we stood in silence, both caught up in our own thoughts. But the silence was broken by cheerful whistling and the sounds of someone quickly descending the hill, not caring if he slipped a little on the way.

I barely stifled my groan when Trey emerged, looking as startled to see the DCI agent and me standing together as I was to see him. A quick glance at my watch confirmed I wasn't crazy. It was still an hour earlier than he was supposed to be here.

The irritation that flashed across Trey's face when he saw us was quickly replaced with a smooth smile. He strode over to us with a cocky grin and stuck his hand out.

"Sergeant Trey Collins. You must be from DCI. We appreciate you coming out to assist," Trey said as he shook the agent's hand.

"Special Agent Vance Weston. Nice to meet you."

I fought the urge to roll my eyes. So much for Trey having to suck up to a woman. These two were going to get along great. Two cocky men who thought they were smarter than everyone else—and I'd have to deal with both of them.

"Wendy, our coroner, and Sheriff McGrath will be here in about an hour, but I had a feeling you'd be early," Trey said, grinning. "I'll give you the rundown on the case thus far and we can start processing the scene. Hawkins, you can go ahead and take off. I'm sure you're eager to get back to your little camping trip with your friends." He stuck his hands into his pockets and gave me a patronizing smile.

Agent Weston studied him the way he'd studied me earlier. "Deputy Hawkins already gave me the rundown," he said flatly. "As for processing the scene, we'll wait for the rest of the team—including my tech from the crime lab, who will need to take samples before anything is contaminated further."

Trey's smile faltered and I did an internal happy dance. I'd never seen Trey get put in his place before, and even though it was incredibly subtle, I could tell that was exactly what Agent Weston had done. I knew it wasn't for my benefit—Agent Weston was probably irritated by Trey's remark about "assisting us." On paper, sure, that's what was happening. It was our jurisdiction and he was here by request. But anyone with half a brain knew that DCI would be in charge and we'd be the ones offering assistance.

"Oh, sure." Trey nodded, trying to look agreeable. "Whatever questions you have in the meantime, I'd be happy to help. Once I saw that bracelet last night, I realized our victim was Katelyn Brown. I spent a few hours reading up on her disappearance so that we can hit the ground running."

Fury flared inside me. *Trey* hadn't been the one to connect that bracelet to Katelyn. That had been Wendy—and me.

But I knew it wasn't worth putting him in his place. If I did, he'd just find a way to make me pay for it later.

Agent Weston glanced at me, then back at Trey. "I appreciate that. Maybe later. Right now, I need to get my gear and bring it back down so we'll be ready when the team arrives."

"Great, I'll help you," Trey said.

"Actually, you should take over here," Agent Weston said smoothly. "I can carry my own gear. Deputy Hawkins has been stuck here all night. I'm sure she's eager to be relieved."

"Of course," Trey said, relaxing. As much as he wanted to stick with Agent Weston, I knew he was even more glad to get rid of me.

Agent Weston stuck his hands in his jacket and headed toward the slope. When he realized I wasn't following him, he turned and looked at me expectantly. "Sergeant Collins has this handled, Deputy Hawkins."

Trey grinned.

"I'm just going to grab my bag," I answered, forcing a smile.

Pricks. Both of them.

Agent Weston nodded and continued walking like he didn't really care if I followed him or not.

As soon as he was out of sight, Trey grabbed my arm and gave me a warning look. "Listen, Hawkins, this is my case. You know what it means to me. Don't try to weasel your way into it."

I wrenched my arm away. "What the hell are you talking about? I'm not doing anything."

"You weren't even on duty last night, and yet you talked Sheriff McGrath into giving you the shift," he said, his eyes dark.

"Forgive me for offering to take a job no one in their right minds would want," I huffed, grabbing my backpack and slinging it on my back.

"I'm just saying, you better not do anything to make me look bad."

I rolled my eyes. "As if I could possibly do that. Don't worry. You and Agent Weston are perfect for each other. I'm sure you'll become best buddies forever working this case together."

He glared at me and opened his mouth like he was going to say something else, but I was done listening.

I walked off, congratulating myself for not flipping him the bird on the way out.

CHAPTER FOUR

Vance

I heard Deputy Hawkins behind me on the hill, catching up quickly despite her short legs. She was fast, even on this steep slope.

And when she caught up, stuck behind me on the narrow path, I could practically feel the impatience vibrating off her.

"In a hurry?" I asked over my shoulder, chuckling.

"I can practically smell the coffee from here," she said, nearly groaning.

The trail gave way to the wider, gentler area close to the campground where her friends were set up. She slipped out from behind me and set her own pace.

And shot me an annoyed glance when I matched it.

I took the chance to look at her again. When she'd introduced herself, I almost hadn't believed she was really a deputy. From a distance, she'd looked like a kid who'd been dared to spend the night alone out there for the thrills.

She barely came up to my shoulder. But she had to be pure muscle based on the way she moved. She wore no makeup that I could tell, adding to the impression of youth. She was tanned like she had spent most her life outdoors, with a scattering of freckles on her nose and her cheeks. Her long blonde hair was a tangle of curls and waves.

It made me think of mermaids—and not the princess kind. Based on the way she'd spoken to me, I had a feeling she was as unpredictable and dangerous as the mermaids in the legends of old.

But behind that fierce exterior, I'd noticed shadows in her eyes. I suspected she'd had a tough night, whether she would admit it or not.

She let out a sigh of relief when we broke the tree line and her friends came into sight. "Please tell me there's coffee left," she called out.

Cheyenne, the one who had led me to the crime scene, slipped on a glove and pulled the percolator off the fire. "Of course there is," she called back, lifting it in salute.

"You should sleep, you know," I said under my breath.

Deputy Hawkins glanced my way. "Why? I slept last night, remember?" The words came out like a challenge.

I looked again at the shadows underneath her eyes—and at the ones that lurked within them. "You may have slept on the job, but there's no way you got any decent rest down there."

She waved me off. "Nothing a good cup of coffee won't cure. We'll share if you want some."

"I'm good," I answered.

"Suit yourself." She shrugged and took off in a jog, catching up to her friends as she called out a question. "What happened to my tent?"

"We packed it up," the long-haired man said, slinging an arm around her shoulders as she reached them. Protective stance—boyfriend, maybe? He eyed me as I gave them a nod, passing by them to get my gear.

A truck emblazoned with the Sage County Sheriff's emblem pulled over on the campground loop, unable to squeeze into the packed campsite. The sheriff jumped out and walked to my vehicle.

"Sheriff McGrath," he said, introducing himself, pumping my hand. "Appreciate you coming out, Agent Weston."

"Of course."

His eyes went to Deputy Hawkins, who had seen him and was walking toward us. He glanced at the vehicles crammed into the site. "Is Sergeant Collins manning the site?"

Deputy Hawkins nodded. "Yes. He just took over."

"Good deal," Sheriff McGrath said. "Have you met Agent Weston yet?"

I answered for her. "Yes, we met down at the crime scene."

Deputy Hawkins gave us a tight smile.

"Great." Sheriff McGrath took a deep breath, staring off at the tree line in an awkward moment of silence before remembering himself. "Claire, go home and get some sleep."

Her head jerked back. "What? I'm already here. I can help process the scene."

Sheriff McGrath shook his head. "No," he said, his tone firm. "You've done enough. We've got this covered."

"But—"

"That's an order," he said, cutting her off. He called out to her friends. "Rhett, Cheyenne—make sure she gets some sleep, okay?"

The man nodded, his arms crossed, while Cheyenne gave the sheriff a salute.

Sheriff McGrath turned back to Deputy Hawkins. "Be at the office tomorrow at eight."

She clamped her lips and gave a little nod, then turned on her heel and joined her friends. She refused to even look at us when Sheriff McGrath and I grabbed my gear and headed down the trail together.

THE NEXT MORNING, I STEPPED OUT OF MY CAR AND surveyed Wildwood's Main Street, my first real look at the town in daylight. You could tell a lot about a place by scoping out the area. This looked like your typical tourist town—minus the tourists.

Main Street was set up like other cowboy towns I'd seen, with false front shop buildings and a western vibe that you'd think had been plucked straight out of a theme park. There were hitching posts out front, and one of them actually had a live horse hitched to it. Either a nice touch for visitors or a holdover from days gone by. The business names promised all your typical touristy fare—a bar with saloon doors, an old-fashioned "trading post" where suckers probably bought over-priced groceries, and a hipster-meets-western coffee shop that likely served eight-dollar cups of coffee. Down the street, I spotted a gallery advertising local art, stores hawking cowboy boots and hats, and a place claiming to sell authentic Native-made goods.

It was like a dozen other towns I'd seen in Wyoming, except that the streets were nearly empty, missing the hordes of tourists that flocked to places like Jackson Hole. And there was something else that felt differ-ent. I leaned against my car, crossing my arms as I thought it over.

Authenticity.

Strange word to give a town like this, but I had to admit, the street gave off vibes that felt different than some of the other places I'd been.

We'd just have to see.

I strolled over to the sidewalk, heading toward the county court-house that also housed the jail and the Sage County Sheriff's Office. I'd deliberately parked a few blocks away, wanting to get my lay of the land before I headed in. As I walked, I studied the buildings that lined the street, casting quick glances in the windows and getting my first look at the citizens of Wildwood. Wondering if one of them knew what had happened to my victim.

It would take time to get an official identification, but my gut said the bones we'd painstakingly removed from their resting place belonged to Katelyn Brown. It all fit, including the charm bracelet. Once I'd seen the photographs of it, I had to agree with Deputy Hawkins' assessment: it *was* identical to the one worn by Katelyn.

But Wildwood was a long way from Laramie. If the remains turned out to be her, my first step would be to start looking for someone here who had a connection to her. That was the ideal scenario.

There was always the chance that the location was random—that she'd either come here or been brought here because it was small and remote. If there wasn't a connection between Wildwood and her or her killer, it would make the case significantly harder. Difficult, but not impossible to solve.

After all, I'd done it before.

But with any luck, there would be some connection here, something to tug at until the pieces fell into place and I had figured out what happened.

Despite being the easier option, it presented a different set of difficulties. In small towns, when the victim was an outsider and the killer was local, people sometimes protected their own—no matter how horrific the crime.

When I reached the entrance to the Sage County Sheriff's Office, I pulled off my sunglasses and stuck them into the pocket of my jacket, then headed into the building. A woman with frizzy brown hair pulled back into a ponytail was manning the front desk.

"Can I help you?" she asked, looking over the rims of her gold-framed glasses. Her smile was friendly but guarded.

"Special Agent Vance Weston here for Sheriff McGrath."

Her eyes flicked over me. Then she rose, smoothing her pink sweater. "Of course. I'm Andrea. I'll take you back to see the sheriff."

"Thank you."

Apparently, Andrea wasn't one for small talk. She was completely silent as she led me down the hallway to Sheriff McGrath's office. When she poked her head inside, she gave him a much warmer smile than she had given me. "Sheriff? Agent Weston is here."

He rose, beckoning me inside. "Good deal. Thanks again for coming, Agent Weston. Andrea, close the door on your way out, won't you?"

Her smile wavered, but she did, leaving us alone.

"Have a seat." He gestured at the two wooden chairs in front of his desk.

I sat, taking a quick glance around the office. It wasn't an inviting place. Wood paneling, wood furniture. Old-school metal filing cabinets. A complete absence of decoration. The windows were small, with plastic blinds blocking most of the natural sunlight. The whole room seemed to be dark and dull. Depressing.

The only bit of life in the room was a single photograph of Sheriff McGrath and a lovely woman who I assumed must be his wife. I glanced at it quickly, committing the details to memory. She had shiny blonde hair that looked to be artificially straightened, a thousand-watt smile, and her hand propped on her hip like a cheerleader. She was beautiful.

She also looked at least ten years too young for the sheriff.

"First things first," he said, drawing my attention back to him. "We set up a private office for you so you don't have to be in the bullpen with the others. It's not much, but it has a door." He retrieved a key and a business card from the top drawer of his desk.

"I appreciate it."

He slid the key and the card my way. "And here's Judge Barrington's personal number. He told me to tell you to call day or night. He'll sign warrants as quick as you need them. *If* this turns out to be a homicide."

"You're hoping it's not," I stated as I pocketed the items.

"Of course I am. Wildwood has always been a safe town, and I'd like to stay optimistic."

"Understood."

"I hope we're jumping the gun here," he said, sighing. "But considering Wendy's concern about the bracelet found on scene, I had Laramie send over the file on Katelyn Brown's missing persons case." He tossed a file my way. "Looks like they were at a dead end there. I'm not sure whether to hope we found her or not. It's a terrible thing either way."

"It is," I agreed, taking the file.

He took off his hat and brushed his graying hair back, then sank back in his chair like he was exhausted. "If it is her, we'll have to hold a press conference, break the news. We'll probably be overrun with reporters."

"Probably," I agreed. "Her case didn't spark a lot of interest when she went missing, but murder draws attention."

He held up his hands. "Let's not use the word murder this early. Even if it's Katelyn, it could have been an accident. A fall, maybe, while she was hiking. Lots of things can go wrong in the wilderness. We're sticking with an accidental death unless the ME tells us otherwise."

I shrugged. "If it's Katelyn Brown, it doesn't matter—at least as far as the press is concerned. You've got a pretty young girl who went missing and whose body was found in a remote area months later. That's sensational. Regardless of where our investigation leads, it will be reported as suspicious. And you won't just have reporters here—you're probably going to get an influx of true crime podcasters, bloggers, and more."

He paled and let out a long sigh. "You're kidding. This town hasn't dealt with anything like this before."

"Consider yourself lucky."

Sheriff McGrath drummed his fingers on his desk, thinking. "If it is her, I expect I'm going to be pretty tied up. I'm hoping I can pair you with one of my deputies and let you take point on this while I try to keep things running smoothly."

My brow rose for a fraction of a second before I smoothed out my expression. Most sheriffs I worked with resented giving up any power, even if they'd called me in because they knew they were in over their heads. They usually wanted to keep their hands in it, to give the appearance to their townspeople that they were in charge and capable of handling anything the job demanded.

"That's fine," I agreed.

More than fine. It was ideal from my perspective. Beyond that, it made me respect the sheriff. He'd called me in right away and didn't seem like the type to play games. He'd only made a perfunctory appearance at the crime scene yesterday before leaving the rest of us to process it, but that didn't bother me, either—I preferred working without someone looking over my shoulder, and I understood the many daily responsibilities of a local sheriff.

"Alright then." He smacked his hands down on his desk and stood. "Let's get you set up in an office and find you a partner."

Chapter Five

Claire

I SAT AT MY DESK, STARING MINDLESSLY AT THE PAPERWORK in front of me.

It was the worst part of the job.

I'd rather be out on patrol. Heck, I'd even prefer serving warrants. Or, as was more likely, spending my day trying to convince old Mrs. Haskins to stop calling 911 every time her new neighbor tried to practice his trumpet in his garage. Even that was better than sitting at a desk. But when I'd arrived this morning, Sheriff McGrath had told us all to stay put so we could meet Agent Weston when he arrived.

I was going to lose my mind if I had to sit here much longer. And I was still irritated I'd been sent home yesterday, as if I was going to break after one rough night.

Still, when the two of them finally made their entrance, I tried my best to give a better impression than the one I'd likely made on the scene. I stood and put a smile on my face while Sheriff McGrath rambled, attempting to impress Agent Weston with our low crime rates and efficiency.

Mr. Hollywood, to his credit, kept a polite smile on his face, too, even nodding in appreciation as Sheriff McGrath bragged. As if someone who'd shown up in a black leather jacket with a swagger to match hadn't worked in places a hell of a lot more impressive than our tiny town.

Finally, Sheriff McGrath made the introductions. Seemed a little silly to me, since Agent Weston had already met two of the three of us, but the sheriff seemed intent on us looking extra professional or something.

Trey, of course, jumped forward with his too-eager smile, saying how great it had been to work with Agent Weston the day before. Agent Weston's face was neutral as he shook Trey's hand, and he didn't return the sentiment. Trey was clearly disappointed.

Next, Sheriff McGrath introduced Joseph Castillo, our night shift deputy. I knew he was ready to get this over with so he could go home and crash. I hadn't worked with Joseph much, but I didn't mind him. He was a quiet type who kept to himself. Worked hard, even though he didn't make the job his whole identity like Trey did. But he and Trey were buddies, which made me question whether he was a good judge of character.

After Joseph, Sheriff McGrath turned to me. "And of course you remember Deputy Claire Hawkins. She's our newest deputy, but she's served ten years on our county SAR team as one of our most dedicated volunteers. It's only thanks to her dedication that those remains were found, and true to character, Deputy Hawkins volunteered to secure the site overnight despite it being her day off."

I clasped my hands behind my back, blushing under the unexpected praise. Trey's nostrils flared with irritation, while Joseph shot me a congratulatory smile.

Agent Weston's face remained neutral, but those piercing blue eyes studied me. He said nothing. Just a nod of acknowledgment before turning to Sheriff McGrath. "I know the remains were found outside the city limits. But does Wildwood have a local police department?"

Sheriff McGrath turned red and let out an awkward chuckle.

"Unfortunately, no. Not anymore. We had a small one—a chief and two officers. But they all decided to quit at the same time over low pay. Thought they'd be able to get a raise if they walked out together, but it didn't work out that way. Right now, it's just us handling things, sometimes with support from state on traffic patrol."

"Things are usually pretty quiet around here, I'm guessing?" Agent Weston asked.

Sheriff McGrath nodded. "Usually." He opened his mouth like he was going to say more but glanced at me and stopped.

I knew what he was thinking. Things hadn't been quiet at all lately. When Rhett had come back to town, not everyone had been happy about it, and we'd had the kind of drama—and danger—that this town hadn't experienced in decades.

But that didn't fit the impression the sheriff was obviously trying to give concerning his tenure. He clamped his lips, straightened, and addressed the room instead.

"Listen up, everyone. I've asked Agent Weston to take point on this investigation. Wyoming DCI has more resources and experience with this kind of thing than we do. Besides that, we need to prepare for a potential influx of people in the community after the news breaks. If it turns out that this is, in fact, Katelyn Brown, Agent Weston has said we'll likely have reporters, podcasters, and more flocking to this area. He's right. We'll need to be prepared for it."

Trey leaned back against his desk, rolling his eyes. "Yep. Watch all the wannabe investigators drive up here, looking for their fifteen minutes of fame. Don't these people know they should stay out of the way so we can do our jobs?"

Agent Weston's eyes narrowed. I wondered if he was thinking about some of the cold cases that had recently been solved by "wannabe investigators" who had refused to give up even when law enforcement was forced to switch gears. There had even been cases solved by SAR teams. My own friends from another county had put in countless unpaid hours in order to bring a victim home—and a killer to justice.

But whatever Agent Weston was thinking, he didn't reveal it, even as his eyes flicked to me.

Sheriff McGrath sighed, giving Trey an annoyed look. "Well, like I was saying. Thanks to the help of DCI, we'll be able to focus on keeping our town running smoothly. But I'd like to partner one of you with Agent Weston to assist him and to keep us in the loop."

Joseph moved backward and looked away, clearly hoping someone else would get picked. I didn't blame him. But I knew he didn't have anything to worry about. Trey, much as I disliked him, was the obvious choice. And by the way Trey straightened, putting on a confident smile as he smoothed out the front of his uniform shirt, I figured he and Sheriff McGrath had already decided the whole thing.

Sheriff McGrath cleared his throat, then turned his gaze toward me. "Claire, you're the one who found our victim. I'd like you to work with Agent Weston and see this through."

My eyes widened. I wasn't sure who was more surprised—me, or Trey, whose head had jerked back in shock.

Or Mr. Hollywood, for that matter, whose face finally revealed a genuine emotion. I tried not to be offended that he was as shocked as the rest of us.

I filled my cheeks up with air and blew it out slowly, not realizing how ridiculous it must look—until Joseph stifled a laugh and looked away. My face burned with embarrassment. "Of course. Thank you, sir." Then I turned to Agent Weston, attempting to be professional. "I look forward to working with you."

The words were a lie, and the twist of his lips told me he knew it.

I SAT ACROSS FROM AGENT WESTON IN THE GLORIFIED closet Sheriff McGrath had repurposed as an office for him, tapping my pen on my thigh as he leisurely flipped through a file. We'd been in here for ten minutes and the man hadn't said a word. He'd merely gestured at the empty seat in front of his desk as I followed him in. Then he tossed his jacket on the desk, took his place behind it, and started reading without even acknowledging my presence.

I disliked him already.

This was Wildwood, Wyoming. We were friendly here—or at least tried to be.

Most of us, anyway.

But he had waltzed in here with his shiny leather and his sharp eyes and acted like he owned the place. Hadn't even bothered to speak to me since I'd been assigned as his partner. Hell, he hadn't even looked up from that file. Every minute that ticked by made me want to crawl out of my skin.

Sitting in silence, with nothing to do, was even worse than being stuck on desk duty with paperwork.

I tapped the pen faster, staring at him with narrowed eyes until he finally looked up.

He gave me a placid stare back. "Yes?"

I raised my hands helplessly. "Do you have an assignment for me? Something you need me to research or someone I should go talk to? Or am I just supposed to sit here, grateful for the privilege of watching you?"

Speaking to a superior like that was way out of line. But sitting quietly for so long had used up all my willpower, and I'd never mastered the art of biting my tongue when I was pissed off.

He smirked. "There will be plenty of work to do, I'm sure. How about you start by getting me a coffee?"

Oh, hell no.

I sat back, putting my hands flat on the arms of the chair, and gave him a death stare. "How about you get your own damn coffee?"

Half of his mouth twitched in a smile before his gaze dropped back to the papers in front of him.

Another four minutes passed without either of us saying a word. Four *excruciating* minutes of silence that had me contemplating all of my life choices.

He had to be punishing me on purpose. No one naturally stayed quiet for that long.

I finally cleared my throat and started to speak, but he held up a single finger in a gesture to be quiet. I crossed my arms and scowled.

"Finished," he said, closing the file and tossing it onto his desk so that it slid my way. "Sheriff McGrath gave me that when I got here. It's the missing persons report on Katelyn Brown, sent over from Laramie PD. You should familiarize yourself with it."

I grabbed it.

"I was serious about needing coffee," he said, standing. "I'm going to get a cup. Do you want one?"

I looked up in surprise. He was offering to get *me* coffee? After I'd smarted off to him?

Was this a trap? I should say no.

Coffee though... It was too tempting. My skin hummed just thinking about it. "Um, sure. Thanks."

He drummed his fingers on the table. "How do you take it?"

"Black."

A nod of approval. "I'll be right back."

I stared as he disappeared down the hallway, wondering if I had misjudged him. But then I remembered him putting me through almost twenty minutes of silence in his office and decided I hadn't.

He was still a prick.

IT TOOK AGENT WESTON HALF AN HOUR TO RETURN—MUCH longer than it took me to read the file. When he did, he held two purple cups from the coffee shop down the street. He came in and handed me one, then took the seat at his desk.

"Why'd you go all the way there?" I asked. "We have coffee in the breakroom."

"One, because breakroom coffee isn't usually very good. Two, because it gave me a chance to meet people and check out a local spot."

"Alright," I said, accepting his explanation. "But just so you know, our coffee here is great. Andrea makes it, and she buys the good stuff. Plus, it won't cost you an arm and a leg every time you need a cup."

"Maybe next time. Did you read the file while I was gone?"

"Yes." *Twice. With time to spare.* But I managed to keep my irritation to myself.

"Any thoughts?"

I took a sip of the coffee, annoyed that it really was better than what we had in the breakroom. "Yeah. I think they didn't work very hard to find her."

"I figured you'd say that, being a SAR operative." He leaned back in his chair, giving me that half grin of his as he gestured for me to hand him the file.

When I did, he opened it and began repeating the facts.

"Katelyn Brown was an adult—age nineteen. Voluntary disappearance. Last seen March thirteenth of this year. Last known location was at a gas station outside of Casper on the same night she left Laramie. She was alone. No suspicious circumstances." He looked up at me, a challenge in his eyes.

I nodded and picked up where he'd left off. "She got into an argument with an ex-boyfriend at a college party. Went back to the apartment she shared with a roommate, packed a bag, told the roommate she was done with college, and left."

"Security camera footage confirmed the roommate's story," he went on. "Katelyn showed up at the apartment visibly angry. Left half an hour later with a bag. Drove her own vehicle away." He looked up at me, watching for a reaction.

I didn't give him one.

So he continued. "She left her cell phone behind at the dorm, so no way to track her with it. But they got a hit on her credit card that night at the gas station south of Casper. Security camera footage showed her alone, in her own vehicle. No further hits after that.

"Police contacted her mother, her friends, her job—all known contacts. Her mother said it wasn't the first time she'd run away. Said she had a long history of being emotionally volatile and would usually show up on her own at some point. Katelyn's picture went out on the news and social media. There weren't any credible leads."

He looked up and gave me a pointed stare as he closed the file and put it on his desk. "So what, exactly, would you have had them do differently?"

"I don't know," I admitted.

"But you think they didn't do enough to find her?"

I let out a frustrated sigh. "Maybe. I don't know. It just goes against everything inside me to give up on a search."

He cocked his head. "That's understandable. But I imagine everyone you've searched for has been anxious for you to find them."

"Something horrible happened to Katelyn. You don't think she wanted someone to help bring her home, too?"

"We don't have confirmation that the remains you found are Katelyn—"

"It's her," I said firmly. I wasn't sure how I knew, but I did.

There was something in his eyes that almost—*almost*—looked like approval. "Maybe. But back to the file. Did anything strike you as odd?"

The fact that he'd asked meant he thought so. But nothing stood out to me.

When I didn't answer, he filled in the blanks. "What nineteen-year-old girl heads out on a trip and leaves her cell phone behind?"

And I finally understood what he was getting at.

Maybe Katelyn Brown hadn't wanted to be found.

Chapter Six

Vance

Claire Hawkins was going to drive me crazy.

She sat in my office, legs crossed, fidgeting and twitching like the pent-up energy inside her was going to explode if she didn't let it out.

It made it impossible to concentrate.

I looked up from my computer and gave her a pointed expression. "You don't have to sit in here, you know. You're welcome to go work at your own desk."

She ran her hands up and down her thighs. "Sure. What do you want me to do?"

I stared at her, realizing she had absolutely no idea where to start. I leaned back and put my hands behind my head, narrowing my eyes at her. "Is this your first investigation?"

"Of course not," she said, bristling.

I cocked my head and gave her a skeptical look .

"Well, it's my first *homicide* investigation," she admitted. "But I've investigated, you know, other things..."

"Reading Nancy Drew as a kid doesn't count."

She bristled again—but the flush on her face told me I was right.

Annoyance tugged. Sheriff McGrath should have assigned one of the others. He'd admitted she was their newest deputy, and it was clear she was also the least professional. I didn't have time to hold her hand and teach her where to start.

On the other hand, if he hadn't assigned her, I'd likely have been stuck working with Sergeant Collins. He would have stuck to me like glue with continual compliments and attempts to make me feel like we were buddies. I also didn't fully trust him—he'd taken credit for identifying that bracelet at Katelyn's even though everyone else I'd talked to said it was Wendy James and Deputy Hawkins who'd made that connection.

Hawkins was probably the better of the two—if I could get her out of my hair.

"I know you think this is Katelyn, but until we hear from the medical examiner, we need to consider all possibilities," I said. "I need you to identify other potential victims. Your background is SAR. Check for unresolved SAR cases in that area or ones where the search radius was close enough to the campground that the victim could have legitimately made it there."

"There aren't any," she said. "At least not from the last ten years."

"You have them all memorized?" I asked, skeptical.

"Yeah."

When I didn't say anything, she sighed. "Don't you remember every one of your cold cases?"

Those shadows filled her eyes again. There was pain there. Guilt and frustration for the people she hadn't brought home.

I understood that. Respected it.

"Point taken," I said, giving her a nod. "Check for older ones. Just in case. When you're done with that, compile a list of missing persons within a two-hundred-mile radius. Narrow it down to females age twelve to thirty, height of five four to five seven. See if any of those reports mention a charm bracelet."

"Got it." She stood up, looking as relieved to get out of my office as I was to get her out of there.

. . .

While Deputy Hawkins worked to create a list of possible victims for us, I kept my focus on Katelyn Brown. It would take time to get an official ID. The bones had been scattered, showing markings from where predator animals had scavenged and feasted. Only a few scraps of clothing had remained. None of them matched what she had been wearing when she left town, and there was no wallet or ID found at the scene to make things easy. We would have to wait for DNA to be extracted from bone or get a positive match on dental records.

Both of those things took time, no matter how many strings I pulled to get to the head of the line. And I'd pulled every string I had.

Our best clue was the bracelet.

I studied the photos of it that Wendy's assistant had taken at the scene and compared them to the photographs of Katelyn. The same charms, in the exact same order.

It wasn't proof, but there was no way it was a coincidence.

A few hours later, when I was deep into Katelyn's social media presence, I got a call from the crime lab.

"Are you about to make my day?" I asked.

The cheerful voice on the other end laughed. "I'm not a miracle worker. But we're working on the DNA. I don't even want to know what you had to do in order to get pushed to the front of the line."

I grinned. "All I did was ask nicely."

"Right." I could practically hear her eye roll through the line. "I'm *hoping* I can have that for you tomorrow, but no promises. I do have something else in the meantime."

"What's that?"

"Preliminary cause of death."

I pumped my fist in the air. "Lay it on me."

"The victim's hyoid bone was broken, meaning she likely died of strangulation."

"Homicide then."

"Exactly."

I frowned, remembering how Sheriff McGrath had mentioned the slope and a possible fall. "Is there any way a fall down a difficult slope could have caused that?"

"No. There were no other fractures noted that would indicate a fall or other trauma. Just the hyoid bone and the damage associated with scavenger animals."

"Got it."

"I have something else for you, too."

I sat forward, hearing the change in tone. "What is it?"

"We pulled a fingerprint off the bracelet. It's a match for Katelyn Brown. Considering the size and age of the skeleton, I'd bet money the DNA is going to match, too."

"Thanks. Call me as soon as you know for sure."

"I will."

I hung up the phone and stared into space. Katelyn Brown had left Laramie on her own, saying she was never coming back. She'd ended up here, of all places. Why?

Wildwood wasn't the kind of place that was on most people's radars. Either she'd had a connection here...

Or she had come here to hide.

SOMEONE RAPPED SHARPLY ON MY OFFICE DOOR.

"Come in," I called.

Deputy Hawkins poked her head inside. "I have those lists for you."

I glanced at the clock. "That was fast. What did you find?"

She walked in and plopped a file on my desk. "The only unresolved SAR cases that correspond with that area are a forty-five-year-old man who went missing on a hiking trip in 1988 and an eight-year-old kid who wandered off from a campsite in 2010."

"Neither of which is our victim."

"Exactly. But there are some potential matches on the second list you asked for."

I picked it up and flipped through it. It was thorough. She hadn't simply compiled the list from a database. She'd done her homework and made a serious attempt at matching up possible missing persons with our remains, making notes about why some of them were more likely than others.

"Good work," I said, glancing up at her. "I don't think we're going to need it after all though. We got a print back on the bracelet."

She sat down and leaned forward. "Is it Katelyn?"

"The print belongs to Katelyn, yes," I confirmed. "And the preliminary exam says we're looking at homicide by strangulation."

She sank back, sighing. "Damn. Part of me still hoped it was an accident."

"I know."

"So, what's next?"

I glanced at my watch. "Nothing for now. It's almost five, and I need to check into my cabin."

"Cabin?" There was a change to her voice, a heightened pitch of anxiety that was completely unlike her usual tone.

"Yes," I said, giving her an odd look. "I grabbed a room at the motel last night, but it doesn't have a desk or the room I need for a homicide investigation. So I booked a cabin rental."

She filled her cheeks with air and then blew it out the way she had when Sheriff McGrath had announced she was my partner.

An announcement that hadn't seemed to make her happy in the least.

"Is there a problem?" I asked, suppressing the desire to laugh. I'd never met anyone who wore their emotions on their sleeve to this extent, who didn't even try to play the game of politics with this job.

It was oddly refreshing.

She fidgeted with her fingers. "What, um, cabin did you rent?"

I glanced at the note I'd made about it. "It's a guest cabin at some place called Falcon Ridge Ranch."

Her face drained of all color. But then she leaned her head back and laughed out loud. "Of course it is."

"Why?" I frowned. "Is it a bad place to stay? It looked great online."

"It's the best place to stay," she said with a funny little smile on her face. "It just also happens to be my home."

Ahhh. So that was the reason for her panic. "Your home?"

She nodded. "Yeah. My parents own the ranch and I–I still live there." Her tone fell as she said the last few words, like she was embarrassed to admit it.

"Well, that will make things convenient."

"Yeah." She looked so glum I didn't know what to make of it.

"Deputy Hawkins, if there's a problem with me staying there..."

"No, it's fine," she said, pinching the bridge of her nose and closing her eyes. "It's great. Um, they're doing a guest dinner tonight. Campfire chili and cornbread outside. It's included in your rental rate. But, of course, if you'd rather have some privacy, you can't beat Whiskey Creek. It's the best restaurant in town. The *best*."

I studied her. She obviously hoped I would turn down the invitation to dinner, yet she'd still felt compelled to make it. That was interesting.

I liked interesting.

"Campfire chili sounds great," I said, grinning. "Why would I pass down an opportunity like that? Whiskey Creek will be there tomorrow, right?"

She flattened her lips into an awkward smile. "Right. Um. See you at dinner."

With that, she fled my office.

She wasn't very friendly. Guarded in some ways, but didn't bother to hide her *strong* opinions. She was unprofessional and had no redeeming law enforcement experience to actually add to this investigation. She couldn't sit still to save her life, and she'd driven me nuts while I was trying to focus.

I had no idea why I found myself grinning at the thought of eating dinner with her.

CHAPTER SEVEN

Claire

I GOT INTO MY TRUCK AND HIT THE STEERING WHEEL WITH the palm of my hand.

Dammit.

I hadn't wanted this assignment. Not when it meant working with Mr. Hollywood. And now, he was going to be staying at my ranch. On top of having to work with him, I'd have to see him at breakfast every morning and at the guest dinners we held once a week. There would be no real break from him, no escape.

I'd watched him today, after he'd sent me out. My desk in the bullpen was angled just right to be able to keep an eye on his office. He'd worked constantly, reading things over multiple times, making careful notes. He never twitched or fidgeted or needed to get up and pace the room like I did. He hadn't been punishing me by being silent. That was just who he was. Calm, capable, and clearly able to handle this investigation without me.

He was like a mirror, showing me my incompetence. My inexperience. How absolutely ridiculous it was for me to be a deputy sheriff—especially one investigating a high-profile homicide.

I'd done my best on the assignment he had given me, despite knowing it was pointless. He didn't need me to find other potential victims; he had just wanted me out of his way while he dug into Katelyn Brown's history.

I was a joke.

Tears pricked my eyes as the truth of it washed over me. That's all I'd ever be, no matter how hard I tried to succeed at this job.

When I'd first told my parents I'd applied for the position, they'd both laughed. "Good one," Dad had said, slapping me on my shoulder. It had taken me half an hour to make them realize I was serious, that I really wanted to work for Sheriff McGrath.

I'd understood their surprise. Sort of, anyway. I'd always been a rebel, a girl who refused to fit into any mold anyone tried to put her in. I was a tomboy who loved to rough it in the wilderness, but who also loved sparkly boots and rhinestones. I was a wild soul who longed to see the world, but who'd chosen to stay put in one tiny corner of it—and who still lived in her parents' house, despite being nearly thirty.

I'd also been on the wrong side of the law a time or two and then decided to make a career of law enforcement. Of course they'd thought it was a joke. But they didn't understand me. Not really.

I stared at myself in the rearview mirror.

Did I even understand myself?

Why *had* I become a deputy? It was a question I'd asked myself more than once. The only answer I had was that I wanted to help people —and that answer rang true to my soul.

Joining the Sage County SAR team had been the best decision of my life, one that had given me purpose. We dedicated ourselves to helping people, saving lives, and putting families back together. That work felt *good*. It made me feel like I mattered. Like I was doing something important with my life.

Working on the ranch didn't make me feel that way.

So when Sheriff McGrath had encouraged me to apply for the job, I'd jumped at it, hoping for the same purpose I'd found in search and rescue. But giving out speeding tickets and breaking up bar fights wasn't anything like performing a successful rescue mission. Plus, I was still working part time at the ranch—and still living with my parents. And they weren't any prouder of me than they'd been before.

Sometimes I wasn't sure why I was still doing any of it.

I snuck inside the house, somehow managing to avoid being seen despite hearing at least three of my siblings laughing in the kitchen. I had a brewing headache and was desperate for a hot shower.

While the water heated, I took a hard look at my reflection in the bathroom mirror. Almost a year later, the stiff deputy's uniform still looked strange on me. Men like Trey wore it well, as much as I hated to admit it. It added to their authority and suited their natural build. On me, it felt awkward, like I was playing dress up. I couldn't wait to shed it every single day.

Off came the uniform, and I stepped into the spray of hot water, sighing in relief. My mind drifted to the investigation as I lathered up with my favorite coconut-scented body wash. The uniform might have felt pretend, but this case wasn't. If I wanted to help people, here was a chance to do it—and maybe prove to myself that I was in the right profession after all.

Or fail miserably and prove I was as much of a joke as everyone thought I was.

When the water turned cold, I shut off the faucet and stepped out, wiping the steam from the mirror. I pulled my hair out the bun I always wore to work, sighing in relief with every bobby pin I removed. My curls never looked great after being forcibly held back all day, but that was what cowboy hats were for. I toweled off and slipped into faded jeans and an aqua flannel shirt. Then I pulled on the soft leather boots that fit me like a glove, appreciating how comfortable they felt compared to the shoes I wore with my uniform. The uniform shoes were supposed to be the better ones, made for running after the bad guys that didn't actually exist in Wildwood. But to me, they felt clunky and odd.

Maybe my parents were right. Maybe I belonged on the ranch after all. I loved the ranch—loved the horses, the wide-open spaces, even the smell of the barn.

I couldn't explain why the thought of spending my life here felt so damn suffocating.

By the time I made it downstairs, everyone else had already headed outside to the area where we hosted the guest meals. It was a casual space, with hay bales for people to sit on and rustic buffet tables where Mom served up meals. But the views were spectacular, especially at this time of day with the glow of the setting sun highlighting the majesty of the Bighorn mountains. The sight of them could sweep you right off your feet.

"Claire!" Mom called from where she was already dishing up chili from the buffet. Her long red hair was gathered back in a messy knot. She grinned at me, looking as fresh-faced as always, with only the sunscreen and lip gloss she donned every day.

I headed straight for her. "Hey, Mom."

"I saw the news this afternoon," she said under her breath as she ladled chili into a bowl for the kid in front of her. "Why didn't you tell me what was going on?"

"Because I couldn't," I said, already uncomfortable. "We have to keep everything quiet until we have an ID."

I hadn't even known that the find had made the news, but I supposed it was stupid to think the local reporters wouldn't notice the flurry of activity from multiple official vehicles heading to the scene.

"I'm your mother," she scolded. "You could have told me. I wouldn't have told anyone."

"Mmm-hmm." I raised my eyebrows. *Right.* She wouldn't have told a soul—except for everyone she knew. Mom was great at a lot of things. Keeping secrets wasn't one of them.

She saw my expression and gave me a sheepish look. "*Anyway*, we booked a new guest today—a Vance Weston. When he asked for an open-ended booking, I figured he was involved somehow. I Googled him. He's a special agent from Wyoming DCI. Isn't that amazing? Maybe you can meet him."

"We've already met," I said, trying to avoid her gaze.

"Oh, so he's already here!"

"He is. I'll be his partner on the case."

She gasped. "Claire! That's wonderful. Did he pick you?"

I shook my head. "Sheriff McGrath did."

"Oh. Well, that's still great. Kind of like a promotion." She seemed hopeful.

I sighed, unable to fake a smile. "All I know is my job is about to get a lot more complicated."

"I bet." She gave me a look of genuine sympathy.

But I barely saw it. Because all I saw was *him* strolling up the driveway toward the yard. He'd shown up, despite the many prayers I'd offered in my truck, hoping he wouldn't.

I shot him a look, tilting my head toward Mom with a subtle shake. Warning him. Willing him to walk away.

He didn't. He walked toward us with a swagger, his hands tucked into the pockets of his leather jacket. Dark sunglasses hid his eyes, and he'd ditched the badge and service weapon.

Though I had no doubt he had a weapon hidden somewhere.

"Hey, Hawkins." His rich voice rang out over the crowd.

I closed my eyes and grimaced.

Mom turned to see who had called my name. Her jaw dropped when she saw him. "Who is that delicious man?" she murmured.

By the way his mouth turned up in a smirk, I knew he'd heard.

I took a deep breath as he approached, then forced a smile. "Mom, this is Agent Weston. Agent Weston, this is my mom, Naomi Hawkins."

He removed his sunglasses, sticking them into his front pocket, and took her hand smoothly. "Call me Vance."

"Vance Weston, of course." A wide grin spread on her face. "I recognize the name from our records. You booked cabin four."

"That's right." He nodded. "Your other daughter—Beth, is it?—got me checked in and settled a few minutes ago. Deputy Hawkins invited me to dinner tonight. I hope that's okay."

"Well, of course it is," she said, her smile growing wider as she flicked her eyes from him to me, then back again.

I could see the wheels turning and knew exactly what she was thinking.

She gestured at the lawn. "Any time we have a meal out here, it's open to all the guests. We do breakfast and lunch every day and dinner once a week. But since you're working with Claire, please feel free to join us in the house for family dinner anytime."

I smacked my forehead with my palm, stifling a groan.

"I just might do that. Thank you." Vance grinned at me like we were sharing a joke—only I didn't find it particularly funny.

"Here you go," I said, grabbing a bowl and dipping out a generous portion of chili for him. I shoved it and a wrapped cornbread muffin into his hands with a pointed look. "I'm sure you're starved. You can find a seat anywhere. Enjoy your night."

"Oh, go with him, Claire," Mom said, quickly making a second bowl for me. "Don't make him eat alone. I'm sure you two have a lot to talk about, with the case and all. Plus, you can help give him the lay of the land."

"I'm sure he'd rather have some privacy," I began.

But Mom glared at me and he kept grinning like he knew I was in a bind and had no intention of helping me out of it.

"Fine," I said, giving Mom my sweetest fake smile. "Save me some apple pie?"

"Of course." She beamed at me.

I took the chili from her hands and stalked off, telling myself for the thousandth time that I absolutely *had* to move out and get a place of my own.

Chapter Eight

Vance

Deputy Hawkins marched behind me as I made my way
to one of the only vacant hay bales left. She plopped down beside me,
keeping her eyes straight ahead and putting as much distance as she
could between our bodies.

She hadn't wanted me here. I'd known that and I'd come anyway,
letting curiosity dictate my decision. Seeing the complete misery on her
face made me regret it.

"Your mom seems nice," I said, trying to smooth things over.

She ignored the comment, letting out an irritated huff before words
bubbled out of her so quickly I could barely follow them. "Listen, you
should know that she's desperate to set me up with someone, and for
whatever reason, she just picked you. I would apologize for that, but you
didn't exactly help the situation, did you?" She began shoveling chili
into her mouth like she was a prisoner eating her last meal.

I laughed out loud, surprised by her honesty. "What do you mean I
didn't help?"

She glared at me. "I gave you a *look*. Don't tell me you couldn't figure out what it meant."

Oh, I'd known what it meant. But I had been too curious to walk away.

"Now she's met you, and you're all"—she gestured impatiently at me—"you know, *you*, and she knows we're working together, so you should be warned. She'll be a nightmare."

I raised an eyebrow, trying to interpret her comment about me being *me*. Me as in ... what? Did Claire find me attractive, despite her obvious disdain? The thought was strangely enticing.

I winked at her. "Should I take that as a compliment?"

She shot me another look—one that said *don't be stupid*. "Only if you consider it to be some sort of *compliment* that you're a male without a wedding ring on your finger." She gave me an exaggerated eye roll. "Congratulations. You're a man *and* you're single. We should alert the newspaper on your incredible achievements."

This girl had a mouth on her.

A mouth I suddenly found very appealing.

"I see," I said, amused. "So is that why you wanted me to eat at Whiskey Creek? So that your mom wouldn't know about me?"

"Yep." She let out a little growl. "I wouldn't even have told you about the guest dinner, but I knew whoever checked you in would, so you'd find out anyway. And if Mom found out we were working together and I *hadn't* invited you, I would never hear the end of it."

"Well, for future reference, if you don't want me to come to something, you should just tell me outright. Trying to manipulate me just makes me curious."

She flattened her lips. "Yeah, I realized afterward that I'd messed up there."

"Lesson number one. Partners have to be honest with each other."

She gave me a look I couldn't quite read. And as I gazed at her, I stopped trying.

Her green eyes sparkled in the fading sunlight, the deep swirls of green, blue, and gold reminding me of the sea. Like the ocean in Maine right after a storm, when the sun finally broke through the clouds again. Those faint freckles spattered across her skin reminded me of the constellations that would soon appear across the Wyoming skies, a sight I'd fallen in love with the first time I'd set foot in this state. It was like she spent so much time underneath them that they'd marked themselves on her. With her hair down again, flowing from beneath her brown cowboy hat, she looked freer. More relaxed than she'd been in uniform.

She was absolutely beautiful.

Her cheeks turned pink. She dropped her gaze, then turned away from me.

I shook myself, realizing I'd stared too long, and followed her line of sight to where a gray-haired cowboy was crossing the yard. He walked quickly, despite a slight limp, heading straight for Naomi. When he reached her, he pulled her into an embrace and kissed her right in front of everyone, dipping her down and earning a cheer from the crowd.

"Is that your dad?" I asked.

Claire nodded. "Yeah. Walker Hawkins."

"Walker and Naomi," I said, repeating their names. "I met Beth and you mentioned your brothers Cole and Rhett. Is that it?"

"Nope." She snorted. "But you have an impressive memory for names."

"Part of the job. How many siblings do you have in all?"

"Six."

I nearly choked on the bite of cornbread I'd just put in my mouth. "Six? Really?"

"Yeah. Travis is the oldest. Then Cole, then me, then Rhett. Rhett and I are just ten months apart, so we grew up kind of like twins. Beth has an actual twin named Finn—he's a professor in Montana. They came next. And that's my baby brother, Jonathan."

She pointed at a lanky kid I guessed to be about eighteen or nineteen. He wore a black cowboy hat and leather chaps, and he had left the top few buttons of his western shirt undone. He walked with an exaggerated swagger and had two teenage girls following him around, hanging on to his every word.

"He looks like quite the ladies' man," I commented.

"Oh, he is." She laughed. "All my brothers have been, to be honest with you, but I think Jonathan will end up taking the prize. He can't fight 'em off."

"Doesn't look like he's trying," I said, winking.

"Those girls are tourists," she explained, a little grin on her face. "I swear, every teenage girl who comes here falls in love with him. Some of them keep mailing love letters for months."

I cracked up. The kid probably enjoyed his job here—maybe too much. Then I whistled as I thought back over all the names she'd listed off. "Seven kids. Wow. That's a lot."

I'd always wanted siblings. Wanted someone to have camaraderie with instead of being the only pawn between two parents at war. With a childhood as cold as mine, I couldn't imagine growing up in such a big, warm family.

Because that was something else I'd noticed watching Claire. The love she had for her family was fierce. It shone in her eyes when she talked about them.

She shrugged. "Mom's a devout Catholic. Took the whole procreation thing pretty seriously. How about you?"

"I'm Protestant."

She rolled her eyes. "I mean how many siblings do you have?"

I grinned. "I know. Sorry. I'm an only child."

"Figures."

"What do you mean?"

This time, she was the one smirking. "You seem like someone who's used to being the center of attention. Plus, I get the impression you don't play well with others."

My eyes widened. "Oh really?"

"Really." She laughed and nudged me with her elbow, letting me know she was just teasing. "So where did you grow up? You're clearly not Wyoming born and raised."

"What makes you think that?"

She gestured to my boots. "Those. No one I know would ever be caught dead wearing them."

I laughed. "What's wrong with my boots?"

"They're too new. Makes you look like a city slicker who's never done any real work."

"So you're saying I should muddy them up."

"That's a start. But I still wouldn't believe you're from here. The accent's wrong."

"You're perceptive," I said, giving her another long look. She'd proven it at the crime scene, and she was proving it here, too.

"You didn't answer the question."

"You're also nosy." I narrowed my eyes, even as my lips twisted into a playful smile.

She grinned. "And you're stalling."

She wasn't wrong. I didn't usually talk about my history, partly because I preferred keeping it to myself and partly because most people didn't ask.

Claire Hawkins wasn't most people.

But I owed her something—something personal. After all, I'd come here, despite knowing she didn't want me to. I'd introduced myself to her mom, knowing she wanted me to stay away. And I'd questioned her about *her* family without a second thought.

"I was born in New York," I said. "But I split my time between there and Maine as a kid. Mostly Maine. Moved full-time to NYC for college. Went to work for the NYPD the fall after I graduated and stayed there until I took the job with DCI. "

She was quiet for a second. "Parents divorced?"

"Yeah."

"That bites."

I shrugged. "I was six. I can barely remember a time when they *weren't* divorced."

She glanced my way, like she was the one trying to read me this time. "I'm guessing your mom lived in Maine, your dad lived in New York?"

I nodded. "Yeah."

"What part of Maine?"

"Seal Harbor. It's a small neighborhood close to Bar Harbor and Acadia."

Her eyebrows went up. "Oh, I've heard of it. A 'small neighborhood' that happens to be the vacation playground for the rich and famous."

I tilted my head toward her in confirmation.

She snorted. "Well, that certainly explains the six-hundred-dollar boots and the fancy leather jacket on a DCI salary. What it doesn't explain is why the hell you're working for Wyoming DCI to begin with. Money like that, NYPD detective on your résumé... That's an odd move, Weston."

I shot her a look. "*Very* nosy," I murmured.

She laughed out loud. "Said the man who showed up for dinner here just because he was *curious*."

"Fair point."

"How's the chili?" she asked, changing the subject.

"It's great. Best chili I've ever had," I said, meaning it.

"Mom's a fantastic cook."

"She is. I'm glad I came." I meant that, too—especially now that Claire had relaxed and the misery on her face had been replaced with a happy kind of calm.

She was different out here.

It hit me that I was, too. Tonight was unusual for me. I typically hyper-focused on my cases, barely taking the time to eat. I couldn't remember the last time I'd relaxed outside on a beautiful evening or even had a conversation that didn't involve work.

"I guess I'm glad you came, too. Maybe it's good you've met Mom," she said, letting out a long breath of resignation. "Now, that's over and we can just focus on the investigation."

"Absolutely." But I was surprised to realize I didn't want to think about the investigation at all.

AFTER DINNER, I STROLLED BACK TO MY CABIN ALONE, enjoying the quiet. Most of the guests were still at the bonfire, chowing down on s'mores while Walker entertained them with cowboy stories. Their voices faded as I walked, until all I could hear was the soft whinnies of the horses in the nearby pasture. Bright stars filled the sky, so clear you could see the Milky Way.

You didn't get skies like this in New York City.

As I walked, my thoughts drifted back to Claire. She was smart. Strong. But she didn't have the personality of a cop, and she seemed much happier out on the ranch—at least when her mother wasn't pestering her. The place appeared to be a successful tourist operation, employing most of the family. She clearly loved her siblings, and it seemed like there was more than enough work to employ her, too.

Why had she chosen a different path?

Not my business, I reminded myself. I was here for one reason only: to solve Katelyn's murder.

One final investigation as a DCI special agent before I moved on.

My new job was waiting for me as soon as I closed this case. It added another layer of motivation. The quicker I wrapped things up here, the quicker I could start the next chapter of my life. Which meant I shouldn't waste time with Claire Hawkins.

She'd done well with her assignment today. And she was surprisingly perceptive, a fantastic skill for a detective. She had a ton of potential. But no matter how bright she was, she was still completely inexperienced and I didn't have time to train her in the field. She could handle the paperwork while I worked the investigation.

Alone.

When I reached my door, I let myself in and tossed my keys into the bowl at the entryway, flicking on the lights to get a better look at the cabin I'd barely glanced at earlier. The place was styled to look rustic, but the quality of the furniture and the included amenities put the rental on par with some of the better resorts I'd been to. It had a fully stocked kitchenette with a solid oak table, a living area with a stone fireplace and full-grain leather furniture, and a private bedroom with luxurious linens and a great view of the mountains. The floors were spotless and the furniture shined. The faint scents of cedar and citrus gave the place a fresh, clean feeling.

The Hawkins family had a great operation, and staying here would be a giant step up from the motel in town. Satisfied, I threw my jacket onto a kitchen chair and grabbed my files. Then I headed to the living area, flicked on the standing lamp, and sank down into the oversized leather armchair, propping my feet up on the matching footstool. Before long, I was lost in my notes, searching for something that would unlock this case. A connection, a clue, a detail nobody had noticed.

A few minutes later, my phone buzzed. I picked it up and scanned the text message.

Good evening, Agent Weston. This is Sgt. Trey Collins from the Sage County SO. I'd love to be of assistance on this case.

I sent him a quick text back.

Thanks. I appreciate the offer.

I put my phone down, meaning for that to be the end of it, but it buzzed again seconds later.

I bet you do, after today lol. I could tell you were as surprised as I was that Sheriff McGrath assigned Hawkins to you. We both know she's out of her league on this one. I'm sure if you request a change, he'll make it happen.

I frowned. This was definitely over the line. And if this was how Claire's colleagues talked about her, no wonder she was so uncomfortable at the office. I decided to be more direct in my answer.

Apologies for being unclear. I appreciate the offer, but Sheriff McGrath assigned Deputy Hawkins to the case and she and I have it covered. I believe the sheriff needs your assistance keeping the town running smoothly.

Dots appeared, showing he was typing again. But after a few seconds, they stopped, and whatever message he'd begun typing went unsent.

Probably a good thing.

I put my hands behind my head, letting my thoughts drift again to Claire. I couldn't figure out why it pissed me off so much that Collins had denigrated her that way. He wasn't wrong—I *had* been surprised. She was still green and lacked investigative experience. And hadn't I already decided that I didn't have time to train her?

I felt bad for her, but I wasn't here to make friends.

One last case. I couldn't afford a distraction.

Chapter Nine

Claire

The next morning, I tried to slip out of the house without getting caught. But Mom, with her special radar, heard me tiptoeing across the living room and called me into the kitchen.

"Leaving without breakfast?" she asked, all doe-eyed and innocent. "I baked this morning. Fresh cherry muffins—your favorite."

My mouth watered. Unable to resist, I grabbed one off the tray and bit into it.

Sugar. Her personal form of truth serum for me. I eyed her, waiting for the questions to start. But she hummed to herself, putting two more trays into the oven to bake without saying a word.

"Where's everyone else?" I asked, unable to keep the edge of suspicion out of my voice. We all ate our breakfast earlier than the guests, since ranch life didn't give us the luxury to sleep in the way people on vacation preferred to. Every morning, the sprawling family kitchen was the meeting ground for the whole Hawkins crew as we filled our bellies and our thermoses and divided up duties for the day.

"You just missed the guys," she said, referring to Dad, Travis, and Jonathan. "They're moving cattle from the summer pasture to the winter lot today, so they needed to get an early start. The rest of them are around here somewhere."

"Uh huh." *Somewhere.* Mom probably told them to clear the kitchen so she could talk to me.

I went to the cabinet and pulled out a thermos to fill with coffee.

"So," Mom said, "you're working the homicide case."

I closed my eyes and counted to ten before turning around. "I never said it was a homicide."

She waved me off. "They called in DCI for a body in the woods. Of course it's a homicide. But that's not the point. I think you should take some time off from working here. With Rhett still helping out, we can cover things and keep you free to devote however much time you need to this."

"That's probably a good idea," I admitted. I only worked for the ranch part-time, and my responsibilities had gone way down with Rhett back. But she was right—I could be clocking some crazy hours over the coming weeks.

"Your Agent Weston seems nice," she said, giving me a little smile.

Here we go. "Don't even think about it."

She lifted her hands in protest. "I don't know what you're talking about. I'm just glad that you have someone nicer than Trey to work with. Nicer *and* nice to look at." She winked. "Is he single?"

"Gotta go," I said, giving an exaggerated look at my watch. "Thanks for breakfast."

"Here," she said, grabbing a paper bag off the counter. "I made up breakfast to go for Agent Weston, in case he needs to get an early start, too. Can you drop it off at his cabin for me? You know, it just hit me that you guys could carpool. I mean, you're going to the same place after all."

"Mom. Stop."

The look she gave me was pure innocence, but I'd watched her play matchmaker with Rhett and Cheyenne and I knew exactly what she was doing. I pointed my finger at her in warning as I stalked out.

. . .

I DID *NOT* DROP AGENT WESTON'S MUFFIN OFF AT HIS CABIN, but I did take it with me so I could give it to him at the office. As I drove into town, I felt a glimmer of excitement about work that I hadn't experienced in a very long time. I was working on an actual homicide case. I was doing something that *mattered.*

On top of that, Agent Weston was actually kind of nice.

Last night had been fun. Outside of the office, he'd been more relaxed, easy to talk to. The teasing between us had been...

Unexpected.

There was a spark there. Chemistry between us that seemed to surprise him as much as it did me. The way he'd looked at me... It was like the way I looked at the mountains, captivated by their beauty and power.

It had been a long time since someone had looked at me like that.

I wasn't silly enough to think that anything might actually happen between us. We were colleagues. But I was looking forward to doing some real work with someone who might actually have my back. Someone who would treat me like a partner.

And maybe I looked forward to a little flirtation on the side, too.

But Agent Weston wasn't around when I got to the office. No one was, except Andrea and Trey, who scowled and didn't speak to me before storming out for his shift on patrol. I shrugged it off. He'd be butthurt for a while over losing the assignment to me, but there was nothing I could do about it. It wasn't like I'd volunteered for the gig.

I settled in at my desk to wait. An hour later, Agent Weston still hadn't shown up, and my good feelings toward him had slid back to annoyance.

I was itching to dive into this investigation. But I knew better than to go out on my own and start asking questions. Until we had an official ID and Sheriff McGrath gave a press conference, I had to keep Katelyn's name quiet. And Agent Weston hadn't given me anything else to do in the meantime.

Another hour passed by.

By that point, I was pissed off. I couldn't just keep sitting there waiting for him to show up.

So I started digging. *Quietly.*

. . .

It was after lunch when Agent Weston finally came into the office, wearing a scowl on his face that was nearly as bad as the one Trey had worn earlier. I jumped up, eager to share what I'd discovered.

He glanced around at the empty building. "Is Sheriff McGrath here?"

"No. But—"

He turned and headed for his office, ignoring me completely.

I ground my teeth and followed him. *What the hell*? What happened to the man I'd hung out with last night?

What was it about this building that made me invisible?

I stomped into his office planning to give him a piece of my mind, but he spoke before I could.

"DNA results are in. It's Katelyn."

"Oh." I sank into the chair across from his desk. I'd expected it, but hearing it still felt heavy.

"They're notifying next of kin this afternoon. The news will break after that." His tone was flat.

"Okay. So, what's next?"

He scrubbed his face, clearly frustrated. "Once her name has been released, we'll start asking questions, trying to find a connection between her and someone from this area. A reason for her to be here. Worst-case scenario, there is none. The fact that she left her cell phone behind makes me wonder if she wanted to hide. If she picked this place at random—"

"I don't think that's what happened."

He stared at the wall absentmindedly, like he was thinking out loud instead of talking to me. "There were rumors she had a new boyfriend, one she was deliberately keeping quiet. No photos on social media, but a few people suspected it, including her roommate. If they're right, there's a good chance he's involved. When people leave in the middle of the night, they're either running away from something or running to someone."

"Not a bad theory, but—"

He ignored me, continuing with his train of thought as he fiddled with a pen on his desk. "If he wasn't local, he could have been someone she met online. We might be dealing with a trafficker who convinced her to come to him. Now that we have a positive ID, I need to get warrants and look through her phone and laptop. Wouldn't be a bad idea to reinterview her roommate, either."

"*Agent Weston.*" I raised my voice, leaning over the table and snapping my fingers in front of his face to get his attention. "Hello? I need to tell you something."

He finally looked at me, his eyes clearing like he was seeing me for the first time that day. "Oh yeah?"

"Yeah." A little thrill of excitement went through me. I'd gone hunting, and I'd scored.

"Go ahead," he said, waiting.

"I found Katelyn's connection to Wildwood."

He straightened, looking dumbfounded. "What?"

"Tony Evans," I said smugly, enjoying the look on his face. "Not a new boyfriend, but an old one. He's a sophomore at the college there, but he grew up in Wildwood. His dad is our mayor."

"You're kidding." Agent Weston grabbed the file on Katelyn and flipped through it, scanning quickly. He looked up. "Is he the one she had a fight with at the party that night? The name wasn't listed in the report."

"I don't know. Maybe." I shrugged.

He sat back and stared at the wall again, his brows furrowed. "They didn't interview him. Maybe they thought it didn't matter since they were looking at a voluntary disappearance. But we need to dig into that more, especially since he's from here." He looked back at me, grinning. "Nice work. This is a great lead. How did you find out about her dating Tony?"

My face flushed. I hoped I hadn't broken any rules. "I called my brother, Finn, the college professor."

"You said he worked in Montana."

"He does. But he has a lot of connections at UW," I explained. "He's been working with a colleague on a joint project, so he's on campus in Laramie a couple of weeks each semester. And you don't have to worry about him saying anything to anyone—he's as discreet as they come."

"What did he know about Katelyn?" Agent Weston was frowning, but he didn't seem to be angry at me—just thoughtful as he mulled over this new information.

At least I hoped that's all it was.

"He said her disappearance caused enough of a stir on campus that it was all anyone talked about for a few weeks. The general consensus was that she'd had some kind of mental health breakdown from stress. One of her professors told him she'd been concerned about her behavior all semester. Said she'd been skipping classes, that her grades had dropped, and that she seemed distracted."

"Hmmm. And Tony? How did Finn know they were dating?"

"He always runs into Tony when he's on campus. Makes a point to say hi, you know, being from the same town and all. Said Tony introduced him to Katelyn last fall. But they'd broken up before Finn was there in February. He said Tony was devastated about it."

"That's very interesting." He grinned again. "Excellent work."

"Thanks." I flushed under the praise.

Heavy footsteps came down the hall, followed by Sheriff McGrath sticking his head in the office.

Agent Weston stood. "We have an ID."

"I know." Sheriff McGrath's shoulders sagged. "I just got off the phone with Laramie PD. They've notified her mother. The news breaks in an hour."

Agent Weston's eyes met mine. "Get ready," he murmured.

"For what?"

He shook his head. "Things are about to get wild."

Chapter Ten

Vance

Sheriff McGrath put out a statement on his social media account and called a press conference to let the citizens of Wildwood know what was going on. I watched the whole thing, observing on the sidelines.

You could learn a lot about people, seeing their reactions to something like this.

It was also interesting to note that Mayor Evans—father of Tony Evans, the apparent ex-boyfriend to the victim—didn't show up at all.

Very interesting.

I told Claire to keep the tidbit about Tony to herself. I didn't want our knowledge of that information to spread before I could get down to the university and interview him personally. The last thing I wanted was for someone to tip him off and give him time to prepare a story—or advise him to lawyer up.

As soon as Sheriff McGrath wrapped up, I headed to my SUV, planning to drive straight to Laramie. I could get there by nine—eight if I ignored the speed limit—and possibly speak to Tony that night.

The faster, the better.

As I opened my door, Claire caught up with me. "Wait," she called, jogging down the sidewalk to where I was parked. She lowered her voice when she got close. "Are you heading to interview him now?"

"Yeah." I closed the door and leaned against it, crossing my arms. "I want to talk to both him and the roommate."

"Can I come?" She bit her lip, her normal confidence gone.

I was torn.

On one hand, she was supposed to be my partner on this case, and she was the one who had gotten this lead to begin with. But she had no training. No experience. And no filter on that mouth of hers.

A mouth that I found terribly distracting.

Besides, I always worked better alone.

"Laramie is outside of your jurisdiction," I began, trying to let her down gently.

"Right." She let out a breath, her shoulders sagging with disappointment.

I almost took it back and told her she could come observe. It would be good for her if she planned on staying in law enforcement.

But I didn't. I left her behind.

One last case, I reminded myself. *No distractions.*

I ARRIVED IN LARAMIE AT SEVEN FORTY-FIVE, BEATING MY own estimate on time. After talking at length with Tony, I grabbed a hotel so I could spend the following day on campus, interviewing Katelyn's roommate and other students who had known her. Next, I stopped by the police department to chat in person with the officers who had investigated her disappearance, then wrapped up my quick trip with a final stop at Katelyn's mother's house.

By the time I pulled back into Falcon Ridge Ranch, I'd been gone for nearly thirty-six hours and had only slept a few of them. The ranch was quiet and the rest of the cabins were dark, everyone else having settled in for the night hours before.

Fatigue hit hard when I let myself into the cabin. I fell into bed and slept like the dead, finally giving my brain the time it needed to process the information I'd crammed into it.

When the sky began to lighten, brightening the room with the first glimpse of dawn, I woke refreshed and ready to work. Needing fuel, I went to the kitchen and grabbed one of the protein bars I'd brought with me, but then I paused, remembering that the rental came with breakfast.

Anything Naomi Hawkins had cooked would be far better than a cold protein bar.

I locked up and started the walk toward the yard, appreciating the view as the sun rose over the land. It made the vista a rainbow of colors: golden light set against hazy blue mountains, pink clouds with purple shadows, green sagebrush in the pastures. I usually preferred the sunrise over the ocean. But I had to admit, it was hard to imagine a scene prettier than this one.

Claire and one of her brothers came over the hill, galloping toward the stables on horseback. I stopped in my tracks, unable to take my eyes off her. She leaned forward in the saddle, her eyes laser-focused on the stables. Her long blonde hair blew behind her in the wind, and her grin was so wide I could see it from here.

And suddenly I realized that the scene could get prettier after all.

Claire and her horse, a dappled gray mustang with a dark mane, flew over the ground like one. A cloud of dust rose behind them as they pulled ahead of her brother.

I thought they were going to blow right past the stable, but as they approached, she pulled to a sudden stop. Then she turned around, threw her head back, and let out a cheerful riff of laughter that reminded me of nimble fingers flying over piano keys.

Just like my favorite Mozart concerto.

"Sucker," she called out as her brother—the long-haired one named Rhett, who I'd originally assumed was her boyfriend—came up beside her on his black stallion.

"You cheated," he announced. "There's no way your horse should have beat mine."

"Bigger doesn't always mean better." She smirked, shaking her head.

I chuckled. Claire was a force to be reckoned with.

At the sound, she turned and watched me walking toward them. The smile dropped off her face. "Good morning, Agent Weston. I didn't know you were back." Her tone changed, the warmth gone.

"Call me Vance," I said without thinking.

Another surprise. I never let deputies call me by my first name, especially if I was investigating in their county. But I'd said it, and I couldn't exactly take it back.

Oddly enough, I didn't want to.

She gave me a tight smile. "Do you need something?"

"No," I said, tucking my hands into the pockets of my jacket. "I'm heading to grab some breakfast. I'll see you at the office this morning. Unless—"

"Unless what?" Those deep green eyes stared at me, waiting for an answer.

I'd been about to suggest we carpool. But my whole plan was to distance myself. To stay focused.

Something about seeing her in her element had nearly made me forget it.

"Nothing," I said. "See you later." I turned around and walked away before I dug myself in even deeper.

She was pissed. Honestly, I couldn't blame her. I was being exactly the kind of agent I'd always hated working with during my days at the NYPD—one who had no real interest in partnering with the local agency and just wanted them to get out of his way.

But this was different, I assured myself. Because unlike how I'd been back then, she wasn't an experienced NYPD detective. She was a sassy cowgirl-turned-deputy who needed to have her hand held in order to work an investigation.

I didn't have time for that.

THE BREAKFAST CROWD WAS SMALL. ONLY A HANDFUL OF people milled around, drinking coffee and eating some sort of breakfast casserole. It didn't look particularly appealing, but when the breeze brought a whiff of it my way, my mouth started watering.

Naomi Hawkins really could cook.

Speaking of Naomi, she spotted me right away and waved me over to the buffet table where she and Beth were serving. Claire's kid brother, Jonathan, was next to them, filling a thermos from one of the carafes.

"Good morning, Agent Weston!" Naomi's green eyes were bright. Sharp. They reminded me of Claire's.

"Good morning. And please, call me Vance."

She beamed. "I was getting worried we'd scared you off. Didn't see your vehicle here at all yesterday."

She was also nosy like Claire. It made me grin.

"No, you didn't scare me off. Quite the opposite actually. Work took me away, but I'm thrilled to be back here instead of at a hotel. I'd like to commend you on your accommodations. I can't remember the last time I've had such a restful night."

She smiled warmly. "I'm glad to hear it. Coffee?"

"Please."

"How do you take it?"

"Black."

She grinned as she gestured for Jonathan to pour me a cup. "Just like Claire. She's over at the stables. Beth can take you over—"

I held up a hand, interrupting her. "That's okay. I'm actually here to talk to you."

Jonathan passed me the coffee, his dark eyes staring at me with marked curiosity. We'd never actually met the other night. He'd been too busy entertaining the girls who'd flocked to his side.

"Vance Weston," I said, sticking my hand out for him to shake. "I'm working with your sister."

Sort of. Guilt tried to creep in.

He grasped my hand with a strength that surprised me. "Jonathan."

"Nice to meet you."

He nodded but didn't say the same.

Beth handed me a plate of casserole, then touched Jonathan's arm gently, pulling him back to give me space to talk to their mother.

Naomi cocked her head. "So, what can I help you with, Vance?"

I took a sip of the coffee. *Divine.* It had a touch of woodsmoke in it, creating the illusion that it had been made over a fire and adding to the cowboy experience for the guests. Incredible.

"Nice coffee," I said appreciatively before getting to my question. "Running this ranch, you probably see most of the tourists who come through this area."

She nodded. "I do, yes. Some stay at the motel of course. It's a lot cheaper. But we get the lion's share of them. There are also a couple of longer-term vacation rentals nearby."

I pulled a photograph of Katelyn Brown from my jacket. "I'm sure you've seen her photo on the news. Did she ever rent one of your cabins?"

Naomi's face grew sad as she looked at the picture. "Poor thing. I saw Sheriff McGrath's announcement. But no, she's never stayed here."

"Are you sure?"

"Positive. We interact with all of our guests. It's part of the experience. You can't just get a code and check yourself in here—we do it that way on purpose. We live here. We want to know the people staying on our property." Naomi shook her head. "She's never been here."

I wasn't surprised, but it never hurt to ask. "She was in this area over Christmas break. Did you see her around town anywhere? Coming to events, hanging out with anyone..."

Naomi's eyes narrowed. She tapped her cheek with her finger and hummed as she thought. "I can't remember ever seeing her, no. Not at any of the town Christmas events. I'm almost always here at the ranch though. Beth, Jonathan, what about you?"

They came closer. Beth took the photograph from my outstretched hand.

Jonathan glanced at it quickly, then shook his head. "Nah. Never seen her."

"You sure?" I asked, cocking my head. He'd barely looked at the photo.

"I'm sure. I've got to go, Mom. Travis is waiting." He gave Naomi a quick peck on the check, then sauntered off without a backward glance.

Beth took her time studying the photograph. Watching her, I was struck by just how different she and Claire were. Claire's hair was a mess of blonde curls; Beth's was soft brown waves. Claire's eyes were green like her mother's, while Beth's were brown. Claire was short; Beth was tall.

But it was more than that. Their demeanors were totally different. Beth was quiet and reserved. She seemed to take an extra moment to think before answering anything—I'd noticed that even when she'd checked me in and given me the key to my cabin.

Claire, on the other hand, seemed to let every thought bubble up out of her mouth before she even knew what they were going to be. And the Claire I'd seen riding that horse today was a free spirit, as wild and untamed as the Wyoming wilderness. I couldn't imagine her sister doing the same.

Beth handed the photograph back. "No, I've never seen her in person," she said softly. "But I feel so bad for her. I hope you and Claire find out what happened."

"I will," I answered, leaving Claire out of it.

It would be me and me alone working this case. There was no *we* about it.

No distractions.

CHAPTER ELEVEN

Claire

I WAS FUMING. OTHER THAN HIS BRIEF APPEARANCE THE DAY we'd gotten the official ID, Agent Weston had stayed away from the office, making it abundantly clear to everyone there that I wasn't his "partner" at all.

Trey was loving it.

Meanwhile, I was miserable. Bored out of my ever-loving mind. Sheriff McGrath wasn't assigning me any normal duties because he wanted me to be "available" for Agent Weston. I'd been stuck twiddling my thumbs for two days straight, on top of having to endure Trey's taunts about the whole thing.

And now, Agent Weston was back, strolling past my pasture like he didn't have a care in the world. No apology, no update on the case. Nothing.

I couldn't believe I'd ever thought he was nice.

Rhett rode his horse over toward me, a lazy smirk on his face.

"Should I ask why you're shooting daggers out of your eyes?" he drawled, leaning forward in his saddle. "And should I warn poor Agent Weston that he's officially on your bad side?"

I clenched my fists. "That. Man." The words came out with a venom I rarely used.

Rhett grinned. "Uh oh. Haven't seen you this fired up in ages. What did he do?"

"I'm supposed to be his partner," I complained. "But he's kept me completely out of the loop."

"I thought you hated working with him." Rhett shot me a puzzled look. "Chey said you called him an arrogant prick. Shouldn't you be relieved he's letting you off the hook?"

I huffed, trying to figure out how to explain it. "Look, I would have been fine if Sheriff McGrath had partnered him with Trey. That's what I expected. But he didn't. He gave the case to me. And now it matters, you know?"

"Yeah." Rhett plucked a piece of straw out of his horse's mane and stuck it into his mouth, chewing the end of it. "I get that. It's like if someone went missing near the county line and they called the other SAR team in, we'd feel fine about it. But if they call us, we're going to see it through."

"Exactly. I'm the one who found her." I swallowed hard, my mind flashing back to images from that night. It was terrible to think that she had been strangled, dumped, and left out there to be eaten by predators. Whoever had killed her had a cold, cruel heart.

I shook myself, shutting the images out of my head, and took a deep breath. Rhett was watching me closely.

"You okay?" His tone was mild, but worry sparked in his eyes.

"I'm fine." I had to be.

He sat patiently, giving me a look that said he was there if I wanted to talk. But he didn't push.

I squared my shoulders and brought the conversation back to the problem at hand. "Like I was saying, I found her, and I was assigned to the case. But he's not letting me do anything." The frustration roared back, taking over the sadness.

Rhett's posture relaxed. He was used to seeing me pissed off. Could handle that. It was the sadness that bothered him because he couldn't do a damn thing about it.

"I've never known you to wait for permission," he said, winking.

It caught me off guard. I laughed, the tightness in my chest easing. "You're right," I admitted. "That's not my style, is it? Easier to ask forgiveness instead."

My brother understood. He got me. He didn't think I was being stupid or that I should be grateful for an easy gig—words Trey had thrown at me yesterday, insinuating that I wouldn't have been able to handle it if Agent Weston had actually wanted me to contribute.

I never should have let those words eat at me. I could handle anything that was thrown my way, no matter what anyone else thought.

"Maybe you should solve this case without him." Rhett smirked, egging me on. "Show him how we do it here in Wildwood."

I grinned. "Maybe I will."

After all, I was Claire Hawkins. I didn't sit on the sidelines.

And I didn't wait for permission.

I SAID GOODBYE TO MY BEAUTIFUL HORSE, SHADOW, stealing a few extra kisses from her for courage. Then I headed into the house and put on my uniform.

I was going to work, whether Agent Weston liked it or not.

He'd never given me his contact information, so I slipped into the office Mom and Beth used to manage the guest bookings and logged onto the computer. It only took a second to find his cell phone number in their records.

Before I could change my mind, I sent him a quick text.

Hi, this is Deputy Hawkins. I won't be at the office this morning after all. I'm following up on some possible leads.

He texted back almost immediately, but I stuffed my phone into my pocket, choosing not to read it. If I hadn't *seen* an order to stand down, then I couldn't get in trouble for failing to do so.

Plausible deniability. My big brothers had taught me that one as soon as I'd been old enough to start getting into trouble.

Next, I tracked down my baby brother, Jonathan.

"Hey, you," I called as I caught him loading up in one of the farm trucks.

He leaned his head out the window. "What's up?"

I opened the door to the passenger's seat and climbed in. "I need some info."

He eyed me suspiciously. "What kind of info?"

"Names. Anyone Tony Evans was close to here who might still be in touch with him."

His eyes narrowed. "Is this about that girl who got killed?"

"You know I can't tell you anything about that. And *you* can't tell anyone I asked you this, got it?" I said it as a precaution, knowing that it wasn't necessary. Jonathan was a vault. He wouldn't tell anyone we'd talked. It was the sibling code.

He ran his hands through his hair, thinking. "Most of the people Tony ran around with have left, either for jobs or college. But there's a couple of people you could try. Rob Dacus for one."

"Rob?" My eyebrows shot up. Rob wasn't exactly who I'd pictured the mayor's son hanging out with. Tony had a dark side—I knew that. But it was the kind that stayed mostly hidden under nice clothes and a winning smile. The kind whose behaviors were often excused because of who his parents were.

Rob was the opposite. He was harmless from my perspective. A gentle soul who'd made some bad choices that didn't hurt anyone but himself. But he was poor and he looked rough. Because of it, he got more trouble than he deserved.

Jonathan shrugged. "They liked to get high together. If Tony wanted a smoke, that's where he went for it. I figure he still does when he's back in town for breaks."

"Got it. Anyone else?"

Jonathan moved his head back and forth like he was weighing it. "It's probably a dead end, but you could try talking to Elsa Jones. They dated senior year. I know they hooked up a couple of times that first year when he came back, but I think it fizzled out after that."

"Rob Dacus and Elsa Jones. Got it."

He hesitated. "Go easy on Elsa when you talk to her, okay? Even though she dated Tony... She's nice. And she's had a rough few years."

The look in his eyes surprised me. There was a tenderness I'd never seen in my baby brother.

"I will," I promised. "I won't even let her know I'm questioning her. I'll just stop by and make conversation, see what I can find out."

He nodded, relieved.

"Thanks, bro. I'll see you later." I snuck a quick kiss on his cheek before he could push me away.

He rolled his eyes but couldn't hide his grin.

It was good to see. Sometimes I worried about him. He'd been so quiet lately, always walking around like the weight of the world was on his shoulders.

Seeing him smile made some of the weight ease off of mine.

Elsa Jones worked at our post office, making it easy to talk to her without it looking suspicious. I went there first, ignoring the phone vibrating in my pocket as I walked inside.

Elsa was alone at the front, restocking the prepaid shipping boxes. "Hi, Deputy Hawkins," she said, smiling at me as she stuck the last of her boxes into a slot and wiped her hands. "What can I do for you today?"

I returned her smile. She was a sweet girl with long brown hair, rosy cheeks, and a shy smile. She was always friendly and kind, patient with customers.

I'd never known what she had seen in Tony Evans.

"I need a book of stamps," I said. "Jonathan still hasn't sent out thank-you cards for his graduation presents and Mom's about to have a fit. Thought I'd help him out by marking one thing off the list."

"That's nice of you." She smoothed back the hair that had fallen loose from her ponytail as she walked behind the counter and took her place at the register. "Just one book? He had quite the fan club at graduation."

"I guess you better make it two, just in case. You know, it's still crazy to me that you've all grown up already. He graduated this year, you graduated last year..." I shook my head and mimicked the expression all the older people in my life used to make about me.

"It's pretty crazy," she agreed, laughing softly as she rang me up. "I don't exactly feel like an adult yet."

"Me either." I fished my debit card out of my wallet and swiped it. "And I *know* Jonathan doesn't."

"I figured he'd be at college this fall," she commented. She kept her eyes trained on the register, but her cheeks turned just a bit more pink.

"He hasn't really decided what he's doing next," I said, trying to figure out a natural segue into the questions I really cared about.

"Does that mean he might be staying at the ranch, making a career of it?" she asked, passing me my stamps and my receipt.

I shrugged. "Maybe. He hasn't really said. Not to me anyway. You know Jonathan—he's quiet."

"Yes, he is." She smiled with the same tenderness he'd had when he told me to be careful with her.

Interesting.

"What about you? You think you'll stick around?"

Her smile faded. "Probably. I wanted to go to college. Even had a scholarship. But Dad's not doing so great and I didn't feel like I could leave. Maybe someday."

My heart squeezed for the girl. Elsa's dad had developed severe early-onset dementia while she was in high school. It had been a huge shock for all of them. He'd only been fifty and had quickly gone from being their sole breadwinner to needing full-time care. I'd always had a feeling that's why Elsa had stayed, but this was the first time she'd voiced it.

"I'm sorry," I said. I was—both for what she was going through and for the fact that I was bringing it up for my own purposes.

She smiled again, even though her eyes looked moist. "I'm glad I can help. Glad Mom doesn't have to do it on her own. There will be time for college later."

I understood that—the mix of emotions. Torn between duty and desire.

"I bet it was hard though, giving that up." I bit my lip, forcing down the guilt about plying her for information. "Were you planning on going to UW with Tony? You guys dated senior year, right?"

Her face turned sheepish. "Yeah. But as they say, every cloud has a silver lining. My staying here gave me a way to end things with him." Her voice had completely changed, the sadness replaced by disgust.

"Oh." I didn't have to fake my surprise. "I didn't realize you'd wanted to. I thought you guys still got together when he came back on breaks."

She looked embarrassed. "He used to call me when he came back to town—that first semester anyway. Thanksgiving break was the last time. I was relieved when it stopped."

"Why?" I cocked my head.

"Tony's ... intense. When he first asked me out, I said yes. Mostly because..." She hesitated, averting her eyes. "Well. For stupid reasons. I never meant for it to get serious. Never thought he'd want it to, honestly."

"But he did?"

She nodded. "I knew pretty quickly that he wasn't 'the one.' Know what I mean?"

I chuckled. "Yeah. I know what you mean."

"But he didn't see it that way." She rolled her eyes. "Tony was obsessive. By our third date, he was trying to plan our entire future together without ever asking me if I even wanted one."

"Really?" I tried to line that up with what I knew about Tony. On one hand, I could see it. He had an ego and he'd never been the type to take no for an answer. But I'd always assumed he was the kind of guy to hop from girl to girl. Never thought he'd be one to want to settle down and make a commitment right after high school.

"Yeah. So even though I wanted to go to college, I was glad to have an excuse to not go with him." Her cheeks were bright red now.

"Why didn't you just break up with him?"

She sighed, averting her eyes again. "Tony's not easy to break up with."

"What do you mean?" My brows knit together in concern. "Did he hurt you?"

"No." She shook her head quickly—too quickly. "Not exactly. I mean, not on purpose. And just once. I shouldn't be telling you this." She tried to laugh and blow it off. "You came in for stamps and I'm talking your ear off. I know you have more important things to do, Deputy Hawkins."

I touched her hand gently. "Elsa, please tell me. What happened?"

I wanted to know. And not just for Katelyn's sake—for Elsa's, too.

If Tony had hurt Elsa, I'd find a way to make him pay.

But she shook her head hard, embarrassed. "It wasn't on purpose," she repeated. "He's just intense. And I'm glad it's over. That's all. He found someone else, and she can have him. He brought her home on Christmas break to meet his family and everything. Sent me a text message beforehand telling me things were over between us, that he'd found the woman he was going to marry. And when that day comes, I'll happily dance at their wedding."

She smiled again, lighter this time. Relieved.

I could tell she didn't know.

The woman he'd found was Katelyn Brown—and Katelyn had ended up dead.

Chapter Twelve

Vance

Claire Hawkins was turning out to be a thorn in my side.

She'd texted me that morning, telling me she was "following up on some leads." Then she'd apparently turned her phone off, because she hadn't read any of my messages or returned my calls.

Following up on leads. By herself. I gritted my teeth as I paced my office, attempting to call her again.

She could blow my whole case.

When she didn't answer, I stormed out of my office to the bullpen where Sergeant Collins was cutting up with some guy in civilian clothes. Collins straightened, putting on a professional smile.

"Can I help you with something, Agent Weston?"

I crossed my arms. "Yes. Do you know where Deputy Hawkins is?"

Collins smirked and cut his eyes to the guy beside him. "No, I can't say that I do." He glanced at his watch, shaking his head. "Forty-five minutes late. I'd like to say that's unusual, but..." He shrugged.

The other guy snickered. "She probably lost track of time painting her nails or braiding her horse's hair or something."

Collins choked back a laugh.

"She's not late," I said, scowling again. I was pissed off at Claire, but hearing these guys make fun of her like that made me want to rise to her defense. "She's working. Following up on some leads."

Collins gave me an appraising look. "If you know what she's doing, then why are you asking me where she is?"

I schooled my features, replacing my scowl with a calm smile—*deadly* calm. "I know *what* she's doing, but she's out of communication. I need access to your office's GPS tracking system so I can see where her vehicle is."

The corner of his mouth rose in an amused smirk. "Be my guest," he said, waving me over to his computer with a shrug. "But I don't think it will be much use to you, since her official vehicle is in the parking lot."

I stopped, my fingers an inch from his keyboard, and straightened.

Of course. She'd taken her own vehicle, which meant I had no way of tracking her down. Meanwhile, she was out there doing God knows what, possibly blowing my investigation to smithereens.

At the look on my face, Collins grinned and patted me on the shoulder. "Is Little Miss Wildwood causing problems?"

"*Little Miss Wildwood*?" I repeated.

"That was her pageant title," his friend said, choking on a laugh. He wiggled his brows. "And you've gotta admit, it fits. She's wild and she always gets *my*—"

Collins elbowed him and gave him a warning look.

Good thing, too. If he had finished that sentence, I'd have been tempted to obliterate his sleazy smile with my fist.

"Don't feel bad," Collins said, his tone empathetic as he turned back to me. He leaned back against his desk, bracing himself with his hands. "You're not the first person to have trouble with her, and you won't be the last."

"Is that so?" My voice was mild, my face a mask.

"Claire thinks the rules don't apply to her. She doesn't belong in this job."

"Doesn't deserve to wear the badge," his friend sneered.

Collins nodded in agreement. "That's why I offered to partner with you instead. I couldn't believe Sheriff McGrath stuck you with her. But that's half the problem. Claire is kind of his ... special pet. The rules are different for her, which, as you can see, has enabled her to continue her problematic behavior."

I took a deep breath. Collins was a snake, but I had to admit that what he was saying made sense. Sheriff McGrath had praised her in a way he hadn't the others, and he'd given her this assignment even though Collins should have been first in line for it.

He chuckled. "I mean, let's be honest. He either assigned the case to her because he wanted to give her special treatment... Or because he resented having to call in an outside agency and wanted to make her your problem instead of ours." He smirked again. "It certainly wasn't because of her experience."

"You're right. It certainly wasn't that," I agreed.

"The offer still stands if you'd like my assistance." He gave me a friendly smile. "I'm sure we can fix it with the sheriff."

"I'll consider it. But first, I need to deal with Deputy Hawkins."

I stormed out to the parking lot, planning on driving all over town until I saw Claire's truck. But she pulled into the parking lot before I made it to my SUV.

I walked straight to her door and yanked it open.

"Where. Have. You. Been?"

She glared at me. "I *told* you. Following up on some leads."

I shook my head. "This is *my* case. You don't do anything without my approval."

Her eyes went wide with innocence. "Oh, gosh, I'm so sorry. I didn't know. I'm new to this, you know. I was just trying to be helpful. I really want to earn a gold star on my report card."

I braced my hands on my hips. "Cut the crap."

She jabbed her finger toward me. "Then you cut it, too. This isn't *your* case—it's *ours*. You may be in charge, but this is *my* county. *My* people. And I'm not just going to sit at a desk, waiting for assignments from you. Especially when you haven't even bothered to show up for two days!"

"That's *exactly* what you're going to do," I said, raising my voice to match hers. "You have no idea how to conduct an investigation. For all I know, you may have blown this whole case today!"

She rolled her eyes. "I did not. When you're ready to pull that giant stick out of your ass, we can sit down and talk about what I found out, compare notes. Otherwise, I have work to do." She pushed me out of the way and hopped out of the truck, slamming the door closed.

"No, you don't," I said, furious at her attitude. "You'll be lucky if you even have a badge after today."

Her head jerked back like she'd been stabbed. Her mouth dropped open, but for once, no sounds came out of it.

"If you want any chance of retaining your job, you're going to do things my way from now on," I said, realizing I'd finally gained the upper hand. "We'll start by you explaining exactly what you did this morning so that I know what damage control I have to do to fix it. My office."

"I need to—"

"My. Office." I lowered my voice, speaking with deadly calm. "Now."

She glared at me, crossing her arms. "Yes, sir." She spit out the words, but the look in her eyes was pure hurt.

And I hated it.

I pushed down my desire to smooth things over and led the way to my office. When we crossed through the bullpen, Collins snickered.

"You screwed up this time, Little Miss Wildwood," he whispered as she walked by, just loudly enough for me to hear.

I looked back and saw her shoulders sag. It pierced something in me.

Claire Hawkins was wild, free, and gloriously unrestrained.

Except here.

Here, she was miserable. And who could blame her? The colleague she needed to be able to trust with her life was constantly backstabbing her, trying to get ahead. He probably made it abundantly clear every single day that he had no respect for her, that he didn't care if the citizens she risked her life to serve did either.

That would make any job hell.

Guilt stabbed hard. I wasn't much better than Collins, thinking I'd keep her busy with paperwork even when it was clear that sitting at a desk was *painful* for her.

I couldn't have her screwing up the investigation. No distractions, I reminded myself.

But I also couldn't stand to see her looking like that.

I opened the door to my office, gesturing for her to enter first. When she sat, looking so damn defeated, I closed the door and took the seat across from her.

"I'm sorry," she began, folding her hands together. "I really was just trying to help. I–I hate feeling useless." She looked down.

I stared at her. Reminded myself that her feelings weren't my problem.

But that didn't make me feel better.

This list I'd made for her this morning caught my eye—a list of research tasks she could complete, meant to make her feel like she was doing something on the case while keeping her out of my hair.

Not one of them really mattered. I'd kept everything that did for myself.

I shook my head, more annoyed with myself at that point than I was with her. I took a deep breath and focused on the situation at hand.

"Tell me about the leads you explored this morning," I directed. "Leave nothing out."

She nodded, then explained how she had talked to Tony's ex-girlfriend and what she had learned. I watched carefully, looking for any sign that she was changing anything to make herself look better. But she was honest. Thorough. Clear.

And she hadn't done a damn thing that would hurt the investigation, I admitted to myself.

"So Elsa didn't seem to know that Tony is connected to Katelyn?" I confirmed.

"Obviously, I didn't ask. But no. She seemed to think he has a current girlfriend and she's happy about it because it means he's leaving her alone."

I weighed it. "You think he hurt her, even though she blew it off. Why?"

She shrugged. "Partially because of her demeanor. I'm the only female deputy here, so I'm usually the one to talk to any female victims of domestic assault. I've seen that look before. And also because of things I've heard about Tony."

"Like what?"

"Rumors."

I raised an eyebrow, willing her to go on.

She sighed. "Tony's younger than me. Not someone I ever hung around with. But my kid brother, Jonathan, was just one year behind him in school. Let's just say Tony had a reputation."

I frowned. "A reputation for what?"

"Getting handsy with the girls. Maybe more."

I shot her a look. "How much more? There wasn't anything on his record."

"There wouldn't be, would there? His dad's the mayor. You know how it is." She shrugged again. "From what I remember, a couple of girls were uncomfortable with Tony because he wouldn't keep his hands off of them. One of the girls came to Jonathan and said she was scared of Tony, that he'd taken her into an empty room at a party and tried to get her to have sex with him."

"Shit."

"He didn't rape her," Claire clarified. "But he was verbally pushy. Stuck his tongue down her throat even when she was pushing him away. It scared her, and she was worried he might not stop next time."

"Did she report it?"

"I'll have to ask Jonathan, but I don't think so. She went to him because she knew he'd do something about it—unlike the school."

My brows rose. "What did Jonathan do?"

She bit her lip and looked away. "I'm not saying he did anything at all. But the next day, Tony had a broken nose." She shrugged. "Must have fallen or something."

I blinked twice, trying not to laugh.

I failed.

When I chuckled, Claire did, too. The tension faded, along with that defeated look she'd had ever since I'd threatened her badge. Seeing her smile again made my heart twist in a way I wasn't at all comfortable with.

"I'm starting to think all of you Hawkins kids are rule breakers," I commented.

"Maybe we are. Ranching is a hard life. You have to make things happen."

"That's true," I admitted. Her childhood had been the opposite of mine in many ways. It was no wonder we had different ways of handling things.

Maybe that could be a strength for our partnership instead of a weakness.

"Anyway," she said, steering the conversation back to Tony. "I never heard about any trouble after that. But when Elsa said what she said…"

"I get it."

"So," she said, her voice going small again. "Am I off the case?"

I looked again at that list I'd made for her. Then I shook my head, crumpled up the paper, and threw it into the garbage.

I had a feeling I was going to regret this.

"Why did you become a deputy?" I asked.

She lifted her head, looking like a deer caught in the headlights. "What—"

"If you're going to be my partner, I want to know why you're working this job. The ranch could easily employ you full-time. You're clearly happier there than here. So, what is it? Did your mom make a vow to God that one of her children would serve in law enforcement or what?"

She stared at me for a beat, then sighed. "I wanted to help people. It's as simple as that. Sorry if that answer isn't good enough for you."

On the contrary. It was the best answer there was.

"Alright," I finally said. "I told you, partners have to be honest with each other."

"I am being honest," she protested, throwing her hands up in irritation.

"But I wasn't," I admitted. "Here's the truth. I was going to keep you tied up with busywork so I could work the case alone—even before that little stunt you pulled today."

Her nostrils flared and fury blazed in her eyes. But then her expression changed. The storm passed, blowing out as quickly as a summer squall, leaving those green eyes sparkling like the sea.

She laughed. It started quietly but took hold of her until her shoulders shook.

I leaned forward, propping my elbows on the desk. "What exactly is so funny?"

She wiped the tears from her eyes and grinned. "The fact that you thought you could."

I just raised a brow.

She scooted forward in her seat, holding up a hand with her fingers splayed out. "Listen, I have five brothers. *Five.* You think I haven't seen this game before? I mastered it before I turned eight."

"I bet you did," I murmured.

"You told me not to make you curious. Well, the same goes for me. You try to cut me out of something and it's a flat-out guarantee I'm going to be right in the middle of it. That list you had typed up over there?" She nodded toward the wastebasket where I'd tossed it. "All it would have done is make me determined to pester you to death. You were right in the parking lot. The only way to stop me would have been to take my badge."

I shook my head, unable to stop my grin. "Nah. Even that wouldn't have stopped you. You would have become one of those amateur sleuths just to piss off Collins. Probably would have solved the case before we could out of pure spite."

She threw her head back and laughed again. Like music.

Like Mozart.

I was as entranced as I had been furious earlier. "You're an interesting woman, Claire Hawkins."

"Damn right I am." She grinned. "Now, what are we doing first?"

"Come on," I said, grabbing my keys as I stood. "I'll fill you in on the way."

Chapter Thirteen

Claire

When we stepped out of Vance's office, Trey straightened, watching us. And when he saw that we were both smiling, his face went dark.

I followed Vance back through the bullpen, trying not to appear too victorious. But I couldn't help shooting a little smirk Trey's way when I walked by.

In the parking lot, Vance gestured for me to get into his SUV. He walked around to the driver's side. "We have a lot to catch up on," he said, as he started the vehicle.

"We do," I agreed. "What did you find out in Laramie?"

"That Tony hasn't changed much," he said, shaking his head.

My stomach knotted. "What do you mean?"

He backed out of his parking spot and headed toward the main road. "Everyone—both Katelyn's friends *and* Tony's—said that he was way more serious about her than she was about him. From my understanding, it started as a whirlwind romance on both sides. But after he brought her here over Christmas break, he started talking about marriage and she started pulling away. By the time of her disappearance, she'd all but ghosted him."

"Really?" That matched with what Elsa had said, but I still couldn't believe that Tony was so focused on getting married so young.

Maybe because I was a decade older than him and still hadn't given the institution a second thought.

"Yeah. Here's the interesting thing, at least compared to what you seem to think about Tony. Every single one of them preferred Tony over her and thought she was crazy for breaking things off. They all described him as a gentleman. I think Katelyn's old roommate was half in love with him herself."

"*Really*?" My jaw dropped.

He nodded.

I tried to think back over the interactions I'd had with Tony. I'd never liked him, but was that fair? He'd never given me any trouble personally. The only reason I disliked him was because Jonathan did— and because of what Jonathan had told me about him.

But I trusted my brother's judgment.

"Tony is well-liked," Vance said. "But Katelyn's friends all described her as a manipulative gold digger. Said she was determined to latch onto someone with money. Does that fit the Evans family? Mayors don't make *that* much."

"It might," I admitted. "Leslie Evans inherited a decent sum of money years ago from some rich uncle in Seattle."

"What kind of money are we talking?"

"I've never heard the figure," I answered. "It was enough to furnish a decadent lifestyle here in Wildwood, but probably not enough to run with the big dogs somewhere like Jackson or Breckenridge. If it was, I think that's where they'd be. Leslie has always acted like she's too good for this place."

Vance mulled things over. "Maybe that's why Katelyn was into Tony, at least initially. He dresses well, drives a slick car. Has the money to rent a nice house with his friends. Lavished her with fancy dinners and flowers."

"But if he got obsessive, she might have decided it wasn't worth it."

"Everyone said she loved the attention. If he hurt her, though, that might have been a different story."

"Or she could have realized he wasn't the catch she thought he was," I pointed out.

"Meaning?" He glanced my way.

I held my fingers up, counting off my points. "Unless he's changed dramatically, he's a lousy student. So he may not have great prospects for a future career. His dad is a mayor, which means there's no family business for him to inherit or some ready-made position for him to step into. Their money came from a one-time inheritance. And at the rate his mom spends cash, there might not be any left for him."

Vance let out a long breath. "So maybe Tony looked great in the beginning, but when she got to know his situation, she realized it wasn't enough for her long term."

"If her friends are right about her, then yeah." I thought it through. "So she breaks up with him. That's rejection. Plus, it makes him look bad. You said Tony is well-liked there. But he has a long history of pushing girls to take things further than they want. He's an only child. Spoiled. Probably thinks the world revolves around him."

"Is that a dig at me?" Vance asked, giving me a smirk.

"If the shoe fits," I answered, grinning. "But let me finish my thought. We'll have to deal with *your* issues later."

"Ouch." He put his hand on his heart like he was wounded.

I rolled my eyes. "Hypothetically, let's say Tony was angry and hurt over the rejection. Were you able to find out if he's the one she had a fight with the night she left?"

"Yes," Vance confirmed. "He and his friends had a party at their house. He invited her, and she went."

"Alone? Or did she take someone with her?"

He glanced at me, giving me the same look he'd given me out at the crime scene. Now that I knew him better, I recognized it as a mix of surprise and approval.

"She went alone," he said.

"Odd choice if she was pulling away because he had hurt her," I pointed out. "It shows she wasn't scared of him."

Vance nodded. "That's a great point."

"So, what did they fight about?"

"Tony made a move on her. Said he wanted her back. She said no and apparently yelled some pretty unflattering things about him. Also told him she had a new boyfriend before she stormed out. He was devastated, according to his buddies."

I put my elbow on the door and propped my face on my hand. "So... He has a motive."

"He does."

"Two questions."

"Shoot."

"First, do you think he did it?" I expected him to say yes quickly. To me, it seemed so clear.

But Vance didn't answer. He stared at the road, his brows furrowed as if he was thinking long and hard. The Wyoming plains whizzed by and the mountains loomed ahead of us as the town of Wildwood faded in the rearview mirror. I took in a sharp breath as I realized what road we were on.

We were heading back to the crime scene.

Vance finally spoke. "I've been asking myself that same question for at least twenty-four hours. He had a motive. They'd had an ugly, public fight. Her body was found in his hometown. He's an obvious suspect."

Obvious, but it had taken Vance a full minute to answer.

"But..." I said, drawing him out. I knew there was more he hadn't said.

"But the kid's grief was real. The news broke a few hours before I got to talk to him, and his eyes were still red from crying. I think he genuinely loved her."

"Doesn't mean he didn't kill her," I pointed out.

"You're right. Love is a strong emotion, and strong emotions can make people do crazy things. Add that to the embarrassment of being publicly rejected and possible rage over her being with someone else..." He shrugged. "The motive is real. But he was cooperative. Didn't ask for a lawyer. Begged me to find out who hurt her."

"Could have been an act."

"Could have been," he agreed. "But to answer your question, no. I don't think he did it."

His answer disappointed me. It wasn't that I wanted Tony to be a killer, exactly. It wasn't even that if he was innocent we'd be back to square one.

It was more that I didn't want Vance to be someone who could be swayed so easily by Tony's charm. By someone who had a friendly smile, wore expensive clothes, and drove a nice vehicle...

Like Vance.

"Are we still going to investigate him?" I asked, biting the inside of my cheek.

"Of course," Vance said, glancing over at me with an odd look on his face. "We'd be fools not to."

His answer settled me—some.

"You said you had two questions," he reminded me. "What's the other?"

"I was going to ask where we're going, but I've figured that out now. You can tell me why though."

"To see if we can establish a timeline," he explained. "Katelyn disappeared March thirteenth. But we don't know how much time passed before she died. Because of the condition of her remains, the medical examiner will only be able to give us an estimated range. So far, they've given me a two-month time span, saying she most likely died sometime between leaving on March thirteenth and the middle of May. Hopefully we can do better narrowing it down ourselves."

"How?"

"It's a long shot. But if the murder wasn't premeditated, maybe Katelyn came here with her killer and there's some sort of record of it. We'll check the visitor registration and camping logs, talk to park rangers, and see if there is any video footage that might help. They might have security cameras in their parking lots and the visitor's center. Maybe we'll get lucky."

I snorted. "I doubt it."

He looked my way, narrowing his eyes. "Why?"

"That campground doesn't open until Memorial Day," I explained. "And that's *only* if the snowpack has melted. Every now and then, we have a crazy year where it's closed until June or July."

"Are you serious?"

"Yep. Last year, it opened on time. But if they're saying she died sometime before mid-May…"

"Then the campground was closed." He tapped his finger on the steering wheel and swore under his breath. "Okay. You know the terrain and you know the conditions last spring. Let's assume the two-month window is correct. How could someone have gotten in?"

I thought back to the past spring. "By May, the roads were clear. If they had gate access, they could have driven in and gone straight to the campsite. There was still some snow left in the mountains, but the campground roads would have been plowed."

"Okay," he said, nodding. "Who all has gate access?"

"National Park Service employees. Any contractors they may have hired to do any work. Local law enforcement. That's about it."

"Do you think the Mayor of Wildwood would be on that list?"

I shrugged. "I honestly don't know. I doubt it. The park isn't in the city limits, so why would he?"

He sat silent for a moment, that mind of his puzzling over it all. "Okay," he finally said. "So, toward the end of the season, the easiest way may have been to go in through the front gate. Maybe someone with access—or someone who was able to bribe someone for it. But that's dangerous. If there are workers around, there are potential witnesses."

"Not if it wasn't premeditated," I pointed out. "What happened to Katelyn meeting someone there to hang out at the park and things going bad?"

He shook his head. "It's a totally different scenario if the park is closed. Seems more likely the park was used as a place to dump the body."

"Makes sense," I agreed. "Unless she was having an affair with someone and they were meeting there because it was closed and private."

"Katelyn doesn't seem like the type to date a park ranger," he pointed out.

"True. But if they bribed someone for access…"

"Are there cabins there where she could have met someone?"

"No. Just camping spots."

He shook his head. "Then that rules that out."

I snorted. "Why?"

He gave me a perplexed look. "Because there aren't any cabins. No beds, no privacy."

I grinned. "There's plenty of privacy out there, and last time I checked, a bed wasn't required for a roll in the hay. In fact, some of us prefer the thrill of the great outdoors."

His jaw twitched and his knuckles turned white on the steering wheel. "Well. Okay. We keep that on the table." He shook his head, like he was trying to clear out the mental image I'd put there.

I bit back a laugh.

He refocused on the conversation. "So, May would have been easy, but with a high potential for witnesses. Maybe that's good. Gives us a place to start. What about earlier? March. Assume Katelyn was killed shortly after she left Laramie and that someone wanted to dump the body at the campground while it was closed. How would they have gotten in?"

"They would have had to hike in," I said. "Either on the main road by walking around the gate or by taking a nearby trail and cutting over."

"Walk me through it."

I closed my eyes, picturing the area. Considering possibilities, eliminating them. Then I found one—a good one.

"There's a trailhead that connects to the primitive campground. It would have been under snow in March, but it's a popular route for snowshoers. To get all the way from the trailhead to the spot we found Katelyn is a long walk for most people though. Fifteen miles or so. That's a long hike in good weather. In snowshoes, it would be even more strenuous."

Incredibly strenuous, actually. It was the kind of thing the SAR team did all the time, but most people? No way. Snowshoeing burned almost a thousand calories an hour, and that was without carrying a body.

I was ready to discard the idea altogether when I suddenly realized how easy it could be. My eyes popped open and I grabbed Vance's arm.

"But take that same route on a snowmobile? Easy."

CHAPTER FOURTEEN

Vance

A SNOWMOBILE. CLAIRE WAS CONVINCED THAT WAS HOW Katelyn's body had gotten into the park. I was starting to think she might be onto something.

There wasn't much security for the area, but they did have cameras on the gates along with a timestamp record of every time it opened. Between March thirteenth and May fifteenth, the gate had only opened a handful of times, and each incident had been connected to specific work being done at the park.

I got the names of every contractor and employee who'd been on site. It was possible one of them was our killer, that they'd brought Katelyn there and dumped her body hoping the animals would take care of it before the park opened. That would have been risky though. You never wanted a body to be found somewhere connected to you.

After talking with the park director, I had Claire walk me through the campground and show me trail connections and possibilities. She knew the place like the back of her hand. We tossed ideas back and forth, running different scenarios, and I was surprised to find how much I enjoyed working with her.

We ended up back where we'd started, standing at the top of the embankment that led to where we'd found Katelyn.

"There are far better places here to dump a body," I said.

"Definitely," Claire agreed. "And I haven't even shown you everything. There are some places here where she would *never* have been found."

I chuckled. "Do you spend a lot of time thinking about where to hide your victims?"

"The opposite, actually." The weight of regret was in her voice.

I turned my head, looked at her. She stared down the slope with a troubled look on her face.

"Your SAR victims?" I asked.

She swallowed hard. "Yeah. We don't lose people often, but... Man, it sucks when we do."

I stayed quiet, giving her space to keep going.

But she squared her shoulders and turned the conversation back to Katelyn. "This is the Bighorns. Most beautiful place on earth, if you ask me. But unlike Glacier and Yellowstone, you can hike for days here and not run across another human being. There's a million places to hide a body. Why here?"

The answer came to me quickly. "Because it was easy."

"It's still not smart," she said, shaking her head.

I turned, looking back toward the campsite. "You're right about that. But if the killer came here on snowmobile, this spot makes perfect sense. This is the most secluded site of all. It's tucked into the trees, and you can't see it until you're right up on it."

"Yeah. That's why I always pick it when I camp here. It's private."

"Exactly. Killers like privacy." I pictured it in my mind, watching it play out. "Maybe he doesn't have snowshoes or isn't physically capable of carrying a body very far. So he comes in on the trail, drives the loop, and finds this spot. It's perfect. Pulls in, starts looking for a place to dump the body. He could have driven the snowmobile right up to the tree line. Getting back up the hill would have been brutal, but pulling a body down it? Not so hard."

"He could have taken the snowmobile way past the tree line," Claire pointed out. "The path is wide enough up here that an experienced snowmobiler could drive all the way to where the trail narrows."

I whistled. "Wide, but steep. I wouldn't want to do that."

"It's not that big of a deal."

"I'll take your word for it."

Claire grinned and started walking down the path. I followed her until she stopped at the spot where the trail narrowed.

"In March, this would have been covered in at least two feet of snow," she mused. "The stones and saplings would all have been buried. If the killer drove here, he could have just pushed her off the snowmobile. It's a straight shot to the bottom. One smooth slide."

I pictured it, realizing she was right. "Easy for the killer. Very little physical effort. And the snowpack would have reduced additional trauma to the body. The ME ruled out a fall, but a slide would explain why she didn't have any additional broken bones."

"Yeah." Claire blew out a breath. "No way to prove it, but... It works."

"It does," I agreed. "I've got to admit, it's a great theory."

She looked up at me with a playful grin. "You've 'got to admit'? What, is it killing you that I might actually be better than you at this?"

"Better than *me*?" I smirked. "I wouldn't go that far. But you're better than I thought you'd be."

She rolled her eyes, and I realized I owed her more than that. Because the truth was that I'd judged her unfairly.

The smile dropped from my face. "I'm sorry, Claire."

"For what?" She looked puzzled.

I stuck my hands into my pockets, struggling to find the right words. "You and I are different. We come from different worlds, and we've had very different experiences, both in life and in work. I assumed your lack of investigative experience meant that you'd be worthless as a partner on this case."

Her eyebrows shot up. I wasn't sure if she was shocked or offended —or both.

"But"—I looked her in the eye, hoping she could see my sincerity— "I'm man enough to admit when I'm wrong, and I was. I was wrong to judge you before even giving you a chance. You're good at this. And I'm honored to have you as a partner."

Her cheeks turned pink. "Thank you," she said quietly. "I–I appreciate you saying that."

Seeing how much my apology meant to her made me angry that she'd worked so long with someone who would never admit how valuable she was on the team. "Collins is an ass. Don't let him get to you."

A little smile played on her lips. "Yes, he is. And he's going to be pissed that you didn't take my badge after all. He was so excited to see me get dressed down."

I snorted. "Just wait until we solve this case and I publicly commend you for your invaluable assistance. He'll have steam coming out of his ears."

She grinned. "Probably. But I do feel kind of sorry for him."

"Why?"

She shrugged. "Working for DCI is his dream. He got turned down due to lack of experience. This kind of thing doesn't happen often in Sage County. It might be his only chance to do something that would get him a shot at DCI."

Understanding dawned. "So that's why he kept trying to get me to ask Sheriff McGrath for a change."

Her jaw dropped. "Did he really?"

"Yep," I said, nodding. "Texted me directly. I told him no, that you and I had it handled."

She blushed again. "Thank you. Again."

"Probably shouldn't thank me for that one, since I was still planning on cutting you out of the case at that point," I admitted.

"So you were just using me as an excuse to not have to work with Collins?"

"Basically."

She punched me lightly on the arm, but then she laughed. "Aw, it's alright. Can't say I blame you on that one."

"I'M STARVING," CLAIRE ANNOUNCED ON THE DRIVE BACK

toward town. "There's a gas station coming up on the left. Pull over. They have great hot dogs."

I glanced at the clock, realizing we'd worked straight through lunch. My stomach rumbled, thanks to Claire's reminder.

But a gas station hot dog? I'd rather go hungry.

"Your mom will be serving dinner in a couple of hours. Wouldn't you rather wait? It's got to be better than gas station food."

"So we'll eat again in a couple of hours," Claire said, shrugging. "That doesn't fix my empty stomach now."

"Alright," I said, chuckling as I turned into the parking lot.

When I parked, Claire jumped out.

I didn't follow.

She turned around and opened the door. "Aren't you coming?"

"No, thanks. I'll wait until dinner."

"Ah," she said, smirking. "I see. You're a snob. Guess I should have realized, with those fancy boots and all."

"I am not a snob."

"What was your favorite food as a kid?" she asked, grinning.

I opened my mouth to answer, then realized all it would do was prove her point. Lobster was a staple in Maine, but it wasn't exactly on most kids' menus out west.

"Fine," I said, unbuckling my seat belt. "We'll eat hot dogs."

"There you go," she said, laughing as she led the way inside.

The clerk behind the counter greeted her by name, giving her a friendly smile before turning suspicious eyes toward me. Claire ordered for both of us, paid, then led me to a booth in the back and handed me mine.

I eyed it warily. It didn't look terrible. It even smelled halfway decent.

Decent enough to make my stomach growl again.

Claire certainly seemed to be enjoying hers, and she couldn't have terrible taste, since she'd grown up with Naomi Hawkins cooking her meals. I bit into the dog and was pleasantly surprised.

"Not bad," I admitted. "Not quite as good as a New York dog, but... Not bad."

She rolled her eyes, laughing. "Wow. First, you don't even want to try one. Then, you have to compare it to the ones in NYC. You're something else, Vance."

It was the first time she'd called Vance, and the intimacy of it sparked unexpected pleasure.

"Right back at you, Claire."

Her lips twisted into a teasing smile. I prepared for her next jab, but she surprised me, asking a personal question instead.

"Does your dad still live in the city?"

"No." Normally, I'd leave it there. But she cocked her head, waiting for me to continue.

And I did.

"He moved to Wyoming right before I graduated college," I explained. "That's why I joined DCI after a few years as a detective with the NYPD."

Her face turned serious. "I get it now. You moved here to be with him."

"Kind of." I took another bite.

"Is that why you went to college in New York? To be close to him?"

"Yeah." Only one other person had ever asked me that question—my mother. She'd thrown it in my face as a guilt trip for years after I'd admitted it. To her, that meant he'd won. That I'd chosen him over her. And that was unforgivable.

Claire studied me. "Sucks that you moved there to be with him and he left. Did he have a job transfer or something?"

"Nosy," I murmured, shaking my head.

Guilt flashed on her face. "Oh. Sorry. I have a habit of that. I'm not trying to be intrusive."

"It's okay. It's just... I don't normally talk about them."

"Why not?" Her eyes were full of curiosity, but as I stared into them, I realized that it wasn't the kind that made me uncomfortable. It wasn't her prying for information she could leverage.

She was just trying to be a friend.

I blew out a breath. "My parents are somewhat well-known. It's always been our policy to keep family drama to ourselves." Especially in New York.

"Oh." Her eyes widened. "Gotcha. I should have known, considering where you grew up. Again, I'm sorry. I won't ask any personal questions."

"No, it's okay." I realized at that moment that I trusted Claire more than I'd trusted anyone in a very long time.

She was the most refreshing person I'd met in years. She didn't play games, and she wasn't constantly looking for an edge or leverage to propel herself up. She was simply herself. Unapologetically, refreshingly herself. A smart and sassy woman who didn't force herself to fit into someone else's box. Because of it, she was breaking down all my walls, coaxing me past my boundaries.

Normally, if someone tried that, I'd resent it. Build my walls higher, thicker. That's what the Westons did. We prized security, privacy, excellence, and self-discipline. Not friendship. Not intimacy. Certainly not love.

But Claire Hawkins was making me wonder what it might be like to live by a different set of values.

Chapter Fifteen

Claire

Despite his initial hesitation, Vance polished off the last of his hot dog. And while he did, he talked.

He told me about his family. How his mom was a New York socialite who had fallen in love with his dad, an FBI agent with a radically different life than she'd ever known. How she'd gotten pregnant, they'd married, and then everything had fallen apart.

"Mom loved the thrill of dating someone with such an exciting job," he explained. "But reality sunk in after they got married."

"What happened?"

He shrugged. "Her life changed, but his didn't. For him, the job came first. Always. 'No distractions.' That was his motto, and it didn't change just because he had a ring on his finger."

I winced. "Man. That really sucks."

"Yeah. And a part-time relationship wasn't sexy anymore when she was stuck at home taking care of a baby she didn't really want. So she split."

He said the words casually, but I knew there had to be pain behind them.

"So that's when you moved to Maine?"

He nodded. "My grandparents had a summer house there. We moved in with them and never left. It was a completely different scene than New York, but Mom loved it. She made a whole new set of friends and traded the nightlife for tea parties and spa retreats. Up there, having a kid was an asset, not a hindrance."

"That's good, I guess?"

He snorted. "I think I liked it better in New York, where she was ignoring me. Having someone value you only as a way to make themselves look good sucks in a different way."

"I'm sorry," I said. I really couldn't imagine. My parents annoyed me sometimes—or often, at least right now. They didn't understand me, but I knew they loved me.

I wondered if Vance had ever experienced that.

"Don't be sorry," he said firmly. "My childhood was cold, but I'm aware of how privileged it was. I don't have any right to complain. If I ever thought that, working the streets of NYC set me straight."

"Money and happiness are two different things."

"They are," he agreed with a small smile that told me he was grateful I understood.

"How often did you get to see your dad?"

"Two weeks every summer."

My jaw dropped. "Wow. That's awful. Travis is in the process of getting divorced. Missy, his ex, only lets him have the girls two weekends a month and that's still not enough for him. For any of us."

"Two weeks was more than enough for Dad." His voice was flat. "The job came first. I understood."

He said it like he'd repeated it to his father a million times—like he'd almost convinced himself it was true. But there was a sadness in his eyes that told me he wished it hadn't been that way.

"If he never cared to see you more than that, why did you move to NYC?" It was another nosy question, but I didn't think he would mind. If anything, he seemed relieved to open up. I got the feeling he'd kept all of this bottled up for way too long.

Some of my siblings were guarded like that—Beth, Finn, and Jonathan. It wasn't healthy. I believed that you had to let things out, lay your feelings out on the table.

They probably wished I would do less of that.

Vance sighed, then gave me a funny grin. "You're too easy to talk to."

"You didn't answer the question."

He chuckled and shook his head. "I think I understand now why you decided to become a deputy. It's the only job where you can get away with questioning people like this."

I grinned. "I told Cheyenne almost the same thing once. But you're stalling."

His smile dropped. "Truthfully? I always saw my dad as a hero. This incredible man who dedicated his life to serving other people."

"Everyone except you," I said quietly.

He gave me a perceptive look. "Yeah. Everyone except me. I think I thought that, if I moved to New York, went to school for criminal justice, and followed in his footsteps, he might finally be interested in me."

I toyed with a paper napkin. "So you were trying to be worthy of him."

He was silent for a long beat. "Yeah. I guess I was."

This time, I was the one to sigh. "I understand that."

"Is that part of why you became a deputy? Trying to prove your worth, too?"

"No." I shook my head. "Not at first. But I've been trying to prove myself ever since."

"Your department doesn't seem very supportive." Irritation flared on his face. I knew that it was for my sake and it warmed my heart.

"Sheriff McGrath has been great," I corrected. "He can be overly protective sometimes, but otherwise, he's good. He's actually the one who encouraged me to apply for the job, and he's been a mentor ever since. But..." I swallowed hard, embarrassed to admit something so personal.

"What is it?" His eyes were curious.

"My parents laughed at me when I told them I was applying."

"Why?" He seemed genuinely dumbfounded. "I know your Mom's a little—"

"Controlling?"

"I was going to say overly invested in your love life." He flashed a grin before turning serious again. "But your family is different from mine. So warm and loving. Connected. And with your background in SAR, I don't understand why they'd laugh about you taking the liaison position."

"Well, they did." My cheeks turned red just remembering it.

His voice softened. "People underestimate you all the time, don't they?"

"Most people. Not everyone." Rhett and Cole never had. Neither had Cheyenne. That was probably why they were my three favorite people on earth.

His jaw tightened. "I know I said this earlier, but I'm sorry I was one of them."

I waved him off. "You didn't know me. Is it irritating when a stranger underestimates me? Sure. But I get it. I'm a woman. I'm blonde, and for some reason, people *still* think blondes are dumb. I'm also short. That's three immediate strikes against me. I get it. The only thing that really hurts is when it's someone who actually knows me."

"Like your parents."

"Exactly."

He shook his head, with a strange smile on his face. "I get that, too."

"Really?"

"Yeah. Why do you think I'm at DCI?"

"What do you mean?"

He wadded up his napkin and tossed it onto the table. "Dad worked his way up to SAC—Special Agent in Charge—of the New York field office. He was a big deal."

"Apparently so," I said, impressed.

"When he retired, he moved to Jackson. Started a private security firm."

I whistled. "So he's making the big bucks providing security for the celebrities that flock there every summer."

"Oh yeah. So much money that even my mom keeps trying to use me as an excuse to get close to him again." He rolled his eyes. "But anyway, when I decided to leave the NYPD, I applied for a position there first. He turned me down."

My jaw dropped. "Are you serious?"

"Yes. I have a bachelor's in criminal justice. Graduated with a 4.0. Made detective in just eighteen months—"

"Whoa," I said, my eyes wide. Eighteen months was exceptional in a competitive place like the NYPD.

"Thanks." He flashed another quick grin. "But even after eight years of experience in New York, my own father still rejected my application to work with him. Said it wasn't enough."

The injustice of it pissed me off. How could his father not see what was right in front of his eyes? Not just Vance's merit as a law enforcement officer, but the fact that he was working his ass off trying to earn a relationship with his dad—something that should have been his all along.

"Why are you even still trying?" I blurted out. "He sounds like a total ass."

He took a deep breath. "It's complicated."

"Maybe it shouldn't be."

"You think I should stop?" Those piercing blue eyes of his focused on me, waiting for an answer. His intensity made me feel like everything was hanging in the balance.

Part of me knew that it was a bad idea to give life-changing advice to someone you barely knew. But I didn't have it in me to hold back.

"Yeah, I do," I said firmly. "You've made it clear you want a relationship with him, but it seems like he keeps blowing you off. That sucks. You shouldn't have to fight for it. Maybe if you stop, he'll realize what he's missing out on."

He took in my words, revealing nothing as he contemplated them. "I have no idea why I told you all of this," he finally said.

"We all need a listening ear sometimes."

"You probably always have that in your family." This time, his smile was wistful. Sad.

It stabbed my heart to realize that the ultra-confident special agent was lonely.

Chapter Sixteen

Vance

Claire and I chatted the whole drive back to Wildwood. I was still surprised by how much I'd opened up to her. How I'd told her things I'd never told anyone else.

Not that I had many friends these days. Since moving to Wyoming two years ago, I'd been entirely focused on work. I'd pushed myself, working around the clock to earn the experience my father said I needed. It had paid off in more ways than one.

But I hadn't realized how empty my life felt until now.

Working cases gave me a sense of purpose. I'd gone into the field trying to find some connection with my father—and probably to piss off my mother—but I'd fallen in love with the job. I was good at it. I enjoyed pushing myself, both mentally and physically. And there was something deeply satisfying about bringing someone to justice or closure to a family.

I'd followed in my father's footsteps and discovered that I shared his personality. That I could make work my entire identity and find fulfillment in it.

I'd never stopped to question whether or not that's what I actually wanted.

Not that it mattered. It wasn't like anything else was available to me at this point. I'd already made my decisions. Two years of giving everything I had to the Wyoming DCI had opened doors for me. Everything I'd done, everything I'd sacrificed had led to this: two offers on the table, either job waiting for me as soon as I wrapped up this case. For me, the only decision left was which one I was going to take.

Option number one was that I could go work for my father, having finally earned enough experience that he'd offered me a position—at the bottom of his company.

Option number two was that I could keep following in his footsteps and take the job I'd been offered at the FBI.

Keep fighting for a relationship with him, or walk away and prove I'd been as good as him all along.

I think I had my answer. The conversation with Claire had sealed the deal.

Right before we hit the Wildwood city limits, Claire told me to take a left.

"Why?" I asked as I turned onto a desolate, narrow road.

"I have another lead. Someone I want to talk to about Tony. But..." She hesitated.

"What is it?"

"Turn right," she said, pointing to another road. "I think I should talk to him by myself." There was uncertainty on her face.

I frowned. "Why?"

"He doesn't like cops."

"You're a cop," I pointed out.

"I'm not like most cops. He trusts me, but...I should talk to him alone."

"What are you not telling me?"

"I don't want to get him into trouble."

I pulled the SUV over so I could turn and look at her. "Partners have to be honest, remember?" Then I softened, seeing the worry on her face. "You can trust me, Claire."

She studied my face. Whatever she saw there seemed to ease her mind. "His name is Rob. He's not a bad guy. Wouldn't hurt a soul. But at his place, you may see ... evidence ... that could get him into trouble."

I smirked. "Let me guess. Weed?"

She nodded, still worried.

"I don't give a shit," I said, shrugging.

"Really?" She looked shocked.

I shot her a look. "I'm a homicide detective. I don't care what people do to relax if they aren't hurting anyone—and I'm sure as hell not going to waste time doing paperwork to write someone up for smoking a joint."

She threw her head back and laughed.

There was that Mozart concerto again, playing in my head against the soundtrack that was Claire Hawkins.

It was a sound I could get addicted to.

"I guess I underestimated you, too." She smiled at me, the worry all gone.

"Apparently so." I returned her smile. "But you're probably right. He might be spooked by me. I'll stay in the car. "

"Thanks. For trusting me."

I could see that it surprised her. But what she didn't realize was that I trusted her more than she could even know. I wouldn't have opened up to her if I didn't.

I winked. "Right back at you."

I pulled back onto the road and followed her directions to a rural area with small, rundown houses spaced an acre or two apart. Half a mile down the narrow street, Claire told me to pull over. As I did, a makeshift pack of mutts crossed the road ahead of us, then watched us from the ditch.

"Is that his place?" I asked, gesturing to the blue house on our right.

"No. I'll walk from here so he doesn't see your vehicle."

"You sure?" I glanced in the rearview mirror at the pack of dogs. They were all honed in on us, their bodies tense and ready to spring.

"Of course," she said, giving me a puzzled look. "It's not far."

I put my hand on her forearm. "Be careful."

She looked down at it, then lifted those green eyes to meet mine. Laughter sparkled in them. "What, are you worried about me?"

"A little," I admitted. "Those dogs don't look friendly."

"I'll be fine," she said, clearly amused. She squeezed my hand and hopped out, tucking her hands into her pockets as she walked away.

The pack of dogs ran into the road and took off toward her.

I threw my door open and put my hand on my pistol. But before I could draw it, Claire squatted, cooing to the dogs. They slowed down and approached her with their tails wagging. She said hi to all of them like she knew them, scratching them behind their ears. The biggest, scariest one of all—an intact male Rottweiler with a spiked collar around his neck—actually licked her face, then threw himself onto the ground and rolled onto his back so she could rub his belly.

She gave the dogs all the attention they wanted. Then she stood and threw me a sassy wink before sauntering down the road.

FORTY-FIVE MINUTES TICKED BY BEFORE I SAW CLAIRE emerge from a house down the street and begin walking toward me. I started the engine and drove to meet her.

"Any luck?" I asked as she climbed in.

She shook her head. "Maybe. My brother told me that Tony and Rob used to hang out together when Tony wanted to get high, so I thought I'd talk to him, find out if he's seen Tony lately. He has, but I'm not sure how helpful any of it is."

"Fill me in anyway," I said, turning the SUV around so we could head back toward town.

"He and Tony hung out a few times over the summer. He said when Tony got high the first time, he started talking about Katelyn. But it sounds like Tony was feeling bitter at that point. Was angry that she'd left him for someone else after everything he'd done for her. Called her a few choice words."

"Interesting," I mused. "He sure didn't talk like that when I spoke to him."

Claire shrugged. "Could be different attitudes for different people. Or that the weed lowered his inhibitions."

"What else did Rob say?"

"Not much—about that, anyway." She laughed. "Rob loves to talk, but he has a hard time staying on track. Likes to rabbit-trail a lot. I let him because he doesn't have many people to talk to."

"That's smart. You never know what kind of information you'll get that way. Plus, you build rapport with someone who could be a helpful informant."

"Not everything's about law enforcement. There's something to be said for just being a good neighbor." It was a gentle reproach. One that reminded me of how different our upbringings had been.

I gave her a smile. "Point taken."

"But he did say Tony wasn't as interested in hanging out as he used to be. Rob got the impression that Tony's parents were watching him more closely than they had before. Tony complained that, even though he was an adult in college, they were being more strict with him than they had been in high school. Wanted to know where he was going, kept trying to force him to have conversations with them. Tony got sick of it and went back to Laramie early."

"Now *that* is very interesting," I said, grinning. "A change in behavior, especially in that direction, means they were concerned. I want to know why."

"Sounds like they're who we need to talk to next," Claire commented.

But I glanced at the time and decided that talking to the mayor and his wife would need to wait until Monday. It was already after five, making it too likely that they would both be home.

Better to talk to them alone, when they couldn't influence each other's answers.

"Later," I said. "We'll talk to them separately. Where does his mom work?"

Claire snorted. "She doesn't, unless you count the 'committees' she serves on."

"Perfect. We'll pay her a visit Monday morning, then swing by the mayor's office."

"We can go tomorrow, if you want," Claire offered. "Mayor Evans hosts a men's breakfast every Saturday morning. Leslie will be home alone."

"We can try it," I said, pleased that there would be an opportunity sooner. "We'll just have to hope she doesn't have plans tomorrow morning."

Claire laughed. "That woman never has plans before ten. She'll be there. But we should wait until nine. She won't answer the door if she doesn't have her makeup on yet."

I grinned. "Alright, nine it is."

We settled into a comfortable silence as we drove back to where Claire was parked so she could drive her truck home. When she got out, she paused before closing the door, then turned and faced me.

"Do you want to come to the house for dinner?" She fidgeted, rubbing her ear.

"Well... That depends," I said slowly.

"On what?"

"On whether you're inviting me because your mom told you to or because you actually want me there." I felt a strange anxiety as I waited for her to tell me which it was, hoping that this time it was the latter.

Her lips twisted. "Which answer would make you actually show up? *I* need to know if you would be coming to torture me or because you want to."

"I'd like to come. But only if that's what you want. I don't want to cause any more tension for you."

Her cheeks turned pink. "Then... I'd like for you to come, too."

"Then... It's a date." Words I shouldn't have said and couldn't take back.

Not that I really wanted to.

She blushed, then gave me a quick nod and jumped out, heading to her truck.

I watched her, wondering how someone I'd just met could make me feel so relaxed and nervous at the same time.

Chapter Seventeen

Claire

When I got back to the house, I managed to avoid my family, sneaking upstairs to jump straight into the shower. The hot steam calmed me and cleared my mind.

I'd invited Vance to dinner. Not because I felt like I should...

But because I'd wanted to.

One day and my feelings toward him had shifted radically. I'd gone from thinking he was the worst and being furious at him for cutting me out of the case to actually ... liking him.

A *lot*.

Yes, he'd underestimated me, just like so many other people had. But unlike most of them, he had changed his mind. *Apologized.* Started treating me like a legit partner.

More than that, it felt like we were starting to become friends. He needed one. But until today, I hadn't realized how much I'd needed one, too.

Things were changing. Cheyenne would always be my best friend.

But she was moving on to a chapter of her life that I couldn't understand. I'd still love her just the same, and I knew she'd love me, too. But things would be different. For her, the change was joyful. She still had me, but she had more, too.

For me, it felt like loss.

I lathered myself in soap, thinking back to lunch with Vance and how different it had been talking to him instead of Cheyenne. I felt like a traitor for thinking it, but the difference was one of the things that had made it so nice.

Cheyenne held all my history. We'd been friends for practically our whole lives. I loved her unconditionally, and I knew she felt the same. But that history colored over everything for us. It was amazing to have a best friend who'd been there for everything, but it also meant she'd had a front-row seat to all the stupid things I'd done in my life.

Vance hadn't. He only knew this version of me. And this version of me had been able to quickly earn his respect. His *trust*.

That gave me a confidence I hadn't felt in a really long time.

AFTER MY SHOWER, I PULLED ON JEANS AND A THICK RED sweater. The temperature had dropped today. It broke my heart a little.

When the weather turned cold, I always found myself dreaming about living somewhere like Miami, where I'd never have to deal with Wyoming winters again. Sunshine and warm days in December—the thought of it made me want to pack my bags and hop on a plane.

The summers there were probably brutal though. No crisp mountain air, wildflower meadows, or wild horses.

I couldn't imagine life without those things.

The people who'd figured out how to have it all, they were the lucky ones. Maybe I should go back to school, I mused as I towel-dried my hair. Become a nurse and sign up with a travel nursing agency. Spend the winters down south and the summers up north. See the country. Save lives in a different way.

It wasn't the worst idea, actually. Except for the whole four years of school thing. Four years of sitting in a classroom, studying textbooks, and taking tests was a high price to pay for a little freedom.

I looked at myself in the mirror and decided to add a touch of makeup. Nothing crazy, just a swipe of mascara and lip gloss. Maybe a hint of blush. There were times when I loved going all out with makeup, really dolling it up with a smoky eye and red lipstick. But I avoided all of it for work, knowing that even a trace of makeup would get some sort of comment from Trey. Thankfully, I was lucky to have Mom's gorgeous skin—although mine was dotted with freckles because I could never be bothered to put on sunscreen. Even so, a natural tan and lip balm was usually enough to satisfy my vanity.

Tonight, though... I wanted a little more.

I tried not to think about why.

Satisfied with my appearance, I headed downstairs to eat. I paused halfway, hearing Vance's deep voice coming from the kitchen. He'd gotten here early and had been intercepted by Mom.

That made me very nervous. There was no telling what stories she might have told him about me. The last time I'd brought a date over, she'd actually pulled out my *baby* book to show him.

I leaned my head back and let out a long sound of frustration, steeling myself before heading down. Beth appeared at the bottom of the stairs and grinned as she headed up to meet me.

"Agent Weston said you invited him to dinner personally." She winked, giving me a knowing smile. "I've always known you to move fast, but family dinner already? That's gotta be a new record."

I glared at her. "Knock it off. He's a coworker. A friend. That's it."

Beth's head jerked back. She was the one person I never snapped at. "I was just kidding."

Guilt struck hard. "I know. Sorry." I closed my eyes and rubbed my chest. "I guess I'm just really stressed out about this case."

"The case. *Right*. That's why you're wearing lipstick. And *earrings*." She flicked one, giving me a look that said she could see right through me.

"Stop," I hissed, ripping the earrings out of my ears and sticking them into my pocket. "The last thing I need is people ribbing me about him—especially if it puts ideas into Mom's head."

"You invited a man to family dinner. I think you put those ideas there all on your own."

I felt my face turn crimson. "I didn't really invite him. You know she's the one who told him he could come to dinner anytime."

She laughed, a look of utter amazement on her face. "What in the world has gotten into you? I've never seen you like this. One little tease and you're flipping out." She leaned closed and lowered her voice, glancing up and down the stairs to make sure no one was close. "Do you actually *like* him?"

"No!" *Yes. Dammit.* "It's just Mom. You know how she's been." I smacked my forehead, more frustrated at myself than at her. "I shouldn't have invited him. I'm just trying to be nice to a coworker, and she's probably already planning the wedding in her head."

Beth smirked, but she tried to reassure me. "Maybe not. From what I've heard, she's in there trying to get the inside scoop on the case. That might be even more interesting to her than fixing you up."

"Maybe," I said, cheering considerably.

Beth hesitated, then gave me a gentle smile. "I won't tell anyone. And you should put the earrings back on. They look great on you."

"There's nothing to tell," I lied. "I'm just being friendly."

"Well, in that case, you better get in there and rescue him," she said, winking. "Because Mom's been giving him the third degree for twenty minutes straight."

I gave Beth a desperate look, then braced myself and walked toward the kitchen. Before I could overthink it, I put the earrings back in and fluffed my hair one more time.

As the voices became clear, I could tell that Beth was right. Mom *was* giving him the third degree, in her casual "this is how I chat with all the guests" way, peppering him with questions about his family and his job. It gave me a smug feeling to hear him answer without giving her any of the personal details he'd shared with me.

When I turned the corner, Vance was perched on a barstool, snacking on cheese and crackers. "Hey," I said awkwardly, trying not to think about how good he looked sitting there in the one space that was normally reserved for family.

Or how good he looked, period.

He'd changed into blue jeans, casual boots, and a slim-fitting sage sweater that showed off the muscle definition in his arms. I didn't normally like sweaters on a man, but the way he wore them changed my mind.

He glanced toward me. "Hey. Your mom gave me a snack while I was waiting."

A laugh sputtered out before I could stop it. It sounded like something a childhood playmate would say, not a DCI agent who was only here because we were working a homicide case together.

He gave me a strange look. "What?"

"Nothing," I said, turning toward the refrigerator. I pulled it open mostly to have a place to hide my face. "Want a beer?" I called out.

"Sure."

I grabbed two and tossed him one. He caught it with one hand, those intense blue eyes looking at me in a way that made my cheeks flush. His gaze lingered, sending a thrill through me.

It was a good thing Mom had her back to us.

The spell broke when she turned around. "Claire, you wouldn't believe how many calls we've had today from people wanting to stay here."

"Oh, really?" I asked, barely paying attention.

I was still thinking about that look on Vance's face.

"It's crazy," she said, shaking her head. "They're coming here because of that poor girl's murder. The news reporters I understand, although I'm not sure why they think they need to camp out here. But some of them are regular people." She lifted her hands helplessly.

"It's a thing now," Vance said. "True crime podcasts and video channels are a big deal, and some of them make a full-time living from the content they create. They'll travel across the country for an interesting case. Some people have a weird obsession with murder."

"That's so strange," Mom said, her eyes wide. "I'm glad you're staying with us and can help keep an eye on things in case some of these people are off their rockers."

Vance grinned. "They're generally harmless. Just looking for content."

"Well, that's good to know. We're booked solid for the rest of the month, which is surprising. Things normally start dying down this time of year."

"Do you not get a lot of tourists in the winter?" he asked, clearly surprised. "That's prime season for some mountain towns."

Mom shook her head. "No. Wildwood isn't much of a winter destination since we don't have any ski resorts here. We occasionally get some snowmobilers or cross-country skiers, but it's pretty dead here after October."

He took a long sip of his beer. "How do you sustain the resort in the winter, then?"

"The tourist side is only part of our operation," I explained. "We started it to sustain the ranch, not the other way around. We used to be cattle only."

"It got harder and harder to make a living that way," Mom added, shrugging. "Some years, ranches our size barely scratch even on cattle. We had to adapt. So I came up with the resort as a way to bring in extra cash flow and to create extra jobs for my kids so that they could all make a living here. If they want to."

I knew it killed her that we hadn't all wanted it.

"Smart," Vance said. "You've done an excellent job with it."

"Thank you," she said, beaming. "I'm glad you're enjoying your stay. I know you're a guest, but can I impose on you to help Claire set the table? Dinner is almost ready."

"I'd be happy to," he said, standing. He looked at me with an expression I couldn't quite read. "Tell me what you want me to do."

My mind flashed with an image of him saying those same words under *very* different circumstances. I blinked it away, hoping he couldn't see how quickly my heart was beating.

"Um. Plates are in that cabinet," I said, pointing. "Grab nine of them. I'll get silverware."

He whistled a tune as he moved past me, giving me a whiff of what was probably ridiculously expensive cologne.

Cologne that made me go weak in the knees.

Inviting him here had been a very, very bad idea.

Chapter Eighteen

Vance

Claire might have asked me to come to dinner, but she avoided me all through it. We'd flirted our way through setting the table, but as soon as everyone gathered and conversation began, she became unusually quiet. She never even looked at me.

Which was probably a good thing since I was having a hard time keeping my eyes off her. The red sweater she was wearing looked incredible on her, a fiery color to match a fiery soul. But the sweet scent of coconut that clung to her matched her easygoing, playful approach to life.

She was a study of contradictions and I was dying to discover more.

Claire's careful avoidance said she didn't feel the same. It might have been awkward had fewer people been there, but the rest of the Hawkins family more than made up for her silence. Dinner was loud and chaotic, with everyone eager to tell their stories from the day. Everyone was welcoming, but they didn't make me feel like some awkward guest of honor expected to answer questions about myself or my job. Family dinner was *their* time, a time for the men to boast and try to one-up each other while the women rolled their eyes and poked fun at them.

My mother would have been appalled by the lack of manners and the level of noise around the table, but I loved every minute of it. They were a family. A messy, teasing, loving family. I envied every one of them for growing up around a table like this. For having that kind of anchor to hold on to through life.

They were damn lucky.

When everyone was finally stuffed, Walker stood at the head of the table and grabbed his dishes. "The men have dish duty tonight," he said, winking at Naomi. "Come on, boys."

Jonathan groaned, receiving a sharp elbow from Travis for it.

I picked up my plate, intending to follow the guys into the kitchen, but Naomi stopped me.

"You don't have to do that. You're a guest."

"I don't mind. It's the least I can do, considering your hospitality."

She smiled. "Tell you what. If you're brave enough to come back for another one of our family dinners, we'll let you help then. Deal?"

"Deal." I grinned. "Thanks again for the invitation. It was delicious."

"You're welcome anytime."

I turned to say goodnight to Claire, but she'd slipped out when I wasn't looking.

As I left the Hawkins home, something drew me toward the stables. The doors were still open and a soft light glowed from within. I poked my head inside, then stopped.

Claire was sitting on a hay bale beside one of the last stalls, her knees pulled into her chest as she faced the starry night sky. Her golden hair spilled down her back, and her dappled gray horse nuzzled her shoulder. Claire leaned into the beautiful animal, stroking the horse's nose, though her eyes stayed on the sky outside.

It made a beautiful picture. But it felt wrong to be there. She'd slipped away for privacy, and the right thing to do would be to respect that.

I found myself walking toward her anyway.

"You found me," she said with her back still to me, before I even made it halfway to her.

"How did you know it was me?"

She let out a little laugh. "I can smell your cologne."

I didn't know why I continued to be so surprised by how perceptive she was. "Is that a good thing or a bad thing?" I asked as I moved toward her.

She scooted over, making room for me on the hay bale. "It's nice cologne," she admitted. Then she looked at me and smirked. "Probably cost a fortune."

I rolled my eyes, despite my grin. I didn't mind her teasing me—as long as she was talking to me again.

But her smile quickly faded.

I bumped my shoulder to hers. "You okay?"

She sighed. "Yeah."

"You were quiet at dinner."

That got a laugh out of her. "Someone needed to be."

"Your family is great."

That earned another smile. "They really are, aren't they?"

So beautiful. Those freckles, that smile… But tonight, it didn't reach her eyes. The shadows had crept back into them.

I desperately wanted to wipe them away. "What's wrong?" *Let me in.*

"It's stupid."

"You listened to my woes today," I reminded her. "Stupid or not, it might feel good to get whatever's bothering you off your chest."

Her throat bobbed. "Rhett and Cheyenne are getting married a week from tomorrow." Her voice was fragile. I'd never heard that tone from her before.

"Is that a bad thing?"

She shook her head. "No. It's wonderful. They've always been meant to be together. Ever since we were kids."

"Then why do you look like you just lost your best friend?"

Apparently that was the exact wrong thing to say, because her eyes filled with tears. She blinked them back frantically, determined not to let a single one spill.

But she failed.

I touched her cheek softly, brushed the lone tear that escaped. "Hey. What is it?"

"I told you it was stupid." She tried to laugh, but like her voice earlier, it sounded strange. Fragile. Fake.

"It's not stupid if it's bothering you. I just don't understand."

"I don't, either." This time, the embarrassed laugh was real. "It's just that everything is changing. Cheyenne and I have been best friends practically my whole life. Now, she'll be my sister, and it's everything I could have ever hoped for. But..."

"But you feel like you're losing her in some way."

She nodded. "Yeah. I don't know. When she and Rhett got together, I thought nothing would change. That Rhett would just be another addition to the party, know what I mean? But it's different now. Different than when we were kids and they were dating. They're building a new life together, one that I'm not part of. And on top of that, she's changing her SAR work and we won't even be partners anymore." Her voice wobbled.

I let out a deep breath. "Cheyenne mentioned her canine training as soon as we sat down to dinner. Is that what you're talking about?"

"Yeah. Like I said, it's stupid. I'm literally the worst friend in the world." She put her hands over her face.

"No, you're not."

"I am. My best friend is marrying her soulmate and training on a new skill she's really excited about. I should be happy for her. We've *always* been happy for each other. I'm being selfish and stupid and I hate myself for it."

I put my hands on her arms and turned her so she was facing me. "You *are* happy for her. But you can be happy for her and also honor the fact that you're losing a partner."

She looked up at me with something like hope in her eyes. "Really?"

"Really. Look, I've been there. I had a partner on the force leave for personal reasons. It was terrible. When you've worked with someone day in and day out, literally trusting them with your life, losing that can shake you to the core."

"You get it," she whispered.

"Yeah. I do. I was so down when I lost my partner that I drank all weekend and ended up with the worst hangover of my life. And he and I hadn't worked together for nearly as long as you and Cheyenne have."

"I haven't been able to tell anyone else this," she admitted. "They wouldn't understand. The family would just think I was being petty. Mom would probably think it's because I need a man." She rolled her eyes.

I laughed. "Probably."

"Even Cheyenne wouldn't understand because she isn't going through the same thing. Rhett's training to join the team. He's a probationary member now, and I'm sure he'll train to be her dog's second handler. She's not losing a partner. She just traded me for him." Her voice wobbled again.

"I'm sorry." It was all I knew to say, but it wasn't enough. I wanted to pull her into my arms and tell her everything would be okay.

She took a deep breath, steeling herself. "You were right. Getting it off my chest helped—especially since you understand." She gave me a timid smile. "Thanks for listening."

"Anytime. And I know it's not the same, but *you* have a new partner, too."

Her green eyes brightened—for just a moment. "For a little while at least." She looked at me like she wanted to say more. Instead, she stood and brushed the hay from her jeans. "It's freezing out here. I'm going to head in. See you in the morning?"

I nodded. "Sure."

She turned and walked away.

My phone rang early the next morning, waking me from a deep sleep. I rubbed my eyes and sat up, grabbing my cell from the table beside my bed.

"Agent Weston," I said, answering it.

A deep, familiar voice chuckled. "Good morning. Did I wake you?"

I scrubbed my face. "Oh. Hi, Dad. Your name wasn't on the caller ID."

Not that it surprised me. He had a multitude of burner phones.

"How's your case going?" His tone was commanding, as if he were my director instead of my father. I tried to remember the last time he'd called to ask how *I* was doing instead of how work was going. I couldn't think of one. The difference between our relationship and the ones I had witnessed last night had never felt so apparent.

"It's on track," I answered.

"Excellent. How soon do you think you'll have it wrapped up?"

I stifled a sigh, pinching the bridge of my nose. How soon? I had no idea. We currently had one real suspect, and my gut said he hadn't done it.

"I'm not sure. I'll know more after the interviews I have scheduled for today."

"Good, good. Keep me posted. If you think you'll be finished within two weeks, I have an ideal first assignment for you. We can make this official and get your contract signed."

I hesitated. And despite how little he really knew me, he noticed.

After all, his ability to read people like a book was what had made him so good at his job.

"You don't think you'll be wrapped up that quickly?" His tone turned sharp, as if I'd disappointed him.

I raked my fingers through my hair. "Dad, I have another offer."

He let out a booming laugh. "If you want to negotiate your starting salary, you'll need to take it up with HR."

"That's not... No. It's not about salary."

"What is it, then? I have to say I'm surprised. You're the one who asked for this opportunity."

Two years ago, I wanted to remind him. But I didn't bother.

"I worked on a joint task force with the FBI a few years back. It went well. They had an opening come up in that department and reached out asking me to apply. I did. They made the official offer a few days ago." I kept my tone casual.

"Well. That's ... wonderful." The sharpness in his voice changed to surprise. "It's not often that they personally recruit people like that. You must have impressed them. Have you accepted?"

"Not yet. I asked for some time to think it over."

"The job is in New York, I take it?"

"It is," I confirmed.

He was quiet for a moment. "Are you still considering my offer as well?"

"I am." I wasn't. But something stopped me from saying so.

Another beat of silence.

"Let me know what you decide."

The line went dead as he hung up.

Chapter Nineteen

Claire

Cheyenne stopped in her tracks, spinning around so quickly that the saddle in her hands nearly knocked me over. "What did you just say?"

"Ow," I said pointedly.

"Sorry. But surely I didn't hear you correctly. Can you repeat that?" Her dark eyes were the widest I'd ever seen them.

I braced myself on Shadow's stall door, put my head in my hands, and sighed dramatically. "I have a crush on Agent Weston."

Cheyenne dropped the saddle, apparently deciding that this was more important than getting a jump start on the morning's work. "Well, he is pretty cute. Not *my* type, obviously, but cute."

"Not *my* type, either," I protested.

"And yet you have a crush on him." She grabbed my hand and tugged me toward our bench so we could talk. It had been our favorite spot for almost twenty years, a location chosen because we could see both barn entrances and the office door, ensuring that none of my siblings could sneak up and overhear our secrets.

When we sat down, she turned to look at me with a happy grin on her face. "We could double-date."

"No." I shook my head. "Nothing can happen. I mean, he's kind of my boss."

"Is he though?" She cocked her head.

"I don't know!" I buried my face in my hands again. I *didn't* know and I was afraid to ask because I knew how stupid and inexperienced it made me look. It was probably something they'd covered in training that had gone in one ear and out the other. I could remember random details that interested me no problem. But something boring? Forget it.

She studied me. "Claire Hawkins, you're legitimately getting hung up on this guy."

I shook my head quickly, trying to deny it to myself as much as to her. "No. This is just me, right? This is what I do. Lose my head, get crazy crushes, make things bigger than they really are... It's my fatal flaw." I sighed dramatically again, holding a fist to my heart.

Her face broke into a smile. "I love you so much it's ridiculous. And yes, you're dramatic. Adorably so. But you've taken a pragmatic and practical approach to relationships as an adult. This is different than anything I've seen in the last several years."

My shoulders sank. "That's because *he's* different."

He was, and it felt like a tragedy. I'd met someone I connected with on a different level than anyone I'd dated before, but our partnership was temporary. He'd be leaving Wildwood as soon as we wrapped up our case. The thought of it made me want to mope in bed with a tub of ice cream.

"How is he different?" She smiled patiently, encouraging me to talk.

"He understands me." I leaned my head back and stared at the ceiling, knowing I couldn't share the depth of it with Cheyenne. I'd never ruin her happiness by telling her how much it hurt to be left behind or how his understanding my feelings had made them bearable.

"It's a good feeling, isn't it?" She leaned back, too, touching her head to mine.

"Yeah." I swallowed hard. "Vance makes me feel like we're a team. Like he has my back."

"Any good partner should. That's true for life *and* law enforcement." I could hear her smile even without seeing it.

"Yeah." I shook myself, sitting up straight again. "But it doesn't matter. It's just a crush. Hopefully now that I've told you, I'll get over it and get back to work."

"What if you don't get over it?" she asked slowly.

"I have to, don't I?"

She squeezed my hand. "What does your heart say?"

I shot her a look. "My heart doesn't apply. This is work."

She rolled her eyes. "Okay, what does your gut say?"

"I don't know. I don't trust it. I know how I am."

"I don't think you're being fair to yourself."

I waved her off. "I'll probably flip back to disliking him by tomorrow. He's a very dislikable man."

"Dislikeable?" She shot me a skeptical look. "What do you mean?"

"Well, for one thing, he wears *six-hundred-dollar hiking boots.*"

"A terrible quality in a man," she agreed, fighting a smile.

"He can sit at a desk, combing through reports for *hours*. Doesn't even get twitchy."

"That sounds like a good thing," she pointed out. "Having different strengths makes you a good team."

"He buys expensive coffee instead of drinking what's in the breakroom."

She rolled her eyes. "You're grasping at straws, Hawkins."

"He probably can't even ride a horse."

She laughed out loud. "So you'll teach him."

"He doesn't live here."

This time, my sigh was real. I slumped, looking down the line of stalls to the mountains beyond. They called to me. Felt like home.

No matter how much I wanted to roam and see the world, something still tethered me to this place. But he would be moving on. And the odds of him ever coming back to Wildwood to work another case were ridiculously low.

Cheyenne sighed too. "That could be a problem. But you know, sometimes things work out. I was hesitant to get back together with Rhett because I thought he was going to be moving on, but look at us now. We're getting married and building a life together."

"I know." I squeezed her hand and gave her a smile. For the first time in a while, it felt real. Vance was right. I could be truly happy for her and honor my feelings, too.

I hated feeling left behind, which was why I absolutely could not get involved with Vance. He was only here for the case. Hell, that was probably the only reason he was even being nice to me and pretending like we were real partners.

When this was over, I'd probably never hear from him again.

At precisely nine o'clock, Vance and I stood on the Evanses' front porch, waiting for someone to come to the door. He'd briefed me on his plans on the way over. My job, for this one at least, was just to observe.

In a perfect world, Leslie would be caught off guard by our visit. But the odds of that were nearly zero. Even if Tony hadn't called to let them know he'd been questioned, we had to assume they knew we'd connect Tony to Katelyn eventually.

When Leslie answered the door, the look on her face told me she knew exactly why we were there. "Come in," she said, sighing. "I've been expecting you."

I glanced at Vance. His face was a mask. The man would make a great poker player.

Hell, I was a great poker player, too. Just wasn't a skill I'd ever thought to use in my job. But interviewing a mother whose son was a person of interest in a homicide case was very different. We had to tread lightly, Vance had warned.

So I followed his cue and kept my face neutral while Leslie led us through the foyer to their sitting room, fighting back the urge to laugh at the sight of her. She was wearing a ridiculously tight pencil skirt and stiletto heels so high that she wobbled on the tile floors, making me worry she'd break an ankle before all this was over.

She waved us into the sitting room with a graceful flick of the wrist.

I perched on the edge of a green velvet chaise lounge, keeping my face as straight as if I were trying to bluff my way into a win against Cole and Rhett.

Leslie reminded me of one of the housewives from reality TV. She'd designed this house herself—a house that was completely out of place in Wildwood. It was like someone had picked up a mansion from some California beach town and plopped it down where it didn't belong. She also loved that her husband held power over the town. His job wasn't much to brag about in my opinion, but it kept Leslie at the top of the pecking order.

She loved being on top.

If I was reading her right, she wouldn't mind being on top of Vance, either. When she sat down across from him, she kept a professional posture, with her ankles crossed and her hands folded lightly in her lap. But she ran her eyes over his body and looked at him through long lashes, giving him a seductive smile.

It took everything I had not to roll my eyes.

"I'm sure you know why we're here," Vance began, giving her an opening to talk.

"Yes." She nodded. "I knew when that poor girl was found so close to us that it would open everything up again. I feel terrible for her, of course, but I hope that Tony's connection to her can continue to be kept quiet."

Vance ignored the plea. "What exactly can you tell me about his *connection* to her?"

She shrugged, but her eyes flitted to the door like she was nervous. "There's not much to tell, really. They barely knew each other. "

A lie.

When we remained silent, she lifted her hands helplessly. "I mean, they went on a few dates. But it was never serious, and it had been over for a long time before she disappeared."

"I understand she came here and stayed with him for Christmas break last year."

Leslie's lips thinned. "Well, yes, that's true. But Tony often has friends come visit. He's a popular guy." She deliberately relaxed her posture. Smiled.

We weren't the only ones wearing masks.

"What was your impression of Katelyn?"

Her expression soured. "Personally, I didn't care for her. I know that sounds terrible to say, considering, and of course I feel sorry for whatever happened to her. But I couldn't help but feel she was trying to manipulate Tony into something much more serious than what he wanted."

Vance cocked his head. "Oh really? What exactly did he want?"

Leslie blinked twice, like she realized she'd said something wrong. "Friendship, of course. He's very focused on his studies right now, but he enjoys ... friendship. As most college guys do."

Right. I worked hard to keep my face blank as I stared at Leslie, trying to figure out if she was lying or genuinely clueless. She was clearly using the word friendship to mean casual sex. But that wasn't at all what her son had wanted from Katelyn—or Elsa. He'd been focused on marriage.

Vance kept digging. "But you felt like she was pressuring him into more?"

"Yes, frankly." She smoothed her skirt, then twisted the gold watch on her wrist. "I understand she didn't come from much. A foster child, I believe. She was beautiful, and Tony enjoyed her friendship, but I think when she saw our home and our lifestyle, she thought she'd landed something big."

"I see," Vance said, nodding along as if we didn't know she was spinning a story that was the opposite of what everyone else had said.

"I didn't trust her," Leslie stated, her voice flat. "And Tony didn't, either. That's why, as I said, things were never serious and why he ended the friendship long before her disappearance."

She smiled and lifted her hands as if that were that. I wondered how many times she had practiced that speech before we came.

"I understand," Vance said, giving her a warm smile. He seemed to have changed tack, moving from neutral to friendly. Odd, since she was lying to us. But maybe that's how he worked. A "keep your enemies close" kind of thing.

Vance studied his notes, then looked back up at her. "Just a few more things. What can you tell me about the fight they had the night she was last seen?"

"Well, nothing, of course. I wasn't there, obviously."

"Obviously," he agreed. "But you're a good mother. You have a close relationship with your son. He listens to you. Respects you. I'm sure he confided in you." He gave her a look of empathy.

I squeezed my toes in my boots to stop from rolling my eyes.

"I'm afraid not." Her smile faltered. "But, if you'll forgive me, I don't understand why it even matters. She left on her own. Stormed off, being overly dramatic as *always*. He had nothing to do with it."

"Oh, absolutely," Vance agreed. "We're just trying to figure out why she came *here*. Wait a second. You said she liked to be dramatic. Did she come to your house, trying to make trouble for you guys?" He said it as if the idea had just occurred to him and he was truly worried for any trouble they might have gone through.

I knew he'd already planned the question ahead of time.

She shook her head. "No, thankfully. I don't know why she came to Wildwood and I don't care. She was trouble, and while I'm sorry for whatever happened to her, I just hope my son won't be dragged into any of this. As I said, he wasn't involved in her leaving, and all of his roommates will back him up on that."

"Yes, I'm aware. We're just trying to get a better picture of her mental state that night. You never know what detail might be the key to breaking things open. The argument may have been almost meaningless to your son, but she might have said something in it that could give us a lead."

"Hmmm. I see what you mean. So you're saying he's *not* a suspect?" Her eyes narrowed.

"As you said, she left on her own and he has a solid alibi for the night she was last seen. We also have evidence that she was alone when she was driving this way." He gave her an encouraging smile.

He hadn't directly answered her question about Tony being a suspect. Leslie didn't seem to notice though. Her body sagged with relief before she pulled herself straight again.

"I wish I could help you more. He really didn't tell me about the fight." The look in her eyes made me believe her.

"That's okay. Thank you for your time." Vance stood, pulling a card out of his wallet and giving it to her. "If you think of anything else, call me. Day or night."

"Of course," she said, staring at the phone number like it was a prize. She looked up at him with a smile that was practically feline.

"By the way, you have a lovely home," he commented, mirroring her smile.

"Oh, thank you." She beamed, tucking her chic platinum bob behind one ear. Then she slipped her arm into his as she began walking him out. "You're welcome anytime, of course. It must be awful being stuck so far away from home, living in a hotel room and investigating such terrible things. If you need a home-cooked meal or a place to decompress, you just stop on by."

"I appreciate it." He stopped to admire the view from a picture window. "You're lucky to have such a great view of the Bighorns."

"Oh, yes," she agreed, nodding.

"This is my first time in the area," he continued, his tone casual. "Makes me want to come back in the winter. I bet this is a fabulous place for winter sports. Skiing, snowmobiling..."

He trailed off, giving her a warm smile.

I bit my lip to hide my grin. I knew exactly what he was doing.

But Leslie was only focused on him. "You absolutely should come back in the winter," she agreed, her eyes lighting up.

"If I do, will you take me snowmobiling? I've always wanted to try it." He winked at her.

She laughed and trailed a finger up his bicep. "I'm afraid you'll have to find someone else for that. I prefer *indoor* sports." The look she gave him was full of meaning.

Gag me.

He chuckled. "I'll keep that in mind."

She kept her arm in his, brushing her body against him as they walked toward the front door together. Both of them seemed to forget I even existed.

Jealousy, fierce and furious, flared inside me. I was grateful their backs were to me so that I didn't have to maintain my poker face for one more second.

Chapter Twenty

Vance

"Nice work in there," I said, offering Deputy Hawkins a compliment as she slid into the front seat.

She scowled at me. "*I* didn't do anything. Although, I'm not sure you did, either, unless you want me to congratulate you on picking up a surefire date any time you want it. Didn't know flirting was part of the job." Daggers shot out of her eyes.

I looked at her, amused. "If I didn't know better, I'd think you were jealous."

"Jealous? Please." She rolled her eyes and huffed.

"If you want me to flirt with *you*, all you have to do is ask." I winked.

"I'm not interested in Leslie Evans' leftovers," she said, shooting me a look.

A look that was still so full of fire I began to wonder if she actually *was* jealous. *That* was a very interesting thought.

"When you're questioning someone, you use the best tool for the job." I shifted into reverse and began backing out of the long driveway. "Leslie was clearly someone who responds to flattery. She's also protective of her son and was giving us rehearsed answers instead of opening up. Best move in that situation is to be nonthreatening, make her feel like I'm on her side. Makes it more likely I'll get something useful."

"You're probably right," she admitted. "I've noticed Sheriff McGrath takes that approach a lot, too. Not the flirting, I mean. But making people feel like he's on their side."

I shrugged. "I'm not surprised. He's an elected official. It's his job to make people feel like he's on their side—even when he's not. Sometimes, winning trust is half the battle."

She screwed up her lips. "Winning trust is not my strong suit."

"I think you're wrong about that."

"Really?"

"Rob trusts you," I pointed out. "So did Elsa. Even Sheriff McGrath trusts you. He wouldn't have assigned you this case otherwise."

"True." She sighed. "But I could never have been as nice to Leslie as you were."

"At least you know yourself," I said, grinning. "But you did a decent job covering up your obvious disdain for her. You didn't screw anything up by opening your mouth like you were dying to do."

She scowled again.

"That was supposed to be a compliment," I remarked, giving her a side-eye.

"Yeah, well, it's not. I was wearing my poker face. It's supposed to be foolproof. How could you tell I was dying to say something?"

I glanced at her again. "Have you ever actually won at poker?"

She slapped my arm. "Yes!"

"Must be some bad players," I said, laughing. "Because you're the easiest person to read that I've ever met."

"Tell that to Travis," she said, smirking. "I took two hundred bucks off him last month."

"Maybe I'm just exceptionally good at reading people," I said, winking.

"Well, then, tell me what you read off of Leslie Evans."

I turned back onto the main drag of Wildwood. "She's scared her son is a suspect. I think part of her is scared he did it, despite the supposed alibi."

"That's the impression I got, too." Claire drummed her fingers on her knee. "She didn't bat an eye when you mentioned snowmobiling."

"Nope. There was no emotional reaction at all."

"Oh, there was an emotion alright." She shot me another annoyed look.

I grinned. Jealous Claire was fun. "Okay, but not a noteworthy one. She didn't connect the comment to the case."

"You didn't push her very hard on Tony." There was an edge of reproach in her voice.

"Setting her at ease, remember?"

"You sure it wasn't because part of you *liked* the fact that she was looking at you like a cougar who'd just cornered a lost little lamb?"

I snorted. "So I'm a lost little lamb now?"

"Maybe in wolves' clothing," Claire muttered.

I pulled my car into a parking spot and turned to face her, delighted by the utter irritation on her face. "You *are* jealous." The satisfaction it gave me was astonishing.

"I am not! Why would I be jealous of some vapid, lonely housewife looking to score?" She waved her hand and looked away.

"Exactly." I touched her chin, bringing her eyes back to mine. "You asked why I knew you were fighting to stay quiet in there."

She nodded.

"It's because you wear your heart on your sleeve. Everything you feel, you feel deeply. Too deeply to mask. You're authentic. Real. You don't play games. And that makes you more special than a thousand woman like Leslie Evans."

Claire's eyes grew big. She held my gaze in silence.

"Don't ever lose that," I said softly. "That honesty. You can learn to wear a poker face during an investigation. I'll even teach you how. But don't ever let it define you."

Her throat bobbed. "I won't."

"Good," I said, dropping my hand.

She took a quick inhale and turned, facing the front. Her chest rose and fell rapidly, like she couldn't quite catch her breath.

I wanted to explore that.

But movement caught the corner of my eye. From where we were parked, I could see the men from the mayor's breakfast slowly dispersing, filtering through the café doors with handshakes and final words before walking to their cars. Mayor Evans was the last, and just like Claire had said he would, he walked down the street from the café to his office.

We'd planned our timing perfectly, but if he stuck to his routine, he wouldn't be there long. I had to choose between exploring this moment with Claire or moving forward with the interview we'd planned.

No distractions. My father's mantra echoed in my head.

We were working a homicide case. There was no question about what had to take priority. It was unprofessional for me to even be indulging this flirtation, no matter how enticing I found Claire.

So when she turned back to me, still wide-eyed, I gave her an easy grin. "Ready to ambush Mayor Evans?"

A flicker of nerves flashed on her face. "You should know that he doesn't really like me," she blurted out.

"Really? Why not?"

She flushed. "Probably for lots of reasons, but the big one? My first month on the job, I gave him a parking ticket."

I blinked twice, then let out a deep laugh. "You gave the *mayor* a parking ticket? As a rookie deputy?"

"Yeah." She let out a long breath. "I should have known better, right?"

"Or he shouldn't have been illegally parked." I chuckled. "You've got balls, Hawkins."

Her smirk came back. "What I've got is more impressive than that. And we need to work on how you give compliments to women you aren't wooing into bed."

I had to bite my tongue to stop from giving a completely inappropriate response to that one. "Fair enough. But listen, maybe we can use the mayor's feelings to our advantage." A plan was starting to form for this interview. A way to get Mayor Evans on my side and make him trust me.

"How?" She gave me a skeptical look.

"Can you handle me being an ass to you?"

She snorted. "I've been handling it just fine, haven't I?"

"I think I've been delightful so far," I said, giving her my most charming smile and earning an eye roll in return. "From everything I've heard, it seems like Mayor Evans is a boys'-club kind of guy. Am I right?"

"Totally," she confirmed.

I nodded. "Wendy told me as much. If he already dislikes you, even better. Odds are, he's going to have a natural reaction against being questioned. Even more so since we're ambushing him on a Saturday instead of during his regular office hours. But if I can get him to side with me—the two of us against you—he'll be more open."

"That won't be hard."

"Alright. When we go in, you take the lead. Tell him we're there to question him about Tony's involvement with Katelyn Brown. Play the part of a rookie who doesn't understand the power games, who doesn't know she's supposed to kiss his ass and play nice."

She leaned forward, tantalizingly close. "In other words... Be myself?"

"Exactly." I grinned.

"Got it. I'll get his feathers ruffled."

"Then I'll smooth them out."

Her lips twisted into a devious smile. "This will be fun."

CHAPTER TWENTY-ONE

Claire

I HAD ALMOST BLURTED OUT MY FEELINGS FOR VANCE. WHEN he'd touched my face and told me that he thought I was *special* for all the things I was usually criticized for, I had felt like my heart was going to burst. All the things I'd told Cheyenne came bubbling back up, forcing their way to the surface.

Thank God Mayor Evans had walked out of the restaurant, saving me from pouring my heart out in a way I wouldn't be able to take back. Flirting was one thing. It was easy to blow it off and call it innocent fun. But telling him that I was actually falling for him?

It could ruin this new partnership. That was the last thing I wanted.

He and I were working together as partners in a way I had never expected. He treated me with respect and valued my opinion. Sure, we teased each other, traded barbs back and forth. But it wasn't like the taunting I got from people like Trey. When Vance and I teased each other, there was respect underneath it. We did the same thing on the

SAR team. Joking and teasing made the work feel lighter and helped build camaraderie. It was all in good fun.

Vance was a great partner. I valued working with him, and in an odd way, it soothed the loss I was feeling about Cheyenne.

I didn't want to blow everything up by losing control of my emotions and making this bigger than it really was.

We got out of Vance's SUV and started walking toward the mayor's office building. I slipped on a pair of sunglasses and strutted a bit. It was fun to play bad cop—even if it meant I was going to get dressed down in a minute.

It didn't bother me. Not coming from Vance, anyway. He respected me and I trusted him.

When we reached the doors to the mayor's office, he looked into my eyes. "You sure you're good with this?"

I straightened my shoulders and raised my chin, finding that fire within. A mask that wasn't a mask at all. "I'm good. Let's do this."

I pulled the door open and walked inside the building, with Vance on my heels. He'd deliberately relaxed his posture, acting nonchalant and slightly amused by my attitude. All part of the act.

We walked down the hallway on the left to where the mayor's private office was. His door was cracked and we heard voices inside. One of them was female—and very giggly.

I shot Vance a look. His brows rose.

Should I knock? I lifted my clenched hand and mimicked the action.

He weighed it briefly then shrugged, leaving it to me.

So I barged in.

The mayor was sitting at his desk, with his administrative assistant leaning up against it. When the door opened, he ripped his hand away from where it had rested on her hip. She skirted away, putting on a professional posture, but she couldn't hide the fact that her top two buttons were undone.

The mayor's face flashed with fury when he saw me, but then his eyes went to Vance. He quickly shifted to the practiced smile he always used when cameras were around.

I stuck my thumbs into my belt loops and cut right to the chase. "Mayor Evans, we need to talk to you about your son."

"Excuse me?"

"You know what I'm talking about," I said, deliberately pushing his buttons. "Looks like Tony got himself into some trouble, huh? What, did you think nobody here in Wildwood would find out he was dating Katelyn Brown and that they had an epic blowup the night she disappeared? What are you trying to cover up?"

His face turned red. "How dare you speak to me that way! First, you barge into my office and interrupt a meeting without even knocking, and now, you're accusing my son of being involved in something that happened *here*, when he was at school in Laramie?"

I stepped forward, putting my hands on his desk. "We both know Tony doesn't like taking no for an answer. Is that what happened? Did she try to run away from him? That's the kind of thing that would make him angry, isn't it?"

His eyes glittered with rage. "You're out of your mind. There *will* be consequences, young lady."

Vance stepped in, holding up a hand. "I am so sorry," he said, acting shocked. "When Deputy Hawkins said she had a lead we needed to follow up on, I had no idea she was planning on accosting you. Otherwise, I would have stopped this sooner. Special Agent Vance Weston." He shook the mayor's hand eagerly, acting like it was an honor to meet him. "Wyoming DCI."

The mayor eyed him suspiciously. "Mayor Anthony Evans," he murmured, looking from Vance to me.

The mayor's assistant slipped out. Vance pretended not to notice.

"Hang on now," I said. "I have some questions that need to be answered."

Vance turned back to me, his jaw open. "Seriously, Deputy Hawkins? Mayor Evans is right. You are *way* out of line." He put his hands on his hips and glared at me. "Tony Evans has a rock-solid alibi for the night Katelyn left town—on her *own* accord, as I have been trying so hard to make you understand. I know you're new to this, but alibis mean something where I come from."

He turned to the mayor, shaking his head and rolling his eyes. "Rookies. When Sheriff McGrath paired me with her, I should have known something like this was going to happen."

"Deputy Hawkins has always been trouble," Mayor Evans muttered, shooting me a dark look.

Anger flared in Vance's eyes. He shut it down almost instantly, too fast for Mayor Evans to notice. But I did. And I loved him for it.

The mayor gave me an insolent smile. "Perhaps you should have stuck with your old title, Little Miss Wildwood. I think prancing on a stage was better suited for you than law enforcement."

Vance glared. This time he didn't try to hide it—he turned his anger into fuel for his performance. "Don't worry. Sheriff McGrath may not be able to control her, but I will. I will personally make sure Deputy Hawkins doesn't give you any more trouble over this."

Mayor Evans took a deep breath and smoothed the front of his jacket before giving Vance that practiced smile again. "Well, I'm glad to know *someone* on the case has some sense. I'd hate to think we were wasting resources looking in the wrong place."

"Exactly." Vance turned to me. "Deputy Hawkins, you need to apologize to Mayor Evans. *Now.*"

"I–I'm sorry," I sputtered. "I just thought—"

"It doesn't matter what you thought." Vance's voice boomed.

He was acting, but I still jerked. He was so easygoing with me that I'd forgotten how intimidating he could be. How naturally that authority came to him.

How most people probably fell in line right away, and how it had likely shocked him that I hadn't.

"*Thinking* is *my* job," he continued, his hands still on his hips. "Go for a walk. We men are going to talk. I'll discuss this with you when we're finished."

He turned his body to where Mayor Evans couldn't see his face and gave me a little wink.

My heart responded with a flutter that nearly knocked me off my feet.

"Uh...yes, sir." My face flushed. Not out of embarrassment over the situation—but because my body was flooded with pure heat from watching Vance take control of that room. From knowing that he was playing Mayor Evans like a fiddle.

And from knowing that the mayor's insult toward me had sparked actual rage in Vance, a protectiveness I'd only seen my brothers and myself. Watching Vance react that way about me... Oh, I was a goner.

I closed my eyes, barely even thinking about what I needed to do. "I'm sorry." Then I turned and fled the room.

I KNEW I SHOULD SIT AND WAIT FOR VANCE. BUT I DIDN'T feel like sitting, so I took off down the sidewalk, barely noticing where I was going. Hot energy coursed through my body.

Energy I didn't have an outlet for. At least, not the kind of outlet I was craving right now.

Vance was off-limits. We were partners. Colleagues.

I didn't want to screw that up.

But, oh, was I falling hard. He understood the worst parts of me. He liked the fact that I wore my heart on my sleeve. And he'd cared enough to get visibly angry when Mayor Evans had insulted me.

There was a ridiculous amount of chemistry between us. Worse, it seemed to be growing, despite the fact that we were spending pretty much all of our waking hours together. That was new to me. Normally, I'd found that the best way to prolong chemistry with someone was to not get too close. I knew myself. I got bored easily.

Vance wasn't boring.

But he also wasn't the kind of guy to be interested in someone like me, I reminded myself. We were great partners, but that didn't mean he wanted anything more.

He was at home with millionaires, wore cologne that probably cost more than my monthly salary, and had lived in New York City. He probably dated fashion models or elegant women like Leslie Evans who spent their summers in the Hamptons. Women who flew to Paris to buy their lingerie and who only drank champagne and chardonnay.

Not women like me, with short fingernails and calluses on their palms.

I sighed, staring at my hands. I was no model, and I'd always thought fancy lingerie was unnecessary. Why spend a fortune on something you were only going to wear for five minutes? I'd never even been to NYC or the Hamptons. And I'd rather have a cold stout over wine any day.

That was me. And I was okay with that. But I had to be realistic. Vance would never be interested in someone like me. He was just a good partner—and a natural flirt.

Here I was getting all worked up and starry-eyed over nothing. *Pathetic.*

I absentmindedly walked into the coffee shop, cringing when I saw every seat in the place filled with someone I didn't recognize. Then I cringed again when Emily came out from the back. She'd come for the summer last year, hooked up with a local, and never left, despite the fact that they weren't together anymore. She had mean-girl energy and I generally tried to avoid her.

"Hi, Claire," she said, giving me a wary smile.

"Hey, Emily. Two black coffees to go, please."

Her eyebrows rose. "Two?"

"Yep." I knew it would annoy her to death that I didn't volunteer an explanation. Emily lived for gossip.

"Who's the other one for?"

I cracked a grin. She couldn't even pretend to not want to know. I lowered my voice, not wanting anyone at the tables to hear me. "Agent Weston. We're working an investigation together."

"Oh." Her eyes got big and she leaned in close like she was sharing a secret, matching my quiet tone. "Are you investigating Katelyn Brown, that poor girl whose body they found in the woods?"

"I really can't say." That was a lie. But I knew it would drive her crazy.

She bit her lip. "Really? Because ... I know something about that, and I've been wondering if I should say anything."

My pulse rose. Part of me hated to take the bait, but if she really knew something, then I needed to know.

"Alright," I said, glancing around to make sure no one was listening. "Yes, we're investigating her death, and any information you have would be very helpful."

She nodded, a serious expression on her face. "I've been debating about whether or not I should say anything. I don't want to get anyone into trouble."

"Anyone who is innocent doesn't have anything to worry about," I said, trying to reassure her. "But at this point, we don't have a lot of leads. Anything you have would be helpful."

"Okay." She took a deep breath, then lowered her voice to a whisper. "When I saw her photograph on the news, I recognized her. I never forget a face. She'd been in here once, around Christmas time. It was right after I started working here. And I thought it was odd, because..."

I nodded eagerly, feeling fresh excitement. "Go on."

"Well ... she wasn't alone."

My excitement fell. We already knew that Katelyn had come to Wildwood with Tony over Christmas break. If Emily's big news was that the two of them had gotten coffee together, that didn't get us anywhere.

"Who was she with?" I asked, even though it felt pointless.

"See, that's what I thought was so strange," she said, glancing around like she was as nervous as I was about being overheard.

If Emily, the queen of gossip, was worried about someone over-hearing her, then she might know something meaningful after all.

"Who?" I asked again.

She looked me in the eye, beckoning for me to move closer. Her eyes were wide and she spoke so quietly that I could barely hear her. "She was having coffee with Sheriff McGrath. And they looked awfully cozy to me."

Chapter Twenty-Two

WHEN I FINISHED UP WITH MAYOR EVANS, I HEADED straight for my SUV, where Claire was supposed to be waiting. But she wasn't there. I frowned and pulled out my phone to text her before spotting her emerging from the coffee shop down the road. Her head was down and her shoulders sagged.

The sight of her looking so dejected made my chest tighten. That scene in the mayor's office couldn't have been easy on her. Mayor Evans was a condescending prick. When he'd called her Little Miss Wildwood, I'd wanted to punch him in the jaw. But my strategy had me siding with him instead, humiliating her in order to earn his trust.

If I'd known that it was going to hurt her, I never would have suggested it. Good cop / bad cop was a proven strategy in my experience, and she was such a fierce, fiery woman that I'd thought we would laugh about it afterward.

I clenched my fists, regretting that I'd ever suggested it.

Claire barely looked up when she reached the parking lot, walking straight to my SUV. She sank into the passenger's seat, staring straight ahead.

I put my hands on the steering wheel, trying to figure out the right words. "Listen, if I was too hard on you in there—"

"What?" She looked at me and jerked her head back. "What are you talking about?"

"You seem hurt. Mayor Evans is an ass. I should have stuck up for you instead of playing along."

Her expression softened. "I'm good."

"Really?" I was doubtful.

She rolled her eyes, but her face stayed soft with a small smile. "Geez, Vance, you think I can't handle a little acting? I agreed to a public dressing down. Don't insult me by apologizing for doing it."

Shit. "You're right. You just looked upset."

"I am," she admitted. "But it has nothing to do with you or our little stunt in there. You played it beautifully and I'm sure he was eating out of your hand by the time it was all said and done. What did you find out?"

I shrugged. "Depends on how you look at it, I guess. I told him we're trying to figure out why she came back here without Tony. Started by playing it off like I was checking in, making sure she hadn't caused trouble for them. He said they hadn't seen her other than the Christmas break trip."

"Not surprised, though if they're smart, they wouldn't mention seeing her even if they had."

"Exactly," I agreed. "Then I said that we suspect she had a new boyfriend and asked if he knew who she might have met while she was here visiting. He said no, but he's lying. He knows more than he's letting on. I just don't know why he isn't telling me when doing so would take the heat off his own son."

That was the head scratcher—unless Mayor Evans *himself* was the new boyfriend. But he wasn't some incredible catch compared to Tony. If Katelyn was after money, she probably would have been better off sticking with the son.

Claire leaned her head back and groaned. "I think I know."

"Really?"

"I feel sick." She was pale and looked like she might throw up any moment.

Worry struck again. "What's going on, Claire?"

She scrubbed her hands over her face. "I went to get us some coffee and—oh, dammit, I completely forgot the drinks. Walked out and left the cups sitting on the counter."

"Don't worry about the coffee. What happened?"

She rubbed her temples like a headache was brewing. "The girl on shift today is kind of a friend of mine. She asked if we were investigating Katelyn's death, because she had information that she was trying to decide if she should report or not."

The look on Claire's face made me very worried about what that information was.

She swallowed hard. "She said back around Christmas, Katelyn was in the shop. She had coffee with someone—a very cozy coffee."

"Not Tony Evans?"

Claire shook her head. "No."

"Then who?" My pulse quickened. If Katelyn's new boyfriend really was from Wildwood, identifying him could crack this case wide open.

Claire's misery was evident. "Sheriff McGrath."

I sat back in my seat, my mouth open in shock. Sheriff McGrath knew Katelyn Brown and had withheld that from us.

It was unthinkable.

My mind raced. "Does she think they were having an affair?"

"That's what she seemed to indicate." Claire held her hands up in defense. "Now, for the record, Emily is a huge gossip. She loves drama, and I could totally see her embellishing the facts for attention. She said they were cozy, but it could have been innocent. Her saying something doesn't mean it's true."

"No, it doesn't," I said, my tone sharpening. "But regardless, the fact that Sheriff McGrath didn't disclose this to either of us sure doesn't look good, does it?"

"Nope. Not at all."

I closed my eyes, realization dawning. "That's why the mayor lied and said he didn't know who she had met. He didn't want to throw a political ally under the bus." I hit my steering wheel in frustration. "Small towns like this, you get a couple of corrupt leaders protecting each other and they think they can get away with anything."

Claire's face was wrecked with devastation. "So, what do we do now?"

"We have two options. We keep this to ourselves and continue gathering evidence, this time with Sheriff McGrath as our prime suspect. Or we confront him and see what he has to say."

"This is terrible," she said, her eyes welling up with tears.

"Murder always is."

An hour later, Claire and I both sat across from an irritated Sheriff McGrath in his office. We hadn't told him why we needed to speak to him immediately, but he was smart enough to tell from our body language that it wasn't good.

"I'm going to cut right to the chase," I said flatly. "You haven't been honest with us."

"Never once have I been dishonest with you," he said, giving me a death stare.

"Alright, let me rephrase," I said, narrowing my eyes. "You've withheld information from us."

He held my gaze for a pause, then nodded. "I'll admit to that."

"Right now would be a good time to come clean."

His eyes flicked from mine to Claire's, then back again. "I'm guessing you found out about Tony Evans dating Katelyn Brown. To be clear, I was never trying to hide that fact from you. I know how things work, and I knew you'd get the information from Laramie PD and do what needed to be done. But by keeping it quiet on my end, I was able to make Mayor Evans feel like I was doing him a favor. Now, he owes me one. Simple politics." He shrugged as if that were it.

It seemed like Mayor Evans and Sheriff McGrath were doing a *lot* of favors for each other. And while I knew that's how it often worked, I didn't like it. At all.

"I appreciate you clearing that up," I said, never breaking eye contact. "But that's not what I'm talking about."

Ah. Those words made him sweat.

"Alright, son, then why don't you tell me what this is about."

Smooth. Call me son to put me in my place and form a connection. Ask me to tell him the details so he would know the extent of what I knew.

But this wasn't my first day.

"Tell me about your personal relationship with Katelyn Brown."

His eyes went wide with shock. "*Excuse me?*"

"We know," Claire said, her voice strained. Broken. "We know about the two of you."

He gave her an angry glare. "Then you need to check your information, because I didn't *have* a personal relationship with Katelyn Brown."

"To be clear," I said smoothly, bringing his focus back to me. "You're denying the fact that you had a relationship with Katelyn Brown, even though witnesses have stated that you were quite cozy with her in public."

The shock in his eyes was real. "I wasn't *cozy* anything. I spoke to the girl once, at the coffee shop down the street. That was it."

There was nothing about his words, body language, or facial expression that indicated he was lying. I'd deliberately left out the coffee shop part, but he'd known that's where they had been seen anyway. That was a mark in his favor, indicating that there weren't multiple locations where he and Katelyn might have been spotted. But I still needed to be sure.

"That's not what we heard," I said firmly. "But I'll give you a chance to tell us your side of the story."

His eyes narrowed. "Don't you forget that *I'm* the one who called *you* in." He smacked his palm on the desk. "You're only here at my request. You think I'd do that if I had something to hide?"

I didn't answer.

He shook his head, rolling his eyes. "Fine. Back, oh... December, maybe? Seems like it was around Christmas. I was working late—bad accident on the highway—and stopped by the coffee shop for some caffeine to keep me going. I see this kid I don't recognize sitting in the back corner with tears streaming down her cheeks. As the sheriff of a small town, I like to keep tabs on things. So I got my coffee and went over to check on her."

"Katelyn was crying?" Claire asked.

I glanced over and saw her mind working a million miles an hour.

"Yeah," he said, glancing at her. "I asked her if everything was okay. She said she'd had a big fight with her boyfriend. The way she looked, I was afraid we might be dealing with a domestic. So I sat down with her, tried to get her to open up."

I frowned. "What do you mean 'the way she looked'?"

He sighed. "She was wearing heavy makeup, but it looked like she was covering up some bruises. And there were some marks on her hands that looked like defensive wounds."

I didn't bother to keep the edge out of my voice. "And you didn't think *that* would be important for us to know?"

He glared at me. "She denied that anything had happened. Said she'd gotten into an accident. The way she was acting, I didn't believe her, but you know as well as I do that you can't force a victim to tell you something if they don't want to. I tried to coax the truth out of her, but she stuck to that story."

I opened my mouth, prepared to bite his head off, but he held up a hand to stop me.

"I followed up on it anyway. When I found out she was dating Tony Evans, I talked to him *and* his dad about it. Tony said she'd gotten the bruises in a car accident. So I called Laramie PD. Sure enough, there was an accident report from a few days before their trip. She was taken to the ER afterward for bruising and cuts on her hands."

I relaxed—slightly. "So the story checked out."

He nodded. "It checked out." But there was the slightest bit of hesitation.

I stared at him. "Why are you still worried it was more?"

He stared back at me for several long seconds before shaking his head. "I don't know. It was just her manner, I guess. She acted like a victim." He shrugged. "And to be honest with you, Tony had a history of getting forceful with his girlfriends. But the police report on the accident and the ER report on her injuries lined up with what I saw—and with her story, no matter what her body language said. She didn't have a history of ER visits for injuries, and the police had never been called for a domestic. There was nothing else I could do."

"You still should have told us," I said forcefully.

"You're probably right," he said between gritted teeth. "But by that point, I'd convinced myself that I'd overreacted to the whole thing."

I stared at him, unwilling to give him any grace on the matter.

He shook his head. "Look, you can think whatever you want of me, but here's the truth of the matter. One, I didn't think my conversation with her had any bearing on the case. Laramie PD agreed, by the way. Two, you and I are on the same side. I called you in because I knew there would be pressure on me to keep things quiet, and I wanted someone who didn't have ties to this town doing the investigating. I want her murder solved—no matter who did it."

I drummed my fingers on the arm of the chair, staring at him. He was right. I was only here because he'd called me in, and that was a point in his favor. And I could easily call Laramie and verify everything he'd said thus far.

But I still didn't like it.

He put his hands on the arms of his chair like he was about to stand, but I wasn't done with him yet.

"You said she was crying because she'd had a big fight with her boyfriend. Tell me what she said."

He squirmed, a frustrated look on his face. "Look, I hate to admit this, because I know how it looks. But she said things weren't working out between her and Tony because he was a child and she was looking for a man. I got the impression she wanted someone to be her knight in shining armor."

"What made you think that?"

He shifted in his seat, his face turning bright red. "Well, she kind of hit on me."

"She *hit* on you?" Claire's voice was incredulous.

He nodded, letting out a little groan. "Yep. That's probably why Emily—it was Emily, right?"

Claire nodded.

He rolled his eyes. "That's probably why she said we looked cozy. Katelyn gave me big doe eyes and said she wished she had a real man to take care of her. Someone to keep her safe. She scooted close and kind of snuggled into me and started crying again. I tried to comfort her at first, but she put her hand on my thigh. Kept creeping up higher. I disengaged as fast as I could and got out of there."

"And that's the only time you ever spoke to her?"

"Yes." His voice was firm. "The only time."

He told his story with the conviction of a man who was telling the truth.

But Katelyn had died last March.

That was a long time to practice a lie.

CHAPTER TWENTY-THREE

Claire

"Deputy Hawkins, I'd like to speak to you for a minute. Privately." Sheriff McGrath had a pointed look on his face as Vance and I stood to leave his office.

"Yes, sir," I said as I sat back down, glancing up at Vance.

Vance gave me a quick nod, then excused himself.

Sheriff McGrath didn't normally make me nervous, but as I waited for him to speak, unwelcome tremors of anxiety made me twitch. The look on his face told me he wasn't happy.

But when Vance closed the door, giving us privacy, Sheriff McGrath's shoulders sagged in relief. He took a deep breath, then smiled. "So, Claire, what do you think about being on a real homicide investigation?"

A little smile emerged before I could stop it. "It's interesting. I'm in over my head, but I'm learning a lot."

"How's it been working with Agent Weston?"

"It's been great," I answered, choosing not to disclose how he'd given me a tough time at first—or how he'd intended to cut me out of the case. We were working as partners now, and I wouldn't throw him under the bus. And even if he hadn't turned things around, I wouldn't complain to Sheriff McGrath about it. You had to have tough skin to work a job like this. Crying wouldn't get me anywhere.

"Any leads he hasn't told me about?" His tone changed just slightly —like he was trying to be casual but couldn't quite hide the edge to it.

My back tensed. Sheriff McGrath had every right to know how the investigation was proceeding. This town was ultimately his responsibility, not Vance's, and the primary reason I was on the case was to keep our office in the loop.

But he'd withheld information from us, at least in part to make Mayor Evans happy. Frankly, that was the best-case scenario.

Worst case... I didn't even want to consider it.

My loyalty had always been to Sheriff McGrath, but all of a sudden, I felt like I was caught in the middle of him and Vance, expected to choose sides for some reason I didn't fully understand.

That wasn't right though. My responsibility was to Katelyn. My loyalty was to justice. To finding the truth. It hit me like a ton of bricks that, in this case, that might mean Sheriff McGrath and I were on different sides. Which meant I couldn't be honest with him about our snowmobile theory, the new boyfriend in Wildwood...

None of it.

"No other leads yet. It's early though," I said, hoping he'd find it reassuring. "We've only just started."

He gave me a long look, then nodded, apparently satisfied. "Let me know if you come across anything. We're all eager to get this case wrapped up. Although, in a situation like this, without any real suspects... Sometimes the case goes cold." He shrugged. "No one will hold it against you if that happens. I want you to know that."

"Right," I said as an uncomfortable feeling spread throughout me. I looked at him pointedly. "I hope it doesn't though. Katelyn deserves justice."

"Absolutely," he agreed. "I just want you to prepare yourself that it doesn't always work out that way. I know from experience that can be tough on an investigator. You need to be ready to deal with that. It's like working SAR. You guys have an exceptional rescue rate. But sometimes, no matter how hard you try, you lose people."

"That's true." My mind flashed to our unsuccessful missions. Times when we got there an hour or two too late. Or worse, times when we never found the person at all. Their faces haunted my nightmares.

But that wasn't the end of it. Because even after we failed, we had to tell their families. Those families put their hope in us, praying desperately that we would bring their loved one back safe and whole. Watching them lose that hope, watching their worlds fall apart...

Those faces haunted my nightmares, too.

You never got closure after something like that. And Sheriff McGrath was right—a case that went cold probably felt the same way.

I would not let that happen with Katelyn.

Sheriff McGrath cleared his throat, drawing my attention back to him. "Claire, you're probably wondering why I picked you to work this case with Agent Weston instead of giving it to one of our more experienced deputies."

I nodded, giving a half laugh. Forcing myself to act like everything was normal, like I wasn't sitting here analyzing every word, every movement he made. "Yeah. Honestly, I was surprised you didn't go with Sergeant Collins. He seemed like the better pick."

"He's not real happy with me about that," Sheriff McGrath admitted. "But you needed it more than he did."

"Needed it?" My eyebrows rose.

"Yep. I know you've struggled finding your place here when there's not a SAR callout to work. I know the rest of the crew gives you a hard time. Some of the townspeople do too."

I dropped my gaze, embarrassed. "I didn't know you knew that."

"Of course I know that. I have eyes—and ears. I'm aware of what goes on with my people." He leaned forward, giving me an earnest look. "A case like this gives you credibility. You won't just be the new girl on the job anymore. People will start seeing you like a seasoned officer—your coworkers and townspeople alike. And that's what you need if you're going to stay and make a career out of this."

"I hope so," I said—though I wondered if I'd ever see *myself* like a seasoned officer.

Or if I even wanted to anymore.

"I hope so too. I know sometimes we get frustrated with each other"—his mouth turned up in a wry smile—"but I care about you, and I want you to succeed in this job."

"Thank you," I said as an odd lump formed in my throat.

I hated this. Hated myself for even suspecting him. I knew he cared about me, and he'd been a great boss. Anyone else probably would have fired me for opening my big mouth one too many times. It was so hard to reconcile the good with the fact that he had deliberately withheld information and was now on our suspect list.

He paused again, drumming his fingers on the table. "Can I give you some advice?"

"Of course."

"There's more than one way to approach law enforcement. Some people take a hard-line approach. They see everything as black and white. I haven't known him long enough to know for sure, but I'm guessing Agent Weston is one of those." He eyed me as if looking for confirmation.

I kept my face neutral. "I don't think I've worked with him long enough to know."

"Maybe not." He cleared his throat and continued. "Another reason I paired you with him is because you understand that different circumstances call for different responses. In a small town like this, taking a hard-line approach isn't always the right way. And in this case, I'd advise you to remember that."

That sweeping discomfort returned. "I don't understand."

He leaned forward, putting his elbows on the table and twiddling his thumbs. "Most of us in Wildwood all want the same thing. Peace. Happiness. Freedom. At the end of the day, what we want most is a safe place to raise our kids. My job here is to protect that way of life. To keep the wolves out, so to speak."

"Sheriff McGrath, what are you trying to say?"

He gave me a friendly smile. "All I'm saying is that you have to know how to differentiate between the good guys and the bad guys. The bad guys are the ones that threaten our way of life here. But the rest of the citizens of Wildwood? They're the good guys. Sometimes they make mistakes. We all do. But that doesn't mean they're bad people."

I studied him, wondering if he was talking about someone else—or himself.

"Working this case," he continued, "is more than just a chance to prove you're a seasoned officer. It's a chance for you to prove that you care about the citizens of Wildwood. That you're on their side. That you're here to protect the good guys."

"Right..." I agreed, trying to sound more convinced than I felt. Because what was I supposed to be protecting them from? It's not like we had a serial killer on the loose. The only victim was Katelyn Brown— and she hadn't even been a Wildwood citizen.

"I'm glad we had this talk," he said, looking relieved. "Be sure to keep me in the loop."

"I will," I said, standing at his dismissal. But my mind was racing.

Was he asking me to protect the people in Wildwood by finding Katelyn's killer?

Or was he asking me to protect *him*?

Chapter Twenty-Four

Claire

When I stepped out of Sheriff McGrath's office and saw Vance waiting for me in the hallway, the poker face I'd maintained in front of the sheriff collapsed. I leaned against the wall and closed my eyes, struggling to breathe as the devastation of it all threatened to break me right there.

Vance came to my side and took my arm, supporting me as he guided me through the hallway toward the doors. It was the kind of thing I'd normally push away, insisting I could take care of myself. Instead, I leaned on his strength, let it be an anchor for emotions that battered me like a stormy sea.

When we pushed through the doors into the sunshine, I finally felt able to take a full breath. The tightness in my chest eased.

But Vance didn't let go.

"What happened?" His eyes searched my face, my body, like he was afraid I'd been hurt.

I shook my head. I couldn't talk. Not here.

He understood, even though I didn't say a word. He relaxed his grip but kept his hand on me until I was inside his vehicle. I stared out the window, mulling over what had just happened as Vance walked around to his door.

Sheriff McGrath wanted this case to go cold.

Worse, he hoped I would cover up the truth, actually help whoever had done this get away with it.

What other explanation could there be for the things he had said?

Everything within me tried to deny it. This was *Sheriff McGrath* we were talking about. Sure, he and I disagreed sometimes. But never on something like this.

Every fiber of my being hoped that I had misunderstood him completely, that the investigation was just making me paranoid. But the swirling storm in my gut told me that's not what I believed.

I was totally and utterly confused. I respected Sheriff McGrath. He was my mentor. The one person who had actually seen something in me and believed I could do this job. And I knew he cared about our town, that he'd done a great job here.

He was also right—I *did* understand that things weren't always black and white. That had been the primary source of contention between us since I'd gotten the job. But I was usually the one wanting to bend the rules, not him.

I felt sick.

If that's why he'd put me on this case, if he truly wanted me to do that with a *homicide* investigation... That was totally different.

He didn't know me at all.

I buried my head in my hands, trying to figure out an explanation for his words that meant anything other than him being a corrupt sheriff at best, a killer at worst.

Maybe he knew something I didn't. Maybe he knew that it had been an accident, that whoever had killed her never meant for it to happen and had panicked and tried to hide the body. My heart sank again. You didn't "accidentally" put your hands around someone's throat and choke them.

Unless it was some kind of weird sex game gone wrong. The thought of that made me shudder.

Regardless, if Sheriff McGrath knew something that big, he was breaking some serious rules by keeping it to himself. I could maybe understand not telling us about the coffee shop. But anything more than that was a crime.

I couldn't respect that.

I looked over and found Vance watching me, his eyes revealing a mixture of worry and anger.

"What the hell happened in there?" His voice was gruffer than I'd ever heard it.

I shook my head. Voicing it, telling him what I feared... I wasn't sure I could do it without vomiting.

He put his hand on mine, stroking it gently with his thumb. Despite everything, my heart fluttered. The weight of his hand felt reassuring, like I was fighting my way through a storm and he was offering me a lifeline.

A lifeline I desperately wanted to grab on to.

"Claire. Come on. What's wrong?"

I found myself wanting to spill it all to him—to trust him with this and for us to figure out what to do together.

But I still couldn't speak those awful words out loud.

His eyes searched mine. "I'm taking you home," he said, his jaw set.

I didn't speak the entire drive back to the ranch. But my mind still raced. I went over every word Sheriff McGrath had said, willing them to have different meanings.

I felt cold. Numb. Like the SAR victims we rescued who were dealing with shock. Only my shock wasn't from physical trauma... It was from utter disbelief. From my whole world being upended.

When Vance pulled up to the ranch house, I took a sharp inhale and shook my head. "I can't." They were the first words I'd spoken since leaving Sheriff McGrath's office and they felt strange on my tongue.

The worry in his eyes grew. "You can't what?"

"I can't be around them right now," I choked out. I was a mess, falling apart in a way I would never let them see. I couldn't take the questions they would ask.

Couldn't handle them seeing me this weak.

Vance gave a sharp nod, then turned his SUV around and drove it straight to his cabin.

"Come on," he said. "Let's get you inside."

I followed him into his cabin, grateful for his understanding.

"Sit," he said, motioning to the rustic kitchen table and chairs. Then he opened a cabinet and grabbed a glass, filling it with water before putting it in front of me. "Drink."

"It's going to take something stronger than that," I said, forcing a laugh. But I drank the water anyway.

He refilled the cup and handed it back to me. "You need food."

"I'm fine." I shook myself, irritated at my own weakness.

A whisper of amusement—and relief—flickered in his eyes. "Okay, then *I* need food. Will you be alright while I go get us something to eat? If I promise to bring something stronger back to drink with it?"

I nodded, then drained the second glass of water.

He sized me up, then returned my nod before leaving me alone with the thoughts I didn't want to face.

I WAS CURLED UP IN THE CORNER OF HIS LEATHER SOFA when he came back an hour later, his arms full of packages. He dropped them onto the kitchen table, then pulled a dark bottle from one of the brown paper bags.

"Something stronger, as promised."

I uncurled myself and crossed the room, eyeing the bottle of single-malt scotch. "You have excellent taste."

"I asked Beth what your favorite wine was. She said whiskey." He smirked.

"She's right." I cracked a grin. "Though I can't say I've ever splurged on a bottle like this before."

His eyes sparkled. "This is nothing. Top-shelf at the local liquor store, but if you really want to taste something incredible, I'll have to introduce you to my father's collection sometime."

"I'll hold you to it."

He pushed a large reusable grocery bag my way. "Also thanks to Beth."

I opened it and found jeans, sweaters, and my cowboy boots. I shot him a quizzical look.

He shrugged. "I didn't know how soon you would feel ready to go home, and I figured you'd rather get out of that uniform sooner rather than later. I asked her to pack up whatever you might need for a day or two. Told her we needed to do some undercover work for the investigation. That should eliminate any questions until you're ready to go home." He winked.

"Thanks," I said, blinking back my surprise at his thoughtfulness—and his total willingness to let me hide out here, even though I hadn't told him why I needed to.

"I'm sure you know where the bathroom is if you want to change before we eat," he said, jerking his head in that direction as he began pulling takeout containers from the final bag on the table.

I hesitated for less than two seconds before grabbing the bag and heading to the bathroom to strip out of my wretched uniform.

Chapter Twenty-Five

Vance

While Claire changed, I set out food and poured us each a generous shot of scotch. I had no doubt that she needed it.

What the hell had happened in Sheriff McGrath's office?

He was pissed that we had confronted him. When he'd told Claire to stay behind so he could speak to her privately, I'd expected him to chew her out. But Claire was strong—wicked strong. She would have handled that and probably walked out rolling her eyes about the whole thing. Instead, she'd walked out and almost collapsed in the hallway.

It had terrified me.

Whatever had happened had shaken her to the core. I *needed* to find out what it was for the sake of the case.

I *wanted* to find out so that I knew exactly how to make Sheriff McGrath regret ever putting that look on her face.

When she emerged from my bedroom in faded skinny jeans and a long teal sweater, pulling her gorgeous hair out of the bun she kept it in for work, I was struck with relief that the color had finally come back into her face.

The relief was joined by a surprising truth: I was crazy about Claire Hawkins.

The realization made me drop the fork I was holding.

Claire didn't seem to notice. "What are we eating?" she asked, sniffing the air.

"Chinese takeout," I said, recovering. "I didn't know what you like, so I got an assortment of things and figured we could eat family style."

"Yum. Does Chinese food go with scotch?" She plucked an eggroll out of a box and bit off the end of it before sitting cross-legged in the chair at the head of the table.

I shrugged. "Who cares?"

She gave me that twisted smile that let me know a playful jab was coming. "I figured growing up all fancy in *Seal Harbor* meant that you know all the right pairings."

"Oh, I do," I said, grinning. "But in my opinion, scotch goes with everything."

"I guess we both agree on that," she said, holding her glass up in a mock cheer before taking a sip. "Whoa." The look on her face was pure pleasure as she held the scotch in her mouth. She closed her eyes and swallowed it slowly, savoring it like she'd never tasted anything so magnificent.

I dropped my fork again.

Those green eyes popped open and narrowed at me. "You're awfully clumsy today."

"Must be hungry," I muttered. I reached for the Mongolian beef and started plating it.

She leaned forward and grabbed the container of sesame chicken, then spooned out a heap of it onto her plate. "I owe you an explanation," she said quietly, the teasing gone from her voice.

"You don't *owe* me anything. But if you're ready to talk about it, I'm here."

Her eyes filled with unshed tears.

It wrecked me.

"Talk to me," I coaxed. "What's going on?"

She swallowed hard. "I'm scared to tell you. Partly because I don't want it to be true. Because I don't want to face it. And partly because I don't want to get him in trouble if I'm wrong, if I … misunderstood." She dropped her gaze, her cheeks flushing with shame. "I do that sometimes."

Rage bloomed in my chest. "Did he hurt you?"

If he'd hurt Claire, taking his badge wouldn't be enough.

"No." She shook her head and closed her eyes. "Not like that, anyway."

"Then how?" I was quiet for a moment.

She opened her eyes and gave me an unreadable look. "It's hard for me to trust my gut. Cheyenne has intuition that's always dead-on. It's amazing. But I've always felt like mine got wired wrong. I jump headfirst into too many situations that turn out to be bad ideas. I think taking the job as a deputy was probably one of those things."

I gave her a look of empathy but stayed quiet, giving her room to speak.

"Sheriff McGrath said he saw something in me. That I would be good at this job." She put her elbows on the table, hiding her face in her hands. "God, I'm so embarrassed."

"Why? Claire, you *are* good at this job. You're inexperienced, yes. But you have natural instincts. You're smart. You're brave." I stopped myself before giving the entire list of reasons why I thought she was one of the most amazing people I'd ever met in my life.

We'd have that conversation later.

"Thank you," she said, removing her hands and giving me a small smile. "But I don't think that's why he gave me the job."

"What are you saying?" My mind was going a million places, and none of them were good.

She tucked her hair behind her ears and took a deep breath. "Today, when he kicked you out of his office, Sheriff McGrath wanted to check up on the investigation. Which is normal, right?"

"Sure." I nodded. "It's still his town. He has the right to be kept in the loop. Although, personally, I think we should keep the details to ourselves until we know he's telling the entire truth about his involvement with Katelyn."

"Agreed. I didn't give him any additional information."

"See? Smart." I grinned.

"Thanks. But the conversation felt weird." She looked more uncertain than I'd ever seen her.

"Weird how?"

She shook her head. "His facial expressions. This is where I wish I had Cheyenne's intuition, to know if I can trust my gut or if I was reading too much into it. But when he asked about the case, something about his face made me think he had an ulterior motive."

I frowned. "I think you should trust your gut."

Gratitude flashed in her eyes. "Then he told me that he gave me this case for two reasons. One, because I needed it to earn some credibility."

"He's not wrong," I pointed out. "It's unfair, but I'm sure he's observed how you get treated by Collins and Mayor Evans. That's never good for a department."

"Yeah. And not just them. Judge Barrington is almost as bad, and half the men in town just roll their eyes at me when I'm in uniform. But the second thing..." She drew in another deep breath, then spit the words like she needed to get them out before she changed her mind. "He basically said he gave it to me because I understand that things aren't always black and white."

"What do you mean?"

"Sheriff McGrath knows I get frustrated by arbitrary rules." She shrugged. "We've argued about it in the past. I prefer taking individual circumstances into account versus going strictly by the book. He said he wanted me to remember that in this case."

My eyes narrowed. "We're talking about murder, Claire. What individual circumstances could matter when it comes to that?"

"Exactly." She gestured in agreement. "When I say I don't always go by the book, I'm talking things like leash laws or restrictions on how many pets you can own. Minor stuff like that, stuff that doesn't hurt anybody. Gray-zone areas."

I took the opportunity to tease her, knowing it would ease more of that heaviness that had settled on her. "Says the woman who gave the mayor a parking ticket. You certainly thought *that* was black and white."

Her lips twitched. "Well, individual circumstances dictate that he *always* deserves a ticket if I catch him breaking a rule." She winked and dug into the food on her plate.

I felt my shoulders loosen. Her fire was coming back and I was more relieved than I could say.

"Fair enough." I chuckled. "But back to Sheriff McGrath. You're saying he picked you for a homicide investigation because you don't always play by the book?"

Her face fell again. "He also said I need to remember who the good guys are. That anyone who wants to protect our way of life in Wildwood is a good guy. That sometimes good guys make mistakes, but that doesn't make them bad people... And that this is a chance for me to prove that I'm here to protect the 'good guys' in Wildwood."

I blinked twice and took a deep breath. "That ... does not sound good."

"He also said that sometimes cases go cold and that nobody will hold it against me if this one does, too."

"Shit." I put my fork down, having lost my appetite.

"Right?" She leaned her head back, looking at the ceiling. "I can't believe I'm saying this, but I walked out of there wondering if Sheriff McGrath really was Katelyn Brown's new boyfriend and if he's hoping I'll cover for him. If maybe the real reason he recruited me for this job was because he's corrupt and he wanted someone weak that he could manipulate."

I blew out a breath. "Well, if that's true, then he made a big mistake there."

"Did he?" She looked at me, her expression clouded with doubt and shame.

I looked her straight in the eye. "There is nothing weak about you. I've known it since the moment we met."

"I was weak today," she admitted, that look of shame flushing her face again. "One conversation and I fell apart. Clung to you like some helpless damsel in distress. Couldn't even face my family."

I shook my head. "Don't you dare think you're weak for that. It wasn't 'one conversation.' It was finding out that someone you trust, respect, and put your faith in isn't who he said he was. I've been there. That's enough to shake the strongest person alive."

"Thank you," she said softly. "For understanding."

She tentatively stretched her fingers across the table, touching mine. I flipped my hand over, taking hers inside my palm, and stroked my thumb over her wrist.

She didn't pull away. And I didn't let go.

I stared at her hand in mine before looking up to meet her eyes. Eyes that made me want to get lost in their emerald depths. Eyes that made me want to throw away the rulebook and explore the vast, swirling ocean that was her.

We were crossing lines, holding hands like this.

I couldn't find it in me to care.

"I like you, Claire Hawkins." I let the words out before I had time to overthink them.

Her lips twisted into the teasing smile that had become so familiar. "Too bad I can't stand you."

The look in her eyes was playful.

But I wasn't interested in playing games.

"We both know you're lying right now." I kept stroking my thumb along the inside of her wrist.

"Am I?" Her eyebrows shot up.

"I know your tells. Plus, I can feel your pulse skyrocketing." I smirked. "You like me more than you want to admit."

She jerked her hand away and grabbed the scotch, taking a swig straight from the bottle. "I think *you* like *me* more than *you* want to admit."

I leaned forward until my face was close to hers, lowering my voice to a dark whisper. "I just admitted it, didn't I? I like you, Claire. I like you so much I don't know what to do about it."

The sassy smirk disappeared when she realized I wasn't joking. Her lips parted slightly. Her chest rose and fell in shallow breaths. She leaned closer. So close that her lips were just a breath away.

"You're the most fascinating woman I've ever met," I whispered, bringing my thumb to her cheek, stroking it down her jawline until it hovered right beside those lips I was dying to taste.

"Should we be doing this?" she asked, her own voice a whisper matching mine.

"Probably not." I dropped my hand and swallowed hard, telling myself to pull back.

But she moved in and brushed those lips against mine.

One taste and the spark between us ignited into flame. Any hesitation she'd had vanished as she practically climbed into my lap, taking control of the kiss. She nipped my bottom lip, then let out a little moan that almost undid me.

I matched her intensity, using my tongue and my teeth to tease. To claim.

I tangled my fingers in her golden curls, swept up in her scent. Pineapples and coconuts, like she really was a mermaid who belonged in the warm ocean waters that mirrored the ones in her eyes.

A mermaid that tempted me to abandon everything I'd worked to build just so I could swim in those depths with her.

CHAPTER TWENTY-SIX

Claire

VANCE LIKED ME. AND NOT JUST AS A PARTNER. HEARING IT had made me lose control and throw myself at him, letting loose all the feelings I'd been working so hard to contain. I started it, but he quickly took charge. One hand tugged at my hair, while the other went to my thigh, his fingers gripping me tightly. His lips were like a hot fire, sending flames through my body.

I was breathless as I rested my forehead to his. "Tell me why you like me," I demanded.

He wrapped his arms around my waist and placed a soft kiss on my neck, sending a wave of pleasure through my body. "Because you're wild and confusing. You're irritating and..."

What? I pulled back and narrowed my eyes at him.

"Amazing," he finished, giving me that smirk of his. "You're absolutely amazing. You constantly surprise me. Every time I think I have you figured out, I see a new side of you."

"So you're saying you like puzzles." I rolled my eyes, trying to hide how much this meant to me. How much *he* meant. "Typical, I suppose, for a detective."

"Yeah. I suppose it is," he said softly, considering. "But there's nothing typical about you, Claire. You're brave. Selfless. Confident. And also... fragile. Soft. Tender. But only when you think no one is looking."

My eyes widened.

"You hide that side of you," he went on, frowning. "From everyone except me. Why?"

I swallowed hard. "They expect me to be strong. They all count on me for that. Hell, *I* expect me to be strong. I have to be."

"You *are* strong. Having a tender heart doesn't change that."

"It feels like I have to choose between one or the other," I admitted. "Being soft, being weak... It's dangerous."

"Dangerous?" He stroked his hand lazily up my back, giving me a contemplative look.

"Life here is harsh. Every year, we lose calves no matter what we do. No matter how hard we try. It's always the weak ones. They get picked off by predators or can't survive the elements." It was all true—basic facts of life on a ranch in Wyoming. But I also knew I was revealing part of myself I didn't share with the others. My fears. What drove me to push myself physically, to be stronger than everyone else.

A fear that I had to be strong enough to save myself—and strong enough to save everyone else too.

Understanding dawned in his eyes. "You've probably seen that a lot."

I nodded. "It's the same with the people we search for. The ones that take days or weeks to find? They only last if they're strong. Resourceful. The weak ones..." I closed my eyes tightly, as if it could block out their faces. "Strength matters," I said finally. "Being soft can get you killed."

Vance touched my face again, brushing his thumb across my cheekbone as if wiping away an invisible tear. "You're safe with me," he said gently.

My eyes widened again at the words. They felt like a balm soothing my heart. How could he have known what I needed to hear when I never would have known myself?

I'd always equated safety with strength. But there was safety in this, too. In having a partner, someone who had your back, someone you could be vulnerable and safe with. I'd always had that with Cheyenne and my family.

Never anywhere else.

And suddenly I realized why I'd never left the ranch even though the thought of working it forever felt suffocating. I'd needed that safety, even if I hadn't recognized it. And I'd never expected to find it anywhere else.

"I like you," he said softly, repeating his words from earlier. "I like your softness and your strength. I like that you let me see it all."

"Why are you telling me this?" My voice was shakier than I was comfortable with.

Vance was saying all of these things that made me feel ... everything.

Excited.

Vulnerable.

Hopeful.

Scared.

Adored.

His eyes never left mine as he spoke words that seemed to surprise him. "Because I want more."

"More?" It came out as barely a whisper.

"More."

He dipped his lips to mine again, softly this time, kissing me with a slow tenderness that made me ache for more. I swallowed hard, trying to get a grip. Men weren't supposed to get to me like this. I was Claire Hawkins, either just one of the guys or a careless heartbreaker, depending on who you talked to. I'd never met someone who had me feeling so ... needy.

I wasn't sure I liked it. But I didn't exactly hate it, either.

"Define more," I said, breaking away and reluctantly taking my seat across from him at the table. I couldn't think straight in his lap, where all I could feel, all I could taste, was him. He was overwhelming, and it felt critical that I regain some sort of control over myself.

This wasn't just flirting anymore. We were toying with something much more dangerous.

"I can't." He shrugged, then ran his hand through his hair, a hint of frustration breaking through his calm demeanor. "That's the thing. I want more. I want *you*."

"I want you, too," I whispered.

His gaze trapped mine, holding me captive. "But I can't define it. I can't offer you anything more than right now. You live here—I don't. As soon as this case is wrapped up, I'm leaving."

"Maybe it doesn't have to just be for right now. Maybe we could visit each other in between cases," I suggested. "Surely DCI doesn't keep you tied up all the time." I tried to say it casually, even though my heart was pounding out of my chest.

He took a long swig of scotch, looking miserable. "There's something I haven't told you."

"A dark secret?" I attempted an easy grin.

"No." He looked away, steeling himself before turning back to me and offering a flat statement. "This is my last case with the DCI."

"What?" The statement completely caught me off guard.

"I was offered a job with the FBI. It's back in NYC."

"Oh." Everything within me sank. The hope, the excitement...

He wasn't just leaving. He was *leaving*.

Now I understood what he meant. Best case, anything more between us would only be for a week or two. Even if we didn't solve Katelyn's murder, he would move on. The FBI wouldn't hold his job forever, and DCI wouldn't devote an agent to this case full-time if it went cold.

He would go back to NYC, to a world where I would never fit in, and this would be over before it had even really begun.

A relationship wasn't on the table. All he was offering was a temporary physical relationship. A fling.

I'd had flings before. Hell, that's pretty much *all* I'd had as an adult, since I'd never been interested in anything serious. But the thought of one with Vance made me depressed. I knew I wouldn't make it out with my heart intact.

I couldn't do it.

But the job offer was a huge deal for him. So I forced a smile, even though all I wanted to do was cry. "That's incredible, Vance. A well-deserved opportunity. I'm happy for you."

"Thank you." The look on his face was hesitant. "Maybe you could visit New York. Fly out for a weekend once a month or something."

"Maybe." But I knew that it was unlikely. He'd be busy with work. I'd be busy with work. My attempt at camping hadn't even worked out, and my job wasn't nearly as intense as his would be, working for the FBI.

He reached for my hand again. "I know it doesn't make sense. But I still want more."

This time, I pulled my hand away. "Long-distance relationships don't work. We both know how this story ends. And getting involved physically would just distract us from the case."

"Yeah. You're right. The case deserves our full focus." He sank back, clearly disappointed.

I was, too. But there was no point in pretending like there might be a future here.

I looked at the food in front of us, forcing myself to take a bite even though I'd lost my appetite. It gave me an excuse to avoid his eyes, and I didn't think I could bear looking at them right now.

"So," I said, forcing the words past the lump in my throat. "I guess we need to make a plan for moving forward."

He was silent for a beat. Then he straightened, putting on the professionalism he'd worn when we first met. "You're right. I'm sorry. I crossed a line. It won't happen again."

"I meant on the case," I said, rolling my eyes. "It was just a kiss, Vance. And in case you don't remember, I'm the one who kissed you. It doesn't have to be a big deal."

Even though it was.

"Right. Not a big deal." He scrubbed a hand over his face, looking weary. Then he stared off into the distance.

"The case," I reminded him. I felt desperate to get back on steady ground. Desperate for proof that my impulsive act hadn't ruined our partnership for good.

He blew out a breath. "Well, I don't trust Sheriff McGrath right now."

"Me either." I breathed a sigh of relief that we were moving in the right direction again.

"There was no indication that he was lying," he said slowly. "None whatsoever. No tells, no body language I'd flag. But I don't know him well. And he might be an exceptional liar. What do you think?"

"I don't know," I said honestly. "I've always assumed everything he's told me was the truth, and he's never given me a reason to think otherwise."

He nodded. "But the things he said to you raise a hell of a lot of red flags."

"Agreed." That sense of betrayal washed over me again, feeling even worse now that I knew that Vance was leaving.

This was the worst day ever.

Vance put his hands behind his head, stretching his legs out underneath the table as he contemplated it. "I want Sheriff McGrath to think you're on his side," he said finally. "He needs to trust you so he'll keep talking. We need his guard down."

I swallowed hard. "So I have to wear a mask."

"Yes," he said grimly. "Which you're not very good at."

"I can do it."

"Any real conversation about the case happens here," he decided. "No talking at the office. But we need to make regular appearances there so he doesn't think we've gone off grid. I'll figure out information you can feed him so he thinks he's being kept in the loop."

"Alright," I agreed. "So, what's our next move?"

He was silent for a moment. "Back when Katelyn left town, there wasn't any reason to get warrants for her cell phone and laptop. No probable cause, since it was a voluntary disappearance. The landlord eventually packed up her things, including those, and sent word to her mom."

I leaned forward. "But you put in for warrants, right? You mentioned that you would."

He nodded. "Yeah. I put in warrants for the phone, the laptop, social media—all of it."

"You should have those by now, right?"

"Takes about a week to get the digital request back from the tech companies. We'll have that in a few days, hopefully. But a judge in Albany County signed off for the physical items right away."

"And?" I glanced around, half expecting to see Katelyn's laptop somewhere.

"It took them some time to track her things down. Katelyn's mom never picked them up. The uncle eventually showed up to get them right before the landlord was going to throw them out. I got a text this morning from a deputy in Albany County that they secured them."

"Great. When will they get here?"

He had a guilty look on his face. "They're short-staffed and their courier can't get here until Monday, so I said I'd drive down after our interviews and get them. But that was before."

"Before I fell apart." I filled in the blank, disgusted with myself.

He put his hand on the table like he was reaching for me again but stopped himself. Withdrew it. "I can stay here."

"No." I shook my head.

I would not be weak again.

"We need that phone and laptop," I said. "Otherwise, we've got nothing but a suspicion about Sheriff McGrath and a suspect you're convinced didn't do it. And there's no way Judge Barrington is going to give us a warrant to search *anything* here without more than that. You have to go."

I almost asked if I could go with him but thought better of it. I needed to start putting some emotional distance between us. His leaving was already going to hurt like hell.

He studied me, then nodded. "You're welcome to stay here at the cabin if you aren't ready to go back home. It's no problem."

I shook my head again. "Thanks. I appreciate it—really. But I might as well start practicing that mask now, huh?"

"Don't ever lose the real you," he said quietly, with a look of pain on his face. Like he regretted even asking me to hide my emotions for the sake of the case.

I flashed him a fake grin that was convincing enough to ease the worry in his eyes.

CHAPTER TWENTY-SEVEN

Vance

THE DRIVE TO LARAMIE AND BACK GAVE ME A GREAT DEAL OF time to think.

The problem was that I kept thinking about the wrong things.

All my focus needed to be on Katelyn's murder investigation. On tying up the loose ends of my life here in Wyoming so that I could start making plans to move back to New York.

Claire was right. There was no reason for me to keep hanging around here, hoping my father would see my worth and want a real relationship with me. That had been nothing but a waste of time—except for the fact that my attempts to prove myself had built a solid career that was starting to pay off. There was nothing left for me in Wyoming.

Except Claire.

But I couldn't let myself think that way. I'd told her I wanted more and she'd said no. I understood and respected it. Who'd want to be in a long-distance relationship with someone working unpredictable hours at the FBI? That kind of thing was hard enough if you lived in the same house—my parents were proof of that. Being seventeen hundred miles apart added a whole new level of difficulty.

For a moment, I'd actually considered staying in Wyoming just to be with her. I knew DCI would let me withdraw my resignation. And if they didn't, there was always the job working for my dad.

But then Claire had said the kiss was *no big deal* and turned her attention back to the case.

I'd spent a decade in law enforcement, and I'd never once kissed a coworker or even flirted with the idea. I'd always kept strict boundaries between my work and my personal life. For me, letting Claire in on such a personal level and crossing those lines had felt monumental.

But for her, it had been no big deal.

I shook my head, irritated at myself. This was nothing more than an infatuation with a woman that, for some reason, I found entirely too bewitching. So bewitching that I'd actually considered turning down the most important job of my career.

No distractions. I understood now. There was a reason my father had always held that line, had never allowed even my mother to distract him from his life's work. You couldn't give everything to an investigation when your energy was split in two different directions.

The truth was that had Claire asked me to, I would have delayed getting Katelyn's cell phone and laptop to stay with her until she'd recovered from her meeting with Sheriff McGrath. There was no excuse for that. Not when the clock was ticking. DCI couldn't justify keeping me on this case full-time if it stalled. We needed solid leads to keep moving forward; otherwise, they would turn it over to the locals and stay on only as consultants. I didn't trust Sheriff McGrath enough to turn it over to him.

No, I had to stay focused. Katelyn Brown deserved it.

So I avoided texting Claire while I was in Laramie. And when I pulled back into Falcon Ridge Ranch on Sunday night, I forced myself to eat dinner alone in my cabin. Then I dove into Katelyn's laptop, hoping it would reveal her secrets.

. . .

MONDAY MORNING BROUGHT PHONE CALLS AND RED TAPE, so I didn't make it to the office until after eleven. When I arrived, the bullpen was empty. So was my personal office. I frowned, having seen Claire's truck in the parking lot, and headed down the hallway to look for her.

Sheriff McGrath's office door was closed, but I could hear his muffled voice. Probably having another meeting with Claire, I thought, tensing.

I started to walk back to my desk but stopped. A clanging noise came from a storage closet down the hall, like something had been knocked over. I backtracked, moving noiselessly toward the door.

Someone was inside, their voice deliberately muted. I put my ear to the door, straining to listen. My eyes narrowed when I realized I was hearing what sounded like a heated one-sided conversation between Collins and someone else. His voice was low, barely carrying over the sound of the footsteps that grew louder then faded away, like he was pacing the floor in the small space.

"I told you I'll take care of it. She won't be a problem." He sounded pissed.

Pause.

"I'm taking care of it *my* way, that's how."

Pause.

"I can't do that."

Pause.

"I can handle her."

Pause.

"I'm telling you it's a bad idea. Better for me to spin it now than to cover it up and risk it coming out later."

A long pause.

"Fine." He sounded defeated. "We'll do it your way. I'll text you if anything changes."

He let out a loud breath, like he'd ended the conversation. But he kept pacing.

The conversation could have been about a million different things, I reminded myself. But considering the circumstances, I had to wonder if he was talking about Claire. He was jealous she'd been given this case, and he threw her under the bus every chance he got. Was it possible someone else was pushing him to do it?

And if so, were they sabotaging her personally in order to sabotage the case?

He'd already tried to get her reassigned, then had thrown her under the bus with some serious accusations about her work ethic and attitude. He sneered at her every chance he got, and he likely had no issue with his friends sexually harassing her as long as I wasn't there to see it. If he was being asked to do something worse, something that even he balked at, that raised concerns about Claire's safety. The undermining had been bad enough, but if he planned to escalate things?

Unexpected rage coursed through me.

I silently backtracked, slipping into the men's room while I waited for him to leave. When I heard the door close and the sound of his footsteps fade down the hallway, I waited another two minutes, then headed toward the bullpen.

When I got there, Collins was sitting at his desk, red-faced as he typed furiously on his computer.

"Where is everyone today?" I asked, keeping my tone casual.

He barely glanced up. "In a meeting." He went back to his typing, then shook himself, like he was remembering who I was. "Sorry. Can I help you with anything, Agent Weston?"

"Nah, I'm good. Everything okay? You seem stressed."

Annoyance flashed in his eyes. "I'm great. I just have a lot to deal with. You know, helping Sheriff McGrath keep the town under control." He stood up, grabbing his jacket. "In fact, I was just heading out to do that. So if you're sure you don't need anything…"

I shook my head, eyebrows raised. "Nope, not a thing."

"Great. Have a good day, Agent Weston."

He snapped his laptop shut, tucked it under his arm, and stormed out, leaving a cloud of anger behind him.

I went back to my desk, leaving the door open so I could catch Claire when she left Sheriff McGrath's office. The electric chime sounded, alerting that the door to the front lobby had opened. Curious, I stuck my head out to look.

A familiar-looking blonde woman walked inside. It took me a second to place her. She was the woman from the photo on Sheriff McGrath's desk. His wife, presumably. Despite having aged at least ten years since the time of the photo, she still kept her hair platinum blonde and straight, just like Leslie Evans. And based on the way her forehead stayed frozen in place when she greeted Andrea, I had a feeling she spent a lot of time and money keeping up her appearance.

"Hey, Andrea," she said, walking up to the front.

"Oh, Serena, it's great to see you. I love that new coat. You look just like a member of the royal family."

"Thank you." Serena beamed, smoothing down the front of the red pea coat with her pink polished nails. "It's not too much?"

Andrea shook her head. "It's gorgeous. Wish I could pull off something like that myself. But it's not practical for what I do."

"We all need pretty things for special occasions," Serena chided. "You should treat yourself more. Especially with as much as they put you through up here."

Andrea laughed. "You're probably right about that. Now, I'm guessing you're here to see the sheriff?"

As Serena smiled, a hint of a blush crept into her cheeks. "Yes. I was hoping to steal him away for a lunch date. Is he in? I tried calling him as I was driving over, but he didn't answer. I haven't been able to get a hold of him all day."

Andrea nodded slowly. "He is. But he's in a meeting right now, and he asked that I not interrupt him. If you want to wait, I'm sure they'll be wrapped up soon."

Serena's smile became pinched. "Oh? Who is he meeting with?"

"Deputy Hawkins. A case update, you know."

A look of displeasure flashed across Serena's face. She quickly replaced it with a practiced smile. "Of course. Have they been back there long? Just wondering how long of a wait it might be."

Interesting. Based on her body language and micro expressions, I'd have bet money that's not what she was wondering at all. Sheriff McGrath's wife appeared to be jealous of Claire. I had to wonder why.

I leaned back against my doorframe, glad that the building layout gave me a great view of the front desk while mostly blocking me from sight. Neither woman had noticed me, which meant I could watch them without making up some pretense as to why.

Andrea glanced at the clock on her desk. "Shouldn't be too much longer. But you know how long-winded the sheriff can be when he gets going!" She was clearly trying to reassure his wife, but based on the look on Serena's face, it hadn't worked.

"Yes, I know," Serena said with a strangled laugh.

Footsteps down the hall caught all of our attention. As she turned her head, Serena glanced at me, her eyes narrowing. But she quickly moved her gaze past me to whoever was walking my way.

I turned and saw Claire. When her eyes met mine, my heart squeezed.

She was back in uniform, her hair slicked back in a tight bun. Her face was pale, her eyes looked sad, and her shoulders were racked with tension.

No distractions, I tried to tell myself.

But something more primal inside me threatened to override it.

Keep her safe.

Chapter Twenty-Eight

Claire

I felt deflated as I walked down the hallway—then annoyed at the way my heart lifted when I saw Vance. The way he made me want to smile. The way I wanted to run into his arms and have him hold me again, like some pathetic weakling who couldn't take care of herself.

I couldn't get caught up like that. He would be leaving soon. I had to stay strong—for myself and for everyone around me. Even if my heart fluttered when he shot me a concerned look and tilted his head slightly, indicating that I should come into his office.

"Everything okay?" he murmured, surveying me as I followed him in and closed the door behind me.

Stay strong. "Everything's fine."

The look on his face told me he knew it was a bald-faced lie.

"We need to talk," he said, keeping his voice low. He glanced at his watch. "Not here. Let's get something to eat and regroup. You said

Whiskey Creek is the best in town. Does that sound good to you, or is there somewhere else you'd like to go?"

"It's my favorite."

It felt bittersweet that he remembered. That he cared about my preferences. Why did I have to meet someone like him if I could only have one kiss? One searing, life-altering, mind-blowing kiss.

It wasn't fair.

We were silent as we walked through the empty bullpen out the back door. But when we got into Vance's SUV, he let out a long breath.

"There's something you should know." He quickly filled me in on the conversation he'd overheard Trey having in the storage closet.

My jaw dropped. "I've always known he was a snake, but..."

"I don't know for certain that he was referring to you. He never said your name, and he mentioned spinning something. That could be about a lot of things. But he does seem to be sabotaging you professionally."

"He wanted this case." I shook my head, clamping my lips tightly. "He even grabbed my arm and warned me not to make him look bad that first day."

"He grabbed you?" Hot rage filled Vance's eyes.

My heart did somersaults. *Dammit.* Why did I have to be such a sucker for the protective thing?

"It's fine," I said, trying to wave it off.

"It's not fine. You need to watch your back around him," he warned.

"I will," I promised. "I can handle Trey. Fill me in on Laramie."

I tried not to think about how he hadn't texted once while he was there, as if our partnership didn't mean half as much to him as I'd thought it did.

"It was productive," he said, starting his engine and pulling out of his parking spot. "I got the cell phone and the laptop. Unfortunately, the laptop doesn't look like it's going to be much use to us."

"Nothing good on it?"

He shrugged. "Who knows? The uncle scrubbed it and gave it to his kid to use for school. Now, the only documents on it are eighth-grade reports and the internet search history is all YouTube and soft porn."

"What?" My jaw dropped. "They just gave her laptop away, without even knowing she wasn't coming back?"

He nodded, irritated. "I told you the mom said she had a history of running away. When I stopped in to talk to her, she said Katelyn had been trouble since the day she'd been placed there. Started running away at age eight, disappearing for longer and longer periods of time. I think they'd given up on her long before this incident."

The lack of concern made me want to punch something. "But she got into college. She can't have been *that* much trouble."

He shrugged. "She was strong-willed. When she wanted something, there was nothing that could stop her. College became one of those things, according to the family. They were happy about it and hoped she would make something of herself. But I think they'd pretty much washed their hands of her."

"Hmmm." My eyes narrowed as I thought it over. "Do you think we're looking in the wrong place? She ran away all those times... Maybe we should look at the mom and the uncle."

Vance shook his head. "I've ruled them out. Mom is in a wheelchair. She's completely disabled and doesn't even drive. That's why she didn't pick up Katelyn's things personally," he explained. "She could barely lift her arms, so there's no way she could have strangled Katelyn, much less have dumped the body. And the reason it took the uncle so long to pick up the boxes is because he was deployed when she went missing. Didn't get back to the States until August."

"So way after our time frame," I said, disappointed. I would have been thrilled to have another suspect.

"Exactly. Beyond that, Katelyn's running away started before this placement. She didn't get placed with Marjorie—her adoptive mom— until age thirteen. She went through seven other families in the meantime and eloped from all of them."

I sighed, hating it. "She really was troubled."

"It sounds like it," he agreed. "From what I was told, Marjorie is the best thing to ever happen to her. But Katelyn was always looking for more. She didn't just want a family—she wanted to be someone. She thought she was better, smarter than everyone else and she craved wealth and power. She had Reactive Attachment Disorder—an inability to form healthy attachments—and delusions of grandeur, according to her psychiatric history."

"How is someone supposed to form healthy attachments when they've never had a stable home?" I asked, throwing my hands up in frustration. "And why is it that when some people are driven to achieve greatness we celebrate it, but when others do we call it a syndrome?"

He glanced over, admiration on his face. "I love that you aren't jaded. Most people in law enforcement are."

I smirked. "Well, clearly, I haven't had much law enforcement experience. And I might never get it."

"What do you mean?" he asked as he pulled into a parking spot in front of Whiskey Creek.

"Mayor Evans issued a complaint about my behavior," I said, trying not to let my emotions show. "I got a warning from Sheriff McGrath today. One more strike and I'm out."

"Shit." He pounded the steering wheel with his palm. "I should have known he would do that. I could have given Sheriff McGrath a heads-up about what we had done and why. But I got distracted." He looked miserable.

I shrugged. "We both did. How could we not have gotten distracted after finding out about Sheriff McGrath and Katelyn? It's alright. It's not my first warning. It'll blow over."

Although, I wasn't so sure this time. Sheriff McGrath had been different during this meeting. He looked exhausted and angry, completely different than his normal easygoing self.

"I'm sorry, Claire." There was true remorse on Vance's face. "This is my fault."

"It's fine," I said, waving him off. "Come on. I'm starving. Let's get some food and you can tell me about the cell phone."

But his face darkened. "I agree about the food. But we have more important things to talk about than Katelyn's phone."

My stomach cramped. That didn't sound good. "What is it?"

"Food first," he said, his mouth set in a firm line.

So I followed him inside and tried not to think about all the ways my life was falling apart.

• • •

VANCE STOOD IN FRONT OF THE SHINY WOOD BAR, STUDYING the chalkboard menu that hung on the back wall.

"What's good here?" he asked, nudging my elbow.

"Everything." My voice sounded oddly hollow. I fought to bring it back to normal. "I'm a big fan of the burgers. The salmon one is my favorite. But if you like red meat, the rest of them use a blend of bison and ground beef. They're grilled fresh to order. You can't go wrong."

"Sounds good," he mused.

Pete, part-owner of the bar, came out from the back, wiping his hands on a towel. "Oh, hey, Claire." He eyed Vance.

"Hey, Pete. This is Agent Vance Weston from Wyoming DCI."

Pete's eyes grew big. "I guess you're here about that girl's murder."

"Actually, I'm here for lunch," Vance said, chuckling. "But if you know anything about what happened, I'll take that, too."

He was back to being the disarming detective with a charming smile, having somehow completely erased the anger and worry that had been on his face outside. He was so much better at that than I was, at moving easily in and out of character and using whatever he needed to gain information.

"I'm sorry, I don't," Pete had said, shaking his head. "Wish I did. First Rhett, then Cheyenne, then this." He cut his eyes to me. "Wildwood doesn't feel the same as when we were kids, does it?"

Vance shot me a questioning look. "What happened with Rhett and Cheyenne?"

"It's a long story. I'll tell you later." I turned my attention back to Pete. "I'll take a salmon burger. You know how I like it. Sweet potato fries on the side."

"Sure. You want a beer to go with that?"

I shook my head. "I'm on duty. Just water."

"Got it. What about you?" He turned to Vance.

"Same as her," he said as he pulled his wallet from his pants. "Lunch is on me." He fished out some bills from his wallet and slid them over to Pete, telling him to keep the change.

Pete's face lit up as he calculated the generous tip. "Thanks. Find a seat wherever, and I'll have it right out."

Vance placed his fingers under my elbow and steered me toward a booth in the back, far away from any of the other customers—more strangers, I noticed. I still couldn't get over how people actually came out here just because a murder had happened.

"You didn't have to do that," I said. "Again. But since you did, next time is on me."

He ignored my words, motioning for me to have a seat. When he sat down across from me, that dark look from the car was back. It was fierce, angry. Determined.

I swallowed hard, imagining that this must be what it felt like to be across an interrogation table from him. It was fascinating. He could be so charming, so easy to like and open up to when it served him. Or he could be completely intimidating when that suited him instead.

But I had no idea why he was turning that look on me. I hoped I hadn't made some mistake that would earn a reprimand from him today on top of the one I'd received from Sheriff McGrath.

And if that was what I was in for, I *really* hoped it wasn't because of the way I'd kissed him, losing myself and climbing into his lap like I'd lost my ever-loving mind. Clearly, I'd crossed a line, and maybe his time away from me had made him decide I needed a reprimand for it. But he'd started crossing lines before that, telling me things that made my head spin. So if he was going to lecture me, well, then I'd lecture him right back.

I crossed my arms and put a stern look on my face, preparing myself.

But nothing could have prepared me for what he actually asked.

"Why doesn't Serena McGrath like you?"

"What?" I dropped my arms, confused. "What are you talking about?"

He studied my face. "She tried to pick Sheriff McGrath up for lunch. When she found out he was in a meeting with you, she presented with clear anger and jealousy."

"*What?*" My jaw dropped.

"Does she have a reason to be jealous?" He watched me closely.

"No," I protested. "Of course not." But then a realization hit and I bit my lip.

"What is it?" His voice was calm, but his eyes were narrowed in on me like I was prey in the water and he was going in.

I shook my head. "Nothing that I've done. But... Serena used to work for him. That's how they met. He was married at the time. They've always said nothing started between them until later, after he got divorced. But the consensus in town was that they had an affair and that's the reason he left his wife." I felt guilty repeating old gossip, but we all knew that it was true.

Vance's eyes lit with clarity. "Ah. I see. She knows her husband is a cheater, so she's worried it will happen to her, too."

"Maybe," I admitted. "But ew. He's my *dad's* age. I've never thought of him as anything except a mentor."

"Maybe you've never considered it. But has he ever given you reason to think that he has a special interest in you?"

"No, of course not," I said, shaking my head. But then I paused. He *had* taken a special interest in me. I knew that was partly why Collins gave me such a hard time. But it wasn't a romantic interest, was it?

"She's blonde, you're blonde," Vance pointed out. "She's younger than him, you're younger than him. She worked for him, you work for him." He shrugged. "It's a pattern. I can see why she'd be concerned."

"Ew." That was the only word that came to mind.

Vance chuckled. "It's clear from your face that you're shocked she would consider you a rival."

"Totally shocked." I grimaced. "I'm kind of disturbed now. But for the record, he's never made any kind of move on me. None whatsoever. I don't know if the pattern is the reason he encouraged me to apply for the job, but he's never once crossed the line, I promise you that."

"Good," Vance said quietly. He looked around to make sure no one was paying any attention to us.

"What?" I asked, leaning in.

"I just have to point out that someone else fits the pattern. Blonde, young. Looking for an older man..." His brows rose.

My jaw dropped as I realized what he was getting at.

Katelyn Brown had also been a young blonde.

And that realization made his coffee date with her look even worse.

Chapter Twenty-Nine

Vance

We ate in silence. The restaurant was too crowded to speak freely about the case, and neither of us seemed to be in the mood for personal chatting.

I'd tried to be angry at her for thinking the kiss was no big deal, but all of that had gone out the window the moment I'd seen her face. Now, I was just angry at how she was treated by her coworkers and for what Sheriff McGrath might have had in mind for her.

I could see the gears shifting in Claire's head as she thought about the implications of Serena being jealous. I knew personally how difficult it was to find out that someone you looked up to wasn't the person you thought they were. Claire was in a tough situation, no matter how this played out.

But I was relieved to know that the sheriff had never made a move on her. It didn't mean he wasn't interested though. The wide eyes and crimson in her cheeks when we talked about it made me think Claire was afraid I was onto something she'd never considered. That his recruiting her and giving her the special treatment Collins resented might have been because of her looks instead of despite them.

I hoped it wasn't true, if only because I didn't want Claire taking that hit to her confidence. She already feared she wasn't good enough for this job. She didn't need another reason to believe it.

Maybe we were wrong about Sheriff McGrath. After all, this was all circumstantial—puzzle pieces that could fit together and paint a very bad picture of him or be totally meaningless. Serena's jealousy could be nothing more than her guilty conscience.

Nothing in my conversation with Sheriff McGrath had indicated that he was lying about his coffee with Katelyn. But he was a politician.

That alone meant he was an excellent liar.

WHEN WE LEFT WHISKEY CREEK, A FAMILIAR CAR DOWN THE street caught my eye.

"Hey," I said, getting Claire's attention. Her head was down, her eyes focused on the sidewalk, clearly lost in her own thoughts.

She looked up at me. "Yeah?"

"See that green Mustang down the street? It was parked outside today when we left the station. Does that belong to Serena McGrath?"

"Yeah. That's her car." She groaned. "And the Beamer she's parked next to belongs to Leslie Evans."

Interesting. "Are Serena and Leslie friends?"

"Oh yeah. Leslie, Serena, and Darla Barrington, Judge Barrington's wife." She rolled her eyes. "They mostly prance around in fancy clothes, forming committees and making up excuses to throw parties."

"Are they all as bad as Leslie?"

"Darla is for sure. Maybe even worse. She's the oldest and kind of the queen bee. I always thought Serena was more down to earth, but she's definitely become more like them over time."

I looked toward where they were parked, unable to make out the name on the front door. "What business are they parked in front of? I haven't been there yet."

"Huckleberry Bistro and Bakery. Their desserts are amazing, but those three go for the fancy salads, tiny sandwiches, and flavored teas." Claire rolled her eyes again.

I was glad to see that her attitude was coming back. After the devastation on her face earlier, it was encouraging to see that spark again. "Not your kind of place, huh?"

"The food is delicious," she admitted. "But I'd rather eat somewhere I can kick back and relax. The bistro wasn't built for that. It's the kind of place where you feel like you should sit up straight, cross your ankles, and hold your pinky out when you sip from your teacup."

"But the desserts are good, huh?"

"The best," she said begrudgingly.

"Great," I said, grinning. "Because that's where we're headed next."

Claire wasn't thrilled with my plan. I knew she didn't want to face Serena after what I'd told her. But my instincts were leading me toward the bistro, so I asked her to trust me.

She sighed dramatically but agreed.

I pushed the bistro door open and was hit with sensory overload. Bells tinkled above the door, and strains of classical violin music poured through speakers mounted in the corners. A multitude of aromas hit. I had the sense that *most* of them would be pleasant if they weren't intermingled with the overpowering smell of women's perfume.

It was immediately clear why the café wasn't Claire's favorite place. She was right about the atmosphere. Even I found myself straightening my posture and feeling like I needed to be mindful not to knock anything over. The place was overly decorated and everything looked fragile. Everything also seemed tiny, from the round tables that couldn't hold four full-sized plates to the straight-backed French chairs that would never allow you to lean back and relax after enjoying your meal.

My mother would love it. But I was with Claire on this one. It wasn't my kind of place.

But I wasn't there for the atmosphere. I was there because two people of interest happened to be sitting together at a table with a third woman. Darla Barrington, I guessed, based on what Claire had told me.

There was no sign of the sheriff, which I thought was curious. Serena's plans to have lunch with him had apparently changed, and I wanted to know why. I began trying to think of a pretext to go over to their table, but the moment Leslie saw me, her eyes lit up and she waved me over. Claire groaned quietly but attempted to put a polite smile on her face as we approached the table.

"Agent Weston! So good to see you again," Leslie said, beaming. "Let me introduce you to my friends. This is Serena McGrath, wife to our excellent sheriff. And this is Darla Barrington, wife to our honorable judge."

Serena shook my hand politely before shifting her eyes to Claire. The coldness in her expression was as plain as day. Leslie and Darla ignored Claire altogether, as if she were invisible.

"It's nice to meet you both," I said, giving them a charming smile. "We stopped in for some dessert. Since I've never been here, I'd love your recommendations."

Darla—who had the same platinum-blonde hair as the other two, along with obvious work done on her face—leaned forward eagerly. "Oh, you have to try the lemon lavender mille-feuille. It's *divine.*"

"It is delicious," Leslie agreed. "Although I prefer the peach tart tatin. The caramelized peaches are absolutely luscious. Positively sensual." She let the word linger on her lips, casting me a meaningful look.

I didn't have to see Claire to know she would be fighting back an eye roll.

Darla shook her head, fighting a knowing smile, and tactfully brought the subject back to the menu. "Really, you can't go wrong. Everything here is fabulous. Wildwood may be small right now, but I'd put any of our offerings up against the top vacation destinations."

"Having been to those places, I think you've got something even more charming here," I said, offering her a charming smile. I meant it, too, although I had to exclude the bistro from my thoughts about the town in general.

"Thank you. We think so too." She beamed. "That's just what we were talking about, actually. We've formed a sort of unofficial committee, you see, to try to get the word out about our little corner of the world. With the right marketing, I think we could easily grow as big as Jackson Hole or Vale."

Claire's voice interjected. "Oh, I sure hope not."

Darla turned toward her and frowned. "What on earth do you

mean? Your family would benefit as much, if not more, from the added tourism dollars than anyone else here in town. And with increased revenue from tourism, we could build additional infrastructure in order to maintain that status year round. You must admit that would be a game changer for your family financially."

"Yes," Claire admitted. "But the best part of Wildwood is that it's still, well, *wild.* Jackson Hole probably gets a million visitors every year. I mean, can you imagine? Having that many people traipsing through here every year would change Wildwood forever."

I could hear the passion in her voice. Again, I agreed with her. Wildwood had charmed me so far because it was authentic, small, and personal. Vastly expanding tourism would change that.

"*Three* million visitors a year, actually," Darla corrected with a tight smile. "That's what's flowing into Jackson Hole—and providing countless jobs and revenue. Changing Wildwood is the point. Most of us want prosperity and financial security more than we want *wild.*"

Darla exchanged a smug glance with Leslie. Serena's face remained cold.

She definitely had a problem with Claire.

Before Claire could open her mouth again, I interjected, changing the subject.

"I appreciate the dessert recommendations, ladies," I said. "And I don't want to keep you any longer than necessary. But I do wonder if you could help me with one more thing?"

"Of course," Leslie said, giving me a coy smile. "Anything you need."

"I'm sure, being as connected as you are, that you're all aware that we're working Katelyn Brown's homicide case. We're trying to find out if she had connections in town. Have any of you ever seen her here, either as a tourist or visiting anyone?"

I deliberately avoided mentioning Tony, knowing that Leslie would never forgive or trust me if I brought his name into it—and also curious about how she would reply in front of her friends.

She sat back, slightly startled by my request, but Darla spoke first.

"Yes, of course," Darla said, looking at me like I was stupid. "Katelyn briefly dated Leslie's son, Tony, and came to stay with them over Christmas. We met her at a holiday dinner party at their house. She was a lovely girl, and Tony was smitten with her. I was quite heart-broken when we heard the news."

Leslie turned white. "Darla, I'm trying to keep Tony's connection to her under wraps," she hissed. "Why would you say something like that in public?"

Darla gave her a cold stare. "You had to know that Tony's connection to her would come out. Frankly, I'm surprised it hadn't already."

"It had," I said. "We were already aware of the relationship."

"See?" Darla said, lifting a graceful hand. "Agent Weston already knew."

"I know *he* knew," Leslie said, fury in her eyes. "I just don't want anyone *else* to know."

Darla shrugged, looking around. "Leslie, we're the only customers here, and Marcia is in the back."

Leslie glanced toward the front, her shoulders sagging in relief when she realized Darla was right. "I'm sorry for snapping, Darla. But you know Tony's had a rough time of things. Everyone was so jealous of him in high school that they made up awful stories, tried to ruin his reputation." She threw a sharp glare at Claire. "He's come so far. I don't want people to assume that he..." Her voice broke off in a sob.

Darla patted her hand. "Oh, Leslie, no one thinks that. It's absolutely unthinkable. We're all so proud of Tony." She looked back at me. "He's a good kid. I assure you, he would never have done something like this, no matter what *some* people may think of him. I'm certain you're insightful enough to realize that not every opinion should be taken as gospel truth." Her eyes flicked toward Claire.

I gave Darla an understanding smile and nodded, letting her think I was convinced. But then I turned to Serena, whose physical reaction to the whole conversation I found to be much more interesting than anything Darla was saying. The moment I'd brought up Katelyn, her back had gone rigid. She had stared straight ahead the entire time, her face blank. Her hand gripped her teacup so tightly that her knuckles were white.

"And what about you, Mrs. McGrath?" I asked her. "Did you ever meet Katelyn?"

Her breath caught. Then she shook her head quickly. "No. We were sick the night of the dinner party," she said, giving Leslie a hesitant look.

"But you knew about her relationship with Tony?" I watched her carefully.

A faint flush crept across her cheeks. She took a careful sip of her tea before answering, avoiding eye contact. "Of course. Leslie told us about her visiting for Christmas. It was a big deal, him bringing a girlfriend home for the first time. She was excited."

I noticed that, unlike Darla and Leslie, she didn't say anything to try to convince me that Tony couldn't be involved.

"A *friend*," Leslie corrected. "I was excited that he was bringing a college *friend* home."

"One more question, Mrs. McGrath. Did you ever see Katelyn in town?"

"Why is that important?" she asked faintly.

"Because we think she returned to Wildwood on her own," I said, leveling with her—curious to watch the reactions at the table. "We suspect she had another connection here. We're trying to figure out who. So if you saw her in town with anyone, that would be helpful for us."

Leslie's head jerked. She cut her eyes to Darla. Darla's eyes had turned thoughtful as she watched Serena.

Another flush, another sip of tea. This time, Serena's hand shook slightly as she set her teacup down on the table. "No, I don't think I did. I'm sorry I can't be more helpful, Agent Weston."

It was a lie.

Chapter Thirty

Claire

I watched closely as Vance questioned the women about Katelyn Brown. Serena McGrath was hiding something. I hoped he would call her out on it in front of the others, but to my disappointment, he didn't. After her lie about never having seen the girl, he thanked Serena and Darla for their help, and then he told Leslie he would follow up with her later in order to protect Tony's privacy. Leslie smiled at that, for reasons that I was certain had nothing to do with her son.

The woman was practically throwing herself at Vance. Telling him to get the *luscious, sensual peaches*. Gag me. We all knew exactly what she was offering him.

Vance would never go for a woman like that. I knew that. Even so, the thought of his hands being on another woman's body made me want to punch something.

Instead, I smiled politely and followed him to the counter, where we both decided to skip the peaches in favor of the vanilla bean creme brûlée and the chocolate croissants. He winked at me when he ordered, and I felt that annoying little flutter in my chest again.

He's just a flirt.

Except he wasn't. He flirted with Leslie because she responded to it. Offered that deferential head tilt and compliment to Darla because she'd respond to that. Was casual and easy with Pete, and acted like part of the boys' club with Mayor Evans. He seemed to have an innate ability to recognize what people needed from him and a willingness to become that in order to further his own agenda.

I wanted to convince myself that he did the same thing with me—that he'd seen my need for a friend and stepped up to be that just for the sake of the case. Believing that would have made it easier to keep my heart guarded from him.

But even without Cheyenne's spooky intuition, I knew better. He wore a mask with everyone else, but with me, the mask came down. He'd opened up to me, sharing things that were real. And the chemistry between us, the feelings that kept growing... They were real, too. On his side *and* mine. I couldn't deny it.

I just had no idea what to do about it.

While we waited for our desserts, I spied my friend Ben in the kitchen. He and Marcia were brother and sister, and they couldn't be more different from each other if they tried. They were both still single, despite being in their forties, and had decided to open the business together. Marcia was responsible for the ridiculous decor and theme of the place. Ben was the talent in the kitchen.

I'd been surprised they lasted a week without killing each other.

"I'm going to say hi to someone," I told Vance before slipping behind the counter.

Ben looked up when I walked into the kitchen, his gentle face lighting up with a grin. "Claire Hawkins. What's a girl like you doing in a place like this?" He gripped a giant stainless-steel mixing bowl in one hand and a whisk in the other. His sleeves were rolled up to his forearms, showing off his impressive muscles. In another life, he'd been a boxer. Now, he used that strength to follow his true passion.

I grinned back. "Wasn't my choice. I'm excited about trying one of your new desserts though."

"Better be careful," he warned. "You'll get addicted, and next thing we know, you'll start dressing like one of those women out there and coming here every day."

"Doubt it." I laughed.

"Yeah, me too." He came over and threw an arm around my shoulders, squeezing tight before going back to the mixing bowl. Whatever he was concocting smelled like a heavenly mix of vanilla and sugar. My mouth started watering.

"What's that?" I asked, walking over to get a look at it.

"Swiss buttercream. Guess what it's for."

"What?" I tried to dip a finger into the mix, but he swatted me away with a scolding look. Then he grabbed a spoon and scooped out a little for me to try.

"It's for Cheyenne's wedding cake."

"Oh." I stopped in my tracks. "Oh, that's... That's in five days." I couldn't believe it. Granted, their engagement had only been a month long. That was warp speed for wedding planning. But still. It had come *so* quickly.

"Right." He cocked his head. "You okay?"

"Yeah." I shook myself. "I just can't believe it's almost here."

"You and me both," he said, shaking his head. "I think we all would have preferred a little more notice, but Rhett and Cheyenne..." He trailed off, realizing I was staring at the video screen in the corner. "What is it?"

The café had security cameras mounted in the restaurant, with monitors in the kitchen so Ben and Marcia could see the whole place. I'd just watched Vance walk out with our bags. As soon as he did, the three women at the table huddled their heads together and began whispering. They were right underneath the camera in their alcove, and the image was so clear that I found myself wishing I could read lips and follow their conversation.

"I wish I could hear what they're saying," I muttered.

Ben picked up a remote and turned on the volume. "Strange request," he said, shaking his head. "Most of the time, I try my hardest to *not* hear whatever nonsense they're talking about. But your wish is my command." He changed the view on the screen so that it only showed their table.

I moved forward and watched the conversation, shocked that I could actually hear most of it despite the ridiculous violin music Marcia kept playing in the restaurant.

Darla looked Serena in the eye. "Don't let it get to you, Serena. You need to start acting like the queen you are."

Serena buried her face in her hands and said something, but I couldn't catch it.

Leslie squeezed Serena's shoulder. "You're the one with a ring on your finger, sweetie."

Darla nodded. "Exactly. And like we've been trying to tell you, it's not the end of the world. Men do these things"—she and Leslie exchanged knowing glances—"but he wouldn't dare divorce you. He knows that my husband will take my side. My friends *always* win at court."

Serena leaned her head back and groaned. "It *feels* like the end of the world, even if he doesn't want to leave. Once was bad enough. I can't believe it's happening again."

"You don't even know that it is," Leslie argued. "You thought he blew you off for her, but look—she's not even with him! She's with that sexy agent."

I startled, realizing they were talking about me. Serena thought her husband had blown her off today for *me*? I'd left the office right after he finished reprimanding me. If he had blown her off, he must have had another reason for it.

Leslie picked up her teacup in both hands, a dreamy look settling onto her face. "Wonder what I'd have to do to get Agent Weston to give *me* a full-body search. Do you think he carries handcuffs? I've never tried that before."

Darla pursed her lips, but she was clearly fighting a smile. "Leslie! You have to stop flirting with every man you see."

"Yes," Serena agreed, frowning. "You really should."

By the look she gave Leslie, I had to wonder if Leslie had flirted with Sheriff McGrath, too.

But Leslie ignored them, rolling her eyes. "Neither of you get to judge me. You're both getting laid. God, I hope our plans to make something out of Wildwood really work. I need some gorgeous celebrity to start vacationing here and fall madly in love with me."

"Love is overrated," Darla said, her lips twitching.

Leslie grinned at what appeared to be an inside joke. "Fine. I need some gorgeous celebrity to start vacationing here and decide he wants to ravish me every time he's in town. Does *that* meet your approval?"

"It's certainly less complicated," Darla said coyly. She turned her attention to Serena. "You know, you might feel better if you followed our lead and let go of these old-fashioned ideas about love and monogamy. Someone new warming your bed would make you realize it's not such a big deal if your husband wants a little variety every now and then. It's natural."

"No," Serena said glumly. "I love him. Only him. I don't think it's natural at all. I just can't believe I'm not enough for him." Her voice cracked and tears filled her eyes.

Darla straightened and gave Serena a scolding look. "Oh, stop it. Self-pity isn't going to get you anywhere. It's not attractive, and more importantly, it doesn't solve anything. What you need is to find your confidence again. You're his *wife*. There's no competition unless you allow there to be."

Serena took a deep breath. "I guess you're right. Maybe I've just been shaken up a bit lately, with everything—you know."

"Of course you have been." Darla cocked her head and gave her an empathetic look. "Anyone would be under the circumstances."

Leslie opened her mouth like she was going to say something else, but the bells that hung over the door jingled and the women instantly stopped talking. Two people wearing reporters' badges settled at another table in the alcove, close enough to overhear anything said. The women exchanged glances and began eating their lunch in silence.

Ben switched the monitor back to normal and gave me a perplexed look. "What was that about? Does Serena actually think you'd hook up with the sheriff?"

"Apparently," I said, gritting my teeth.

"That's ridiculous," he said, shaking his head. "Don't let it bother you, Claire."

"I'll try. But listen, can you get me a copy of this?" I couldn't prove it, but if the first affair Serena mentioned was with Katelyn, this conversation might be important. And because it had happened in a public place, we could use it as evidence.

"I think so," he said. "The recordings stay in the cloud for twenty-four hours."

"Great." I scribbled down my email address on a piece of paper and tucked it into the pocket of his apron. "Shoot a copy to me as soon as you get a chance. And don't mention this to anyone, okay?"

"Okay," he said, giving me a weird look.

"Is there a back way out of here? I don't want them to know I heard any of that."

"Yeah." He nodded and pointed toward a door tucked into the corner. "Leads to the alley."

"Thanks, Ben." I gave him a quick peck on the cheek. "See you at the wedding!"

Then I slipped out to find Vance.

We had a lot to talk about.

Chapter Thirty-One

Claire

Vance gave me a funny look when I hopped into his SUV. "Why did you come from the alley?"

"Long story," I said, buckling my seat belt. "I just overheard a very interesting conversation between those three women and I didn't want them to know I heard it. Even better, it's all on video. Ben, my friend in the back, is going to email me a copy."

He backed out of the parking space onto the road. "What did you hear?"

I gave him a quick rundown of their conversation.

"Hmmm," he said, mulling it over. "So Serena thinks you're having an affair with Sheriff McGrath, and apparently, it's not the first time."

"Apparently not." I let out a loud groan. "I feel sorry for her, but I'm also furious she would even think that. Regardless of what he may have done in the past, I'm offended that anyone would think *I'm* capable of screwing up some other woman's marriage."

He glanced over. "Goes against your code, huh?"

"Absolutely." I shook my head. "I'm live-and-let-live about a lot of things, but not that. I guess I'm old-fashioned, but I think marriage is sacred."

"We have that in common."

"Really?"

"You sound surprised," he said, frowning.

"Not exactly," I mused. "But you did flirt with Leslie Evans, and she's married."

"I didn't flirt. I was charming," he corrected. "Charming serves me well in my profession. She interpreted it as flirting because that's what she wanted to see. I knew it and allowed it. But I didn't say anything to her that I wouldn't have said in front of her husband. I would never *actually* flirt with a married woman."

"What if Leslie was single? Would you flirt with her then?"

"Maybe if I was single, too," he admitted. "Don't get me wrong. I don't find her attractive in the least. But for the case? Sure."

"Hmmm." I frowned.

He eyed me. "But if she was single and *I* was with someone, I'd take a different approach."

"Meaning?"

He shrugged. "I think it's disrespectful to be so ... charming ... to other women if you're in a committed relationship."

I brightened. "I think so, too."

"Well, there you have it." He looked over and gave me a little smile. Not the charming smile he gave Darla and Leslie or even the easy grin he gave Pete. The one he gave me was almost tentative. Unsure. Hopeful.

It was a smile I'd never seen him give anyone else.

And I fell in love with it.

I looked away, focusing my eyes on the road in front of us. My heart thumped in my chest as I tried to think of something insightful to say instead of blurting out my feelings like I was tempted to do. I was only saved by the realization that we were pulling into the ranch. I'd been so distracted by our talk that I hadn't even noticed where he was driving.

He pulled into the parking spot in front of his cabin, got out, and headed toward the front door.

I hopped out, then froze. This was the cabin where I'd practically attacked him a couple of days ago, climbing into his lap and kissing him like I'd die if I didn't. The place where he slept and showered. The place where the tantalizing scent of his expensive cologne had lingered even when he'd left to get us food. The place where we'd shared a bottle of scotch and I'd opened up my heart.

That was the problem with me. Unlike Beth and Cheyenne, who were slow, steady, and stable, my feelings always felt like a tornado ripping across the prairie.

And my feelings for Vance?

Those were an EF5. Stronger than anything I'd ever withstood. Strong enough to make me destroy everything I'd built in my life.

He stood at the door, waiting. Then a flash of realization washed over his face. "Oh, I'm sorry," he said, shaking his head. "I didn't even think. We left your truck at the office. We can run back and get it."

He moved back toward the vehicle, but I stopped him. "That's okay," I said. "We can get it later. But do you mind if I run home and change?

"Of course. I'll make coffee while you're gone," he said, wiggling the dessert boxes. "We can fuel ourselves with sugar and caffeine, then dive into Katelyn's cell phone."

I gave him the most awkward wave ever, then started walking up the driveway, hoping a break and a cold shower would knock some sense into me.

Then I would go back inside that cabin, act like a freaking professional, and solve a murder.

Chapter Thirty-Two

Vance

I PUT ON A POT OF COFFEE, THEN SET UP A CRIME BOARD while I waited for Claire to arrive. I was adding photographs to it when she knocked.

"Come on in," I called.

She opened the door and stepped inside. "Whoa."

"Whoa what?" I turned around. When I saw her, my breath caught.

She'd changed into the soft jeans she preferred, a dark-green sweater, and suede boots. A beaded necklace hung around her neck, flowing down between the valley of her breasts. The bun was gone, and her beautiful hair fell in a soft cascade. I loved how varied it was, a mix of different textures. Ringlets beside soft waves, like even her hair refused to be put into a box. It was completely unlike the perfect heat-styled hair most women seemed to prefer. It was messy and wild and totally Claire. She was the most beautiful woman I'd ever known.

And she was staring at me like she'd said something I hadn't caught.

"Cat got your tongue?" she asked, dropping her bag on the kitchen table.

I shook myself. "Sorry. What were you saying?"

"You've got a murder board." She grinned, shaking her head in amazement. "An actual murder board."

"Even with tech, it's still my favorite way to organize evidence," I said, returning her grin.

"I've never seen one. Not in real life, anyway." She moved toward me, gazing at the board with an intrigued look on her face. She then pointed to the photograph hanging beside Katelyn's. "You still have Tony as a suspect."

"I do. I don't think he did it, but until we rule him out, he stays up there."

"Sheriff McGrath is also a suspect," she said, swallowing hard as she looked at his photo.

"Yeah." I cast a glance her way, pained at the tight lines around her eye. It would take a while for her to get over his betrayal.

"And I guess that's Katelyn's mom and uncle over there?" she asked, pointing to the left side of my board.

"Exactly. I like to keep track of everyone I've talked to, even if they're not an active suspect." I walked to my briefcase and pulled out some additional things to tack onto the board. "Snowmobile registrations. Everyone within a one-hundred-mile radius who has one registered. Gotta love public records."

Claire grinned. "Nice work." She turned back to the board. "Um. Okay. What about the Evanses? Are they on the registration list?"

"Negative," I confirmed. "They don't own one. However..." I tapped a name on the list.

She exhaled. "Sheriff McGrath does." She smacked her head. "He would also have access to the SAR snowmobiles. They're housed in a storage unit that belongs to the Sage County Sheriff's Office. I can't believe I didn't think of that."

"You weren't thinking of him as a suspect at that point," I reminded her. "But that's good to know. Is there any way for us to find out if someone accessed one of those for a non-SAR event?"

"No," she said, shaking her head. "Unless the storage facility has security cameras and kept the footage from that far back. But the place is locked with a regular deadbolt. Everyone at the sheriff's office has keys to it. So does Hank, our base command operator."

"We can check on footage," I said, making a note. "But I agree. That's a long shot at this point."

"The evidence is stacking up against him, isn't it?"

"It might be," I said gently.

She sighed deeply, staring at his picture. "Alright. So he had snowmobile access and Tony didn't. But there are places around here that rent snowmobiles in the winter. We should get a list of people they rented them to in March and April. Maybe we'll get lucky and Tony Evans will be on that list."

I shook my head. "We can ask them if they'll share, but right now, we don't have enough for a warrant. Having a theory that the killer used a snowmobile isn't enough. If we had more, I could push for the DA to draft a subpoena. But we don't even have enough for that."

"Alright, so we ask nicely. What else?"

"Katelyn's phone," I said, grabbing a marker to make some notes on the board. "The only calls or texts to or from a Wildwood phone number were the ones to Tony Evans, and those were few and far between after January. But get this. Her roommate said she was texting someone before she left that night. And there were no texts sent or received during that time on her phone."

"Maybe she deleted them?"

"That's what I thought, too. But I checked her cell phone carrier's metadata. There weren't any."

"She was probably messaging on a social media app," Claire pointed out. "That's the way most of my personal messages are sent these days."

"I've checked the apps on her phone and didn't see any messages for that time frame."

"Some of those apps automatically delete them after a period of time—that's why some people use them to try to find hookups online without leaving evidence behind for their spouse," she said, rolling her eyes. "Will your data warrant cover that?"

"No. We might get metadata, but not message content."

"Crap." Claire looked disappointed.

"Metadata still helps," I assured her. "But my gut says that's not where we're looking anyway."

She turned to me, her lips twitching. "You have a different idea."

I did. The thought had hit me earlier, and it made perfect sense. "What if she had a second phone? A burner used only for her new boyfriend."

Claire's eyes lit. "That would explain why she left hers behind. It didn't matter to her. Only the one she used to contact him did."

"Exactly," I said, grinning.

"So how do we prove that?"

"Normally, I'd do a geofence for that night, use it to identify all the electronics that had been used at her residence. But it's been seven months. That data could be gone. And a geofence gets tricky in an apartment building full of college students. A lot of judges are going to see that as an invasion of privacy, since it would tag all of their devices, too," I mused, thinking it over. "Besides, that only works if her phone was connected to the internet and used apps that collect voluntary data like Google. If we're talking about a flip phone with wireless only or a true burner, we're out of luck."

"What about cell tower data?"

I shook my head. "Seven months later, full tower dumps will be long gone. We would only be able to get data if we knew the phone number."

"So there's no way to prove it." Her shoulders sagged again.

"There's always a way."

She shot me a skeptical look.

"Maybe we'll get lucky." I shrugged. "Once we get the social media returns, we might find another device connected that way."

"So much waiting around," she complained.

"Welcome to my world." I loved every minute of it, but being a detective was slow work for the most part.

"It's fun," she admitted. "Most of the time. But I do get antsy. I'm used to more action, less thinking and data."

"You get used to it." I pulled another photo from my files and stuck it up on the board.

"*Trey*?" Claire's jaw dropped. "You think *Trey* might have killed Katelyn?"

"I think we should consider him as a possibility, especially after the conversation I overheard. Let's think him through as a suspect."

"Okay," Claire said with a heavy exhale. "We know he wanted this case. I assumed it was to give him a leg up with the DCI, but if he killed Katelyn, that's a whole new level of motivation to be in on things."

I nodded. "He came to help process the crime scene and made sure his DNA was there."

"That's true." Claire's eyes narrowed. "If Katelyn was looking for attention when she was here and Sheriff McGrath blew her off, maybe she tried getting it from Trey. He'd love playing that protective hero role in someone's life just to feed his own ego. Plus, he's closer to her age than Sheriff McGrath."

"Exactly. Or he could be helping someone else."

"Sheriff McGrath?"

I shook my head. "He couldn't have been on the phone with him. You were in the office with the sheriff during that phone call. But there's another possibility for Katelyn's affair partner—someone else Sergeant Collins would be eager to help." I stuck another photo up on the board. "We know they met, and we know he has a pattern of infidelity."

Claire smirked when she saw Mayor Evans in my row of suspects. "As much as I want to slap a pair of handcuffs on him, I have a hard time seeing Katelyn pass up Tony for him. Tony is at least attractive. Mayor Evans is not."

"Agreed. And while I know you're not a fan of Leslie Evans, I have a feeling she's smart enough to make sure the money stays with her if they divorce. If Katelyn really was a gold digger, she'd be stupid to go for the mayor."

"Totally. But Sheriff McGrath doesn't have money, either," she pointed out.

"That's true," I admitted. "That would go against Katelyn's supposed MO."

"Unless she really was just looking for a man who would make her feel protected." Claire let out that deep sigh again. "Sheriff McGrath would be good at that. Better than Trey. But I still can't imagine Sheriff McGrath committing murder."

"Maybe he didn't," I said slowly, as a new thought began to form in my mind. I paced the room, thinking it through before I turned back to Claire. "What if Sheriff McGrath didn't kill her? What if his only mistake was having an affair?"

She looked at me blankly. "Then it would be a moral failing. It might cost him his career, but it isn't criminal."

"It *is* criminal," I corrected. "If they had an affair and he lied about that during a homicide investigation, that is *absolutely* criminal. Even if he didn't kill her, knowledge about why she came back here and who else she may have had contact with could be the key to solving her murder."

"True. Which makes me think either he killed her or he's telling the truth. Why hide an affair to save his job if doing so is a crime that he'd lose his job for anyway?"

"Maybe he believed he did such a good job of covering it up that we would never find out."

Annoyance flashed on Claire's face. "I can see him underestimating me, but you're DCI. You think he would be that confident about hiding it from you?"

"Maybe." But I had another theory.

One that made a hell of a lot more sense.

"What is it?" Claire asked, sensing my shift.

I couldn't believe I hadn't thought of it sooner. The woman was angry, cold, and paranoid. She had means and motive. And it would explain every move Sheriff McGrath had made.

I turned to Claire. "What if *Serena* killed Katelyn?"

Her mouth fell open as the implication hit. "Oh my God."

She put her hands up to her head and started pacing the floor, her mind working a million miles an hour as she put the pieces of the puzzle together the same way I had.

"It would explain everything," she finally said. "Sheriff McGrath and Katelyn have an affair. Serena finds out and confronts him. Loses it and kills her. Maybe Sheriff McGrath knows or suspects, or maybe he thinks Katelyn just got tired of him and moved on."

She stopped pacing and sank down onto the couch. "He's relaxed and casual when he gets to the crime scene because he doesn't know it's her. But then Wendy shows him the bracelet and he knows it's Katelyn —and that Serena killed her."

I nodded, picking up her trail. "So he calls in DCI and excuses himself from the case because he knows it's a conflict of interest to work it. His moral code won't allow him to cover it up completely."

"Then he puts me on the case. I'm inexperienced. A liability for you."

"A distraction," I said, groaning.

"*And* because he knows I've let things slide for other people. He hopes I'll protect Serena. *That's* why he hinted about that during that weird conversation. She made a mistake, but she's a good person, and he feels guilty because it's partly his fault. He hurt her." She filled up her cheeks with air. Blew it out slowly, the way she always did when she was nervous. "It all makes sense."

"He loves his wife," I said quietly. "So he can't tell us about the affair."

"Not because he's trying to save his job," Claire said, the realization dawning.

I nodded. "But because it would give away Serena's motive."

CHAPTER THIRTY-THREE

Claire

"So, what do we do?" My body felt like a snake coiled, ready to strike. I wanted to rush over and arrest Serena right now.

But Vance was the voice of reason. "We make our case." He held up fingers as he ticked off points. "One. We believe the body was dumped via snowmobile. That's the most logical explanation for how someone got into the park that time of year. Two. We know Serena owns a snowmobile. Three. We know what her motive was. But we have to be able to prove it."

My eyes lit up. "The video. From the bistro. It has proof that Serena knew Sheriff McGrath had cheated on her."

"Did she say Katelyn's name?"

My shoulders sank. "No, I don't think so."

"It might still be enough. We have a witness statement that they were seen cozying up at a coffee shop, plus video proof that Serena knew he recently had an affair and was upset by it. That, along with the snowmobile registration, might be enough for a warrant."

"An arrest warrant?"

He shook his head. "A search warrant. If she used the snowmobile to dump the body, there will probably be forensic evidence on it. Blood, hair, skin cells. That would make our case. Has your contact sent the video yet?" Vance's eyes were sharp, like a predator ready to pounce on his prey. But unlike me, he knew how to slowly stalk a victim. How to wait patiently for exactly the right moment.

I wanted desperately to know what it might feel like to have that slow intensity focused entirely on me.

"Well?"

I shook myself, realizing I'd gotten lost in a fantasy and hadn't responded to his question. "Um. Let me check." I pulled my phone out of my pocket and looked. "Yes! He did."

"Here." Vance took my phone from me, typing quickly before handing it back. "I just emailed it to myself. We can watch it on my laptop."

"Perfect. But I need coffee first."

I felt my eyes sparkle. Knowing that *Serena* was our bad guy had improved my mood immensely. I felt no loyalty to her, no sense of betrayal because of her actions. And it redeemed Sheriff McGrath somehow, too. Hiding the truth from us had been wrong, but he had done it to protect his family.

I could respect that.

"Help yourself," Vance said, shooting me a grin. "I'd ask you to pour me a cup, too, but..."

I blushed, remembering how I'd snapped at him the day we'd been paired together, thinking he was going to treat me like I was less than all the others because I was a woman.

I was so glad I'd been wrong.

I went to the kitchen and poured us each a cup of black, carrying both mugs in one hand so I could grab the bag of desserts, too. While Vance pulled up the video on his laptop, I settled in on the couch, taking a sip of the delicious dark blend before diving into my creme brûlée. The combination was as heavenly as I could hope for.

"Ben's a genius," I said around a mouthful of sweetness.

Vance cut his eyes toward me. "Genius, huh? Should I be worried that he's going to swipe my partner away from me?"

"Yes," I said, laughing. "I'd marry Ben in a heartbeat, just so he'd make me breakfast every day."

Vance attempted a casual smile, but the jealousy in his eyes was clear.

It gave me a thrill to see him as jealous over me as I was over him. I was tempted to tease him just to see a little more of it. But I smoothed it away instead.

"Unfortunately, I'm not his type," I said, winking. "You'd have better luck seducing him than I would."

Vance relaxed. "I guess it's a good thing I don't have much of a sweet tooth."

"Try this and see if you feel differently." I held out a spoonful of the delicious dessert for him to taste.

He locked eyes with me and wrapped his lips around the spoon as I held it, heating my blood and sending a delicious ache between my thighs when he licked off the last of the cream.

"Delicious," he murmured, those eyes still locked on mine. "But unless Ben's a blonde with the eyes of a mermaid, I'm not interested."

"The eyes of a mermaid?" My voice was almost breathless, like all the air had been sucked out of the room. Vance's intensity held me captured.

He nodded, his gaze darkening. "Those eyes of yours are dangerous. A swirling ocean. And you're tempting enough to make a man want to drown in it."

Serena, the case, the creme brûlée, all of it—forgotten. One more second of his smoldering gaze on me and I would have climbed into his lap again, savoring the taste of his lips more than the dessert in my hands.

I didn't know whether to be disappointed or grateful when his phone buzzed, pulling his attention away from me.

"Who is it?" I asked, trying to be casual even though my heart was still racing.

He frowned. "My father."

"Do you need to take it? I can give you some privacy."

He thought about it, then shook his head and flipped the phone over to where he couldn't see it. "No." He swallowed hard. "No distractions."

I knew he was talking about more than just his phone.

His face hardened as he started the video on his laptop and turned all his attention back to the case.

Hours later, I stretched my arms above me and yawned. "I'm starved," I announced.

Vance looked up from his computer. "Really?"

"Really." I pushed to standing and slipped my feet into the boots I'd discarded earlier, bending to tug the suede up my calves.

After watching the video, Vance had drafted a warrant request for the Sage County SO storage locker and the McGraths' home. We had debated long and hard about whether we were ready to tip our hand. Both of us would have preferred to find rock-solid proof of Serena's guilt before letting them know we were onto her. But the only hard evidence might be on that snowmobile. So he called Judge Barrington and pleaded our case, asking him to keep the request quiet so we could execute the warrant without giving them time to get rid of potential evidence.

Judge Barrington had been shocked and said he needed to process all of it before he made a decision.

All we could do was wait—and plug away at every potential lead we could think of. I'd called motels and cabin rentals, trying to find out where Katelyn had stayed when she got here. Vance had called snowmobile rental places and checked with the storage unit to see if they had footage from back in March. We'd combed through photographs on Katelyn's phone, looking for anything that might give us proof of her affair with Sheriff McGrath.

It had been a long day with very little to show for it. Some businesses had been cooperative, but others hadn't. Vance had submitted warrant requests for a couple of hotels and some cabin rentals in between the park, and he had sent them over to Judge Barrington to sign, too. The judge had signed those right away—those didn't threaten to blow up our entire town with controversy.

Everything we'd done was important work, but I was going to lose my mind if I didn't get a break. "Come on," I said, pouting. "Let's get some dinner."

"Sure," Vance said. "On one condition." He had a mischievous twinkle in his eyes that made my heart beat just a little bit faster.

"What's that?"

He closed his laptop and tossed the papers beside him onto the coffee table, then stood. "Your mom said I was invited to dinner anytime, even if it was just the family."

"Oh, no," I began, shaking my head.

"Oh, yes." He gave me a pleading look, but there was humor in his eyes. "Come on. We already did Whiskey Creek for lunch. Don't take away my chance for a home-cooked meal."

"Fine." I relented. "But I have a condition of my own."

"Anything," he said, giving me that charming smile.

"Eat fast." I winked. "And as soon as we're done eating, you tell them we have more work to do and we leave."

He laughed. "Deal."

We locked up, then slowly walked up the driveway toward the two-story eastern-white-pine cabin that made such a pretty picture against the background of the Bighorns. The ranch was winding down for the day. A handful of people milled around the front of the horse stables, likely just back from one of the daily trail rides Rhett and Cheyenne provided for guests. A mom snapped photographs of her kids petting the horses that had meandered over to the pasture gates. Travis and Jonathan were in the pasture, leading horses one by one to take their saddles off. Behind it all, the sun hung low in the sky, painting the mountains purple. It was one of my favorite times of the day—both because of the beauty of a Wyoming sunset and because it meant the day's work was nearly done. As a ranch-raised kid, you learned to appreciate that more than most.

Vance glanced my way. "You're happy here," he commented.

I took a deep breath and let it out, smiling before I answered. "Yeah. I am."

"But it's not enough. You want more."

I looked up at him in surprise. How could he know that when the people closest to me didn't seem to have a clue? "Yeah," I finally said. "I do."

He focused his eyes on the mountains ahead, sticking his hands inside the pockets of his black jeans as he walked lazily toward the house, like he wasn't in any hurry to get there. "It's hard. Being torn between two things you love."

"Sounds like you're speaking from experience."

Silence hung between us until he finally answered. "Yeah."

"What did you choose?" I held my breath, waiting for an answer—maybe because I was hoping his answer would tell me what mine should be.

He looked back at me with a strange expression on his face. "The job. I chose the job."

There were layers of emotion there. Pride. Regret.

I knew some of the choices he'd made. He'd chosen between Maine and New York, between his mom and dad. Now, he was choosing New York over staying in Wyoming and pursuing a relationship with his father.

But something in his eyes told me he was talking about more than that. Something even deeper. Something that had truly broken his heart.

I wanted to pry. But something stopped me. Maybe I was afraid to know. Afraid to hear the truth. Afraid that there was someone else he'd loved but left anyway.

Afraid he was talking about me.

Either way, the outcome was the same. He'd chosen the job. And that broke my heart, too.

CHAPTER THIRTY-FOUR

Claire

"Claire, I'm so glad you're here tonight. I've been dying to tell you something," Mom said. She dished some salad onto her plate, then passed the bowl to Travis. He shot me the kind of grin that said he was glad I was the one on the receiving end and not him.

"Oh yeah?" I reached for the mashed potatoes and plopped a giant scoop onto my plate, then passed them to Vance. His fingertips met mine as he took the bowl from me. My breath caught from that brief moment of contact.

I forced my attention back to Mom, hoping my face wasn't as red as it felt. If it was, she ignored it, too eager to tell me her news.

"Do you remember Rhett's best friend from high school?" She beamed.

"Um, yeah," I said, giving her a strange look, then cutting my eyes toward Cheyenne. "She's sitting right there. Hard to forget her."

Mom rolled her eyes. "No, not her. Rhett's *other* best friend, Cody."

My eyebrows shot to the ceiling. Best friends? That was news to me —and apparently to Rhett, too, based on the look on his face.

I poured a generous amount of gravy over my potatoes. "You mean that scrawny kid that used to follow Rhett around and always tried to dress just like him?"

"He wasn't scrawny," Mom scolded. Then she sighed. "Well, maybe he was. But he was a kid back then, and that's beside the point."

Vance coughed beside me, clearly trying to cover the laugh that had slipped out.

"What *is* the point, Mom?" I asked between gritted teeth.

"Well, Cody still has family here and I found out he's in town this week visiting. Rhett and Cheyenne said it was okay, so I invited him to the wedding. He said he'd love to come, and I thought it would be nice if you sat by him and made him feel welcome. You know, since the four of you used to run around so much."

"Mom," I groaned. "Seriously?"

"Rhett and Cheyenne will be busy, obviously, and someone needs to keep him company. Besides, you might enjoy reconnecting with him. He's a dentist now. Very successful, from what I hear, with his own practice in Billings. You two might have a lot to talk about."

"You're right. There's nothing I love more than talking about dental hygiene," I said, keeping my face straight. "Flossing, brushing. Types of toothpaste. It's riveting, really. Is there a drink limit at the open bar? Asking for a friend."

Mom shot me a look that made me feel like a heel.

But I just couldn't. "Why can't Beth hang out with him?" I protested.

Beth blushed and looked down, fiddling with the napkin in her lap. "I, um, sort of already have a date for the wedding."

My jaw dropped—along with everyone else's at the table.

"Well, that's wonderful," Mom said, smiling. "Who is it?"

"I–I'd rather not say. Not yet, anyway," Beth said, blushing furiously.

Unfortunately for Beth, that only made my brothers want to tease her—and made Mom more curious.

But for me, it created an opportunity.

"Eat faster," I whispered to Vance. "That way, we can get out of here."

HALF AN HOUR LATER, VANCE AND I SAT ON THE WOODEN fence overlooking my favorite pasture. Neither one of us had been ready to get back to work, but he had followed my lead and gotten me out of the house as quickly as possible. I'd snagged a bottle of whiskey and two glasses on the way out, and now, I poured him a shot as thanks for telling Mom I had to work.

My shot was to take my mind off the fact that Mom had set me up with a wedding date I had zero interest in.

"It's gorgeous out here," Vance remarked, oblivious to my inner turmoil.

Only a faint hint of light remained on the horizon. The first stars had already popped up over the mountains, but we could still make out the silhouettes of the horses who preferred the pasture over the barn at night.

"Prettier in the summer," I said, refilling our glasses.

He took a sip of the whiskey and made a low sound of appreciation. "Is that your favorite season?"

"Definitely. I'd love to be one of those people who spends their summers up here but heads to Florida for winter."

"Florida, huh?" There was a touch of humor in his voice.

"Sure." I shrugged. "Or any place warm, really. Somewhere with sunshine."

"Wyoming winters can be brutal," he agreed. "The wind, the snow. Temps so cold it hurts to breathe."

"Yeah. I hate the cold," I said, sighing unhappily. "But I also hate how everything here just kind of slows down. Roads close, the tourists stop coming. The nights feel way too long. Search and rescue slows down—for a couple of months, anyway. Then it picks up again when you're rescuing stranded snowmobilers or skiers, but you're doing it in the suckiest weather possible."

"So you like warm weather and a fast pace, huh?"

"Yeah." I looked over at him and held my glass up in toast. "To sunshine and fast living. Just eight months to go."

He clinked his glass to mine and grinned. "Speaking of toasts. When are Rhett and Cheyenne getting married?"

"Saturday."

His eyes widened. "*This* Saturday?"

"Yeah." A wave of nerves hit. "That won't be a problem, right? I mean with the investigation. I know it comes first, but…"

He waved me off. "Of course not. We'll make sure you're there."

"I also have the rehearsal Friday night. And Thursday night, we have SAR training. I have to be there—it's part of my official job duties."

"So you're saying I only have a few more days before I have to start sharing you." His voice was low, and his eyes suggested he didn't want to share me at all.

I didn't want that, either.

"Until after the wedding, anyway. I'm sorry. I know the timing is terrible with an investigation like this. I'm surprised Sheriff McGrath didn't consider that before choosing me to work with you. I'd already put in to have those days off of work."

"It's fine. I'll let you know if anything breaks on the case. Though I'd hate to distract you from entertaining Cody." He winked. "How did you describe him again?" He tipped his glass up and emptied it.

I groaned and joined him in downing my whiskey. "I can't believe my mom. She's never going to give up."

A smile tugged at Vance's lips. "You know what you need to do?"

"What?"

"I had this buddy in college. When his parents were harassing him about settling down, I told him he should make them think twice about it. One of my friends was a theater major who loved drama. I paid her to pose as his fiancée. Only we purposefully made her act like the worst fiancée ever—to his family at least."

I grinned. "How so?"

Vance laughed, low and deep. Warmth spread through me at the sound of it.

"Well, his parents were highly conservative, so she showed up with blue hair, ready to argue politics. She hinted that she was an ex-stripper with four kids by three different dads. She gave backhanded compliments to everyone in the family and called their house 'ironic.' Covered her ears and hummed loudly every time the family prayed over dinner. Stuff like that. Funny thing is that she's the opposite of all that in real life, but she had a blast playing the part."

My jaw dropped. Then a grin spread across my face. "Why, Vance Weston. You're not as straight-laced and uptight as I thought you were."

He let out an even louder laugh that echoed across the pasture. "No, I think you may have misjudged me."

"What did the family do?"

"Well, he and the girl kept up the charade for a few weeks. When he finally broke things off with her, the family was so relieved they never hassled him again. I guess his mom decided there were worse things than being single."

I mulled it over. "Hmm. Maybe I *should* do something like that."

"Do you have any friends who get a kick out of being deliberately annoying?"

I shook my head. "No. And I don't think that part of it would work anyway. Trust me, I've brought home some terrible boyfriends. That won't get Mom off my back. If anything, she'll just start trying harder to set me up with someone else. But if she thought I was with someone awesome, someone she'd totally approve of..."

"There you go," Vance said, shrugging. "Get her off your back by thinking the problem is already solved."

"Exactly." Although, for the life of me, I couldn't think of anyone awesome to invite—except Vance. And while everything in me wanted him next to me that day, I knew there was no way I would be able to pretend it didn't mean anything.

With him, I couldn't pretend at all.

He cleared his throat. "You know, I could go as your wedding date. Keep you from having to hang out with Cody, at least."

I swallowed hard. "I don't think that's a good idea."

"Why?" He kept his eyes focused on the dark scene in front of us.

"Because I want more than just a date with you," I said softly.

He turned toward me and stared into my eyes. Then his hands were in my hair, pulling me to him. His lips crashed onto mine in a kiss that was as demanding as it was arousing. The taste of him mixed with the whiskey we'd shared was intoxicating, and all I could think was *more,* until I found myself whispering it against his mouth.

"Define more," he said roughly, his lips still tantalizing close as he repeated the question I'd asked him what somehow felt like a lifetime ago.

I closed my eyes and put my hands on his chest, pushing away, trying to get a moment of distance from him so I could put together a coherent sentence. Then I put my hands beside me on the fence, gripping the rail like my life depended on it.

Nothing else could make me lose my head the way Vance Weston could. Not wine, not whiskey, not another man. Nothing compared to the pure intoxication of his hands on my body while he teased me with his tongue.

If just kissing was this good, I couldn't even imagine what it would be like if we went further.

His hand came to my chin, gently turning my face toward his. "I asked you a question," he said, his piercing eyes holding my gaze.

"I don't have an answer. My version of more doesn't work for you."

"Because of New York?"

I nodded.

He released my chin, putting his hand over mine on the fence rail. "It's great there. You might like it. You could visit, give it a try. You never know, you might fall in love with the energy of the city. There's lots of fast-paced work you could do there."

I forced a smirk. "The winters are still cold, but without the beauty of Wyoming to make up for it. And me, living in a place with millions of people and no wilderness?" I pulled my hand away. "I don't see that working."

"Yeah, I guess I don't, either," he said slowly.

He started to say something else, but my phone buzzed. I pulled it out and read the text with a sinking heart.

"What is it?" He nudged me, a concerned look on his face.

"I–I have to go." My brain felt fuzzy from the whiskey—from *him* —but I jumped off the fence, knowing I had to pull myself together. Quickly.

I fired off a couple of quick texts and began to formulate a plan in my head. *Coffee.* I needed coffee.

He stared at me. "What do you mean?" When I didn't answer him, he jumped off the fence and grabbed my arm. "Claire, what is it?"

I looked up at him and took a deep breath. "There's a missing girl. I have to respond."

"Okay." He grabbed the whiskey and the glasses. "Let's get back to the house so you can go."

"Vance." My heart thudded, knowing the potential ramifications of what I was about to tell him.

"What?" He turned and gave me his attention.

"Her car is parked at Lost Creek Trailhead."

"Okay..."

I took a deep breath. "That's the trail I told you about when we were talking about ways someone could have gotten into the park last March. It's the one I would have taken if I were going to dump Katelyn's body."

CHAPTER THIRTY-FIVE

Vance

What were the odds of a woman going missing from a trailhead that we suspected had been used to dump our victim's body? I'd been convinced Serena McGrath was our killer, but a second victim would change everything.

We'd been looking for people who had a connection to Katelyn. But maybe we'd been wrong from the beginning.

Even though my legs were longer than hers, I had to quicken my pace to keep up with Claire as she marched toward the barn. Her feet seemed to know the path by heart, because her head stayed buried in her phone as she fired off messages in rapid succession.

Rhett and Cheyenne were already waiting in the barn when we got there.

"What's the scoop?" Cheyenne asked, arms crossed. The look on her face said she was ready for battle.

"Missing hiker last seen at trailhead around seven this morning,"

Claire answered. "Was expected back early this afternoon and didn't take supplies for an overnight. Female, age twenty."

Only one year older than Katelyn.

"Hiking alone?" The disapproval was clear on Rhett's face.

"Not sure yet. I've got the number of the guy who made the report. I'll give him a call and get more info on the way. I've alerted Hank. He's heading there to set up base camp."

"Rendezvous point?"

Claire flinched. "Lost Creek Trailhead."

The realization hit Rhett and Cheyenne at the same moment. They knew the area as well as Claire did—even without knowing our theory, they knew how close that trail ran to our crime scene.

"Shit," Rhett muttered as Cheyenne looked up at him with dismay on her face. But she quickly wiped it away, and turned back to Claire.

"Horses?"

Claire nodded. "We'll need horse teams to cover ground quickly, especially since she wasn't prepared to spend the night out there."

"Got it." Cheyenne nodded. "We'll load up Shadow for you, then head to our place to grab Wildfire and Diablo and meet you there."

Rhett was already moving toward the tack.

"What about me?" I asked.

Claire turned, like she'd forgotten I was there. "What about you?"

"I'm going with you."

Her head jerked back. "Like hell you are."

I shook my head. "We've got a missing woman who disappeared near the same place our victim's body was found. This isn't your call. I'm coming."

Claire's face turned red. "Can you even ride a horse?"

"Of course I can ride a horse." I rolled my eyes.

"I mean *actual experience*. Not just attending the Kentucky Derby or whatever your mom does for entertainment." She scowled, but her lips twitched like she wanted to smile.

I grinned. "Yes. Actual experience. I may not be a cowboy, but I know what I'm doing in the saddle."

She eyed me up and down, then shook her head. "Until I've seen you ride, I can't approve you to ride with the horse team. If you're not a skilled rider, you could get us all in trouble. But"—she held a hand up, seeing that I was about to protest—"it's fine. You can come."

She turned back to Cheyenne. "Skip Shadow. Just get your horses. You'll be lead on the horse team anyway. I'll be a ground pounder today."

Cheyenne smiled. "Got it, boss." Then she turned and jogged toward where Rhett had disappeared.

Claire turned toward me. "I need to change, and I've got to get my badge and my gear. Go back to your cabin and change into hiking gear if you have it. Grab your coat, gloves, hat—whatever you have. It's going to be cold tonight. Meet me back here in fifteen."

"Got it, boss," I said, echoing Cheyenne's words. I winked at Claire and thought I saw a little hint of pink flood her cheeks before she turned and marched toward the house.

CLAIRE'S TRUCK RATTLED AS SHE FLEW DOWN THE HIGHWAY, one hand on the wheel and the other on her phone.

"Take notes for me," she said, pointing toward the glove compartment before putting the phone up to her ear.

I opened the compartment and found a notebook and a pen tucked inside. I pulled them out and waited.

"This is Deputy Claire Hawkins with the Sage County Sheriff's Office," she said to whoever had answered her call. "I'm following up on a missing person report. Who am I talking to?"

She switched the phone's audio to speaker and put it in the console with a silent warning to me to be quiet.

A male voice came on the line. He sounded nervous. "Mitch. Mitch Donaldson."

"Hi, Mitch. You can call me Claire. Are you the one who made the report?"

"Yes."

"Okay. Why don't you go ahead and tell me what happened?"

"My friend Robin Frey went hiking this morning. She left at seven and said she would be back after lunch. But she never showed up and she's not answering her phone."

"Okay. Dispatch said her last known point was Lost Creek Trail-head. Is that correct?"

"Yes." But there was hesitation in his voice.

Claire heard it too. She shot me a look.

"What are you not telling me?"

He didn't answer right away. "Look, I don't want to get her in trouble."

"Being lost in the wilderness means she's already in trouble," Claire said. Her voice was firm but soothing. "I'm only here to make sure she's safe, okay? That's what I do. So tell me the whole story."

His words came out in a rush. "Robin has a true crime podcast. She wanted to get some footage of the place where Katelyn was found. But the campground was closed. She looked on the map and saw that the trailhead runs right through there. She thought she could cut over, take a look at the crime scene, and get back without anyone knowing. Worse case, she would get told to leave, but she could say she was just a hiker who wandered off the trail."

Claire's lips flattened. I could see her visibly fighting back the responses she *wanted* to make, instead responding calmly.

"Okay. Have you heard from her at all since she began her hike?"

"No."

"Where was she supposed to meet you after?"

"Back at the motel. I've been here all day—she's never come back."

"I was told her vehicle is still parked at the trailhead. I'll need to confirm that. What kind of vehicle was she driving?"

"A white Honda Civic. Wyoming tags."

Claire gestured for me to write it down, but I already had. She gave me a brief smile.

"Does your friend Robin have any hiking experience?"

"Some," he said doubtfully. "Like, day hikes and stuff. But not back-packing or anything like that."

"Does she have any medical conditions that you know about?"

"She has asthma," he said eagerly, like he was glad to finally be helpful.

I noted it down.

"Do you know if she has her inhaler?"

"Of course. She never goes anywhere without it."

Claire nodded, relieved. "Tell us what she looks like and what she was wearing, the best that you can remember."

"She's beautiful," he said, emotion washing through his voice. "Um. She's shorter than me, like five four maybe? Long blonde hair. She had it in a ponytail today, with a red baseball cap. Regular workout kind of clothes. Sneakers, white sweatshirt, and a blue jacket."

"That's good," Claire said, encouraging him. "What all did she have with her? Do you know? Food, water, first aid kit..."

"She had a backpack, but it was mostly her podcast stuff. Cell phone for filming, extra mic, some makeup, notebook, you know. She did take water and a Snickers bar. But I don't know what else."

"Do you have any of her other clothes? Unwashed. Just in case we need to get a scent."

"A scent?" His voice became fearful.

"We probably won't even need it," Claire soothed. "Our local team is going to handle the search on the front end. But if we get stuck, we'll call in a canine unit from the next county over. And if they come in, they'll want a scent pack. That's all."

"Uh, yeah... I mean, her suitcase is here."

"Great. Don't touch anything in it, okay? Leave it uncontaminated in case they need it. And keep your phone on. I'll call you if I have any more questions. If you hear from her, call me right away. This is my personal number. If I don't answer, it's because I don't have reception. In that case, call dispatch again and they'll get the message to me. Okay?"

"Okay."

"Don't worry. We're going to do everything we can to find Robin and bring her back safely."

"Thank you." As another wave of emotion crashed through his voice, he hung up the phone.

Claire grabbed the thermos of coffee that sat in her cupholder and chugged it down like her life depended on it. "Drink up," she said, nodding toward the one she'd brought for me. "My gut may not be as good as Cheyenne's, but I have a feeling we're in for a long night. Robin Frey. That name ring any bells?"

I shook my head. "No. I Googled her while he was talking. Looks like she's new to the game, doesn't really have many followers. Her podcast only has a few episodes, and they're all about Katelyn. But get this: she's a student at UW."

"*That's* interesting," Claire mused. "She may have known Katelyn."

"That's what I'm thinking."

Then she let out a long sigh. "I hate that she's blonde."

"I know." I'd had that same thought.

"This could totally change our case. And if Serena's not guilty? Sheriff McGrath is going to kill us for putting in that search warrant."

I didn't have to answer for her to know we were on the same page. The look we exchanged said it all. I grabbed the second thermos of coffee and started chugging it the way she had.

I'd never been on a SAR call. But I had a feeling Claire was right. It was going to be a long night.

Chapter Thirty-Six

Vance

Claire threw her truck into park at the trailhead and hopped out, taking long strides toward a middle-aged man who was setting up a table underneath a pop-up tent.

"Hank," she said, reaching out to shake his hand. "You made good time."

He shook his head, grimacing. "Helps that I live so close, but I don't know how to feel about someone going missing right in my own backyard. This is a well-marked trail. Makes me worried she got hurt."

"I know," Claire agreed. She angled her body, inviting me into the circle. "This is Special Agent Vance Weston. He's working with me on a case right now. Vance, this is Hank. Hank runs our base command. He's practically a legend in SAR circles."

Hank's weathered face broke into a sheepish smile. "Not a legend. Just someone who likes to push himself. My knees don't cooperate with search ops anymore though, so I help out here." He grabbed my hand, giving it a hard shake. "Honored to have you here, Agent Weston."

I liked the guy immediately. "Call me Vance. Nice to meet you. I hope I can be of some help tonight."

Claire tossed me her keys. "You can start by grabbing my gear from the truck while I help Hank set up. There's an orange hiking backpack, plus a smaller black pack. Grab both. They're in the back of the truck"

"Got it."

While I retrieved Claire's things, several other vehicles arrived, including Rhett and Cheyenne, who were towing their horse trailer behind Cheyenne's truck. Before long, the trailhead parking lot turned into a full-blown staging area for the search, with map boards and flood-lights and a flurry of activity as people checked radios and prepped their packs.

Eventually, Claire's voice called out above the commotion. Everyone instantly grew quiet and looked at her.

She gave them a brief rundown of who we were looking for and the circumstances surrounding the search before giving assignments.

"So, we know where she was headed, but we don't know if she made it. That gives us a starting point, but there's a lot of terrain to cover. I want to run a modified Type II grid. We don't have enough light for a full sweep, but we'll work high-probability zones and hope we get lucky. Sound good?"

There were nods around the group.

"Team One, I want you to conduct a hasty search at the campground where she was heading, in case she made it through. There's a park ranger at the entrance who has been briefed and will let you in. Start with the primitive campsites, since that's the location she was aiming for. He'll be able to escort you down to her target destination."

Three people nodded. "Got it," one of the guys said. "We'll radio if we see anything." They broke away and headed to one of the vehicles.

Claire turned to Rhett and Cheyenne. "Team Two, I want you to cover the loop trail on horseback. I know her friend indicated that she was going to take a shortcut, but the terrain's a hell of a lot easier on the trail. Sticking to it would have added some mileage to her hike, but it would have eventually taken her right into the campground and she could have doubled back to her target on the road instead of blazing her own way. That's a lot of miles on foot though—too many for most hikers to cover in a single day. Let's hope that's why she hasn't made it back yet. She might still be walking. See if she's still out there and if you can bring her home."

Rhett and Cheyenne nodded. "On it," Cheyenne said before they turned and walked toward their horse trailer.

Claire turned to me and the three other people who remained waiting for orders. "The rest of us are going to investigate possible shortcut routes. We know where she was headed, but we don't know where she may have left the trail to try to cut over. Team Three, you take the lower forest." She gestured to an area she had marked on the map. "It's dense through there, way too easy to get lost, but since she isn't familiar with the area, she might have thought that was the easiest short route to the campsite."

One of the guys gave her a high five and a grin. "Dense forest. My favorite. Maybe I'll have a chance to use my new machete."

She laughed. "Glad you're excited about it, King. But watch that ankle. You're still recovering. Don't push too hard."

"I will. Aren't you heading out with us?" He gave her a curious look.

"Of course I am. But I'm with Agent Weston today. We'll be Team Four." She nodded my way.

The guy flicked his eyes to me, surprise registering. "Oh. You're going out on the search? That's cool."

"I am." I felt an odd jealousy at the easy chemistry between the two of them. I was out of my element as Claire's partner in this situation, and I liked it about as much as I liked the idea of her going to Cheyenne's wedding with another man.

"We'll be heading toward the campground perimeter through the ravine. It's the most direct route from the trail to where she was going," Claire said, grabbing her hefty backpack and swinging it onto her back. She gave her radio one last check, then grabbed the black backpack and shoved it into my arms.

King whistled. "Most direct, but also most dangerous."

"Exactly," Claire said.

King threw his arm around her shoulder and gave her a quick kiss on the head. "Be careful out there."

"You too."

Oh, yes. That was definite jealousy I felt—even if I didn't have the right to.

The guys headed out.

Claire turned to Hank. "We may be out of comms in some low spots."

"Yeah, I expect you will be," he said, giving her a stern look. "You know, you don't always have to take the worst assignment. You could have given yourself an easier one—especially since you've got a civilian with you."

Civilian? I winced.

Claire grinned. "Where's the fun in that?"

Hank laughed, shaking his head.

When Claire turned to me, all the humor was gone from her face. "If you see anything—a broken twig, a candy bar wrapper, a sock, *anything*—don't touch it. Call it out and let me handle it."

"I *am* a detective, you know," I said drily.

"Yes. But you're not a SAR operator. Out here, I'm in charge. Got it?"

"Fair enough," I conceded. It was fascinating to see Claire like this. In this world, she was the expert, and she took charge in a way I'd never seen her do. She was bossy, fierce, and confident.

I loved it.

She put her hands on her hips. "Stay ten feet behind me."

"Why?"

"Because that's close enough to talk without having to shout, but far enough that we can see clues between us."

"Alright." I held up the black backpack. "What do you want me to do with this?"

Her eyebrow shot up. "*Carry* it. It has some extra supplies in there. There's bottled water—you need to stay hydrated. Also has some snacks and emergency supplies." She grabbed an extra radio off the table. "Clip this to your belt. There's bear spray in the bag. You might want to clip that to your belt too. And there's an extra flashlight and red flagging tape in the side pocket. We flag anything we see. You ready?"

I took a deep breath. "I'm ready."

"Then let's go."

She turned on her heel and headed toward the trail. Hank came over and clapped my shoulder. "Good luck."

I eyed him. "Think I'll need it?"

He threw his head back and laughed. "With that one? Hell yes I do."

Darkness settled as I followed Claire down the trail. At first, we followed behind the others. But before long, Rhett and Cheyenne were out of sight, moving much faster than us on their horses. Then the three guys turned off the trail into the forested area, leaving just me and Claire. The teams kept in touch on the radios, letting everyone else know their positions. Soon, everyone was in place, working their assigned areas—except for us.

After another half hour, Claire stopped, waiting for me to catch up.

"This is where we leave the trail behind," she said quietly, shooting her flashlight beam into the dirt beside the path to show me what she'd spotted.

"Are those boot prints?" I asked, squatting to take a closer look.

"Yep. This is close to where I planned on cutting over, and that looks fresh. So we're going to follow it."

"You called it," I murmured, judging the size of the print. It was small, about the size of Claire's boot. "She tried to take the shortest route."

"Maybe," Claire interjected. "We don't know that those prints are hers. Could have been another hiker who stepped off the trail to pee."

"Could be. But you don't think so." I shot her a look.

She nodded, sighing. "Yeah, unfortunately, I'm afraid it's hers. All too often, people take the shortest route possible without knowing what they're getting into."

"Is this path really more dangerous than the rest?" I stood, studying Claire's eyes the best I could in the dark.

Claire shrugged. "Depends on how you look at it, I guess. There are a hell of a lot of ways for a person to get in trouble out in the wilderness. But the ravine's tricky. Lots of loose rocks, uneven terrain, and steep drop-offs. Plus, there's the rattlesnakes. They like the way the rocks heat up in the sunlight."

"Shit. That doesn't sound fun." I was starting to feel *very* out of my element.

Claire didn't seem fazed. "Flag the spot. I'll radio it in."

I pulled the flagging tape from the pocket of the bag and wrapped a piece of it around a branch beside the prints while Claire made the call. Then she gave me a quick nod of approval and headed off the trail into the darkness.

Chapter Thirty-Seven

Claire

Our progress was slow moving through this part of the woods. The vegetation was a lot thinner than the lower forest where I'd sent King and the others, which made it look like the easier path. But the closer we got to the ravine, the worse the ground became for walking. It was the kind of rocky ground where you could twist an ankle no matter how careful you were.

Not to mention everything else that could go wrong out here off the beaten path.

I didn't have Cheyenne's intuition, but the farther we went, the more certain I was that we were following Robin's footsteps. The signs were few and far between, but there were enough disturbances to tell me someone had come through here recently. And who would have done that other than Robin?

Unless she wasn't the only amateur investigator with the bright idea of trespassing into the campground.

The thought made me groan, but it also gave me hope. Hope that, unlike we had initially feared, this wasn't a second victim. And hope that, if multiple people had been pulling this kind of thing, maybe the trail disturbances were from someone else. For Robin's sake, it would be much better for her to be slowly trekking her way home on the long loop trail, exhausted and hungry—but safe.

If she was in the ravine, this could end very badly.

We never give up hope. The words came to me in Cheyenne's voice, the way they always did on a search. It was practically her tagline. Even now, I missed being on horseback with her and Rhett, trading jokes back and forth as we worked the search.

Everything was changing, and things would never be the same again. I was tempted to take comfort in the fact that Vance was with me, that my new partner had my back here the same way he had it everywhere else.

But this partnership was temporary, too.

It would end the day he left for New York.

It was nearly midnight when we made it to the edge of the ravine. Rhett and Cheyenne had radioed in, telling us they had come up empty on the loop trail. Same news from the team that had done the hasty search at the campground.

I scanned my flashlight into the darkness, calling for Robin. My voice echoed. But there was no answer.

Vance came up beside me. "What are you thinking?"

The words squeezed at my heart. They were the ones I usually asked Cheyenne at this point.

I turned to Vance, struck with a whole new appreciation for him. Exhaustion was written all over his face, but he was calm and steady. He hadn't complained once, even though I'd pushed him hard.

It made me like him even more.

I pulled off my heavy pack, dropping it to the ground. "Well, I have some bad news for you."

"What's that?" He brushed his hair off his forehead and dropped his bag onto the ground beside mine.

I gulped down some water. "It's late. We're exhausted, visibility sucks, and the risk of injury is too high for us to move forward. But it would waste too much time to turn back."

"So we camp here," he stated. There was no irritation on his face. Just acceptance.

"Yeah. I'm sorry."

"Why should you be sorry?"

"Because we'll be roughing it," I said, wincing. "Like ... really roughing it."

"You didn't force me to come. I insisted. Remember?" He brushed his thumb across my cheek.

It killed me how he could make my heart flip upside down with a single touch.

"True," I said, giving him a little smile. "You're stubborn like that."

"We both are." He held my gaze for a long moment, then let his hand drop, sticking it into his pocket with a sigh. "So, what's the plan?"

I took a deep breath. "We'll grab a few hours of sleep and start searching the ravine at first light. I'll let everyone know we're staying put."

I turned away from him and radioed in. Cheyenne was the first to respond, saying that she and Rhett were going to crash at base camp and would resume searching at daybreak. King said they were going to push forward for an hour more, then bed down in the forest if they hadn't found her yet. They were following a potential trail and hopeful it was hers.

Vance built a small fire at a spot about fifty yards away while I did my check-ins. When I wrapped up, I grabbed my pack, walked over, and warmed my hands on it.

"Nice," I said, smiling in appreciation.

"It's not much. But maybe it will help keep you warm. I know you hate the cold." He stuck his hands into his pockets and rocked back on his heels, giving me a tentative look like he wasn't sure I would approve.

But the gesture blew me away. He'd built a fire for *me*. The whole SAR team was supposed to take care of each other, but normally, I was the one taking care of these things. It came naturally to me and I didn't mind it at all. But Vance's fire felt like a gift. One that meant the world to me.

"Thanks," I said, my voice raw. "It's great."

He gestured at the area around us. "I wasn't sure where you would want to sleep, but this is the flattest spot I could find. I moved a few rocks out of the way." He pointed at the tree line. "There are some pine branches down over there that I could drag over for makeshift pillows or something."

I hid my smile. "I know I said we were going to be roughing it, but we don't have to rough it quite *that* much."

"Oh really?" He turned to me in surprise, putting his hands on his hips. "You holding out on me, Hawkins?"

I laughed and unzipped my pack. Now, *I* was the one feeling nervous. It only made sense for us to share my gear—it would be safer and more comfortable for both of us. But it was also highly intimate.

"I'll share," I said, keeping my voice light. "But when you see the size of this thing, you may prefer the branches." I pulled my ultralight pop-up tent out of my bag.

"What the hell is that?" He eyed the small pouch.

"Magic." I pulled it open, laid it on the ground, and popped up the support pole. Instant tent. It wasn't much more than a place to sleep. Too low to stand up in, barely even high enough to sit in without hitting your head on the top. But it was waterproof and helped keep the heat in on a cold night. I never went on a search without it.

His jaw dropped. "Damn. That *is* magic."

"It's tiny," I warned. "But if we leave our gear out here, we can both fit. I also have an ultralight sleeping bag, a sleeping pad, and a blow-up pillow. It's not great, but..."

"It's a hell of a lot better than rocks and pine branches. I'm sold. I'm surprised you carry all that with you though."

I shrugged. "On long searches, it's easier to camp on the trail than to hike back to base camp. And the extra weight is worth it to me because it gives me a dry place to sleep without a lot of effort. It also puts a barrier up between me and the rattlesnakes."

"Don't want one trying to slip into your sleeping bag at night?" He grinned.

I returned the grin. "Exactly. I'll gladly carry a few extra pounds, even if it's giving me a false sense of protection."

"So we've finally found out what Claire Hawkins is afraid of," he teased, dropping to a seat beside the fire.

"Who said I was afraid of anything?" I pulled the pad, pillow, and sleeping bag out, put them in the tent, and zipped it up tightly so that nothing could crawl in before I did. Then I sat down beside Vance and passed him a granola bar from my pack.

"Thanks." He unwrapped it and ate half of it in one bite. "I can't believe I'm already hungry after the dinner your mom made."

"Hiking burns a ton of calories," I said before biting into a bar of my own. "How are you on water?"

He lifted the liter bottle from my extra pack and showed me what remained. "Low. I drank more than I expected, too."

"I'm glad you drank it. It's important to stay hydrated. There's a stream that runs close to here. We'll refill in the morning before we head down the ravine. And there's a creek at the bottom where we can fill up again."

He raised his eyebrows. "Do you have a way of purifying the water?

"Of course." I grinned.

"Of course," he echoed. "I should know by now not to doubt you." His sparkling eyes looked at me with undeniable affection, and I felt my breath catch. The smile faded from his face and those eyes turned serious. He stared at me, then shook his head. "You're amazing. You know that?"

"Me?" I felt my cheeks flush.

"Yes, you. What you do out here? It's incredible. Your knowledge, your dedication, your skill—I'm blown away. I've never met anyone like you."

I felt caught in his eyes, lost in this moment where it was just us. For a moment, everything else disappeared—the search, the investigation, the betrayal. Even the grief over feeling like I was losing my best friend. It all faded away, and all that was left was me and Vance, sitting underneath a starry sky beside a fire he had built to keep me warm.

"I've never met anyone like you, either," I whispered.

He held my gaze for a long moment before speaking. "I could stay. You make me want to."

"At DCI?" Hope flickered in my heart.

"DCI or working for my father. He offered me a job, too." Vance took his hat off and pushed his hair back.

"Are you serious? That's amazing," I said, unable to stop my smile—until I realized Vance didn't look happy.

He nodded. "Yeah. I'd made up my mind to say no. That day at the gas station."

I flashed back to the moment he'd stared at me intently, asking if he should give up on a relationship with his dad—and how I'd known I shouldn't give advice on something that big, but I'd done it anyway. The weight of it crashed down, feeling like the worst sort of punishment for my impulsive tongue.

"You had two job offers," I said, closing my eyes as the puzzle pieces fell into place. "The FBI or your dad."

"Yeah. My dad's offer was an insult. Grunt work at the bottom of his company, a chance to prove myself—again. I don't think I realized until that conversation with you that I shouldn't have to."

"You shouldn't," I said, hope dying like the flames in front of us.

"But if I took it now, I wouldn't be staying for him. I'd be staying for you." The look in his eyes was so earnest.

"You can't." I had to say it even though it broke my own heart. "You're meant for more, Vance. More than DCI and definitely more than grunt work for your father. You'd be miserable—you're miserable right now even thinking about it. You'd end up hating me if you passed up the FBI for my sake."

His jaw clenched. "I'd never hate you for a choice I made."

"You would." I could barely force the words out over the lump in my throat. "You know you would. Maybe not at first. But you'd end up resenting me for it. And if things went sideways between us, you'd never forgive yourself for passing up the job of a lifetime for a temporary romance."

His face hardened. He opened his mouth like he was going to say something but stopped. He shook his head and looked away.

I turned my eyes to the dying coals in front of us. They felt like an hourglass, counting down the little bit of time we had left. All I wanted was to get some of it back, but I couldn't.

Just like everything else.

We sat in silence until the last coal darkened and the fire went cold.

"We should get some sleep," I said, my words sounding strange as they pierced the silence. "Sunrise will be here before you know it, and we need our strength."

"Yeah." He kept his eyes on the ground. "Are you sure you're okay sharing your tent?"

For half a second, I thought about asking him not to. The thought of being so close to him all night felt almost painful—the kind of pain my heart felt when I watched the wild mustangs running free and knew no matter how fast I ran I could never keep up.

The kind of pain that came from wanting something desperately and knowing you could never have it.

But I couldn't ask him to sleep out here. This was the wilderness, and the night was already freezing.

"Don't be silly," I said, forcing myself to act casual. "We don't need you to be our next rescue. It's cold out and it's practical to share."

"Yeah," he said, nodding. "Practical. No big deal, right?" There was a trace of bitterness in his voice.

"Right."

"After you."

He finally looked up. My heart skipped a beat when our gazes caught. His eyes held the same depths I felt swirling in my own heart. But the look of steel on his face told me he was doing the same thing I was and putting it all aside.

We had no other choice, really.

I crawled into the tiny space and slipped my shoes off, tucking them into place beside the tent flap. Then I unzipped the sleeping bag all the way so that we could both cover ourselves with it and rolled to my side on the sleeping pad to make as much room for him as possible

My heart throbbed against my chest as Vance climbed in after me, putting his boots beside mine.

"Tight in here," he commented, his voice strained.

"Yeah, but the great thing about a search is that you're so tired from hiking that you pass out quickly and don't mind the lack of comfort," I said, trying to keep things light.

"Exactly," he agreed.

He was careful not to touch me as he crawled forward and lay beside me, but even so, he filled the space in a way that made it hard to breathe. I could feel the length of his body stretched out a mere inch from mine, the heat from his chest radiating into my back. I closed my eyes, breathing in the faintest trace of cologne that still lingered on him, mixed with the woodsmoke in our hair and the pine needles that clung to our clothes.

It was like heaven. A painful, heartbreaking heaven.

I didn't want to close my eyes and miss a moment of it.

CHAPTER THIRTY-EIGHT

Claire

DESPITE MY INTENTIONS, EXHAUSTION TOOK OVER. I FELL asleep quickly and slept hard. When I woke, Vance's body was curled around mine, his chest pressed up to my back and his arm slung around my waist.

It shouldn't have been sexy. We were crammed into a one-person tent, still wearing our thick winter coats and dirty clothes from the night before. I'd seen myself after a search enough times to know there would be nothing cute about the way I looked this morning, with tangled curls and dirt smudged on my face and wrinkled clothes underneath my coat.

I also knew we were only snuggled up together because it was cold—cold enough to see my breath, even inside our little cocoon.

Even so, I let out a contented little sigh. Because, to me, this *was* sexy. Damn sexy. There was nothing I liked more than the Wyoming wilderness. Nothing that felt better than the kind of sore you got after a long hike. Adding Vance into that mix, with his arms around me and his warm breath on my neck as he snored lightly? In another world, one where we had met for different reasons and had gone camping as a couple... Man. This was the stuff of fantasies.

He was much taller than me, but his body fit perfectly around mine, curled up like this. I wanted to linger in this moment as long as I could, no matter how bad of an idea it was to get even more attached to him. But Robin was still out there—without the benefit of a tent and a man's body to warm her. I checked my watch. The sky was already getting light and the sun would be up soon. We had to get moving.

I gently pushed his arm, trying not to wake him so I could wiggle away while he slept. But he grabbed me and pulled me even closer, nuzzling his face into my neck with a little moan. His hard body pressed against mine, tempting me even more.

I groaned. He was killing me.

His body tensed. "Claire?" He sounded disoriented.

"That's me." I bit my lip.

His fingers tightened on my arm. Then he rolled away, letting me go. "I'm so sorry. I didn't realize I'd—"

"It's fine," I said, sitting up quickly. My hair pressed into the top of the tent as I rubbed the sleep out of my eyes. I grabbed my boots and shoved my feet into them, forcing myself to focus on our mission. "I'm going to refill our water bottles. We'll get a quick bite to eat, check in with the other teams, pack up, then hit the trail again. Can you be ready to go in fifteen?"

"Yes." That edge of steel was back in his voice.

I unzipped the tent and crawled out of our cocoon, missing it the minute I walked away.

As promised, we prepped quickly, barely talking while we got ready to head out. But despite the difficult conversation we'd had the night before, the silence wasn't awkward. We settled into an easy camaraderie, working together as well as teams that had been together for years.

The only thing different were the soft looks of affection and longing between us.

We didn't address it. There was no point in wishing for something we knew we couldn't have. But as we shared a quick cup of instant coffee and protein bars, the sadness and regret I'd seen in his eyes the night before remained.

And I didn't need a mirror to know that the same feelings were reflected in mine.

After our quick meal, we broke camp.

"You ready?" I asked, swinging my backpack onto my back.

"Yeah." He grabbed the second bag, then hesitated. "Do you want to switch? I feel dumb carrying the lighter load."

I laughed. "Not a chance. No one carries my pack for me."

His eyes grew serious. "You've got a partner now. You don't have to carry it alone."

"For now. I have a partner for now." I was reminding myself as much as him.

His face fell.

My radio crackled, offering welcome distraction for both of us. The other teams were up and on the move, and by the sounds of it, everyone was cheerful and ready to get to work. A few hours of sleep and the promise of daylight brought the familiar surge of optimism that we'd find our target soon.

Vance and I began our careful descent down the ravine, moving slowly even though daylight gave us an advantage we hadn't had the night before. Loose rocks rattled and slipped underneath our feet, threatening to send us tumbling with one wrong step. We stayed closer to each other than we had in the forest, frequently helping each other out with a steady hand while the other crossed tricky terrain. And we flagged a few more signs that someone had been through here recently. Each clue gave me an extra hit of energy.

We were on target. I knew it.

I was about to say as much when King came over the radio, giving us the bad news that the trail they'd been following turned out to be a dead end. They were retracing their steps and would move to a new section of their grid.

I looked at Vance. "You know what that means, right?"

He tilted his head. "I'm not the SAR expert here. But it looks like everyone's at a dead end except us."

I nodded. "Exactly. I don't have Cheyenne's gut, but I'd bet money Robin's in our section."

In my excitement, I turned too quickly and put my foot down on a loose rock. I slipped, but before I could fall, Vance's hand gripped mine. I skidded to a stop, my heart pounding.

"Thanks for the hand," I said, glancing back at him.

"Anytime." The look he gave me said he was talking about more than our search. But then his eyes shifted to the side. "Hey," he said, his face lighting up in excitement. "Look at that."

I followed his gaze. Ahead of us on the trail, something bright blue flashed in the sunlight. I slowly made my way toward it, using my hands on the steep slope to stay steady.

"It's fabric," I called over to him, fresh excitement hitting me as well. "Looks like it got torn. And it's the same color as what Robin was reportedly wearing."

He carefully worked his way toward me. "I bet she slipped right where you did. Her jacket probably got caught on the way down."

"I bet you're right." I scanned the area and called out for her but got no reply. "Flag it and I'll call it in."

He wrapped tape around the branch and snapped a picture of it while I entered our location into my GPS and tried to radio.

"Dammit."

"What's wrong?" He frowned.

"We're too far down. I'm out of comms."

"Does one of us need to hike back up and radio?"

I shook my head. "She's down there and she's probably hurt. We keep going."

CHAPTER THIRTY-NINE

Vance

CLAIRE'S EXCITEMENT WAS OBVIOUS AS WE CAREFULLY picked our way toward the bottom of the ravine. I knew now why Hank had said it was the hardest path. The sun beat down on us, making me sweat despite the cold temperatures. Every step had to be deliberate—one wrong move could send you flying down the side of the rock face. It was exhausting.

And I was having the time of my life.

Seeing Claire out here was like seeing the version of her that had raced Rhett on horseback. The one who threw her head back and laughed in the face of danger but got tears in her eyes when she looked at the beauty of the mountains.

Claire Hawkins was a badass adrenaline junkie. She didn't just handle all this well—she thrived out here. Her eyes came to life in a way they didn't at a desk.

The sheriff's office was stifling her, and I had a feeling it wasn't just because of her shitty coworkers. She had to be bored senseless working for a sleepy little town where her primary job was probably responding to domestics that never went anywhere. She needed more. Her soul was going to die if she stayed stuck there. I knew because I had once been the exact same way.

Before I'd pursued my career in law enforcement, I'd spent six months working for my grandfather at his investment company. I'd been bored out of my mind, needing a challenge to feel alive. Those feelings had made me walk away from a cushy job where I made more money than I knew what to do with to a job with long hours and very little thanks at the end of the day. But it fed a need inside me, and I loved it.

This fed a need inside her, too.

Our souls were more alike than I ever would have predicted when I'd met her. Because of it, I knew she was right—no matter how much I hated to admit it. Working as a grunt for my father would make me miserable, and there was a limit to how far I could go with DCI. I loved my job, but it didn't compare to the excitement of the FBI or the opportunities a bigger agency could offer me. I never would have resented *her* for my choice. But I also wouldn't be happy with either of the jobs available to me here.

I hated that she'd turned me down—again. But when the initial sting eased, I knew she had done it because she cared about my happiness the way I cared about hers.

I had a feeling that someday I'd thank her for talking me out of taking a job I'd despise.

I started to say so, but Claire stopped suddenly in the trail, holding her finger up in a sign to be quiet.

"Did you hear that?" she whispered, turning to me.

I strained to listen—then I did. It was faint and still way too far away. But down at the bottom of the ravine, a frail voice was calling out for help.

Claire's eye's sharpened, honing in on the sound. She tried her radio again, frustration flashing when it wouldn't work.

"Okay," she said, slipping the radio back onto her belt and giving me a serious look. "I can tell you're straining at the bit there. I get it. We're both feeling a surge of adrenaline right now, but that makes this extra dangerous. The terrain is just as shitty as it was up there. We go slow, okay? Look twice before every step. This is where we can get ahead of ourselves, make mistakes, and get hurt. And that won't help Robin."

"Got it, boss." I winked at her.

Her face relaxed. "Let's go get her."

Although we moved as carefully as before, time seemed to fly by twice as quickly now that we had our target within sight. Adrenaline pumped through my veins the same way it did on a chase. It was an addictive feeling.

I knew that Claire felt it, too. But you'd never know it unless you knew her well enough to see that glint in her eyes, the thrill of excitement she kept contained as she did her job. And when we finally found Robin, cold and weak at the bottom of the ravine, Claire's energy was more calm than even I would have been able to pull off.

She spoke to Robin in soothing tones, even as her eyes darted over her, assessing—and seeing, as I did, that there was no way Robin was going to walk out of this ravine on her own two feet. Robin's face was pale and her lips were nearly blue. Beyond that, her leg was broken. Sharp bone jutted out from her shin, caked in blood below the makeshift bandage Robin had made from her torn jacket.

Claire dropped to her knees, quickly pulling medical supplies out of her bag. She covered Robin in a thermal blanket, tucking in heat packs to help bring her body temperature up. Then she gave her a few sips of water to wet her parched lips before checking her pulse. Claire's lips pinched and she shot me a worried look.

"Thank you," Robin said, her voice trembling. She cast grateful eyes first to Claire, then to me. "I thought I was going to die alone out here."

"Not on my watch." Claire smiled gently. "We're going to get you taken care of."

"I was so stupid."

"We all make mistakes," Claire said, her tone still calm and soothing. "Can you tell me what happened?"

A look of distress crossed Robin's face. "I was trying to make my way down the ravine. I lost my balance and fell. Only about halfway. But my leg... I knew I couldn't make it back up to the top. I called for help, but nobody came. My phone wouldn't get a signal. I didn't know what to do. The skin wasn't broken yet..." She looked helplessly at her leg. "But I couldn't stand on it."

"What happened after that?"

"When I realized no one was coming, I knew I needed to get somewhere safer to spend the night. Plus, I needed water. I knew there was a creek down here, so I worked to slide myself down. I tried to keep my leg protected, but... I got in a hurry and slid too hard there at the end. That's when the bone broke through. I didn't make it to get water after all."

Claire winced. "That had to have hurt. I can offer you some ibuprofen or acetaminophen. It's not much for that kind of pain, but it will help."

Robin nodded her head gratefully. "Please."

Claire fished the meds out of her bag and handed them to Robin along with a fresh bottle of water. "Just a sip, okay? Don't overdo it. Do you have pain anywhere else?"

Robin swallowed the pills and handed the water back to Claire. "No. Just my leg. I mean, some bumps and bruises elsewhere." She held up her arm. "I hit my elbow pretty hard on a rock. But nothing else feels serious."

"Did you ever hit your head or lose consciousness?"

"No. I *wish* I would have lost consciousness." She made a pathetic attempt at a smile.

"I bet." Claire gave her a look of sympathy, then reached for more supplies from her bag and slipped on a pair of latex gloves. "I need to check your leg, okay? First, can you wiggle your toes?"

Robin winced. "A little."

"Great. That's a good sign. I'm going to take your shoe off so I can check for blood flow to your foot. I'll try not to jar your leg." She gingerly removed the hiking boot and peeled down Robin's sock. Then she lightly ran her fingers across Robin's toes. "Can you feel this?"

Robin made a half-hearted nod.

Claire gave me the same worried look from before. "I'm going to clean and dress this wound to help prevent infection, okay? I can't set the fracture, but I'm going to splint your leg to keep it from moving."

She caught my eye, directing her words to me as much as to Robin. "We're going to need a helicopter to transport you out. It could take a couple of hours to get one here. I can pretty much guarantee they're going to want to do surgery on that leg, so I'll have to limit you to sips of water. But we'll keep you as comfortable as we can."

"Thank you. I'm just so grateful that I'm not going to die."

"Hopefully you still feel that way after this," Claire said, chuckling. "I'm going to pour some antiseptic on this wound. It will burn, but we've got to do it. Hold Vance's hand," she said, nodding my way. "Squeeze as hard as you want. He's strong. He can take it." She winked at me.

I offered Robin my hand. She gripped it tightly and let out a moan when Claire poured the antiseptic over the wound. It bubbled up, turning light red as fresh blood mixed with it and oozed out, dripping down onto the rocks below. Claire gently wiped away the excess, then covered the wound with sterile gauze from her pack and carefully wrapped the leg.

Robin let go of my hand as the pain eased, sighing in relief. A bit of color came back to her face.

"Worst part is over," Claire said cheerfully.

Too cheerfully. The tension in her jaw revealed the truth.

But Robin bought it and smiled gratefully.

"The signal down here is bad," Claire said. "We're going to walk up just a ways to call for that helicopter."

"Please don't leave me," Robin said, trying to scoot herself up.

"Try not to move," Claire said, putting a hand on her shoulder. "Keep that leg stationary. I promise we won't even be out of sight." She pointed to the trail we'd come in on. "We'll be right there. You can watch us the whole time. But the faster we make this call, the faster we get them here—and the faster you can get some pain meds that are a hell of a lot better than anything I can give you."

Robin let out a breath and nodded.

Claire gave her another sip of water, then stood and grabbed my arm, heading back up our trail.

"Normally, I'd leave someone with her," she said, keeping her voice low. "But you're new to this and I want to loop you in on the plan. I'm going to tell the rest of the team to hang back. There's no sense in any of them risking this descent when it's going to take a chopper to get her out of here."

"Agreed. I saw the worry in your eyes. Tell me what you really think about her condition."

"She's strong. Responsive, which is good. But that's a serious injury, she's lost a lot of blood, and she spent the night in the cold with nothing more than a torn coat to keep her warm. She's not getting full blood flow to that foot, either." Claire shook her head. "Honestly, I'm surprised she's doing as well as she is. She's got some signs of shock—blue lips, weak pulse. But she's talking, and she's in good spirits. That's a good sign."

"How long is it really going to take to get help down here?"

She let out a sigh. "A few hours if we're lucky. Longer if we're not."

TIME TICKED SLOWLY AS WE WAITED FOR THE MED EVAC. Robin had to have been in severe pain, but Claire was right—she was strong, and her relief at being rescued kept her spirits bright.

Claire was a marvel. She was patient, kind, and reassuring. Never let even an ounce of the exhaustion she must have felt show through. She monitored Robin's vitals and kept her distracted from the pain.

This was her passion, and she was damn good at it. If the people who had underestimated her could see her in action out here, they'd be blown away. I was proud of her.

Proud to be her partner.

I'd worked with a lot of good people over the years, but there was something special about working with her. I had a nagging feeling that anyone else would be a disappointment after this—even at the FBI.

At the top of every hour, one of us would climb part of the way up the ravine to radio in. Seven minutes up, seven minutes down. It was a punishing exercise, but it kept us warm. By midday, the sun beat down from overhead, bringing welcome heat to the ravine floor after the cold of the night. Robin shifted, wincing from the pain, and asked how much longer.

Claire glanced at the watch on her wrist. "Shouldn't be too much longer now. Last time we checked in, they said the heli was en route. Another fifteen minutes or so, I'd guess."

Robin let out a breath and smiled. "Thank you. Again."

"You're welcome. Again." Claire's lips twitched in a gentle smile.

"You probably think I'm stupid, coming out here by myself like this," Robin said, blushing.

"Nah. We all do stupid things sometimes. Doesn't make us stupid people."

Robin gave her a grateful smile. "Thanks. But I *was* being stupid." She groaned. "I don't even know what I thought I'd find out there."

"What were you hoping to find?" I asked casually.

Claire's ears pricked.

Robin shrugged. "Anything. The girl they found—Kate... I just wanted to find out what happened to her." She swallowed hard.

"We heard you're a student at UW," Claire said, her tone matching the ease I'd kept in mine. "You knew her then?"

"Yes." She paused, looking away. Her grief was palpable.

"Seems like you two were close," Claire said gently.

Robin nodded. "Yeah. She was... She was my sister."

"Your sister?" I asked, frowning. We weren't aware of Katelyn having had any siblings, biological or adopted. "Like, a sorority sister?"

Robin shook her head. "My foster sister. We both grew up in the system. We were in some of the same foster homes when we were kids." Shame coated her features.

"Oh, man," Claire said, her face falling. "I'm so sorry."

Tears welled up in Robin's eyes. "Me too. Nobody cared when she disappeared. Not really. But I did. I tried to find her. Started a podcast, hoping I'd get clues or something. Or that she'd hear it and reach out, let me know she was okay at least. We'd... We'd always looked out for each other. Even after we were moved to separate homes. Then I saw the news." Her voice broke. "I just wanted to help find out who hurt her. I was so stupid, thinking I could."

Claire squeezed Robin's hand. "You were trying to help your family. There's nothing stupid about that."

"And maybe you still can," I added.

Robin looked at me, confused.

"Claire and I are the ones working the investigation," I said, laying our cards out on the table. "We have a suspect, but we're still trying to make our case. You were Katelyn's sister—I would have talked to you immediately had anyone told me. If you know anything at all, either something Katelyn told you or something you've uncovered through your podcast, it could help."

She blinked twice. "You... You guys? You're the detectives on the case?"

Claire grinned. "Yeah. We wear a lot of hats."

"But I already talked to a detective," Robin said, confused. "I told him everything."

"In Laramie?" I asked.

Robin shook her head. "No, here. The Sage County Sheriff's Office. I went there as soon as I got into town. I gave him everything I had and he said he'd take care of it."

Claire and I exchanged glances.

I pulled out my badge to show Robin. "I'm Special Agent Vance Weston from the Wyoming DCI, and I'm the lead investigator on Katelyn's case. Whoever you talked to did *not* turn the information over to me."

"He didn't?" The distress returned as she looked from me to Claire. "But—"

"Shhhh," Claire said, giving me a warning glance. "It's okay. It was probably a mistake. I need you to stay still, okay? Take a couple of deep breaths."

Robin took a deep inhale, nodding as she settled.

"Good," I said. "But we don't have much time before the heli arrives. I need to know who you talked to and everything you gave them."

Robin took another deep breath to steady herself. "Okay. I'll tell you everything."

Chapter Forty

Claire

"A lot of people didn't like Kate," Robin said, her voice wavering. "But that's because they didn't understand her. Foster care isn't always a good thing. It can be brutal. You learn to survive, but survival isn't always nice and pretty."

"No, it's not," I said, understanding.

Robin nodded. "Over the years, we ended up in three different homes together. One of them was pretty good, but the other two were shitty." Her face turned bright red. "One of the dads was into little girls."

I wanted to vomit.

"Kate was my protector." She blinked back tears. "Even though I was the oldest. She was fierce. She wouldn't let him touch me, even though it meant she endured it all. She was always like that. Taking the worst to shield the rest of us."

My eyes filled with tears, thinking about the girl so many people had spoken badly of during this. How everyone had judged her, called her names. Would they have done that had they known what she'd sacrificed to protect the people around her?

I knew that the sad truth was they probably still would have.

Vance put a steadying hand on my back. I leaned into his strength as Robin continued her story.

"Kate always wanted one of two things. She either wanted enough money to ensure her security—*our* security. Or she wanted love. The movie kind of love where he would adore her and protect her." Robin's face darkened. "When she started dating Tony Evans, she thought she'd found both."

Vance and I exchanged glances.

"Did Tony hurt her?" I asked gently.

She shook her head. "Not physically. But he's got a sick desire for control. It's something we got used to seeing, growing up the way we did. It can get dangerous. So when Kate started seeing the warning signs, she started looking for a way out."

Vance interjected. "What do you mean?"

"Tony's obsessive," she said flatly. "He's into the whole sub/dom thing. Kate was kind of cool with it when she thought it was just kinky foreplay, but that wasn't enough for Tony. He wanted to control her whole life."

"Her whole life?"

Robin nodded. "He has this fantasy of marrying someone who would be entirely submissive to him. He wanted to control everything, even who she was friends with and what shows she could watch on TV. He thought he could just claim her as his and it would sweep her off her feet or something. But when you've lived most of your life with absolutely no control over what happens to you, the last thing you want to do is give it up when you finally get some."

"What happened when she started looking for a way out?" Vance asked. "Did Tony get angry?"

"Yes, but I don't think he killed her, if that's what you're thinking.
"

"I don't, either," Vance agreed. "But it might help if you can tell us why you think that."

"Because he didn't know where she'd gone," she explained. "He thought I did. He tried to make me tell him. Said it was to *protect* her. But I couldn't tell him because I didn't know, either."

"Did he hurt *you*?" I asked. My jaw clenched. I'd had just about enough of Tony bullying young girls. All I wanted was one good reason I could go after him.

She shook her head. "No," she said softly. "He scared me, but he didn't hurt me. And after that, he was just so sad. He kept checking in with me every week, asking if I'd heard from her. I think he was about the only person who actually listened to my podcast. And when we heard that she had died, he was as devastated as I was."

I glanced at Vance, hoping he could see the question in my eyes. He seemed to, because he nodded.

"We think she had a new boyfriend and that she might have left Laramie to be with him. What can you tell us about that?"

Robin hesitated, biting her lip.

"It's okay," I said. "You can tell us."

I glanced at my watch again, realizing I needed her to tell us *quickly.* The heli could be here any minute.

Robin's face turned red. "I told her it was a bad idea," she blurted out. "Worse than Tony. More dangerous."

"Why?" I asked, heart pounding.

"Because he was married. That never ends well."

"No," I said, shaking my head. "It doesn't."

Regret settled onto her face. "He whisked her off her feet, just like Tony had. I tried to tell her it was just a fantasy, that he could never give her what she wanted. But she said he was different. That the *situation* was different."

"How so?" Vance asked.

I heard the faint sound of the chopper in the distance. I caught Vance's eye and saw that he heard it too.

We were almost out of time.

"She said he was powerful enough to give her anything she wanted. That it was different because she had no illusions about him leaving his wife for her. She didn't even want him to. He was just a stepping stone."

"What do you mean?" I asked, gripping her hand.

"He offered her protection, money, even a place to live. He told her he would help her make connections, meet other people with money. That he could help her get into graduate school or land a good job that would put her in the right circles to find the kind of husband she wanted. He was the exact opposite of Tony—he wanted to be a benefactor, not someone who controlled her or kept her for himself. All he wanted in exchange was some fun and excitement. She said he was a great lover and that it was a win-win for both of them. I told her that things that sound too good to be true usually are."

"Wasn't she worried about the wife finding out?" I asked.

Robin shook her head. "No. The wife knew. She didn't care."

"The wife *didn't care?*"

"Back up," Vance said. "He offered her a place to live?"

The sound of the helicopter grew louder.

She glanced at both of us, unsure who to answer first. "They had an open marriage," she said, choosing me. "Kate had met the wife and everything. The wife assured her she was welcome to have a relationship with the husband as long as she remembered her place and kept things discreet. The wife had a boyfriend of her own."

She turned to Vance. "They had a guest house on their property. For discretion, they said. Kate wasn't the first girl, obviously. She planned on spending the summer with them, but when Tony tried to rape her at that party, I guess she decided to leave sooner."

"Tony tried to rape her?" Now, I was furious.

She nodded, biting her lip. "I got to the party as she was leaving. She was crying. She told me what he had tried to do. But she didn't tell me she was leaving. She didn't even say goodbye." Tears welled up again.

The helicopter came into sight, spotted us, and hovered over the ravine.

"Do you know the boyfriend's name?" Vance asked quickly.

Robin shook her head, blinking back her tears. "No. She was very secretive about the whole thing. She said they made her sign a non-disclosure agreement because it could get him in trouble if it got out. She wouldn't tell me where he lived, where they had met—nothing like that. Only that he was married and that he has a guest house."

I racked my brain, trying to figure out who here had something that might be called a guest house. The McGraths had an apartment over their garage. They usually rented it out during the summer when temporary hires needed seasonal housing. The Evanses had a building out back that I'd always assumed was a gardening cottage. Maybe it was a guest house. I couldn't see Katelyn wanting to stay there over the summer, though, if their son had tried to rape her.

Robin's face brightened. "Oh, and that they own horses. He even bought a gray pony that he said would be hers to ride while she was with them, and he gave her a silver charm bracelet with a horse on it."

The truth slammed into me like a hurricane.

I knew who Katelyn's boyfriend was—I'd sold him that gray pony last January.

"I need to know who you spoke to at the sheriff's office," Vance shouted over the rising noise of the incoming chopper. "Was it Sheriff McGrath?"

Two men began descending from the chopper on rappel lines.

"No," she shouted back. "It was a sergeant something or another."

"Sergeant Collins?" I yelled.

Her face lit up. "Yes! That's the one. I told everything to Sergeant Collins. He said he would take care of it."

Then the medics pushed us back so they could hoist Robin up to the chopper and fly her away.

Chapter Forty-One

Vance

"I'M COMING WITH HER!" I SHOUTED AS TWO MEDICS IN flight suits attached Robin's stretcher to the hoist.

"No room!" the medic shouted back, shaking his head.

"She could be in danger!" I grabbed his jacket.

He gave me a look like I was stupid. "That's why we're getting her to a hospital! Now back up, we need to move!"

I yelled into his ear. "You don't understand! She could be a witness in a homicide case. I need to stick with her."

His eyes widened. "I'm sorry," he shouted back. "We can't carry anyone else. You'll have to meet us at the hospital. We're heading to the trauma center in Casper."

"Then don't leave her side," I thundered. "Don't land this chopper until you get there, got it? I'll have someone waiting at the landing strip."

He gave a sharp nod.

I backed up to where Claire was and watched them ascend on ropes into the chopper. Then the helicopter rose into the air, carrying our most important witness far away from us.

"We've got to move," Claire said darkly, shoving a candy bar and a fresh bottle of water into my hands.

I scarfed the bar and gulped the water as we jogged to the ravine wall to begin yet another ascent. "Sure wish *we* could get a helicopter ride out of here."

"Same. Some day, our SAR team will get its own heli. Then, in a situation like this, it would actually come back for us. But for now, we're going to have to hoof it on foot." She put her hands on the punishing incline and started the long walk back to the top.

I fell in line behind her and decided the climb back might not be too bad, considering the view. "Why don't you guys have one? A lot of other counties do."

"Money." She shrugged. "We're fundraising, but we're still nearly half a million away, and—"

"—and Sage County doesn't have the revenue to foot the bill," I said, putting the dots together.

"Yeah. Although that might change if Darla Barrington gets her way and brings in that increased tourism she's so desperate for." Her voice was full of bitterness. "Vance, we have a problem."

"Other than the fact that our best witness is on a chopper headed for Casper?"

"Oh yeah. Way worse than that."

Her tone alarmed me. "What is it?"

She turned her head, catching my eye over her shoulder. "Katelyn's affair wasn't with Sheriff McGrath."

"I figured that since she said the wife was okay with it. Do you know anyone here with a guest house and a gray pony?"

I didn't bother pointing out the fact that *her* family had plenty of guest houses *and* horses. Walker and Naomi Hawkins didn't seem like the types to have affairs. They were the real deal. Married and still so in love you could practically feel it radiating out of them when they were together.

"Yeah," Claire answered between heavy breaths. "I do. I know who the boyfriend was. I sold him that pony myself, right after Katelyn's Christmas visit. He said it was for when his niece came to visit."

"Why do you sound so disappointed? I thought you'd be happy it's not Sheriff McGrath." My own breathing started to labor. A climb like this was bad enough on its own. But after very little sleep and insufficient calories, it was killer. The SAR team was badass. And my partner was the most badass of them all.

"Oh, I'm thrilled it's not him. But we're screwed."

"Why?"

"Because she was dating Judge Barrington. And apparently, he has Trey in his pocket."

Judge Barrington.

The pieces clicked into place. Him meeting her at the Evanses' house when she came for Christmas. Darla Barrington not caring about his infidelity and encouraging Serena to have an affair of her own. The non-disclosure agreement. The conversation where Sergeant Collins had talked about spinning something instead of risking it coming out later—he'd been talking about the information Robin had just given us, information that could connect Katelyn to Judge Barrington.

It all fit.

"Shit," I said between gritted teeth.

"Yep. And now you know why we're screwed."

I did. Judge Barrington was the only one who knew our entire playbook. I'd called him for warrants and told about the snowmobile theory, about Sheriff McGrath having coffee with Katelyn, even about the video where Serena discussed an affair. All of it. I'd held nothing back, needing to prove probable cause in order to get my warrants.

If Judge Barrington owned a snowmobile and had used it to dump Katelyn's body, he could ditch it before we searched it. If he'd had Sergeant Collins do it with one of the SAR snowmobiles, he could have had Collins destroy the evidence during the time he'd said he needed to "think things over" before granting my warrants.

Worse, he could have used that time to plant evidence at the McGraths', framing the suspect we'd handed him on a silver platter.

My mind began working, trying to figure out a plan to fix everything as we scrambled up the side of the ravine, racing to try to salvage our case.

We almost made it to the top.

When the edge of the ravine came into sight, a shot rang out. One bullet whizzed by my head; a second one hit the ground beside me.

Claire and I both hit the dirt.

A third bullet struck, shattering a stone beside Claire's shoulder. Her eyes, full of fear, met mine.

We had to get under cover.

There was a boulder back behind us, to the left. One that jutted out of the side of the ravine and would provide a shield if we could get beneath it. I grabbed Claire and rolled backward, bracing my feet against anything I could find to stop our slide before we got too far. We landed just below the outcrop and scrambled underneath it.

"Are you okay?" I asked, my breath ragged as I grabbed her shoulders and looked her over. She had scratches on her face and hands, blood mingling with the dust that now coated her. But she was alive.

"Yes." She nodded, fighting to control her breathing. "You?"

"Yep." Anger settled hard as I looked at her pale face and wide eyes.

A torrent of rocks fell, pelting the ground around us. I pulled Claire to my chest, making us as small as possible beneath the meager protection of the outcrop.

"He's trying to cause a rockslide," she gasped. "It could bury us."

"And it would look like an accident," I said grimly. I reached for the radio on my belt, but it was gone. "I lost my radio in the fall. Can you call for help?"

She pulled hers and tried it, cursing when it failed. "It must have gotten damaged when we rolled."

Another barrage of rocks let loose, bigger than the last. The ground beneath us trembled in response.

"I'm sorry," Claire said, miserable. "I shouldn't have let you come out here. It's my fault."

"No," I said, gripping her shoulders. "I insisted, remember?"

"I knew we were in trouble," she whispered, tears pricking her eyes. "SAR reports go straight to the sheriff's office."

The meaning of her words sank in. "Trey would have seen Robin's name and known that you and I found her. If they were going to cover it up, this was their last chance."

He'd probably headed this way as soon as he found out about the mission. One conversation with Hank and he would have known we were in the ravine with Robin. Even if he was smart enough to stay hidden, it would still have been easy reconnaissance. We'd checked in via radio every hour. Our GPS location was undoubtedly circled on one of those maps Hank had set up at base camp.

Three sitting ducks. Three loose ends he could take out in one fell swoop if he made it to us before Robin was rescued. And there were a million ways to make it look like an accident out here.

Claire gripped my hand. "I hoped we could get up the ravine in time, make it to cover. I'm sorry, Vance. I don't know how to get us out of this."

"This is not your fault," I said, forcing her to look at me. "We're partners. We're in this together, okay? And everything is going to be okay."

She nodded. But I knew she didn't believe me.

Robin was safe—for now.

Claire and I were still sitting ducks in a ravine, with only one way out and nowhere to hide.

Chapter Forty-Two

Claire

"I'm going to take a look," Vance whispered. The barrage of rocks had stopped and things had grown quiet.

But another shot rang out the moment he lifted his head above the rock protecting us.

I grabbed his shirt and yanked him down. "Don't," I whispered, desperate.

I couldn't lose him. Not like this.

Grim determination settled onto his face. "He's still at the top of the rim. The way I see it, we have two options. We can try to wait him out. Maybe he'll get spooked and leave. Someone had to have heard those gunshots."

I nodded. "Yeah. You're right." There was no way Rhett and Cheyenne would stay put if they'd heard them. I looked at my watch. "We're due to check in again in just four minutes. If we don't, Rhett and Cheyenne will come find us, if they're not already on their way."

"Waiting is the safest move for us, but it puts them in danger," he said, weighing it. "They're civilians. Can they handle themselves in a situation like this?"

I nodded, knowing it was true. "Cheyenne's always armed and she's a great shot. Rhett has some martial arts training. They can handle themselves. I still haven't told you the story of what happened to them this past summer."

"Save it for when we get out of here," he said, attempting a grin. "You can tell me over a bottle of scotch."

"Deal." It hit me that we might be about to die. I grabbed his collar and kissed him on pure impulse. None of my worries about the pain of him leaving mattered anymore. If this was our last day, I didn't want to die knowing I'd held myself back from him.

He gripped the back of my neck with his hand as he took the kiss deeper, somehow telling me that his feelings were as strong as mine without saying a single word. But the sound of movement above had him tensing and breaking away.

"I wish I could look," he said, cursing.

"Here." I dug into my backpack and pulled out a small mirror.

He grinned as he took it from me. "I didn't think you were the type to carry a mirror into the wilderness."

"It's a cheap, easy way to signal a helicopter," I said, returning his grin. "Use it on a clear day and it can be seen ten miles away."

"I like you, Claire Hawkins." His eyes twinkled with pure affection.

I shot him a wink, even though my heart squeezed with sadness. "It's too bad I can't stand you."

He smirked, then used the mirror to look around the boulder. "He's standing," he whispered. "Looks like he's on his cell phone, distracted..."

I could tell he was weighing something. Alarm went through me.

Then that grim determination came back on his face, and I could read his thoughts as easily as he could always read mine.

No.

I gripped his arm. Made him look at me. "What was option two?"

But I already knew what he was thinking.

He gave me a final look, one that was full of affection, regret, and longing. Then he placed his lips back on mine, gently this time.

He was kissing me goodbye.

When he pulled away, I grabbed his face and tried to pull him back to me.

But he took my hands in his, looking deep into my eyes. "You're going to run, Claire. Leave your pack. Go sideways—out of his line of sight—while I have him distracted. Use your hands, crawl, do whatever you need to do. But get yourself safe. Don't come back for me, okay? No matter what."

"No, Vance." I shook my head, lips trembling. "We're partners. We get out of here together. You're not going to sacrifice yourself for me."

He brushed his thumb across my lips. "You sacrifice yourself for everyone else all the time. It's my turn to do the same for you."

"Vance—" My voice broke into a sob as tears flowed down my cheeks.

But he pulled away, took one more look with the mirror, then shoved it into my hands. With a sad smile, he winked, then pulled his service weapon and stepped out from the boulder.

I lunged after him, but he was too quick. Before I could stop him, he scrambled up the hillside toward the man who was waiting to kill him.

I bit back my cry and hid behind the boulder. My heart raced and throbbed at the same time, from fear and pain that threatened to overwhelm me.

No.

It wasn't going to end like this.

I took a deep breath, steadying myself. Then I thrust the mirror out to get a look at what was happening.

Vance had made it halfway up the hillside, going faster than anyone should on the unstable rocks. At the noise, Trey spun around, dropped his phone, and reached for his rifle. In a horrifying moment that seemed to move in slow motion, he aimed at Vance and moved his finger to the trigger.

But Vance was faster. He pointed his pistol and fired, nailing Trey's left shoulder without breaking stride.

Trey jerked back.

Vance kept charging.

And I moved.

I pulled my own weapon and ducked out from the other side of the boulder, ignoring Vance's instructions to go sideways. I went straight up, parallel to the path Vance had taken. The terrain was even more unforgiving, with gravel that sent me falling to my knees. But I grabbed onto the branches of a desert shrub that jutted out from the rocky surface and hauled myself to my feet again, forcing myself to move.

Vance had almost made it to the top. But as his hands gripped the flat ground at the surface, a swift kick to the face sent him careening backward.

My heart nearly stopped.

But Vance held on, grasping for leverage, then hauled himself up and over the ledge.

And I kept running.

Vance stayed low this time, tackling Trey's knees. The men fell to the ground, locked in combat.

One final push. I hauled myself to the top and ran straight for them.

The men grappled, both stretching for the rifle that lay a few feet away from their outstretched arms. Vance punched Trey in the chin, then rolled and reached for the weapon.

But Trey yanked a hunting knife from his belt.

No.

I threw myself onto him, pinning his bicep with my knees. I grabbed his wrist with both hands and slammed it onto the rocks, knocking the knife from his hand. Trey wrenched his hand from mine and grabbed my neck, squeezing so hard I couldn't breathe.

Then Vance delivered a blow that knocked Trey unconscious.

"Are you crazy?" Vance yelled as he grabbed me, pulled me to him. "You could have been killed!"

I gasped for breath, clinging to him as tightly as he clung to me. "We're partners," I croaked. "We get out of here together."

Chapter Forty-Three

Vance

Claire went back for her packs and found my radio a few feet away. She used it to call in an update while I restrained Trey with the zip ties she carried in her kit. Then I called one of my DCI contacts in Casper and asked for someone to meet Robin at the hospital, both for security and to get an official statement. After a moment to catch our breaths, we started the long haul back to the trailhead, dragging our sullen prisoner with us.

When we emerged at base camp, the entire SAR team was waiting for us—along with a red-eyed Sheriff McGrath, who wordlessly took custody of Collins and hauled him to the back of an official vehicle

"Great work," Hank said, shaking my hand and throwing his arm around Claire. "You guys had a tough assignment this time—and that's *before* you had to deal with that one." He shot a disgusted look toward Collins. But he turned back to us with a smile. "You persevered and got another rescue on the books. "

"Claire deserves all the credit," I said, grinning. "She was amazing. I was just along for the ride."

Claire's eyes met mine. She gave me a cocky smirk, but her eyes shone with something deeper.

It made me want to tell her how incredible she was every single day of her life.

Cheyenne pushed past Hank and grabbed Claire in a tight embrace. "I'm so glad you're okay." Her voice broke.

"Me too." Claire gripped her friend, closing her eyes tightly.

"When we heard the shots, Rhett and I started saddling the horses to go after you." Cheyenne pulled back, her eyes teary. "I was so scared. I love you so much. I don't know what I would have done if..."

"We're okay," Claire said, though her own eyes were teary as well. "Thanks to Vance. He put himself in the line of fire to give me a chance to get away."

Rhett came over and shook my hand. "Thanks for taking care of my sister," he said, his voice rough.

"I tried to," I said, giving Claire a wink. "But instead of getting away, she threw herself down in front of a dagger and saved me instead."

He grinned. "That's our Claire. She's a hell of a woman."

Claire blushed under his praise.

"Yes, she is," I murmured, catching her eye.

The rest of the team had held back, giving Claire a few moments with Rhett and Cheyenne. But with their patience gone, they swarmed us, thrusting hot sandwiches and thermoses of fresh coffee into our hands. The energy was contagious and gave us a much-needed boost—as did the calories. The hot ham and cheese sandwich tasted like the best thing I'd ever had in my life.

Maybe the second best thing, I thought, eyeing Claire as she traded stories with her team and laughed at SAR jokes. It was a lot like dinner with the Hawkins family. The SAR team was a family of its own, and I realized how lucky Claire really was.

She wanted more. I understood that. Respected it.

But she had something incredible here, too.

. . .

SHERIFF MCGRATH HUNG BACK FOR A FEW MINUTES, GIVING us time to eat and hydrate. When he finally approached the edge of the group, Claire's laughter faded. She caught my eye and jerked her head toward the sheriff.

The celebration was over. It was time to work.

He was silent until the three of us had walked to the other side of the parking lot beside the car that held Collins, well out of earshot from the SAR team.

When he spoke, his voice was gruff. Weary. "There's a hell of a lot I want to say to you two," he said, removing his hat and brushing back his graying hair. He shook his head and gave Claire a look of reproach. "Serena? Really?"

The betrayal in his eyes mirrored the hurt I'd seen in Claire's the day he'd talked to her in his office.

Claire's face fell in devastation. "I'm sorr—"

I cut her off before she could apologize for doing her job. "I'm guessing you found out about our warrant request," I said, bringing Sheriff McGrath's attention back to me. He could be pissed if he wanted, but he wasn't going to make Claire feel like shit over this.

He pulled his eyes away from hers and gave me a short nod.

I crossed my arms and gave him a pointed look. "I'll be happy to have a conversation with you whenever you're ready about why our investigation pointed in her direction. Clearly, you had some responsibility in that. But right now, we have more important things to talk about."

He pinched the bridge of his nose, sighing. "Right. When Hank called me, he said Trey had attacked the two of you. Fill me in. What the hell happened out there?"

"He didn't just attack us," Claire said, the strength returning to her voice. "He tried to kill us. Took shots at us with a rifle and tried to start a rockslide. Pulled a knife on Vance."

Shock rippled on Sheriff McGrath's face. "Why would he..."

"He's involved in Katelyn Brown's homicide," I said flatly. "He helped cover it up, at the very least. Maybe more."

"*What*?" It was clear this was news to Sheriff McGrath.

"Our SAR victim, Robin, was a close friend of Katelyn's with valuable information concerning her relationships here in Wildwood. When the identification was made public, Robin came here and reported that information—to Sergeant Collins."

"He's been sabotaging the case from the beginning," Claire added, fury in her eyes. "He withheld Robin's information from us because he's in Judge Barrington's pocket." Claire's disgust was evident. "And Robin can prove that Katelyn and Judge Barrington were having an affair."

Sheriff McGrath's mouth tightened. "I see."

"You don't seem surprised by that," I said, arms still crossed.

"Serena's told me that the Barringtons have a unique arrangement," he explained. The look on his face changed to disgust. "But I had no idea he'd hooked up with Katelyn. Good grief, he's old enough to be her grandfather. Judge Barrington. Well, that's going to be complicated." He shook his head, crossing his arms tightly.

"Maybe not as complicated as you think," I said thoughtfully.

"You figured something out," Claire stated, the brightness sparking in her eyes.

I grinned. "Just a theory. But if it proves true..."

"Well?" Sheriff McGrath prodded. "What is it?"

"I don't think Judge Barrington killed Katelyn."

"You think Collins did it?" Sheriff McGrath glanced at the car behind us. Trey's sullen face stared straight ahead, refusing to make eye contact.

"No. I think we were right about Katelyn being killed by the wife of her affair partner. We just had the wrong wife." I shrugged.

"Darla." Claire inhaled sharply.

I nodded. "Robin said Judge Barrington thought of himself as a benefactor to Katelyn. Katelyn had no illusions of a future with him— apparently didn't want one. She was discreet, willing to play by their rules. His wife already knew about the affair. So, what's the motive for him to kill her?"

"They could have had a fight," Sheriff McGrath pointed out. "Katelyn may have changed her mind about what she wanted from him when she got here."

"Maybe," I conceded. "But I spoke with Judge Barrington about the investigation. I've replayed that conversation ever since we found out about the affair, and my gut still says he genuinely wanted the case to be solved. I think he delayed the warrants because he knew we were wrong—that there's no way Katelyn was having an affair with you because she was with him."

"Alright." Sheriff McGrath sighed. "Tell me why you're thinking Darla."

"Robin said something that's been bothering me. She said Darla had given her blessing—as long as Katelyn remembered her place. That's a mild threat. And Darla is as cold as ice. I could see that as clear as day when I met her."

"That's pretty weak. I agree with you that Darla Barrington is a sharp, cutthroat woman. But that doesn't make her guilty of murder."

"Think about it," I said. "We know Darla had a boyfriend. What if Trey wasn't in the judge's pocket—what if he was in *hers*?"

Sheriff McGrath put his palm over his face. "Serena told me Darla was a cougar. Said her boyfriend was half her age. That fits. But again, what's the motive? She has a boyfriend of her own and already knew about Katelyn."

Claire inhaled sharply. "Other than whatever Katelyn might have done that crossed a line? I can think of two."

Sheriff McGrath looked at her. "How do you figure?"

"Darla's whole goal is to bring tourists to Wildwood. What happened as soon as the news broke?"

Sheriff McGrath squeezed his eyes shut. "The motel booked up."

"Exactly," Claire said, her jaw set. "It's not an ideal way to bring people in, but it sure gave the town exposure. Second, Trey is her lover. What is the one thing Trey wants most?"

"To work at DCI," Sheriff McGrath said. He looked sick. "And his lack of homicide investigation experience was the one thing standing in his way."

"It's a win-win for both of them," I agreed.

"We need proof. And that's going to be tricky, seeing as how we can't go to Judge Barrington for a warrant." He shook his head. "This is a mess."

"I'll go to the district court judge," I decided. "We'll get a search warrant for their home and guest house. They'll have cleaned it, but I bet we'll get proof Katelyn was there. We'll get the DA to offer Sergeant Collins a deal. He'll talk—eventually. We've got Robin's testimony, and we'll get Serena's, too."

"Serena?" Sheriff McGrath's head jerked back. "Why does she have to get involved in this?"

I leveled a look at him. "Because I'm pretty sure Darla Barrington is the reason Serena thought you were having an affair with Katelyn. She was whispering in Serena's ear while Sergeant Collins dropped hints about you and Claire. It was all part of the plan. Darla was setting you—or Serena—up to take the fall. And we walked right into it."

"Son of a bitch."

Chapter Forty-Four

Claire

The forty-eight hours after the search were a blur. There was no time to catch up on the sleep we desperately needed. Vance and I pretty much worked around the clock, building our case against Darla Barrington.

Our hard work paid off.

Serena confirmed what we'd suspected. She'd driven by the coffee shop that evening after dinner out with her friends and had seen Sheriff McGrath and Katelyn together on a night when he'd said he had to work late. The next day, she told Darla and Leslie, looking for reassurance that she had nothing to worry about. A few months later, Darla started actively feeding Serena's concern about Katelyn. She needed a viable suspect for when Katelyn's body was discovered.

When Sheriff McGrath assigned the investigation to me, Darla and Trey started planting seeds about a second affair, making Serena question everything about the husband she loved. She wanted to trust and protect him but was overwhelmed with fear and betrayal. She never even realized she was being manipulated.

The moment Trey was offered a deal in exchange for testimony, he dropped all loyalty to Darla and filled in all the missing pieces.

Darla had killed Katelyn. Not because of anything Katelyn had done, but because Judge Barrington had fallen in love with her. For the first time since they'd opened up their marriage, he started talking about the future, dropping hints that he wanted one—with Katelyn.

One night, Darla overheard him telling Katelyn he was going to file for divorce. After all, he'd never wanted an open marriage to begin with. That had been all Darla's idea. Now that he'd found love, he wanted to make Katelyn his wife.

That was a threat Darla couldn't endure.

Judge Barrington had no idea Katelyn was dead until we'd found her body. Darla had texted him from Katelyn's phone, telling him that she'd changed her mind and was leaving. Then she'd recruited Trey to help cover it up, promising him the one thing he wanted—and threatening to pin the whole thing on him if he didn't cooperate.

I'd been right about the snowmobile. Trey had used one of the SAR ones from the storage locker to dump Katelyn's body in the park, knowing she'd eventually be discovered—in Sage County. That was the only way Trey would get the homicide investigation experience he needed.

When we told Judge Barrington the truth, he crumbled. He told us how he'd met Katelyn and had become taken with her. He'd made up excuses to bump into her while she was there, trying to lay the groundwork for a connection.

Then one day, she'd shown up at his office, crying and making him believe that Tony had hurt her. He'd never realized she was playing the same game he was, looking for a conquest of her own.

He gave us full access to everything, including her second phone. He had no interest in protecting himself from the consequences of his affair.

Only in taking down the woman who'd killed his lover.

.   .   .

"Seems like we have a solid case," I said, snagging the last egg roll from the carton. We were at Vance's cabin, finishing up a late dinner of Chinese takeout—paired with scotch, of course. It was the first chance we'd had to even be alone since making our arrests.

"Yeah." Vance grinned. He grabbed the fortune cookies and tossed me one. "Darla never counted on both of her men turning against her like that."

"I'm glad they did. She's awful," I said, shaking my head. "I feel terrible about what she did to Katelyn—and to Sheriff McGrath and Serena."

"Think they'll be okay?"

I nodded. "I do. He loves her. And now that she realizes she was being manipulated, she knows that. I think she feels really stupid for listening to Darla's lies."

"She is stupid." He leveled a look at me. "She should have known better about *you*."

"She doesn't really know me." I shrugged. "But she apologized. And I think we'll be okay, too."

"What about you and the sheriff?"

Sheriff McGrath had asked to speak with me privately earlier that afternoon, but Vance and I hadn't had a chance to talk about it.

"I think we'll be fine. Eventually." I blushed. "I definitely read too much into that conversation with him. He admitted that he figured Tony was our guy, which was why he wanted his hands out of it. And he hoped we would go gentle on Leslie if she lied to us to protect her son. That's what he meant about the good people in Wildwood."

"Politics," he said, rolling his eyes.

"Exactly."

He cracked open his fortune cookie and pulled the fortune out.

"Did you get a good one?" I asked.

He smiled, but it didn't reach his eyes. "Says I have a long journey ahead of me."

I swallowed hard. "Guess they nailed that one."

"Guess so." He looked away, then said the words I'd been dreading. "I'm leaving tomorrow. I have to go back to the field office in Laramie to wrap things up there before..." He trailed off like he couldn't bring himself to voice it.

No. I wanted to scream it, wanted to rage, even though we'd both known that this was coming. There was really nothing more for him to do here.

But I wasn't ready to say goodbye.

He held my gaze. "It's been really great working with you, Claire."

No.

"Sure," I said, forcing a laugh. "Minus getting shot at and roughing it in the wilderness."

He didn't smile. "All of it. I wouldn't trade any of it."

My heart thundered against my chest. "When do you leave for New York?" I asked quietly.

"Friday." He drained the last of his scotch and stared straight ahead. He looked miserable.

"That's ... fast." *Too* fast. I wasn't ready.

"I'll be back and forth for a few weeks. I need to find a place to live there, then pack up and get things moved over. Plus, I need to be available to the DA." He gave me a tentative look. "Maybe we could see each other when I'm here."

"Maybe. But I know we're both going to be busy over the next few weeks." I toyed with my fortune cookie, afraid to crack it open and see what it said. "Rhett and Cheyenne's wedding is this weekend, remember? Did I tell you that my brother Cole and his wife, Willa, are flying in for it? She's pregnant and they were afraid she might not be able to fly, but the doctor approved it. They'll be staying for a week."

"No, you didn't tell me." He took a swig straight from the bottle, then passed it to me. "But I need to point out that you changed the subject."

My pulse quickened. "Did I?"

"Yes." Those sharp blue eyes honed in on me. "I wasn't done talking about us."

I threw up my hands in frustration. "There is no *us.*" My eyes filled with tears, but I refused to let them fall. "I'm crazy about you, Vance. I don't—I don't even want to think about you leaving. But your future is in New York, and mine isn't. And I'm scared that, if we drag things out, it's going to hurt even worse when you leave for good. Saying goodbye to you is already going to be one of the hardest things I've ever done. I don't think I can do it over and over and over again."

His eyes darkened. He let out a sigh that was half growl. "What if I'm not okay with saying goodbye at all?"

"I don't think you even know what you want," I said, letting out a shaky laugh. "You keep contradicting yourself. You want to stay in Wyoming, but you want the job in New York. You want more, but—" *But not enough to do anything about it.* I stopped myself before finishing the sentence, blushing as I realized that my words could describe me as well as they described him.

"Must be contagious." He smirked. "Tell me, Claire. What do *you* want?"

"I—" I stopped, realizing I didn't have an answer.

At least not one I could give him.

"Tell me," he demanded.

"I don't know what I want." *Liar.*

His eyes narrowed. "Are you talking about life or about us?"

"Life." I knew exactly what I wanted from him. I just couldn't have it.

His gaze heated. "So put life aside. Life is complicated. What do you want regarding *us*?"

I knew all the things I should say. But only one word made it past my lips. "More."

A look of satisfaction settled onto his face. "Me too."

"But you're leaving tomorrow."

"I am. That's the reality of the situation. But life is short, Claire." He leveled a look at me. "We both could have died on that rock face. And in that moment? You mattered more to me than the job."

"I felt the same way." I couldn't deny it. It's why I'd kissed him, even knowing I couldn't ask him to stay if we made it out of there alive. With our survival uncertain, all that had mattered was the one thing we had— that one moment.

"I don't know how we'll work it out," he said, shaking his head. "Maybe we'll have to settle for eating Chinese food over video chat and taking turns flying in for weekends when we can. I'm not asking you to give up the life you love and come with me. I'm just asking for you to give this a chance, even if we have to figure it out as we go. I don't want to lose you."

A chance. It made me hopeful and terrified at the same time.

But I was Claire Hawkins. I'd never let fear stop me before. I'd risked my life countless times.

Maybe it was time to risk my heart.

I took his face into my hands and kissed him, pouring everything I felt into that moment. "I don't want to lose you, either," I whispered. "And if all we have is tonight, then I want to make it count."

Vance's eyes smoldered with heat. He pulled me into the cabin bedroom and kissed me deeply, his hands tangled in my hair. I reached for his belt, but he stopped me.

"Slow down," he murmured, trapping my hands behind my back as he trailed kisses down my jaw. "You're always in such a rush, Claire. I want to take my time."

I huffed in protest until he began focusing that same patient intensity on me that I'd seen him apply to his work. There was no rush, no frenzy—no matter how much I pushed for it. *He* was in control here— teasing, touching, and exploring each curve in turn as he slowly peeled every piece of clothing from my body.

"You're driving me crazy," I said in a tone that sounded like a complaint, even though I was loving every bit of it more than I would ever admit. I'd never been with anyone so patient, so entirely focused on *my* pleasure. Every moment he lingered on my skin, his hot breath and rough hands working together to play a symphony, I became more and more dizzy with desire.

"Good," he said with a smirk. "That's exactly what I'm going for."

"Please," I begged, desperate for release, desperate for *more.*

I reached for him again, but he captured my wrists and held them firmly above my head as he continued that exquisite slowness, holding himself back until I exploded in waves of ecstasy.

Then he ravished me with all the fast, furious energy I could ever desire.

· · ·

I woke up the next morning in Vance's arms. It was different this time. We were in an actual bed, for one thing. We weren't numb with cold or filthy from hours of hiking.

And the way he'd touched me the night before hadn't been a fantasy.

I'd spent more time than I cared to admit imagining what it might be like if Vance took me to bed. The reality had been a thousand times better than anything I could have dreamed up.

But this—the sweet intimacy of him holding me against his chest the next morning—was the best part of all.

"I hate to leave," he whispered in my ear.

"I know."

"I'll call you when I get back into town next week. Maybe you can drive down to Laramie and spend a night."

"Yeah." But my answer was hollow. Rhett and Cheyenne would be on their honeymoon. The ranch would need every minute I could spare. I wouldn't be able to get away for a trip to Laramie, much less New York when he settled there.

I was crazy about Vance, but I knew there was no telling when we'd actually be together again. My life stretched out ahead of me, empty and sad.

Lonely.

CHAPTER FORTY-FIVE

Vance

I WATCHED THE CITYSCAPE OUT MY WINDOW AS THE PLANE made its final approach to Laguardia. I was finally home, back where I belonged.

But instead of the excitement I'd expected to feel, all I felt was emptiness.

It would be better when I got to the FBI field office, I assured myself. It was natural to feel a sense of sadness. After all, I'd genuinely loved Wyoming. It would always hold a piece of my heart.

Or all of it, I thought glumly, since the odds of Claire ever wanting to move to the city were less than zero.

She'd hate living here. I couldn't fool myself into thinking there was even a chance of her wanting to move her life to the city. She might enjoy an occasional visit. I could take her to Central Park. We could eat hot dogs, see the sights. Order cheap takeout and pair it with a five-hundred-dollar bottle of scotch just for the hell of it.

Just thinking about it put a smile on my face.

But my smile disappeared the moment I stepped outside of the terminal and hailed a cab. Had New York always been this crowded? It was a shock to the system after being in the wide-open land of Wyoming.

It was too early to check into my hotel, so I had the cab drop me off a couple of blocks from the FBI field office. I slung my messenger bag over my shoulder and began my walk, glad for the chance to stretch my legs after my flight.

Horns blared, tires screeched, and a man shouted profanities at someone who had cut him off. Sirens wailed in the distance, and a jackhammer pounded incessantly.

What the hell was I doing here?

I stopped in my tracks in front of the federal building where I was supposed to report. It loomed above me, bringing back memories of my dad. It had always seemed so important then. So defining. Part of me had always thought that if I made it there, I'd know I was as good as him. That it would make us cut from the same cloth, give us an identity to share that went beyond biology.

But I didn't want to be cut from the same cloth as him.

In a moment of clarity that felt like a lightning strike to the soul, I realized following in his footsteps would prove nothing—except that his opinion still held entirely too much control over my life. Yes, he'd had an amazing career. But that's all he had.

I wanted way more than that.

CHAPTER FORTY-SIX

Claire

COLE'S VISIT AND CHEYENNE'S WEDDING PREPARATION KEPT me busy enough that I didn't have much time to think about Vance's absence. But when the ceremony was over and I was no longer needed for maid-of-honor duties, I snagged a glass of champagne and slipped away from the reception for a moment alone.

Then Vance's absence hit hard.

I sat dejected at a table underneath the stars while everyone else danced the night away on a temporary dance floor set up by Rhett and Cheyenne's pasture. They'd known from the beginning that they wanted to get married on the land that belonged to them. The land where they'd fallen back in love again.

The wedding was beautiful. Cheyenne looked stunning in her white long-sleeved dress, her new sparkly blue cowboy boots poking out underneath the bottom. They were a gift from me—her something blue for the day she promised forever to my brother.

I wore a matching pair. A grownup substitute for friendship

bracelets, something practical but fun that would always remind us of this day. Cheyenne had told me to wear anything I wanted for my role as her maid of honor. I'd found a shimmery dress that faded from emerald green to navy blue. The skirt hugged my hips, then flared out at the bottom—a mermaid dress, the saleslady had told me.

I'd bought it before Vance had forever linked that word to him, picking it primarily because it came with a matching sweater I could wear to the reception to keep me warm when the sun went down.

But now, the mermaid dress did nothing but remind me of him.

I picked up my champagne glass and downed it, then snagged two more from the tray the caterer carried past my table.

"Sorry I'm late."

My entire body went tight at the sound of that warm, sexy voice. His hand dropped, resting lightly on my shoulder, as his thumb gently stroked the nape of my neck.

I whirled around, nearly dropping my champagne at the sight of Vance.

He was here. *Here.* And he looked like James freaking Bond in a gray tuxedo.

"What are you doing here?" My face lit up with a smile. "I thought you flew to New York yesterday."

He grinned. "I did. And as soon as I got there, I realized there was somewhere else I'd rather be."

I couldn't stop smiling. "I'm so glad you're here. So, so glad." I threw my arms around his neck, trying not to think about the future. About how he'd leave again.

He was here now, and that was all that mattered.

His arms wrapped tightly around my waist. "Can I have this dance?" His voice, low and sensual in my ear, sent shivers down my spine.

"Yes," I said breathlessly. "God, yes."

He led me to the dance floor, then took me back into his arms. I closed my eyes, sinking into the feeling of being held by him.

Home. The word vibrated through my very being, shocking me so that I opened my eyes.

Cheyenne was staring at us, her face lit up in a dazzling smile. She gave me a questioning look and I just shrugged.

I didn't know and didn't care. Didn't know how long he would be here, or when he was going back, or how we would make this work. I wouldn't let thoughts of the future ruin this moment with him.

"Don't you want to know why I came back?" he asked, like he could read my thoughts.

"Doesn't seem to matter much right now," I answered, half drunk on the feeling of being back with him.

He chuckled. "Odd for you to not be nosy. I figured you would start peppering me with questions the minute you saw me."

I pulled back so he could see my smirk. "Bold of you to think you have me figured out."

His head tilted, giving me the point, as his lips twitched into a smile. "Nosy or not, I'm going to tell you anyway."

I sighed dramatically. "Fine, then, since you obviously want attention. Why did you come back?"

His gaze turned serious. "Because I want more."

My heart railed against my ribs. "Define more."

"More everything," he said simply, before twirling me, bringing me even tighter against him when I spun back. "I thought I needed to take the job in New York to prove that I was as good as my dad. And I thought I needed to be like him—to live by his mantra. No distractions. That's what made him good."

I bit my lip.

"But that's not what makes me good," he said before brushing his lips softly against mine. "And I don't want a life like his."

I nearly came apart right there on the dance floor.

"We're good together," he continued.

"Yes, we are." *So* good together.

He whispered into my ear. "So I have a proposition for you."

"Oh?" I asked, feeling weak.

"I was late because I didn't come straight here. I stopped to have a conversation with my father first."

I pulled back and blinked. "Okay." This was not where I'd thought this conversation was going.

"I used the FBI offer as leverage to get a better one from him."

My heart soared. "Wait, what? You mean you're staying in Wyoming?"

"Yes." He sent me for a spin, then brought me back, clasping me tight against his firm body. "I also convinced him that he needs a second center of operations—here in Wildwood."

My eyes went wide. "How did you do that?"

"By showing him the possibilities and the benefit of having a safe house for his clients that's far off the grid and out of the busy tourist zones."

"So you're going to live here in Wildwood? Seriously?" I was almost dizzy with excitement.

He grinned. "I am. And he gave me full hiring capability. So here's my proposition: be my partner."

"Your partner?" I blinked again. "At the security firm?"

"Yes. At the security firm and ... more." He brushed his lips against mine again, then dipped me.

When he pulled me up, I realized my entire family was staring at us. Mom was beaming. My brothers were staring Vance down.

I couldn't help but laugh.

"You're amazing," Vance said, grinning as he took in the sight of everyone watching us.

"That's not why they're staring," I whispered, flushing red.

"I don't care." He nipped my neck with his teeth, earning a death glare from Jonathan.

"Stop," I laughed, pushing him away. I dragged him from the dance floor back to the table where we could talk. "So let me get this straight. You're offering me a job."

"Yes. Claire, you're too good for the sheriff's office. You know you'll never be happy there."

"True." And it had been even worse since this investigation. Even with Trey gone, things remained awkward between me and Sheriff McGrath. My days there were numbered and I knew it.

He gave me a piercing look. "I'm offering you a job where you can do more. Where you can color outside the lines. Where you'll never have to answer to people who don't understand how valuable you are to the team."

"So you're saying you'd be my boss?" I said, raising an eyebrow.

"No." He shook his head. "Partner, not boss. You'd be an independent contractor. An equal. I wouldn't have it any other way."

My heart soared again.

"That sounds very tempting," I admitted. More than tempting. I'd already made up my mind to take it, but what he said next sealed the deal.

"SAR is your passion." He grabbed a glass of champagne for himself and tasted it, shooting me a surprised look of approval. "The firm will understand and work around that. In fact, we plan on utilizing it. I had a long discussion with my father about that very thing. He's been searching for someone who has those abilities. I told him about you and he's as convinced as I am that you're the perfect addition to the team."

"Wow," I said, shaking my head. "This is ... amazing."

"There's more," he said, grinning.

"How can there be more?" This was already everything I could ever hope for.

He leaned in, his lips tantalizingly close to mine. "My first assignment is in Florida. I'll be there for December and January."

"We're spending the winter in Florida?" I squealed.

"We are." He gave me a sultry smile. "Can you come for a drive?"

I nodded.

I'd go anywhere with him.

TWENTY MINUTES LATER WE PULLED INTO A FIELD. HE jumped out of his SUV and motioned for me to follow him.

"What are we doing?" I asked, pulling my sweater tight to shield against the cold breeze.

He stopped. "Wait for it," he said, glancing at his watch.

Seconds later, I heard the unmistakable sound of a helicopter and shot him a questioning look.

He just smiled.

"What is this?" I asked when the chopper landed in front of us.

He slipped an arm around my waist. "*That* is the new Sage County Search and Rescue helicopter."

"*What*?" My jaw dropped.

"Crazy thing. My father mentioned that he was looking to sell this one and get an upgrade." Vance grinned. His excitement was adorable. "As the final part of my contract negotiation, I convinced him to donate it to the SAR team instead. It's a tax write-off and great publicity for him. Plus, I told him it would probably convince you to accept the job."

"Hell yes it does!" I hiked up my dress and jumped into his arms, wrapping my legs around his waist. I kissed him feverishly, not even caring that the helicopter pilot could see us.

Vance didn't care, either.

When we finally broke apart, he gave me a cocky smirk. "I take it you're in?"

"I'm in." I grinned.

In for all of it. The job, him... Everything we could have together.

Then I blurted out a thought. "I'm not good at relationships."

He laughed, stroking a lazy hand up my spine. "That's okay. We'll take it slow."

I smiled coyly. "I'm not exactly good at slow, either."

"*You*? Not good at slow? I'm shocked." He rolled his eyes.

I bit my lip and gave him a devilish grin. "Your cabin is still empty. How about we steal a bottle of scotch and go take things fast, instead?"

His smile became a smolder. "I knew I liked you, Claire Hawkins."

"It's too bad I can't stand you." I winked.

The following March

I SLAPPED AT MY PHONE, TRYING TO STOP THE INCESSANT buzzing that disturbed my sleep.

"You should answer it," Vance murmured before nipping my neck with his teeth.

I smiled lazily, stretching a hand behind me to feel the glorious body that wrapped around my own. "It's my day off."

He grabbed my phone from the nightstand. "It's Beth."

"Shit." I yanked the phone out of his hand and sat up, answering it. "Hello?"

"Claire, we need you." Beth's voice was frantic.

"What? Why? What's wrong?" I rolled out of bed, grabbing the bra and panties that had been discarded on the floor the night before.

"It's Jonathan."

My heart stopped. "What happened? Is he hurt?"

A million things could go wrong on a ranch.

"No. He's ... gone."

"Gone?" I blanched, looking helplessly at Vance.

He pulled the phone out of my hand and took over while I threw my clothes on. "Beth? It's Vance. Tell me what's going on."

He listened, saying little, as I stuffed my feet into my boots and grabbed my keys. He made a motion for me to wait for him.

I paced frantically, wanting to rip the phone back out of his hands.

"We'll be right there," he finally said. Then he hung up and put his hands on my shoulders. "Breathe."

"He's missing," I said, pain stabbing my chest. "I have to—"

"No." He shook his head. "He's not missing."

"What do you mean? Beth said he's gone. He—"

"He pulled a Rhett," Vance said calmly, letting go of me so he could pull his jeans on.

"A Rhett?" My jaw dropped. Rhett had left in the middle of the night over ten years ago, breaking all of our hearts in the process.

Vance nodded. "A Rhett—and a Cole, for that matter."

I sank onto the bed, his words becoming clear. "He joined the military."

"Yep. Didn't tell anyone he was doing it. Left them a letter. He's safe, but your mom is a wreck. We need to head over. Beth asked us to stop at Travis's on the way."

"Why?"

"She said he'd take the news better coming from you."

"He doesn't know yet." My stomach clenched.

This would *kill* Travis. Jonathan was his right-hand man running the cattle side of the ranch. Travis was already overworked and stretched too thin.

Plus, he'd take it personally. Feel hurt that Jonathan hadn't cared enough to stay. He'd already lost two brothers that way—Cole, Rhett.

Then Missy had left him too, taking his beautiful girls with her.

This would wreck him.

"Alright," I said, swallowing hard. "We stop by Travis's on the way."

Not that it was actually on the way. We were back in cabin four, the guest house Mom kept available for us while we looked for a place of our own. We were a quick jog from the family home, but we'd have to drive to Travis's cabin. It was all the way on the other side of the property.

But I understood. They were right.

He'd take it better coming from me.

I knocked on Travis's door, a sinking feeling in my gut.

He didn't answer.

I knocked again, then hollered. "Travis, it's me. Open up!"

Footsteps slowly came toward the door. He pulled it open an inch. His eyes were bloodshot and he looked like he hadn't slept a wink. "What do you want?"

"I need to talk to you about something," I said, trying to push the door open.

He held it firm. "This isn't a good time."

"This is important. Make time."

"Not now." He tried to push the door closed.

"Travis, what the hell—"

Then I saw movement behind him.

"Hi, Claire."

Travis groaned and let the door swing open.

Missy, his ex, was standing in his living room, looking pensive.

And wearing nothing but one of his long flannel shirts.

I gaped at her, then looked back at my brother.

"What the actual hell, Travis?"

He scrubbed his face. "It's a long story," he muttered.

THANK YOU FOR READING *SHADOW SABOTAGE*! I CAN'T WAIT to bring you the next Wildwood story. In the meantime, you might want to get to know Claire's brother, Cole, in *Mountain Secrets*.

Reviews are invaluable to authors. If you enjoyed this story, I would so appreciate you taking the time to leave a review at your preferred vendor. It truly means the world.

Want to stay in touch? Connect with me on Facebook or Instagram. I love getting to know my readers! You can also sign up for my mailing list and receive a bonus scene from Rhett and Cheyenne's wedding!

Acknowledgments

Is it okay for me to thank a fictional character? Because I'd really like to thank Claire Hawkins for taking me on the unexpected wild ride that was writing her book.

I thought Claire's story would be easy–high on adventure and laughs, low on emotion. Instead, she pulled me into deeper waters than I ever planned, teaching me some important truths in the process. For me, she truly was like a mermaid, beckoning me to leave the shores behind and dive into an untamed ocean. Writing her story was a journey that I never expected, and I am deeply grateful for the experience.

I'm also grateful for two fellow mermaids who were by my side the entire time: Camille and Abbey. You encouraged me and cheered me on, as I pushed to meet a deadline for what turned out to be the longest book I've ever written. Camille, you were always there to remind me that it was okay if I didn't follow the rules with this one, that I could trust the flow of the tide and follow where it led. Abbey, you pushed me to go deeper, to fully explore the emotions I kept trying to keep on the surface. The book is better because of both of you. *I* am better because of both of you.

Thank you to Detective Jacob Higdon for not laughing too hard when I said I wanted to write a police procedural, even though we both know I hate following the rules. I appreciate you taking time to answer my endless questions about search warrants and procedure. A note to my readers: any mistakes in the police details of this book are entirely mine. I tried to be as accurate as possible, but every good story requires at least a little bit of creative license.

Thanks also to Mike Poulsen, the Wyoming SAR operative whose insight inspired so much of the first two books of this series.

The beautiful cover for this book was designed by Esther from Meraki Cover Design. It's absolutely perfect, and I'm thrilled to have you on the team!

Thank you to Jessica, my faithful beta reader. I'm so glad you love Claire as much as I do.

To my editor, Mickey Reed: thank you for being by my side for seven books now! I'm so grateful for you—and for your patience, despite my extravagant love of unnecessary commas and em-dashes.

To Brandon, my husband: thank you for your understanding as I hid away in my writing cave, for sharing my excitement over every epiphany, and for believing in my dreams even when I started to doubt them. You are the shore to my waves.

To Aiden and Will: thank you for still being willing to curl up for storytime with your mom even though you're teenagers. I treasure every moment with you both.

And as always, I'm grateful for YOU—my readers. Creating these stories and sharing them with you is one of the greatest honors of my life.

About the Author

Nicole Gardner lives in NE Arkansas with her husband, their two sons, and their two crazy dogs. If she's not at her desk, you'll likely find her either in the garden, or creating teas and tinctures in the kitchen.

Nicole's background is in psychology. This fascination with human behavior and relationship dynamics plays a significant role in her writing and the way she shapes her characters.

www.nicolegardnerbooks.com